HER DYING BREATH

HER DYING BREATH

RITA HERRON

The characters and events portrayed in this book are fictitious.
Any similarity to real persons, living or dead, is coincidental and
not intended by the author.

Published by Montlake Romance
PO Box 400818
Las Vegas, NV 89140

ISBN-13: 9781477805930
ISBN-10: 1477805931

Prologue

———— o ————

<u>A journal entry, March 2</u>

The first time I died, I was only five years old.

I remember seeing rainbows and carousels and the golden wings of an angel dancing in the wind, ready to sweep me to the heavens and save me from the monster who chased me through the endless dark forest of child-eating trees.

But then he was there again, blotting out the angels, and the darkness came. The minutes that bled into hours. Hours where I fought for my life. Hours where the carousels turned into evil beings with dragons' wings, with fangs and claws that reached for me and twisted my neck until it snapped.

I didn't want to die.

But I had no control.

The Commander would kill me over and over again. All while the piano music played in the background, as if Mozart's music could soothe me as I took my last breath.

It was a game, he said. A test of wills. A regiment to make me strong.

Even then, when I begged for him to send me to my grave, he didn't.

Because he liked to listen to my dying breath rasp out. He said it brought him pleasure.

Voices rumbled in the common room, and I carried my journal with me, anxious to see what the commotion was about.

But there was no one except Six there. The TV was on—a newscast about the story in Slaughter Creek.

A picture of the Commander flashed on-screen, and I wanted to run. But my eyes were glued to his face in the same morbid way rubberneckers are drawn to the scene of a fatal accident. You can't turn away.

"This is Brenda Banks coming to you from Slaughter Creek, Tennessee, where a shocking case has just been uncovered," the dark-haired reporter said. "Arthur Blackwood, a commander in the armed forces and the former director of Slaughter Creek Sanitarium, who went missing ten years ago, is not only alive but has been arrested and charged with multiple counts of homicide.

"In a bizarre twist, Commander Blackwood, who is believed to have been working with the CIA, was arrested by his own sons, Sheriff Jake Blackwood and Special Agent Nick Blackwood, who discovered that the Commander had spearheaded a research project called the CHIMES at the local sanitarium.

"At this point, the CIA disavows any knowledge that Blackwood was working with them or that they sanctioned the project, which used unsuspecting children as experimental subjects. Commander Blackwood is now in custody, but word is that he is not cooperating with the police and refuses to reveal the names of his victims."

I lifted my hand and stroked the tiny number that had been branded behind my ear.

The Commander wouldn't release names because to him we had no names. Just numbers.

I am Seven.

My friend who sits beside me, Six.

The reporter continued to babble about the experiment and its horrific effect on the subjects they had identified.

The subjects, that's what they called us. Guinea pigs. Freaks was more like it.

"If you have any knowledge or information pertaining to this case, please contact your local law enforcement agency or Special Agent Nick Blackwood." The reporter smiled, stirring a faint memory in the back of my mind.

I had seen her before. Years ago at the sanitarium…would she remember me?

"Again, this is Brenda Banks coming to you from Slaughter Creek. We will bring you more information on this case as it becomes available."

Six turned to me with an evil glint in his eyes as the broadcast finished airing. "Everyone must pay."

I nodded and glanced at the keeper of the home we shared. Six pulled a pack of matches from his pocket and gestured toward the back, where our rooms were.

His devious mind already had a plan.

Five minutes later, a blaze erupted in the bathroom, and I grabbed my bag from my room and slipped out the back. Blood soaked Six's pocket, but I didn't ask what had happened. I didn't want to know.

Flames shot into the air, smoke billowing in a thick cloud. I heard a scream from inside, and then Six appeared through the cloud of smoke, his eyes scanning the property.

I hooked a thumb toward the car on the corner, and we ran toward it, ducking our heads as a siren wailed and a fire engine roared past us, heading to the blaze.

Silence fell between us, deep and liberating, as we climbed into the car. I hot-wired it in seconds and pulled away. With Six, there was no need to talk. We had bonded years ago in the sanitarium.

I could read his mind now.

We would go back to Slaughter Creek, to where it all began. Where the Commander started his reign of terror.

Where the townspeople had allowed it to happen and ignored our pleas for help.

Heat flooded my veins as I imagined him chained to some godforsaken table, where he became the pincushion for the doctors' needles and drugs. Where the CHIMES drained his blood and watched the life flow from him, one breath at a time. While he screamed for help that would never come.

Prison was not good enough for the man who'd tortured and deceived me and the others.

The police, the federal agents—they thought they knew the Commander's secrets.

But they knew nothing.

Red Rover, Red Rover, send Seven right over...

I would show him what he'd turned me into.

And then I would kill him, just as he'd killed me.

Over and over and over again—seven times, I'd take his life, until he begged me to extinguish the light and finally let him slip into peace.

Then I would kill again, just for the fun of watching him die.

Chapter 1

———— o ————

Special Agent Nick Blackwood hated his father.

The bastard had ruined the lives of dozens of young, innocent children in the name of his research.

He'd ruined the lives of his two sons as well.

Nick had his own stories to tell.

Stories that he'd never shared with a single living soul. Not even his brother, Jake.

But they were his secrets to keep, and he wore them like a badge of honor. The painful memories had shaped him into the man he'd become.

A cold, ruthless killer for the government. And now a cold, ruthless federal agent who hunted down the most wanted, the sick and depraved.

Psychopaths like his father.

The scars on his back ached as he walked into the interrogation room where Arthur Blackwood sat, scars his father had inflicted from the time he was three, but he refused to massage the pain away. Seeing his discomfort would only bring the Commander pleasure, and he refused to give him that, just as he refused to react to his father's pleas to get to know him again.

Instead, Nick wiped all emotion from his face and mind.

This man meant nothing to him. Nothing but a means to an end. He had information Nick wanted.

The interrogation techniques Nick had learned in the military taunted him. He'd like to use those on the Commander. In fact he would *enjoy* using them, making his father suffer as he'd made others suffer.

Unfortunately the TBI didn't allow torture as part of their tactics.

The downside of being a fed—he had to play by their rules.

He and several other agents had already questioned the Commander a half dozen times and gotten nowhere.

But they kept hoping he'd slip somehow and reveal the names of other parties involved in the mind experiments they'd conducted at Slaughter Creek Sanitarium.

They also wanted a list of all the subjects.

If their theories proved correct, the Commander had created a slew of mentally unstable twentysomethings who ranged from trained murderers to psychopaths to sadistic serial killers without a conscience.

Not only had the people of Slaughter Creek been affected by the loss of loved ones, but these psychopaths could strike anywhere, anytime.

Already they'd uncovered one who'd been a sniper.

Worse, a handful of the subjects and two doctors involved had been murdered in order to cover up the project, murders his father had ordered to save his own ass.

"Hello, Nick," the Commander said in that eerily calm tone he'd adopted since his capture.

Did the bastard think he could hypnotize Nick like he had the children he'd used in his project?

Nick dropped into the chair facing him. His father was shackled and chained on the other side of the wooden table, the only furniture in the room.

"The guards said you asked to speak to me."

The Commander gave a clipped nod, his gray eyes trained on Nick as they used to be when he forced an impossible physical test upon him. They flickered with contempt, just as they had when Nick failed.

And then that glint of challenge, just before he doled out whatever punishment or torture his evil mind had concocted in the name of catapulting his son into manhood.

A sick smile tilted the corner of his father's mouth. "I always knew you'd grow up to be a killer."

Nick ground his teeth. Of course his father knew about his military background. According to his sources, the CIA had given him a new identity and helped him hide out for the past ten years.

Gray hair now dusted the tops of his father's hands as he folded them on the table. "You are so much more like me than Jake is. That's the reason I was harder on you. You had that killer instinct, that same intense ability to focus. To kill."

Emotions Nick thought long buried rose to the surface, his temper flaring. But he had to remain calm. His father had been famous for pushing his buttons.

And then punishing him for reacting.

Men—soldiers—did not react.

"I'm nothing like you," Nick said. "I fought for my country, yes. But I didn't prey on innocent little children like Amelia Nettleton or Grace Granger."

"They were casualties of the cause."

Nick shook his head. "If you called me in for your same old song and dance, then I'm out of here." The chair scraped the hard floor as Nick shoved it back and stood. Then he headed toward the door.

"Jake has his head buried in that Nettleton girl's ass just like he did ten years ago." Disgust laced his father's cold voice. "But you, Nick. You're a worthy adversary. You won't give up. I know that. You have to know the truth. All of it."

Nick turned and cut him a scathing look. "Does that mean you're ready to talk?"

A cynical chuckle escaped his father. "Now what is the fun in that, son?"

"This is not a game, or one of your training exercises," Nick said tersely. "If you have any shred of humanity left, you'll give us a list of all the subjects, so we can investigate the effects of your project on them and get the victims psychological help. We might even be able to save lives."

"What you've done is expose the subjects, which will make things worse for them. They may want revenge."

"All the more reason for you to give me that list."

"The list was destroyed," his father said simply. "The names of the Slaughter Creek subjects are lost."

The slight inflection in his father's voice aroused Nick's suspicions. Another lie, or was his father toying with him?

Nick walked back to the table, planted his hands on top of it, and leaned forward, eyes narrowed. "What do you mean, the *Slaughter Creek* subjects' names are lost?"

"Just what I said. We destroyed records when the project was terminated to avoid leaving a paper trail."

"CIA protocol?"

His father nodded.

But a knot formed in Nick's belly, the same fear that had slithered through him when he'd been cornered behind enemy lines. "Are you saying that the project wasn't contained to Slaughter Creek?"

The handcuffs clanged as his father shifted. "That's for you to find out, Nick."

Nick silently cursed. Of course the project could have taken place in other cities. Why confine it to this small town? "I told you I'm not here to play games." He started to walk away again, but his father cleared his throat.

"But you will play this one."

The Commander opened his folded hand to reveal a slip of paper. Dammit. There was probably nothing on it.

But Nick couldn't gamble that it wasn't a clue of some kind. He took the bait.

When he opened the paper, though, his heart began to hammer.

There once was a child with a mind
Till he stole it from her for all time
Then they played Red Rover
And he said, "Come over"
And she crossed the line to the dark side.

Nick raised his gaze to his father's. "Did you write this?"

"No," his father said simply. "It came in the mail, no return address."

Nick wanted to punch something. The bureau was supposed to be checking his father's mail. The son of a bitch had received hundreds of letters. Some hate mail. Some letters from individuals who claimed they were part of the experiment.

The bureau had had to assign a special team to investigate those. So far none of them had panned out, though. They were all crackpots and attention seekers looking for their ten minutes of fame.

Then there were the love letters from depraved women who claimed they were in love with the Commander. Some twisted souls thought they could redeem him. Others offered conjugal visits. He'd even had two marriage proposals.

What kind of sick woman would want to marry his father, knowing what he'd done?

"I believe it's a warning," the Commander said.

A warning from one of the CHIMES children, who knew what he'd done to her?

She'd crossed the line to the dark side...

What did that mean? That she was going to hurt herself?

Or somebody else?

Or was she coming after the Commander?

Hell, if that was what she wanted, Nick would leave the cell door open and let her have at his father.

Still, he had to find out who she was, because she might lead him to the others—the victims who, their minds warped by the experiments, might have become killers.

———— · ————

Brenda Banks straightened her skirt and jacket as she waited outside the prison for Special Agent Nick Blackwood to emerge.

She wished like hell she'd been a fly on the wall, so she could have eavesdropped on his conversation with his father.

The tall stone prison with its massive gate and barbed wire fencing housed almost a thousand inmates, including some of the worst criminals in Tennessee, on twenty-four-hour lockdown with no chance of parole, some on death row.

Would Arthur Blackwood receive the needle for his crimes?

Frustration coiled inside her. She wanted an exclusive interview with the mastermind behind the project, but the feds had refused to put her on the list of approved visitors.

She wouldn't give up, though. Brenda Banks was not the woman everyone thought she was.

Sure, she could don a pleasing face for the public, but that talent had been drilled into her as a child by William and Agnes Banks.

Much to their displeasure, though, she refused to simply be a pretty face on a man's arm, like her daddy wanted. Or the socialite entertainer her mother tried to mold into being.

Maybe there was a reason—technically she wasn't their child.

Of course, her father, now the mayor of Slaughter Creek, demanded that his dirty little secret be kept safe, so she had to keep her mouth shut. Be a Southern lady, Agnes insisted. Use your charm and support your man!

Brenda intended to support herself, and have a man stand behind her. Or maybe they would stand side by side.

Finding out the harsh truth, that the Bankses had bought her as a baby, had changed her. Made her tougher.

Explained why she felt like a stranger in her own family's house.

She liked digging into people's lives, liked digging into their secrets, liked exposing what lay beneath their polished exterior.

This winter, she'd clearly landed the biggest story in Slaughter Creek's history, maybe even in the history of the state of Tennessee.

There was more to the story, too.

More victims. More people involved in the project. More involved in the cover-up.

She wouldn't quit until she exposed them all.

No matter what she had to do.

The wind swirled around her, and she folded her arms, rubbing off the chill. Her piece about the CHIMES had landed her a position at the local TV station as an investigative reporter. No more covering the annual dog pageant or the cornbread festival. Or the Labor Day festivities with the deep-fried Oreos and Twinkies.

The front doors of the prison suddenly whooshed open, and Nick Blackwood, stepped outside. Her heart stuttered.

Nick had grown even more handsome and masculine with age. He looked three inches taller, and had developed muscles that hadn't been there when he was a teen, massive broad shoulders, and a chiseled jaw that made her want to run her finger along it, make him smile.

The intensity in his dark eyes implied that he was untouchable, though. That cold, angry look screamed that he'd seen the dark side of the world.

And he hated everyone in it.

She remembered when he'd joined the military and left town. Had heard he'd joined Special Forces. Even now he exuded that military aura—the steely eyes and focus, the harsh mouth, the cropped haircut, the posture that indicated he was always in control.

He paused on the steps, adjusted his sunglasses, then scanned the parking lot as if he were searching for someone. She had the uncanny sense that he was always on guard. Always suspicious.

Always braced for a bullet to come flying at him.

She took a deep breath and strode toward him, steeling herself for another brush-off.

"Nick," she said as she stopped in front of him a second later.

He heaved an exasperated sigh before she could say anything. "I have no comment for the press, Brenda."

She felt a sliver of unease as his gaze swept over her, condemning her to the ranks of lowly civilian.

Even worse, lowly *female* civilian.

"I know you and your brother think I'm the bad guy," she said. "But really, Nick, I just want the story. People in town deserve to know how your father got away with what he did for so long."

"Jake gave you the exclusive when we made the arrest," he answered in a gruff voice.

"Yes, but I also know you're looking for other victims, subjects of that experiment. I'd like to interview them, run a personal story on each of their lives and the effects the experiment had on them and their families. The series would garner sympathy for the families and victims."

His only reaction was a fine tightening of his mouth. "I'm sorry, but I can't help you."

"But I can help you," she said, determined to find some common ground.

He brushed past her, dismissing her, but she grabbed his arm.

A mistake.

He stiffened, removed his sunglasses with careful precision, then leveled his cold eyes at her.

A tingle of awareness she hadn't expected shot up her spine.

Brenda instantly dropped her hand, disturbed by the feeling. She could not be attracted to Nick Blackwood.

"If you won't talk to me, maybe your father will," she said, desperate to remain professional. "Maybe he wants to tell his side of the story."

Nick wrapped his big, long fingers around her wrist. "I don't give a damn about his side of the story, Brenda. Lives may be at stake, so take your pretty little ass and go interview the women down at the country club."

Rage volleyed through her. His snide comment sounded exactly like something her father would say. "That's not fair, Nick. I've earned my position as an investigative reporter."

His gaze darkened. "This is serious business, Brenda." His voice dropped a decibel. "You have no idea what you're doing. Leave the police work to the cops."

"People have a right to know the truth," she snapped. "Otherwise, how will the citizens know that you aren't covering up what your father did, just like he covered it up for years?"

Anger blazed in Nick's eyes, betraying him—this cold, harsh man did feel something, after all. In that brief moment, she sensed a well of pain beneath his steely veneer.

He had been hurt by his father's actions, shamed by the horrible accusations against Arthur Blackwood.

Had Nick known or suspected his father was capable of the crimes he'd committed?

Did Nick have his own secrets from the past?

What had it been like growing up with the Commander for a father? He'd been cruel to the children in the experiment. Had he been cruel to his sons, or abused them?

Her heart raced. Yes, there was an angle she hadn't thought of before. One everyone in Slaughter Creek would be interested in.

"I'm not covering up for that bastard," he said through clenched teeth. "I intend to find his victims, get treatment for them if necessary, and protect the public."

"Then let me help," she said. "Some of the victims might talk to me before they would a federal agent."

Tension stretched between them as his gaze locked with hers. A police van pulled up and unloaded a string of prisoners, then led them through a series of gates. One of them shouted a lewd remark at her, but she ignored it.

A muscle jumped in Nick's jaw. "I'm warning you, Brenda, stay away from my father."

"Why?" Brenda asked, a challenge in her voice. "Are you afraid he'll tell me your deep, dark secrets?"

His fingers gripped her wrist so tightly that she bit her tongue to keep from wincing as pain ripped up her arm. A second later his gaze dropped to his hand, and he must have realized he was hurting her because he released her.

Still, rage darkened his eyes. But he didn't respond to her challenge. Instead, he strode down the steps, his shoes clicking on the cement.

Brenda rubbed her wrist, curious at his reaction. She'd obviously pushed a button. That rage meant she was right—he had suffered at the hands of his father. She had no doubt.

But how much? And what had his father done to him that he didn't want to be revealed?

The dim glow of the lamp on the table painted her lover's chiseled face with a sickly yellow glow as his eyes bulged in shock. His name was Jim Logger.

A decent name.

But he still had to die.

"What are you doing?" he rasped.

His face blurred, and the Commander's replaced it. He was hurting her. Punishing her. Laughing.

She twisted the piano wire around Logger's neck, tightening it with her fingers.

The whites of his eyes bulged. "Enough, babe, please…"

She shook her finger in his face, brushing her bare breasts against his chest. His erection stood tall and stiff below her, the cock ring holding him hard and thick, just waiting for her to climb onto him.

She hadn't yet decided if she would, or if she'd make him wallow in unsatisfied anticipation.

"I can't breathe," he whispered.

She ran one finger along his jaw and straddled him. "Just go with it. Soon you'll feel the euphoria, then the hallucinations will come. Colors and images like you've never seen before."

His chest rose and fell, panic creasing his face as he struggled for air.

The bastard had been speechless with lust when she'd performed her striptease, then undressed him.

He'd barely blinked when she'd wound the ropes around his wrists and ankles. And he'd nearly exploded all over her face when she'd planted wet licks along the insides of his thighs as she secured his restraints.

"Seriously," he gasped. "Stop it and let me just fuck you."

Her smile faded, the pain of what the Commander had done fueling her fury. All men were like the Commander. She saw him in every face on the street.

"No, I'm going to fuck you." She increased the pressure against his throat. "Do you feel the high? Do you see the lights twinkling?"

He kicked and jerked his arms, rattling the bedrails. She glanced at the clock, timing him as she impaled herself on his rigid length.

Ten seconds, twenty…thirty…

He jerked again, desperate to escape, but she rode him hard and fast, her senses taking over. The pressure of her orgasm rippled through her as he began to gag and choke.

His penis was big, long, felt delicious inside her. Heat sizzled along her nerve endings, the rhythm building as she gripped the wire and moved up and down on his cock. Over and over until a tingling started in her womb and her climax seized her.

Blinding colors of pleasure washed over her as she thrust deeper, so deep he touched her core. She threw her head back and groaned, moving her hips in a circular motion and riding the waves as sensation after sensation pummeled her.

His body jerked and spasmed, his own orgasm teetering on the surface.

But she climbed off of him, denying him the release.

"Please," he moaned.

She squeezed the wire harder, repeating it seven times, lifting it from his skin and pressing it to another spot, each time increasing the pressure so hard she cut off his oxygen. His breath rasped out, his pallor turned gray, then a gurgling sound erupted from his throat.

Finally his eyes rolled back in his head and his body went slack.

She paused to listen for the sound of his breathing, but barring the ticktock of the clock, the room was silent.

Puny son of a bitch. Not even two minutes, and he'd passed out.

She loosened the wire, leaned over and blew air into his mouth, then began chest compressions to bring him back from the brink of death.

When he finally opened his eyes again, shock glazed his irises, the realization that she'd choked him evident in the panic on his face.

"Get off of me, you freak!"

His shout sounded more like a croak. "No, babe," she said, using the pet name he'd given her. "The fun is just beginning."

She straddled him again, gripped the ends of the piano wire and wound it together until the fleshy skin around his neck bulged in fatty rolls. Again, seven squeezes, each one more intense, each one marking him.

She checked the clock. "The first time you die is always the worst. Let's see if you can make it longer the second go-around."

Pure terror shot across his face, and he struggled frantically, then shouted as loud as his sore vocal cords allowed, "Help! Someone help me!"

She chuckled softly, then stuffed her panties in his mouth to muffle his screams. "If you last more than two minutes, I'll save you again," she murmured.

The pupils of his eyes dilated as he fought, but he was weak from dying the first time. He flailed, tears rolling down his ruddy cheeks.

The fight drained from him as her fingers worked the wire. Seconds later, he lay limp again.

A sad excuse for a specimen.

The Commander would have been disappointed.

She studied his face, the slack jaw, the listless eyes. Really, he was a handsome man.

Maybe she would save him again.

She ran a finger down his chest, through the thick, dark hair, then down to his waist.

Yes, she'd watch him die one more time.

But first she'd mark him as she'd been marked.

She took the knife she'd brought with her and carved a number behind his ear: *1.* Her first kill.

Now for more fun.

Then she'd alert that reporter who broke the story on the Commander and tell her where to find him.

Brenda Banks would give the message to the Commander.

Then all the world would see what *she'd* done in his honor.

Chapter 2

———— ○ ————

Nick tried to force thoughts of Brenda Banks from his mind as he left the prison. The infuriating woman had dogged him and Jake ever since the story broke about their father.

Actually, Jake admitted that she'd pestered him and Sadie when Sadie first returned to town because of her grandfather's murder, the chain of events that had set in motion Arthur Blackwood's need to cover up the experiment he'd conducted years ago.

Then the bodies had started stacking up, and Jake called Nick in. Neither of them had been prepared for the revelations that eventually surfaced.

First, their father was alive. He'd gone missing ten years before, and they'd presumed he was dead. And second, their father was a sadistic monster who'd orchestrated mind experiments on innocent kids, then killed countless people and almost killed Sadie to hide his abominable acts.

Nick opened the door to the black sedan the FBI had issued him, wishing to hell he had a Jeep or Range Rover. The downside of the federal bureau—the conservative clothes and vehicle.

The upside—the resources he needed to track down notorious criminals. He'd just never expected the first case to center around his own family.

His military training kicking in, he scanned the streets and area for anything suspicious. For all he knew, the Commander had ordered hits on both him and Jake. After all, he'd killed others who tried to expose the truth about him.

But the streets looked clear. Except for Brenda. She still hadn't left.

Good God. She was standing by that fancy Bimmer, watching him like a hawk. He paused to meet her gaze, irritated at the heat building inside him. She wore a skintight little blue suit, the skirt hugging her curves in all the right places, the jacket barely covering her breasts, which strained against the buttons. Jesus, she had turned from that skinny teenage cheerleader into a voluptuous woman. But she had never had eyes on him. She'd fallen for Jake in high school. Back when *he* had had a crush on her.

He'd always been second best to his brother.

As his father had pounded into him over and over during his incessant drills and beatings.

His insecurities had created a wedge between him and Jake. As an adult, he realized that wasn't Jake's fault, and he was trying to mend fences. But the lessons that had been imprinted in his brain haunted him.

Another reason he had to steer clear of Brenda. She'd grown sexier with age.

And he was too tainted and broken to tangle with her.

Those coffee-colored eyes of hers drew him in, the fiery heat sizzling in them when she pushed to get what she wanted only lighting the flames of desire inside him.

Desires that hadn't been lit in forever.

Desires that made him vulnerable.

Nick did not do vulnerable.

He snapped his sunglasses back into place, started the engine, and sped away from the prison and from Brenda.

The seductive vulture would have to dig her claws into some other man.

After all, all she wanted was a story. Any flirtatious gleam in her eyes was simply predatory. And he knew from experience that you had to either attack the enemy head-on or steer clear entirely, before you got in so deep they could destroy you.

———————.———————

Brenda watched Nick drive away with a mixture of emotions. She needed to focus on the investigation; this was her one chance to prove to her new boss that she could handle the job.

And Nick might be the key to helping her.

She had to find a way to convince him to give her the scoop.

As she drove away from the prison, she decided to visit Amelia Nettleton. According to Sadie, her sister was making great strides in merging her three personalities. Maybe she was ready to talk.

God knows the poor girl had been through hell and back.

Brenda didn't want to add to her pain, only offer her a way to vindicate herself by publicly naming the man who'd destroyed her life.

Brenda already had her angle, her way in, she hoped, so that Amelia would confide in her. She would divulge her own secret to Amelia, confess the truth that she'd never told anyone: that she had no idea who she was, either.

On her sixteenth birthday, she'd found documents from her father's safe on his desk. An adoption file—Brenda Banks had not been born the daughter of William and Agnes Banks. She had been thrown away by some other woman.

Only there had been no birth mother's or father's name listed in the file, and when she confronted the man who'd raised her, he exploded and ordered her never to speak of it again.

For months, she'd tried to find out on her own, had even suffered a meltdown and spent a couple of short weeks in that horrid sanitarium.

Of course, no one knew about that either. William Banks, prominent citizen in town and now the mayor, had covered it up well.

Did Amelia remember seeing her there?

If so, that would be a start in forging a friendship, in winning Amelia's confidence.

She drove straight to Amelia's complex, expecting guards and a hospital atmosphere, but the facility looked more like a condo development than a mental care hospital. Flowers garnished the flower beds flanking the front door, a pair of crystal wind chimes dangled from the awning, and the door was painted Williamsburg blue, lending a homey appearance.

She'd managed to pilfer the address from a sheet of paper she found in Jake's desk when she tried to corner him for more information, so she checked the numbers on the units: 23B.

She parked in front, then checked the surrounding area, but again didn't see a guard or Sadie's car. Hoping her impromptu visit would pay off, she hopped from her BMW, tucked her notepad and mini-recorder in her shoulder bag, then sashayed up the sidewalk to the front portico. She tapped the knocker twice, then waited, but seconds passed with no answer, so she punched the doorbell.

Again, no one answered. Curious, she peeked through the small windows on each side of the door. From that vantage, she saw a comfy-looking living room with a myriad of artwork on the walls, then an adjacent studio, with paint tubes filling the shelves and blank canvases lined up along the wall.

A series of morose paintings of Slaughter Creek were stacked to one side. One depicted the graveyard by the old river mill, where Blackwood's body had been buried before he'd risen from the dead. Another showed twin girls, each locked in a dark prison with blood dripping down the walls. Then another must have reflected the basement torture room where Blackwood and his staff had conducted their hideous experiments in the sanitarium. Wires and electroshock machines dotted the black background.

A dark, hollow tunnel that seemed to go nowhere had been painted on another canvas. In the center of the tunnel, a lone hand suggested a lost child desperately reaching for help, her tiny fingers curled over the end in an attempt to claw her way out.

A shudder coursed through Brenda. She'd heard that Sadie used art therapy techniques with her patients and realized Amelia was working out traumatic memories from her past in the paintings. Maybe Amelia would allow her to photograph some of her pieces as part of a personal profile.

She rang the doorbell again, then peeked through another window, but the rooms were dark, and no one answered the bell.

Deciding that Amelia wasn't home, Brenda walked down the sidewalk. A series of gardens lay to the left, an immaculately maintained array of roses, azaleas, and daylilies, with cozy seating nooks carved through the walkways; at the center, water gurgled in a two-tiered fountain with a bird feeder beside it.

A middle-aged woman sat reading a book on a bench, while other residents strolled through the bird sanctuary. A clearing with several outdoor tables offered areas where patients congregated to chat, read, play cards and chess. Easels had been erected in a corner of the garden, and another set of tables held lumps of clay that four residents were pounding and molding into their own creations.

Brenda didn't spot Amelia, so she gravitated to the middle-aged woman reading *Wuthering Heights*. "Excuse me, ma'am. I'm looking for Amelia Nettleton."

The woman glanced up as she turned the page, a small frown puckering her brow. "Amelia left a couple of days ago."

Brenda rubbed the leather strap of her bag. "Do you know where she went?" Maybe to visit Sadie?

"No, I sure don't. But I heard she saw that horrible news story about that man named Arthur Blackwood being arrested. Amelia got upset and ran out."

Brenda drew a deep breath. "Are the patients free to come and go at will?"

The woman looked offended. "Of course we are. This is not a prison."

Brenda bit her lip. Surely family members were notified when a resident left, especially one who'd once been considered dangerous and had an arrest record, like Amelia.

Brenda thanked the woman and headed to her car. If the story had upset Amelia, maybe she'd remembered something. Maybe she could name others involved in the experiment.

She started the engine, then turned her car back toward Slaughter Creek; perhaps Amelia might have gone back to the Nettleton farm.

Rather the studio—the farmhouse had been burned down in an attempt to kill Sadie. But Amelia might go back to the guest-house.

When Brenda found her, she'd persuade her to talk. She wanted the inside scoop on Amelia, to get inside her head.

Just like you want to know the real story about your own past.

What would she find if she searched for the truth? Something terrible? Was her mother a criminal, or maybe she just had babies and sold them to make a living?

Was that the reason the Banks had kept her adoption a secret?

Nick contemplated the note his father had received as he drove through the winding roads of Slaughter Creek. Odd, how tourists saw only beauty in the rolling valleys and hills, yet for him they just awakened memories of survival exercises and running from monsters in the woods. Human monsters like his father, who'd knowingly forced predators on him when he was a child, just to see if he was tough enough to survive.

He had to forget about his past and focus on the case. He assumed the victims wanted help, that they might even testify against his father, but so far no one had come forward.

Brenda Banks wanted their personal stories.

What if the subjects' stories triggered a need for revenge, as the Commander had suggested? Not that he cared if one of them came after his father, but he was concerned that the psychopaths created by the experiment might harm innocents on the streets.

How could he protect any of them, if he had no idea who else was involved?

A breeze stirred the leaves in the trees on the mountain, the fluttering noise filling the chilly spring air, echoing in a domino effect. The sea of green blended into the dark, the ridges enfolding the town of Slaughter Creek like a mother's arms, protecting the residents from outsiders. Yet innocent children had suffered, while the town remained oblivious.

Even Nick and Jake hadn't known.

Nick passed the road leading to Jake's, and was tempted to drop by. But he still felt like an outsider.

In spite of his father's abuse, Jake had turned out to be a loving father to his daughter. Ayla attended kindergarten at the same school he and his brother had attended years ago. Jake obviously had fond memories of growing up in Slaughter Creek, or he wouldn't have brought his daughter here.

Nick's memories weren't so pleasant.

He drove to the homestead where he and Jake had grown up, but the place had been destroyed long ago. Still, he parked and climbed out, his shoes crunching dry, brittle grass as he crossed to the giant live oak he'd climbed as a kid. A few fond memories flashed back. He and Jake building a fort at the edge of the woods near the property. The two of them fishing in Slaughter Creek as boys. The campouts that had started out fun when they were young—hikes in the woods, catching frogs at the edge of the creek, roasting hot dogs on sticks.

But as they'd grown older, those campouts turned into strenuous hiking sessions—basic wilderness training. Days of being left alone in the woods with no food or water, to teach them how to live off the land. Nights of sleeping in whatever cave they could find to protect them from the frigid mountain temperatures and mountain lions when winter set in.

And then the times when the Commander took Nick out alone. His father always saved the worst tests, the harshest conditions—the beatings—for times when Jake wasn't around.

Nick's shoulder throbbed as he crossed the field to the edge of the creek that ran through the property, and the images he'd tried to banish for years bombarded him. Suddenly he was launched back in time, as if he were eight again, reliving one event.

"You must learn to survive to be a good soldier," his father said.

Nick stood perfectly still, his gaze trained on his father's face. To look away meant he was afraid. Stare down the enemy, his father had taught him.

His father was the enemy.

The thick ropes cut into his wrists as his father tied him to the stake in the middle of the circle of rocks. Next came his legs, his father kneeling on the dirt to secure the knots around his ankles.

Nick scanned the area for a way to escape. If he could reach the rifle leaning against the boulder, he could take off his father's head.

He almost smiled at the thought.

But his father looked at him, and he erased any trace of emotion. Instead, he focused on analyzing his surroundings.

If he passed this test, he'd need to find his way home again.

The trees stood tall and thick around him, hiding him from other hikers and campers in the woods. They'd hiked north for approximately two miles, then veered to the east, then...he couldn't remember; it had been so dark.

But he could hear the creek…If he followed it, it would lead him home.

Other night sounds echoed off the mountain walls. Animals. Gunfire. The sound of fire sizzling jerked his attention down to his feet, where his father was lighting the sticks surrounding him.

When they caught, his father muttered a cold good-bye and disappeared into the woods.

Nick's breath formed a cloud of white in front of him as he breathed in and out. The sticks crackled as the flames began to eat at the dry wood.

He struggled to untie his hands, twisting and yanking at the knot.

Remember how he formed the loop, he told himself. Then work it backward from there.

Heat singed his bare feet as the flames grew higher, sweat trickling down his jaw as he worked at the ropes. Blood streamed down his arms and dripped onto the flames from where the rough hemp clawed at his skin, but he bit his tongue to keep from crying out. The flames licked higher, teasing his fingers, and smoke curled upward in a fog, making it hard to breathe.

He had to hurry, or the flames would eat him up.

Seconds passed, maybe minutes, the heat intensifying, the fire catching the tail end of the fraying rope. The rope began to blacken in the flames, his fingers burning and aching as he finally slid free the knot.

He jerked the rope away and dropped it to the ground just as fire engulfed it. The flames shot higher, closer to his feet, and he bent over and quickly untied the restraints at his ankles. But he wasn't fast enough, and the flames caught the leg of his jeans.

Pain ripped up his calf as he ran through the circle of fire, then dropped to the grass nearby and beat at his leg to put out the flames.

His father's laughter echoed in the woods nearby. He had been watching, timing Nick to see how fast he could escape.

And he had failed the test.

Nick opened his eyes, breathing through the pain as if his leg were on fire once again. That night Jake had found him slathering burn cream on his leg.

Of course he'd lied.

He'd lied to cover his father so many times.

Never again.

If it was the last thing he ever did, he'd track down his father's victims.

He wanted them to see his father rot in jail.

——————— , ———————

Brenda drove past Amelia Nettleton's studio, planning her strategy as she parked. The charred remainder of the Nettleton farm adjacent to the guesthouse still looked stark, the embers dirty brown, soggy from rain and weather, a sad reminder of the family whose life had been destroyed by Arthur Blackwood.

Crickets chirped nearby, the March winds rocking the trees and making the wind chimes on the front porch clang violently. Whispers of honeysuckle, wildflowers, and new grass scented the air, yet the wind also brought the stench of burned wood and rubble that lingered from the fire.

She peeked through the windows of the studio, not surprised to find more paintings in the front room, dark, sinister reflections of Amelia's tormented mind. Would the woman ever truly recover?

Brenda's cell phone buzzed that she had a text, so she clicked to check it.

Tell the Commander I left a present for him.

Slaughter Creek Motel. Room 7.

Brenda's pulse clamored, and she immediately texted back. *Who is this? Where are you?*

She waited several seconds but received no response, so she grabbed her keys and raced back to her car, then sped toward the old motel.

The person who'd sent the text must have seen her news-cast. They'd asked for anonymous tips, but this one sounded ominous.

What exactly would she find when she reached the motel?

Chapter 3

---o---

T he night sounds picked up as Brenda wound around the curves of the mountain, then turned onto the road leading to the Slaughter Creek Motel.

The motel was ancient, situated off a beaten path from the main road but close enough that truckers and other travelers needing a layover before they reached the deserted thick forests of the great Smokies could see it.

For a brief moment, she considered calling Nick, but she quickly dismissed the idea. She'd wait until she saw what was in that motel room. After all, this text could be a prank, someone who got his jollies by sending her on a wild goose chase.

Or it could be some crazed person leading you into a trap.

Maybe someone who didn't want her snooping around. Hadn't Arthur Blackwood murdered everyone who'd tried to expose his secrets?

She shivered, then patted her purse, where she kept her revolver. After being mugged in an alley in Nashville when she was a student, she'd bought herself some protection the next day.

Her instincts told her that this text was for real. Maybe whatever the person had left in the motel would lead her to the names of the subjects in the experiment. Or to the other people who'd been involved—Jake and Nick suspected that someone higher up in the military or CIA than their father had run the experiment. If she broke the story, Nick couldn't leave her out of the investigation.

Her decision made, she focused on the road. Headlights nearly blinded her as she raced around Blindman's Curve, tires screeching as she rounded the switchback. An eighteen-wheeler barreled past from the opposite direction, and she slowed as an SUV pulled out from a dirt road and turned in front of her. Frustration made her curse, and she blew the horn to prompt the driver to move on, but he ignored her.

Minutes crawled by and two other cars whizzed past, lights flickering off the asphalt. A warning sign for falling rock glowed from the rocky wall beside her, and water trickled down the side of the mountain.

Finally the driver of the SUV turned onto another dirt road leading to a fishing lodge that rented cabins, and she waved him on and sped up. By the time she reached the motel, her palms were sweating and she'd imagined a dozen different scenarios, half of which left her dead.

The person who sent the text could have been a psycho. Someone who intended to do God knows what to her. The one-story motel backed up to the woods—a murderer could leave her body in the forest, and no one would ever find her.

She hadn't told anyone about the text either, so it might take days for someone to even realize she was missing.

Maybe she should alert her boss.

But if this lead turned out to be nothing, she'd look like a fool and lose his respect. Being an investigative reporter meant digging in the trenches and taking risks. If she showed weakness now, no one would take her seriously as a professional.

Still, as she parked at the motel, she checked the .22.

The blinking lime-green lights of the motel sign created a strobe-light effect as they swirled across the nearly deserted parking lot. The lights on the word CREEK had burned out, so the sign read SLAUGHTER MOTEL.

A rusted pickup truck, minivan, and RV were parked in the lot, but all of the rooms looked dark.

She stepped from the car, then scanned the row of rooms in the L-shaped building.

Room 7 sat at the end of the row, shrouded in shadows and wedged up against bushes that bordered the woods beyond.

For the briefest of moments, she considered asking the motel owner to accompany her to the room, but decided to check the room first. If the person who'd texted her had left something inside, the door was probably unlocked.

Nerves on edge, she scanned the parking lot again, then raked her gaze across the woods and vehicles in the parking lot, looking for someone lurking around to jump her.

She could already envision the headlines: "Reporter Mutilated at the Slaughter Creek Motel. Body Parts Sent to Arthur Blackwood."

What if the person who'd texted her was working for Blackwood and planned to eliminate anyone investigating him? He'd already killed half a dozen people to cover up the project.

She might be next.

She slid her hand over the gun in her purse, stiffened her spine, and forged ahead.

She didn't intend to die today.

The gravel in the parking lot crunched beneath her shoes as she crossed to the room, and she looked through the window, but it was too dark to see inside.

She slowly reached out and touched the doorknob. Just as she'd expected, the knob turned, and the door swung open.

The room was pitch-black, and an acrid smell assaulted her. She flipped on the light by the door, but it didn't work, making her more uneasy, and forcing her to take another step inside the room.

Vile odors swirled around her, and her stomach churned, her ears honed for the sound of someone inside. She covered her mouth with one hand to keep from gagging and bumped into the lamp on the end table nearest the door.

Heart racing, she flipped on the lamp, then gasped in horror.

A naked man lay on the bed, his arms and legs tied to the post. His face and neck were discolored, and a piece of wire was wound around his throat. But it was the wide-eyed terror in his unblinking eyes that would haunt her forever.

He hadn't died in his sleep or by his own hand.

He had been murdered.

Nick parked at Jake's, noting the feminine touches Sadie had added to the Victorian house—a wreath of dried grass with spring flowers woven into it, the birdbath, the white bench where Ayla had left a doll, propped up with a toy teacup beside it.

He couldn't believe his macho brother, the sheriff of Slaughter Creek, had a little girl. Judging from the few times he'd been around them, Ayla had him wrapped around her little finger, too.

Just like Sadie had, ever since the summer before their senior year in high school. Their father's efforts to stop Jake from dating Sadie hadn't worked.

Now they both knew Arthur Blackwood's reasons for trying to keep them apart—he'd been afraid Jake would discover the truth about his project and what he'd done to Amelia.

Nick knocked on the door, determined to stay on an even keel with Jake. For too many years there'd been a chasm between them. Too bad it had taken the arrest of their father to bring them back together.

Jake opened the door, a worried look on his face. "Come on in."

Nick glanced around for Ayla and Sadie. "Where's the family?"

"Ayla's in bed," Jake said. "Sadie just left to drive over to Amelia's studio."

"What's wrong?"

"Amelia left the facility where she was staying."

"Can she do that? Check herself out, I mean?"

"Yes. No." Jake raked a hand through his hair. "Patients leave, but they're supposed to receive clearance from their therapist first."

"Amelia hasn't been cleared?"

"Not to leave without supervision." Jake sighed and led him to the den. "Anyway, Amelia has made progress, and Sadie thought she might show up at the studio."

"I hope you find her," Nick said, hating his father again for the pain he'd caused Sadie and her sister.

The comfortable leather sofas were Jake's, but a corner held Ayla's dollhouse, and he was sure the throw pillows and painting of wildflowers on the wall were compliments of Sadie.

Jake offered him a drink, but he shook his head. "What's going on, Nick?"

Nick removed the note his father had given him. He'd bagged it to send to forensics, although he doubted they'd get prints off of it, but he wanted Jake's take on it first. "I saw the Commander." He refused to call him Dad.

"Anything new?"

"He wouldn't give up the list of subjects or anyone else involved in the project," Nick said. "But he showed me this."

Jake's eyebrows arched in question as he read it. "Who sent it?"

"I have no idea," Nick said. "It's possible that it came from one of the subjects who wants revenge on the Commander."

"What does he expect us to do? Put the bastard in protective custody?"

Nick barked a laugh. "He may be a masochist, but he's no fool. He knows we'd just as soon leave him to his victims and let them dole out his punishment."

Jake nodded, but Nick's cell phone buzzed. He checked the caller screen, surprised to see Brenda Banks's number.

"You gonna get that?" Jake asked.

Nick shook his head. "It's Brenda. I ran into her at the court-house. She's pushing for more on the story."

"I wish we had more," Jake muttered.

The phone stopped buzzing, then started up a second later.

"You might as well answer it," Jake said. "When Brenda wants something, she doesn't give up easily."

Like when she'd wanted to date Jake.

Nick connected the call, prepared to blow her off. "Listen, Brenda, I told you—"

"Shut up and listen," Brenda said in a strangely high-pitched voice.

Nick's hand tightened around the handset. "What?"

"There's a body, a dead man," Brenda choked out. "At the Slaughter Creek Motel."

"You're there now?"

"Yes," Brenda said. "You have to see this, Nick. He was mur-dered."

Nick's mind raced. "How did you find the body?"

"I'll explain when you get here."

Nick began to pace. "Is anyone else with you?"

"No," Brenda said. "I called you first. I'm in room seven."

"Sit tight and don't touch anything," Nick said. "I'll be right there."

Nick headed to the door as he ended the call. "There was a murder at the Slaughter Creek Motel."

"Let me call Sadie, and we'll ride over together."

Jake shoved the limerick back into Nick's hand. Nick glanced at it, and a sudden feeling of trepidation came over him. "What if this murder has something to do with the note the Commander received?"

A tense second passed. "We can't assume that," Jake said.

"No, but it's possible."

"True. Or the note could simply be someone toying with the Commander. For all we know, he could have written it himself, just to mess with us."

Nick hadn't considered that.

"I wouldn't put it past him." Although the timing hit him as odd. "What if Amelia sent Dad that limerick? The fact that she's missing now is suspicious."

"Don't go there, Nick. Let's get the facts first. For all we know, Amelia just took a long walk somewhere."

"Find her," Nick said. "If anyone has reason to send the Commander hate mail, Amelia does. I'll call you from the motel when I see what we're dealing with, and you can meet me there."

Jake reluctantly agreed, and Nick jogged to his car. Questions pummeled him as he drove down the road, then around Blindman's Curve, and he couldn't help but think about Sadie and her sister. Their parents had died on this road, all because the Nettletons had discovered that the doctors were mistreating Amelia.

He passed a stalled SUV on the shoulder of the road, then flew the few miles to the motel. The gaudy green light from the sign blinked, streaking the sky and road with puke-green lines, reminding him of a cheap Vegas strip club.

A pickup and RV sat at one end of the parking lot, Brenda's Bimmer a few spaces down. The door to room 7 stood slightly ajar. Nick gripped his gun as he climbed from his car, scanning the property.

If a man had been murdered, the killer could be lurking nearby.

The area appeared clear, but his senses were honed. The trees rustled in the wind, mosquitoes buzzed nearby, an owl hooted from the woods, followed by the wail of a cat. He approached the door slowly, checking over his shoulder just before he stepped inside the doorway.

Except for the dim glow of a table lamp, the room was dark. Brenda stood by the table, her face ashen.

He quickly scanned the room, but the metallic scent of blood hit him before he even spotted the corpse. He immediately noted the position of the body on the bed, and the fact that he was naked and had bruises on his chest, arms, and legs. His color was gray, his eyes wide open in the death stare, his wrists and ankles raw from straining against his restraints.

The setup suggested S & M behavior, and the wire—asphyxiation sex. Had the sex been consensual?

Kinky sex that went too far and turned into an accidental death? Or was this premeditated murder?

Another step closer, and he touched the man's neck, where a pulse should have been. But the skin felt cold to the touch, and when he lifted the man's arm, it was rigid and heavy, indicating rigor had set in.

"What were you doing here?" he asked as he looked up at Brenda. "Do you know this man? Were you meeting him?"

She released a breath, then seemed to pull herself together. "No, I don't know him." Her voice took on a brittle edge. "And no, I wasn't meeting him."

She indicated the ropes and piano wire around the man's neck. "And I'm not into that kind of sex either," she said sharply.

For the briefest of seconds he wondered what kind of sex she was into, but decided not to broach that subject. He did not want to get personal with Brenda Banks.

"Then why *were* you here?" he asked.

Brenda pushed her phone into his hands. Her fingers were clammy, her sigh shaky as she gathered her composure, and he had the sudden urge to pull her into her arms and comfort her.

"I received this text about a half an hour ago."

Dread balled in his stomach as he read it.

Tell the Commander I left a present for him.

Slaughter Creek Motel. Room 7.

Now he understood why Brenda had been so certain this was murder.

He jabbed Jake's number into his phone. Jake answered on the second ring. "Did you find Amelia?" Nick asked.

"Not yet."

"Brenda was right," Nick said. "You need to get over here asap and send a crime unit, Jake. We've got a homicide."

Amelia let herself back inside her condo, her body coiled with tension as she eased into her artist smock and picked up her paintbrush. She'd desperately needed some fresh air.

To clear her head.

And quiet the voices in her mind.

She also had to find some relief for the sexual urges that seized her when Viola whispered in her ear.

But she'd lost a few moments, actually hours, and that worried her. She thought the blackouts were behind her...

What had she done during that time?

She glanced down at her tattered shirt and rumpled skirt and smelled sweat and the scent of a man on her.

Her therapist assured her that her sexual urges were normal, and that as a young woman, she had a right to enjoy sex. But she wanted to make real love, the way the doctor said it was supposed to be. To be with a man without Viola's propensity for rough, edgy escapades. To have a man love her with tenderness and affection. But most of all, she wanted to remember every minute of it.

She began to paint, purging the demons inside her head, letting her artistic side flow. Long black strokes, images of a woman and man engaged in violent sex, of whips and chains and ropes, of dominance and submission, images Viola placed in her head with her books and whispered words and…pictures.

It took three canvases to capture the darkness Viola liked, but with each stroke, Amelia's determination to thrive grew stronger. She had to keep Viola at bay. Because Viola liked to steal her nights and days, just as Skid had done for years.

Just a few months ago, she had finally killed Skid. She refused to let another personality dominate her.

She glanced at the bulletin board on her wall, at the article Brenda Banks had written about the Commander. Brenda had portrayed him as a cruel, depraved man who'd preyed on innocents.

Amelia intended to show the world that he hadn't destroyed her, that she wasn't the nutcase everyone thought.

That she would survive, in spite of what Arthur Blackwood had done to her.

Chapter 4

_____ o _____

Nick checked the dead man's eyes and saw definite signs of petechial hemorrhaging. The acrid odor of body wastes and death permeated the room, but he'd have to wait on the ME to establish time of death.

He glanced around the motel room, searching for clues to the killer's identity. A tacky orange flower-print bedspread on the floor. A dusty, ancient TV. A cheap painting of a grizzly bear on the wall. A bathroom with a rusting toilet and cracked tile flooring that needed cleaning badly.

No personal items. No toiletries left behind.

"Did you touch anything, Brenda?"

"No." Brenda fidgeted. "Well, nothing except the doorknob."

"Was the room locked when you arrived?"

The color was finally returning to her face. "No. I considered going to the manager for a key, but figured since I received the text that the door was probably unlocked."

Nick nodded. "Go on."

"I scanned the perimeter outside, just in case I was walking into a trap. A pickup truck and an RV sat in the parking lot, but the lights were off in all the rooms, including this one."

"So you did touch the lamp?"

"Yes, the light by the door didn't work," Brenda said. "The stench hit me, and I...had to see what had happened."

"Then what?"

"Then I found the body," Brenda said in a shaky voice. "And I called you."

"So the room looked exactly like this when you arrived?" Nick asked. "You didn't see any clothing or a wallet?"

"No—I understand the importance of not tampering with a crime scene," Brenda said in a defensive tone.

Nick yanked a pair of latex gloves from his pocket, then checked the bedcovers, the dresser, and the bath again. "No clothing anywhere. No wallet. Not even a condom."

"Whoever killed him probably took everything to foil forensics," Brenda said.

Nick grunted. "You sound like you know a lot about a murder scene."

Brenda shrugged, then gripped her phone and started to punch in the newsroom number.

Nick pressed a hand over hers. "Wait, you can't air this on TV. We have to determine the victim's ID, notify next of kin. Process the crime scene."

Brenda glared at him. "This is news, Nick. I found the body, it's my story."

"Yes, but we can't tip the public on crucial aspects of the crime."

"Fine," Brenda said. "I know the boundaries and will make sure my people follow them." Still, she snatched her phone and began snapping pictures.

"Brenda," Nick growled.

"I promise you nothing goes into print without your permission. But you can't shut me out, Nick. The killer invited me to this crime for a reason."

He cursed. "Because the killer wants publicity."

"You're probably right—the coverage will give him notoriety."

"She," Nick clarified.

"How do you know the perp is female?" Brenda asked.

"Instinct. Just look at the setup."

"Still, it's possible the killer is male. Maybe a gay male."

"Or confused sexually," Nick conceded. They couldn't rule anything out at this point.

A siren wailed in the distance. Jake was on his way, and hopefully the ME and crime unit.

"All right, it's your story," Nick said, giving in. "But listen to me, Brenda—you have to run everything by me first. If you become a problem, I'll arrest you for interfering with a homicide investigation."

She lifted her chin in challenge but nodded. "Don't worry, Nick. I won't interfere. In fact, I'm probably going to be an asset."

He mumbled something ugly beneath his breath. No reporter was ever an asset. "More like a thorn in my side."

"Deal with it. For some reason this killer sent a text to me, not you." Brenda started toward the bathroom to take more photos.

Nick stepped in front of her, using the fact that he towered over her to intimidate her. "After we're done processing, you get your chance. You might contaminate the evidence."

Brenda gave him a saccharine smile. Apparently she didn't intimidate easily. "Come on, Nick, I might grow on you if you give me a chance."

He glared at her, then ordered her back to the doorway.

"Fine," Brenda said. "But I am calling my cameraman. We can take shots of the outside of the motel."

He wanted to wring her neck, but she disappeared out the door, and he used his own phone to snap some photographs.

Jake's squad car zoomed up and barreled to a stop, the sound of doors slamming echoing from the street. Seconds later, his brother and his deputy, Mike Waterstone, appeared in the doorway.

"The crime unit will be here any minute," Jake said as his gaze raked across the scene. "Jesus. Have you identified the victim?"

"No, no clothes or wallet," Nick said.

Deputy Waterstone appeared behind him. "Shit," Waterstone said as he spotted the dead man tied to the bed. "Are you sure this was murder? Some people are into this kinky sex. Maybe it just got out of hand."

"It's possible, except that Brenda received a text telling her to come here. That she'd find a present for the Commander."

"Some sick bitch," Waterstone muttered.

Which made him wonder if the killer had been one of his father's subjects. Of course, other people were also incensed over what his father had done. Family members of victims, friends, anyone with a pulse. "Hopefully the ME can give us more information."

Jake cleared his throat. "I'll talk to the motel manager, inform him we have a crime scene and find out who rented this room."

Nick turned to the deputy. "Waterstone, see who those vehicles in the parking lot belong to. We need to know if anyone saw anything."

"How about Brenda?" Jake asked. "She's going to be a problem."

"For some reason the killer contacted her, probably wants Brenda to make her famous."

"Probably," Jake agreed.

"I gave her strict orders not to show any photos or reveal any details she hasn't cleared with me."

"Good," Jake said. "I didn't see any security cameras when I drove up. But I'll ask the manager. Maybe he has one at the check-in desk."

The sound of two more vehicles rumbled into the parking lot. First the crime unit. The other—Brenda's news van.

As if Slaughter Creek hadn't suffered enough from the recent publicity.

Now another circus would begin.

————————— , —————————

Brenda met her cameraman, Louis Bellamy, at the news van. Now that the shock of finding the dead man was wearing off, her adrenaline had kicked in.

The killer wanted Brenda to tell his or her story, and she intended to do that.

"What's up?" Louis asked as he hoisted his camera from the back of the van.

"A murdered man in room seven."

Louis raised a brow. "How did you get here so quickly? Are you on the police scanner?"

Brenda shook her head. "I can't say just yet. Sheriff Jake Blackwood, his deputy, and Special Agent Nick Blackwood are on the scene. For the sake of the victim and until the family is notified, we can't divulge details or photograph the inside of the room. But we can shoot some preliminary footage."

Dr. Barry Bullock, the medical examiner, parked and climbed from his vehicle, giving Brenda a look of disgust, then charged toward the motel room. She'd heard the man enjoyed his job a little too much, that he was obsessed with bugs and weird particulates.

She ignored him, and directed Louis to start shooting live footage.

"This is Brenda Banks coming to you outside the Slaughter Creek Motel, where a man's body has been found. Special Agent Nick Blackwood and Sheriff Jake Blackwood are both on the scene, along with Deputy Mike Waterstone." She gestured toward the police car and ME's van.

Jake appeared from the motel lobby with the motel manager, a thin rail of man with a bad toupee, smoke-stained teeth, and a set of keys jangling from his left hand.

Brenda made a beeline toward them.

"Sheriff Blackwood, what can you tell us about the victim?"

Jake shot her a look of disdain. "Unfortunately we have found a deceased man, but the ME has not confirmed cause of death yet."

"Have you identified the victim?"

"Not at this time." Jake gestured toward the crime scene tape that his deputy was beginning to roll out to cordon off the area. "Now, please stay behind the tape and let us do our jobs."

"Of course." Brenda faced the camera. "Ladies and gentlemen, as soon as we have details on this case, we will inform you. What I can tell you right now is that an anonymous tip was received tonight, alerting authorities to this crime. Details are not clear as to the circumstances surrounding the death, but we should know more soon."

Jake and the motel owner had reached the doorway. "Get a shot of the manager," Brenda said to Louis.

Louis already had the camera trained on the man. A moment later, Jake led the manager back outside. The man looked peaked, leaning against a tree as if he might be sick.

Brenda rushed to him. "Sir, you are the manager here, correct?"

Jake gave her a warning look. "Don't say anything, Mr. Feldon. This is an official investigation."

The older man rubbed his head, sending his toupee askew. "I don't know anything."

"Who rented room seven?" Brenda asked.

"Brenda," Jake said. "I told you we have no comment. Next of kin has to be notified before we can disclose the man's name."

"That means the dead man *did* reserve the room, not another party?" Brenda pressed.

Nick glared at her again, then motioned for Jake to join him and the crime techs heading into the room. Mr. Feldon pulled out a Marlboro and lit up, his hand shaking as he flicked the lighter.

"Mr. Feldon, was the man alone when he checked in?" Brenda asked.

"I didn't see anyone with him," Feldon muttered as he took a deep drag. "Man paid cash."

"Do you have security cameras in the lobby?"

"Don't have a camera," the man said. "But after this, I guess I need to install one."

Brenda gestured toward the pickup and RV. "Was he driving one of these vehicles?"

The embers of the cigarette sparkled against the night sky as Feldon flicked the ashes onto the ground. "Didn't see the car. I was watching TV and barely looked up when the man dropped cash on the counter and took the key."

"You don't have your renters leave their car tag numbers with you?"

The manager's eyes, which were set a little too close together, narrowed in anger. "Lady, look where we are. We rent by the night, by the hour sometimes. I mind my own business. Now mind yours."

"A dead man is lying in one of your rooms, and it appears to be murder," Brenda fired back. "If you saw something, you need to help the police."

He dropped the cigarette into the dirt and smashed it with his boot, then strode back toward the office. "Like the sheriff said, lady, I ain't got nothing to say to you."

Brenda bit the inside of her cheek as he stalked off. He was already lighting another cigarette by the time he reached the office. Deputy Waterstone had finished winding the crime scene tape, so she headed toward him.

"Deputy Waterstone, did you find out who the two vehicles in the parking lot belong to?"

The deputy ran a hand through his thick blond hair. He was handsome, a flirt with the ladies in town. But he did nothing for Brenda.

"Pickup belongs to the manager," he said. "The RV, to a family who left it here while they drove the Jeep they were towing to Nashville. Had plans to see the Grand Ole Opry. They're supposed to be back tomorrow."

"A dead end," Brenda murmured.

Two more cars turned from the road into the motel parking lot, the people jumping out. "Is this where that murder was?" a middle-aged man asked.

The teens in the next car whipped out their cell phones. "Cool, man. Can't wait to post this on YouTube."

Deputy Waterstone jogged over to circumvent the rubber-neckers while Brenda watched the door, waiting for Nick or Jake to appear. Hopefully soon the ME would exit with the body, and they could get a shot of the medics wheeling the corpse to the ambulance to transport him to the morgue.

Questions pummeled her. Nick would need to run a trace on her phone. But why had the killer chosen her? Was the perp from Slaughter Creek? Would she hear from the killer again? And why had the killer chosen this victim—as some kind of statement to Commander Arthur Blackwood?

"What can you tell us about the body?" Nick asked the ME.

Dr. Bullock pointed to the red slashes and bruises on the man's neck. "It appears he died of asphyxiation, but I'll verify that when I get him on the table."

Nick scanned the room again, noting the thick ropes used to bind the victim to the bed. "He weighs, what, about two hundred pounds?"

The ME nodded. "That'd be my guess."

"So he probably agreed to be tied up. That is, unless the killer held a gun to his head."

"That's possible," the ME said, "although he wasn't shot."

"Man probably thought he was in for a night of fun," Jake muttered. "But the fun got out of hand, just like that damn choking game kids have been playing."

"I haven't seen one of those yet, and don't want to," the ME commented as he scraped beneath the man's fingernails.

The crime unit had already photographed close-ups of the man's body, including the cock ring around his penis.

"Any scratch marks or body fluids evident?" Nick asked.

"Not so far." He shone an instrument onto the man's genital area, then on the sheet. "Looks like she probably made him use a condom. I don't see any evidence of vaginal or seminal fluids." He began to untie the man's wrists, and Nick untied the legs, allowing the CSI team to photograph close-ups of the bruises made by the ropes.

Nick pointed to the torn, rope-burned skin. "Looks like he struggled."

The ME peeled back the wire from the victim's neck. "Probably realized that his partner wasn't playing." He indicated the depth of the bruises and cuts in the man's throat. "In fact, if I'm guessing right, the killer was sadistic. It looks like the victim was subjected to repeated strangulation."

Nick swallowed hard, contemplating the text on Brenda's phone. *A present for the Commander.*

Was the text connected to the limerick his father had received?

Seven felt the sweet satisfaction of watching Brenda Banks airing the story about the motel murder while she relaxed in a hot tub of lavender-scented water. She had to wash the stench of the vile man from her skin.

Not the scent of the man she'd fucked.

Arthur Blackwood's black scent.

His evil had permeated her years ago, and the only way she could purge the darkness he'd birthed inside her was to show the world what he'd turned her into.

And to exact revenge on other men like him.

She closed her eyes, the memories of her earlier years starting to take on new meaning. Memories of friends who had not been friends. Of babysitters and caretakers who, she realized now, had been guards.

Red Rover, Red Rover
Send Seven right over.

She had obeyed the Commander because he was the only father figure she'd known. He was her family.

Now she had no one.

Only the mindless games of survival he'd taught her. Disappear into the dark for days and survive, and he would finally love her.

The image of Jim Logger's eyes bulging as he drew his last breath taunted her. The Commander had looked into her eyes and watched her die so many times, only to revive her.

And for what?

To make her suffer and die again.

Her laughter pierced the air.

Now it was his turn to suffer.

Chapter 5

———— o ————

Nick jotted down notes on the details of the crime scene while the crime techs dusted the motel room for prints and searched for clothing fibers, strands of hair, and other forensics.

"There are dozens of prints in this room," Marc Maddison, the lead investigator, said. "Apparently whoever cleans this dump doesn't do a very good job."

"That's obvious," said Nick. Water rings marred the scarred dresser top, clumps of dust were stuck to the lampshades, and a nasty brown stain colored the ugly chair in the corner. He motioned to Jake, and they stepped to the threshold of the door for some air. Three more vehicles had appeared, people climbing out to see the murder scene after Brenda's story aired. The deputy worked to maintain control in the parking lot and keep curiosity seekers behind the crime scene tape.

He'd seen Brenda talking to the motel owner, but she must have ticked off the man, because he stalked back to his office in a huff.

Jake cleared his throat. "The owner, a Mr. Feldon, said the man who checked in signed his name as Jim Logger. I got a copy of his signature for analysis."

"You don't think that's his real name?" Nick asked.

Jake shrugged. "We'll run his prints and DNA and find out."

"What kind of vehicle was the victim driving?"

Jake shook his head. "He didn't see the automobile or the person with him. Logger signed in, then dropped his cash on the desk and left."

"Obviously the killer drove off in the car."

"Yes. But we have nothing on the vehicle. Feldon doesn't require guests to leave their tag numbers when they register." Jake paused. "But I'll find out what he drove and put out an APB for the vehicle."

"Let me know if you find it," Nick said. "What time did Logger check in?"

"Around midnight."

"Dr. Bullock," Nick said, addressing the ME, "what is the estimated time of death?"

"Judging from rigor, I'd say several hours ago."

Nick frowned. "Did Logger rent the room for two nights or one?"

Jake checked his notes. "One."

Nick contemplated the timing. "Maybe a midday rendez-vous."

Jake glanced around the room, then went to check the door. "Looks like either the vic or the killer left the Do Not Disturb sign on the door to keep the cleaning staff out."

"Feldon didn't bother to see if the man checked out?" Nick asked.

Jake shrugged. "He said the only vehicles in the parking lot were his and the RV, so he assumed Logger had left."

Nick made a low sound in his throat. "Not a very observant guy."

"That's putting it mildly," Jake said. "I asked about business—if Logger had been here before—but he said no. He claims business was slow, that it usually picks up mid-March."

"I wonder if the killer knew that," Nick said.

Jake shrugged. "Could be, especially if she's from around here."

"Brenda suggested the killer could be a man."

Jake raised a brow. "I suppose, but my bet is on a female."

Dr. Bullock cleared his throat. "I found some fibers in the man's throat. Probably from a rag or whatever the killer used to muffle the man's cries for help."

Nick and Jake both walked over to examine the fibers, but it was impossible to tell the source. "Looks like satin," Nick said.

Jake nodded. "Maybe a scarf that belonged to the killer."

"Or satin underwear," Nick suggested. "Bag them. If you can identify where they came from, it might help with the case."

Maddison carried an evidence bag over to the ME to collect the samples.

Nick confiscated the Do Not Disturb Sign and gave it to the analyst. "Maybe the killer hung this on the door before she or he got down to business, and you can lift some prints from it."

Jake's phone buzzed, and he punched connect. "Yeah. Okay, good. Stay there with her. I'll be there soon."

"Did Sadie find Amelia?" Nick asked as Jake ended the call.

"Yeah, she's back in her condo."

"Where was she?"

"She wouldn't tell Sadie," Jake said. "She said she was tired and just wanted to sleep. Sadie's trying to give her some leeway, to prove she trusts her."

Nick hated to consider Amelia as a suspect, but she had mental problems. According to Jake, one of her alter personalities, Viola, was promiscuous. Another personality, Skid, was violent. The combination could be volatile.

"You still need to find out where she was," Nick said. "What if Viola took a lover, then Skid emerged and killed him?"

Jake's gaze met his, tension thrumming between them. "I know, but Sadie will be upset. Amelia has made progress in merging the personalities."

"But she could have suffered a setback," Nick said. "Maybe she saw the news story and snapped."

A mixture of emotions tightened Jake's face. Then he sighed, resigned. "Don't worry. I'll question her."

"Okay—I'll see if Logger has family or friends. We need to find out everything we can about him." Nick addressed the crime team. "Copy me and the sheriff on your findings. And let me know asap about the prints and DNA results."

Maddison agreed, and Nick left Jake to monitor the crime scene. He needed to talk to Brenda and to trace that text.

Determining its source might be the best chance they had to track down the killer.

Brenda gestured for Louis to capture the medics transporting the dead body to the ambulance.

The teens who'd first arrived protested as Deputy Waterstone ordered them to stay behind the line. "It's a free country, man. You can't make us go."

"I can arrest you for interfering at a crime scene," the deputy said.

"We're not interfering," one of the boys shouted.

"Let me see your IDs." The boys argued at first, but the deputy took them and made a note of their names and contact information.

For a moment, Brenda wondered if he suspected the boys of the murder, although after seeing the body, she didn't think they fit the profile of the killer. Still, killers often return to the scene of the crime to watch the investigation. She searched the crowd, then used her phone to take random shots of the crowd in the parking lot.

Louis photographed the deputy and the group, then followed Brenda to question the ME. "Dr. Bullock, can you confirm the cause of death?"

Bullock's eyes narrowed below the rims of his glasses. "Not at this time. When I'm finished with the autopsy, I'll release the results to the police."

"Thank you, Dr. Bullock." She turned to the camera as the doctor climbed in his car. "As I stated earlier, we will bring you more on this late-breaking story as more information becomes available."

Nick exited the motel room and walked toward her while Jake remained inside with the crime team.

She braced herself for a battle.

"The crime unit is finishing processing the scene," he said when he joined her. "I need to trace that text."

"Of course." Brenda removed her phone from her purse. "As long as I get my phone back."

"Actually, I don't need the phone. I can use your number from my caller history. But I figured I'd get your permission."

"Of course."

"Thanks. I'll get a warrant for the wireless provider, and then we're set."

"I texted the caller back, but she didn't respond," Brenda said.

"Keep trying. And let me know if you receive any more communication from her."

"Of course," Brenda said. "You know, Nick, it's not like I asked for this. The killer chose me."

Nick's dark eyes flashed with annoyance. "Maybe you did ask for it," he said gruffly. "You dogged Jake to report this case from the beginning."

Brenda's heart thumped at the intensity in his expression. She had tried to persuade Sadie to talk to her about her grandfather's murder, but that was because she'd wanted to help her and her sister. Maybe she'd wanted to atone for her less than stellar behavior in high school. She'd had her own problems back then. She'd been upset over finding out that she was adopted, insecure, but that didn't excuse her rudeness.

She couldn't share any of those feelings with Nick, though. "Yes, I did," she said. "If I hadn't pursued the story, someone else would have. And they might not have been as easy on Jake as I was."

"Because you're still in love with him," Nick said sharply.

Brenda sucked in a breath. "That's not true." In fact, she'd never really been in love with Jake. She'd dated him to fit in, at a time when she felt out of place.

Nick grunted. "Not that it matters to me, but you know he loves Sadie."

Of course it didn't matter to him. He didn't feel anything for her. So why did it hurt so much? "Nick, I wrote the story the way I saw it," Brenda said. "What your father did wasn't Jake's fault or yours."

He licked his lips, drawing her gaze to his mouth. She chided herself for reacting, but forced herself not to look away.

"Not unless you knew what your father was doing."

Nick glared at her. "Is that what you think?"

"I don't know," she said softly. "But I'm a good listener."

He cursed. "Yeah, you'll listen, then plaster my personal thoughts all over the fucking television."

"No, Nick, that's not what I meant—"

"Just stay out of my way," Nick snapped. "And keep your end of the deal."

Brenda started to assure him she would, but he stalked toward his car without giving her time to reply.

Frustrated, but knowing she'd gleaned all the information she could from him, she motioned to Louis to wrap it up.

Maybe Nick would have some luck with the trace. Meanwhile, she'd try again to open up communication with the killer. Jordan Jennings, the weather girl who'd wanted Brenda's job, would kill to have this lead.

Brenda didn't intend to waste it.

Her thumbs quickly typed another text: *Call me and tell me your story.*

Maybe she'd arrange a meeting with the killer.

It would be dangerous, but it would be worth it if she uncovered her identity.

Nick fumed as he drove back to his cabin. Damn Brenda Banks.

She was persistent, so pushy that if she were a man, he'd have slugged her for digging into his personal life.

There was no way he would discuss his feelings or past with her or anyone else. Did she really think that he and Jake had known what their father was doing?

It was too late to go to the TBI office, but he'd installed a state-of-the-art computer system linked to their national database at his cabin, so he could do some research tonight.

He wound around the mountain, then turned onto the road to his cabin, grateful he'd found a place close to town but also tucked into the woods for privacy. A small group of cabins had been built on Slaughter Creek years ago, but the builder had nestled them into the trees and situated them miles apart for seclusion.

He parked, crickets chirping as he walked up to his door. Instincts always on alert, he scanned the perimeter and woods beyond for an attacker, but barring the sound of an animal skittering in the bushes, everything seemed quiet.

Forcing thoughts of Brenda from his mind, he let himself inside and flipped on the light. A profiler would have a field day with his obsessive-compulsiveness, the way he kept everything in perfect order. They'd say it was his military training, but Arthur Blackwood had beaten it into him long before he joined the service.

He went to the kitchen and poured a shot of whiskey, then sat down at his office nook and booted up his computer. Scanning in the picture he'd taken of the dead man, he input the name Jim Logger and sipped his drink while the computer program searched its databases.

Brenda's face kept flashing in his head, making his body tighten with agitation...and something else. Lust.

He could not be attracted to that woman. She was infuriating and nosy and...her scent had invaded his pores.

Fuck.

He took another sip of his whiskey and stood, needed to expel his frustration. His phone beeped. Jake.

"Hey, brother, what's up?"

"Logger drove a 'ninety-six black Jeep. My deputy found it abandoned out on Bogger Hollow Road."

Nick perked up. "Anything in the Jeep?"

"I've gone over it myself. Just an old coat of Logger's, pair of work gloves, tool kit. Nothing that looked as if it belonged to a woman."

"How about prints?"

"The Jeep was wiped clean."

Nick cursed. "She's covering her tracks."

"Yeah, looks like it." Jake paused. "Oh, and I talked to the crime lab about that piano wire. Apparently you can order it online through dozens of websites. And Home Depot carries an almost identical wire that's cheaper. I checked with the stores in Nashville and Knoxville, but they had no big orders for it."

"Our unsub probably paid cash for it anyway."

Nick rubbed the back of his neck where it was stiff as he hung up. A second later, the computer dinged, and he glanced at the screen and saw Jim Logger's name appear, along with a photograph.

Logger's military photo. He slid into the chair and scrolled down. Logger had spent four years in the marines before receiving a medical discharge.

After his release, he went to rehab for a gunshot wound and physical therapy for an injury to his leg. Notations also indicated he suffered from PTSD.

Logger hadn't worked for two years, but a few months back he'd taken a job at a security agency.

Questions mounted in Nick's mind.

How could a tough marine, a man adept at security measures, have ended up dead in a cheap motel?

Several scenarios raced through his mind.

One—the killer had lured Logger into trusting her because he knew her. She'd obviously seduced him, so he didn't sense the impending danger.

Two—he'd been forced at gunpoint to submit to being tied up.

Three—the killer had an accomplice who aided in restraining Logger.

But the most likely scenario was that Logger had met up with a lover, expecting a hot night of sex. After all, Logger had checked into the motel and paid for the room. No one had been seen with him, not a woman or a gunman, when he'd reserved it.

He studied Logger's profile. Six-four, 230 pounds.

A big guy with military training would be difficult to subdue.

"Who killed you, Logger?" he murmured.

He skimmed the man's personal information, searching for family. According to records, he had married five years ago and divorced six months ago. No other living family.

It was too late to visit the wife tonight, or search Logger's apartment, but tomorrow he would. Besides, he wanted the ME's report before he questioned the ex.

Tracking down the victim's actions and behavior the last few months might lead him to the killer.

———————— . ————————

A journal entry, March 4

Now I know the truth. The Commander lied to us at the hospital. What other lies did he tell?

Was any of what he'd said true?

The school where he sent me, the teachers, the caretakers... had they helped him continue his experiment on us once we left the Slaughter Creek Sanitarium?

Memories fought their way through the fog in my brain. Just as the news story said he'd done to Amelia, he'd stolen my mind, and I'd left the memories of what was real behind.

But suddenly one memory broke through the wall.

When I was four years old, I saw one of the other girls in the hospital with a pretty lady with silky blond hair and eyes that glittered like stars when she looked at her daughter.

The little girl had to get a shot, and the mommy hugged her and shielded her face while the doctor gave the injection.

I told the Commander I wanted a mommy like that.

But he said my mommy died. I cried and yelled and called him a liar. Then he punished me by locking me in the dark tiny room he called the hole for hours until I cried myself to sleep.

When he let me out, I asked again about my mommy.

A sinister look crossed his face, then he drove me to the graveyard and showed me her grave.

He made me lie down on the cold dirt for hours and hours.

Seven hours, he said, because I was number seven.

After that, seven became my number. Seven times I walked up and down my room before I crawled under the covers. Seven times I checked to make sure no monsters were under my bed.

Seven times I'd chant, "Yes, sir," when he ordered me to walk to the basement.

Seven times I counted over and over in my head as he filled the needle with the drugs to make me sleep. And when I slept, and he played with my mind, I heard him calling my name, Seven.

I glanced at the newspaper picture of him I'd cut out and taped on the wall of my room, then stood and began my pacing regimen.

Seven steps across the room. Seven steps back. Seven times in one direction, seven times in the opposite.

A block just the size of the hole where I spent so many nights.

If everything he'd told me was a lie, was my mother really dead? Or had she left me with him to be killed over and over again?

I slumped down against the wall, the terrifying memories bombarding me. The shrill screams of the others. The cries and pleas, the children begging not to be taken to the basement.

My hand shook as I gripped the piano wire and wound it around my wrist. I clenched it tight and pulled and twisted with one hand, watching as it began to cut off my circulation.

Seven times I squeezed it, seven times I thought about lying on that cold grave as night set in, and ghosts rose from the ground and reached for me. I closed my eyes and tried to read the name on the tombstone, but shadows covered the name and I couldn't make out the letters.

It was a good thing my mother was dead.

If she was alive, I'd kill her for leaving me with the Commander.

Chapter 6

───────── o ─────────

B renda's phone was ringing as she let herself into her condo.
Hopefully it was Nick with more information on the murder, but the caller ID indicated that it was her father.

Stalling, she dropped her keys on the kitchen counter and
opened the back patio doors. The moon shone dimly over the
treetops, stars glittering like diamonds in the sky.

She had chosen the new housing development for its security and the fact that it had been built on one of the ridges that
jutted out over the valley and hollows. Her patio spanned the
length of her unit, offering a panoramic view of the mountains
and Slaughter Creek. The last of the snow was melting, the buds
on the trees bursting to life, the smell of spring wafting in the air.

Her phone buzzed again, and she clenched and unclenched
her hands, dreading the conversation that inevitably waited.

But her father would send one of his goons over to check
on her if she didn't pick up. When the case had broken before,
and he'd seen her name on the news story featuring Arthur
Blackwood's arrest, he'd insisted on hiring her a bodyguard.

She had adamantly refused and told him she would no longer
answer his calls if he persisted.

The phone buzzed again. Resigned, she punched connect as she walked to her bedroom and slipped on her PJs. A strong odor hit her, and she glanced around. It smelled like…hospital soap.

She didn't have hospital soap in her condo. In fact, the smell always made her nauseous, just as hospitals did. It was almost as if she had a phobia.

"Brenda, what took you so long to answer?" her father bellowed. "Your mother and I have been worried sick."

"You're always worrying, Dad." Nerves on edge, Brenda checked the condo, but nothing seemed amiss.

She must have imagined the odor.

Shaking off the unsettling feeling, she returned to her kitchen and examined her refrigerator for dinner. Nothing substantial, but she had grapes, red pepper hummus, and a block of Gouda cheese. She pulled them out, grabbed a box of Triscuits from the cabinet, and made herself a meal.

"Of course I'm worried," her father said, his voice uneven. "You insert yourself in the middle of the most horrific crime that's ever happened in Slaughter Creek. Hell, the worst in Tennessee, for that matter."

"Dad, I'm just doing my job." Brenda poured herself a glass of her favorite pinot noir.

"A job doesn't require putting your life in danger." Her father heaved a breath. "You don't even have to work," he said. "If it's money—"

"No, Dad, I like my job."

"But it's not safe," he argued.

"I'm fine, Dad," Brenda said. "Home, locked safe in my condo."

"For now, maybe," her father said. "But I saw that newscast of you at the Slaughter Creek Motel. For God's sake, first you tangle with Arthur Blackwood, who you know murdered everyone who was involved with that experiment, as well as everyone who tried to expose him, and now this."

"He didn't kill Jake or Nick or Sadie," Brenda said, irritated.

"He hired someone to kill Sadie," her father said. "And who knows—he may hire someone to kill you."

Brenda opened her mouth to argue, but he continued on his rant.

"I know you had a breakdown years ago over the adoption, but do you have a death wish?"

Brenda tensed at the reminder. "That was years ago, Dad," she said, striving for calm. "I've moved on and worked hard to earn respect in my field. I wish you'd try to understand that."

A long, tension-filled minute pulsed between them.

Brenda sipped her wine. "Dad?"

"Just promise me you'll come to Sunday dinner." Emotions thickened his voice, triggering Brenda's guilt.

"I—"

"No excuses, Brenda," her father said. "It took me a half hour to calm your mother down after she saw that newscast. I had to give her a Xanax."

Along with her vodka tonic, Brenda thought. "All right, Dad. I'll be there."

She could hear her father's relieved sigh. "Thank you, darlin'. We're looking forward to it. And oh…wear a pretty dress."

"Dad—"

"I have to go—your mother's calling from the bedroom." He said good night, then hung up, and Brenda took her plate of food and wine to the patio.

Wear a pretty dress?

What did her parents have up their sleeves? She always dressed nicely for dinner. Agnes Banks had instilled the rules of etiquette in her as a child. But the fact that her father had suggested a dress made her wonder if they were having other guests.

Good grief. They weren't planning a setup for her, were they?

No, surely not. She'd warned them about meddling before.

Maybe it was some kind of intervention—they intended to try to convince her to drop the story.

She dipped a cracker in the hummus, took a bite, and stared out at the mountains. There was no way they could persuade her to do that.

Just like there was no way they would keep her from finding out the truth about her birth parents.

———————— , ————————

The next morning, Jake called Nick to discuss a strategy.

"I'm going by the ME's office to see what he found," Nick said. "Then I'll visit Logger's ex and search his house."

"Good. Amelia was too tired to talk last night, but Sadie and I are going to visit her today. I'll meet you at Logger's house."

Nick agreed, then showered and drove to the ME's office, an urgency needling him.

Dr. Barry Bullock was deep in concentration over the body as Nick entered the morgue. Nick paused a second to stave off the vile odors of the autopsy and the chemicals, grabbed a paper cover-up, and approached Bullock. "I checked his fingerprints in the database last night and verified that the vic is Jim Logger."

Dr. Bullock was peering at some organ in a dish. "I'll run his blood and DNA," he said.

"How about the tox screen?"

"A little Ecstasy in his system, but nothing that would have incapacitated him to the point of being unconscious when he was strangled."

Meaning the poor bastard had known what was happening to him.

"What else can you tell me about him?"

The doctor lifted his protective goggles. "Man was not a smoker, liver and heart look good. He was fit, too, probably worked out regularly." He hesitated, then gestured toward his abdomen. "Looks like he took a bullet once, and he had some shrapnel in his leg."

"Fits with his time in the service," Nick commented.

Dr. Bullock nodded. "Now, to the cause of death, asphyxiation. In this case, death resulted from autoerotic asphyxiation." Bullock looked up at him. "Did you know that cases similar to this were noted dating back to the seventeenth century? The practice of autoerotic asphyxiation came about when it was noted that subjects who were hung developed erections. Some actually ejaculated, while in others the erection remained."

Bullock was a wealth of information. "No, I didn't know that."

"It's called a death erection," Bullock continued. "You see, the carotid arteries in the neck carry oxygen-rich blood from the heart to the brain. Compression on the arteries, as in strangulation or hanging, creates a sudden loss of oxygen to the brain, which makes carbon dioxide accumulate. This accumulation increases feelings of giddiness, pleasure, and lightheadedness.

"There are also abnormalities in the cerebral neurochemistry involving the interconnected neurotransmitters dopamine, 5-hydroxytryptamine, and endorphin."

"It creates a rush?"

"Exactly. Some people also experience hallucinations." Bullock poked at the brain with one of his instruments. "One of the most famous cases was in Japan in the 1930s. A woman killed her lover, cut off his penis and testicles, and carried them around in her pocket for several days."

"Ouch," Nick muttered. "She was sick."

Dr. Bullock shrugged. "Definitely." He indicated bruises on the man's chest. "It looks like she strangled the man, then revived him. My first thought was that it was accidental and she tried to save him. But—"

He indicated the ligature marks on the man's neck. "Judging from the number of ligature compressions, she saved him only to strangle him again."

"My god," Nick said as he counted them. "There are twenty-one different slash marks in his skin."

"Like I said, I think the unsub killed him, then revived him and killed him again."

Nick tried to comprehend the mindset of a person who would repeatedly strangle another human. Was the crime personal? Someone who had a grudge against Logger?

Or a crime of passion where the sex act turned ugly?

"Did you find any other forensics?" he asked.

Dr. Bullock shook his head. "So far, no hair or skin cells. Looks like she was careful and knew what she was doing."

Nick frowned. "You think it was a female?"

"Judging from the sexual act and the position of the body, yes. If a male, a gay man, had committed this murder, he would have left him facedown. There are also no signs of anal sex."

Nick contemplated his comment. "Which brings us back to the fact that Logger is a big muscular guy who walked into that motel room expecting a good time."

"It may have been good until his lover turned psycho on him," Bullock said.

Nick nodded. "Either way, this perpetrator has a sadistic side. If she knew him, the kill could be personal. If not…"

"Then you're dealing with a psychopath." Bullock rolled the body sideways. "Take a look at this."

Nick leaned over, his heart racing when he saw what Bullock was pointing to. "Jesus. She carved a number behind the man's ear."

"Number one."

"Because this was her first victim," Nick muttered.

Nick removed the paper cover-up he'd put on and tossed it in the trash. "Call me if you find anything else. I'm going to check out the victim's apartment, and talk to his ex-wife. Maybe she had a reason to kill him."

Bullock frowned. "Men don't usually hook up with their exes in motels."

"Unless that was part of some sex game. At this point, I can't rule anything out." Besides, if the man had been cheating on her, his wife might give him the name of Logger's lover.

There was another factor that weighed into the case. The text Brenda had received indicated that the perpetrator had left a present specifically for his father. Which meant that the killer wanted the Commander to know what she'd done.

Because Logger was connected to Arthur Blackwood? Or because the unsub was?

Was she another one of his victims, one who'd been programmed to kill for him?

And if Logger was number one, how many men did she plan to murder?

———— . ————

Brenda rose early, showered, and drove to Amelia's place again. She hated to disturb the poor girl, but she couldn't discount her as a suspect in the motel murder without talking to her.

Besides, Amelia knew Arthur Blackwood firsthand, had suffered from his cruel mind experiments.

Amelia might know who'd sent her the text.

She checked to make sure her mini-recorder was in her purse, then climbed out and walked up the stone path to the front door. More hints of spring showed in the tulips popping through the earth along the walkway.

The wind chimes tinkled in the breeze blowing off the mountain, a musical sound that reminded her of her piano lessons as a child.

Lessons she'd hated because she hadn't been interested in music or attending a cotillion or impressing her mother's snobby friends. Instead, she'd had her head buried in mystery novels and preferred helping the gardener dig in the earth to keeping her dress white and her social status pristine.

She knocked, taking in her surroundings while she waited. The complex seemed quiet, but she noticed several people congregating by the community center and wondered what was going on. Maybe therapy sessions or classes?

Today she hadn't brought her cameraman with her, knowing that would intimidate Amelia. She wanted to broach the subject of a personal profile without scaring her off.

To do that, she needed to win her trust.

She knocked again, and a moment later Amelia opened the door. Even though Brenda had known the twins for years, Amelia looked so much like Sadie that it was still startling.

"Amelia, it's Brenda—do you remember me from high school?"

Amelia's eyes darted past her as if she was expecting someone to be with her. "I know who you are," she said. "You used to gossip about me."

"I'm so sorry for that," Brenda said sincerely. "We were just kids, Amelia. I…wish I could change how I acted back then."

Amelia studied her as if she was dissecting her. "You mean that, don't you?" she finally said softly.

Unexpected emotions rose in Brenda's throat. "Yes, I do. I know everyone thought I was so confident, but I was really insecure. I took that out on you and Sadie, and that was wrong."

Amelia tucked a strand of her auburn hair behind her ear. "Is that why you're here? To apologize?"

Brenda hesitated. "That's part of the reason," she said. "Can I come in? I'd like to talk to you."

Amelia looked wary for a moment. "I don't have many visitors. Or friends."

Because Arthur Blackwood had toyed with her mind. "I'm sorry, Amelia. I'd like to be your friend."

"You would?" Childlike hope laced Amelia's voice.

"Yes," Brenda said, realizing she meant it.

A slow smile tilted Amelia's mouth, and she gestured for Brenda to enter. Brenda followed Amelia into the living area, which was attached to a studio where Amelia obviously spent most of her time. She'd seen some of the macabre paintings through the window when she'd peeked inside, but the dark colors and lines, the image of the black tunnel out of which the little girl was reaching for someone to pull her out, sent a shiver up her spine.

Today she noticed another canvas against the wall—an erotic portrayal of a couple engaged in disturbing sex acts.

No doubt some of the paintings were therapeutic, probably renditions of the horror Amelia had suffered at Blackwood's hands.

But the S & M? Was that Amelia's preference in sex? If so... it made her a viable suspect in the strangling death at the motel.

"Do you want some tea, or something else to drink?" Amelia asked.

"Whatever you're having is fine," Brenda said.

Amelia smiled, walked over to the L-shaped kitchen, and poured them both a glass of iced tea. Brenda's gaze strayed from the dark, haunting paintings to another of two little girls holding their dolls in front of a Christmas tree. The girls were twins, obviously Amelia and Sadie. A happy memory.

Brenda had always wanted a sister; now she understood the reason she'd never had one.

"I saw you on television," Amelia said, drawing Brenda's thoughts back to the reason for her visit. "You told the story about the Commander. And then you were at that motel."

"Yes, I'm working with the TV news crew now." Brenda hesitated, carefully constructing her thoughts. "Amelia, I know you suffered terribly from what Arthur Blackwood did to you."

A haunted look flashed across Amelia's face, her smile fading. "I don't like to talk about him."

Brenda sipped her tea, willing herself not to react as the image of the dead man crept into her head. Amelia seemed so calm now, so desperate for a friend, not like a killer.

"I understand that," Brenda said. "And I don't blame you. But I'd like to help."

Amelia wiped at the condensation on the outside of her glass. "How can you help?"

"I'd like to do a personal in-depth profile on you, tell your side of the story and explain what Commander Blackwood did to you, so people will understand."

Amelia jerked her head from side to side. "Sadie wouldn't like that."

"Maybe I can talk to her," Brenda said. "Assure her I won't disparage you or your family. You deserve for everyone to know that you're not crazy, that Blackwood messed with your mind."

"I'm not crazy," Amelia said, her tone sharpening. "You can't say I am."

Brenda touched Amelia's hand. "I know you're not—that's why I want you to tell me what happened to you. Sometimes it's cathartic for victims if they confront their abusers."

Amelia shot up from the sofa and paced over to stand in front of the picture window that overlooked the mountains. "No, no, no—I just want to forget what happened."

"All right," Brenda said. "I didn't mean to upset you."

Amelia traced her finger over the windowpane, relaxing slightly. Outside, the wind chimes swayed and tinkled, making Brenda wonder why Amelia had so many of them.

"I stopped by to visit yesterday, but you weren't here," Brenda said softly. "Where did you go, Amelia?"

Amelia's eyes darted back and forth from her to the wind chimes. "I can't tell you that."

Brenda set her glass on a coaster on the table. "Why not?"

"Because it's personal," Amelia said, lifting her chin.

Brenda removed her phone, walked over, and showed the screen to Amelia. "Someone sent me a text, Amelia. I thought it might be from you."

Amelia reluctantly took the phone and read the text.

"Did you send this?" Brenda asked again.

Suddenly the door opened, and Sadie and Jake barreled in. "Don't say anything to her, Amelia," Jake said.

"What are you doing here, Brenda?" Sadie rushed to her sister like a mother bear protecting her cub.

Brenda's defenses rose. "I just wanted to talk to Amelia," Brenda said.

Sadie rubbed Amelia's back. "Are you okay, sis?"

Amelia nodded, a confused expression clouding her face as she looked back and forth between Brenda and Sadie.

"Amelia has suffered enough." Jake took Brenda's arm and ushered her toward the door. "Don't come back and harass her, do you understand?"

"I'm not harassing her." Brenda dropped a business card on the foyer table. "I want to be friends with her, to tell her side of the story so everyone will understand."

"Maybe she doesn't care if everyone understands," Jake warned as he hauled her outside. "She deserves privacy."

Brenda barely suppressed her temper. "I don't want to hurt her, Jake. I think going public might be good for her."

"You're not a therapist, Brenda."

"I know that, but I've read—"

Jake cut her off. "Please just leave."

Brenda dug in her heels. "Did you ask her if she sent me that text about the motel murder?"

Jake spoke through gritted teeth. "Her phone records prove it didn't come from her phone. It came from a burner phone."

Brenda sighed. "Amelia left the premises here the night of the murder, Jake. She could have bought a burner phone while she was out and disposed of it." Brenda slanted her eyes toward the erotic artwork. "How about those?"

Jake pointed to her car. "I thought you said you wanted to help her. It sounds like you're trying to hang her."

Brenda shook her head. "I just want the truth, Jake." Two residents walked by, and she lowered her voice. "As an officer of the law, I think you would, too."

Jake's eyes turned to slivers of ice. "Stay away from my family."

Brenda yanked her arm away. "Does that include your father and your brother?"

Jake's breath hissed out. "Yes."

"I can't do that," she said. "I'm going to get the story, with or without your help."

"You're playing with fire, Brenda."

"Maybe." She flashed her phone at him, then opened her car door. "But like I told Nick, the killer invited me to this one for a reason. And I'm going to see it through to the end."

———— , ————

Amelia pressed her hands over her ears to drown out the voices. Not Bessie's or Skid's this time, but the voices of Jake and Brenda outside, arguing.

"Amelia, please sit down," Sadie said.

Amelia allowed her sister to pull her into a chair in the sunroom, where they usually sat when they chatted. "Are you okay?" Sadie asked.

"Yes." Amelia struggled to control herself. She'd worked hard to prove that she wasn't crazy, like everyone thought. Brenda said she wanted to tell her story, so the town would know that.

Was she lying, or could Amelia trust her? She had seemed sincere...

"Amelia," Sadie said, taking on that worried edge, as if she was her mother. "What did Brenda want?"

"For me to tell her what happened."

Sadie's eyes looked troubled. "What did you say?"

"Nothing. But she showed me this text about finding a present for the Commander in a motel room." Tension vibrated in the air. "What was in that room?"

"Have you been to that motel?" Sadie asked.

Amelia twined her hands. She wished Sadie wouldn't worry so much about her. And if she told Sadie the truth, that her memory of the night was foggy, she would. "No," Amelia said. "I've never been there."

Jake stepped back into the room, his badge glinting in the sunlight. Sadie loved Jake, but he was the sheriff. He was also the Commander's son.

He'd arrested Amelia and locked her in a cell before, and he might do it again if he thought she was dangerous. Amelia had to watch what she said.

"Why is everyone so upset?" Amelia asked.

Jake and Sadie traded looks that sent alarm through Amelia. "Tell me," Amelia insisted. "What was in that motel room?"

Sadie inhaled before she spoke, the way she always did when she was delivering bad news. "A dead man."

"He was murdered," Jake said as he looked down at Amelia. "He died of asphyxiation."

Amelia bit her lip.

She had been to the Slaughter Creek Motel. She just couldn't remember when, or whom she'd been with.

But Sadie didn't need to know that. All she needed to know was that Amelia was getting better. She might not be well yet, but she was working on it.

Even though a new voice had climbed into her head. Amelia understood what that meant, too. Another personality was trying to emerge.

But Sadie didn't need to know that either.

Chapter 7

———————— o ————————

Nick knocked on Linda Logger's door, his posture ramrod straight. He wasn't looking forward to delivering the bad news about Logger's death.

Of course, watching an ex's reaction when she received the news was vital in deciding whether or not she was a suspect.

But the text that Brenda had received had changed his way of viewing the crime in a way he didn't like. Not that he hadn't already been looking for the other subjects of the experiment, but he'd hoped to find them and help them receive treatment.

Instead of learning that another one was a killer.

He knocked again, and the door opened. A tired-looking thirtysomething woman with short brown hair stood on the threshold, juggling a toddler on her hip.

"Mrs. Logger?"

The baby girl tugged at her mother's hair, and the woman grasped her hand in her own, then affectionately tweaked the little girl's cheek.

"I'm Special Agent Nick Blackwood."

She frowned as he flashed his credentials, the freckles on her nose prominent as the sun streaked her face. "Actually, it's Linda

Robertson," she finally said. "I took my maiden name back when the divorce was final."

Nick nodded and quickly glanced into the house. Judging from the mess, she had her hands full. Children's toys littered the den, dishes were piled up in the sink, her shirt was stained with something green, and she smelled like bananas. The Cartoon Network blared on the TV in the background.

"I hate to bother you this early, ma'am, but I need to speak to you about your ex-husband."

Apprehension and some other emotion he couldn't define creased her face. "What about Jim?"

Nick debated what to say. The toddler babbled something that sounded like "Da Da," and pain darkened her mother's eyes. "Are you here alone with the baby?" he asked.

"Yes, why?"

"Can I come in?"

She reluctantly nodded, then gestured for him to follow her to the den. The couch was piled high with unfolded laundry. She set the baby down inside a Pack 'n Play, then handed her a rubber squeaky duck and pointed to the sofa.

He took a seat and braced his legs apart while she claimed the chair near the baby. "What's Jim done now?"

He frowned. "Why would you ask that?"

"When he returned from Iraq, he wasn't the same. The physical injuries were nothing compared to his psychological state."

"He suffered from PTSD?"

"Yes." She reached down and handed the baby a stuffed dog with ears that looked worn from loving. "He adored little Ginny, but he couldn't sleep. He was in pain, too, and got hooked on oxycodone. His mood swings turned erratic."

"How do you mean?"

"He had a hard time with his temper. He even..." She let the sentence trail off.

"He hit you?"

Linda rubbed a hand over her face, embarrassment heating her cheeks. "No, he just…liked things rough."

"You mean sex?"

She squeezed her eyes shut as if to block out the memory. "Yes."

"I'm sorry," Nick said quietly.

She looked up at him again, her breathing ragged. "I loved him, even then," she said. "I tried to convince him to go to counseling, but he never was one to talk about his problems. He saw it as some kind of weakness, that it made him less than a man."

"That's a shame."

"I know." She sighed wearily. "But I couldn't live with that kind of violence in the house, especially with a baby."

"When did you last see him?"

She hugged a throw pillow from the couch to her. "About a week ago. Now please tell me what this is about." A frown pulled at her eyes. "Did something happen to Jim? Did he do something?"

So far, Nick believed everything she'd said. "I'm sorry to have to inform you, ma'am, but he's dead."

Linda gasped and covered her mouth with her hand. "No, he can't be…gone."

Nick waited silently, giving her a minute to absorb the information.

"How? When?" she asked. Then as if something had clicked in her mind, she released a low, shocked sound. "Oh, my God, was he the man who died in that motel?"

Nick sighed. "I'm afraid so."

"I can't believe this," she cried. "What happened?"

The baby squealed, her chin wobbling as if she was about to burst into tears, and Linda scooped her up, soothing her by rocking her back and forth.

"I'm afraid I can't divulge all of the details yet, as we're still investigating, but it appears he was murdered. Can you tell me about your divorce? Did you instigate it? Did he?"

She stood, walked to the kitchen, grabbed a handful of tissues, then wiped her eyes and returned to her chair. The baby snatched a plastic maraca off the end table and banged it, the sound echoing in the quiet.

"I asked for it." Her voice cracked. "I couldn't have him exploding around little Ginny."

"How did he take it?"

"Not well. Jim was a prideful man."

The killer had taken that pride from him. But Nick refrained from commenting.

She leaned her head on her hand. "He even accused me of cheating on him, but that was ridiculous."

"Did Mr. Logger have a job?"

Linda chewed her bottom lip. "He had a hard time getting one when he first returned, but he finally started work as a security guard. I don't think he liked it, though. His drinking got worse. He quit the job or lost it, I'm not sure which. We separated around that time."

"Do you know the name of the security company?"

"He didn't mention it." She rocked the baby back and forth, holding her tightly as if she didn't want to lose her as she had her marriage. "He finally started driving a big rig for some freight company. Mountain Truckers, I believe it was."

"Thanks. I'll look into that."

"How about his personal life? Was your ex-husband involved with anyone else?" Nick asked.

The baby started crying, and Linda unfolded the top of a bag of Goldfish, shook some into her hand, and let the child eat out of her palm. Like magic, the little girl quieted, munching greedily.

"He saw women," she said in a voice laced with disgust.

"You mean he was dating?"

"I'm not sure you'd call what Jim was doing dating."

She sounded resigned.

"Was there anyone in particular?"

"Not that I know of. He just...needed to sow some oats, still feel vital, he said." She gestured down at her daughter. "I guess he needed something more than us."

"He was a fool," Nick said, then wondered why he'd made such a statement. But something about the woman and the baby tugged at his heartstrings.

Heartstrings he didn't even know he had.

"If you think of anyone, a name, that might be helpful, give me a call." He laid a business card on the table.

She followed him to the door, patting the baby's back. "Jim doesn't have any other family," she said. "I'd...like to see him. To give him a proper funeral. For Ginny's sake."

"The military will help with that. I'll have someone contact you when the body is released."

"Agent Blackwood," she said just before he stepped outside. "You...aren't related to that man Arthur Blackwood who headed up those awful experiments in Slaughter Creek, are you?"

His gaze met hers, his heart pounding. "Yes, ma'am, I'm sorry to say I'm his son." Then his instincts kicked in. "Why? Did you know Mr. Blackwood?"

She shook her head no, and pressed her baby to her more tightly, as if she feared he was his father incarnate. "No—he was a monster, though. Hurting all those kids like that."

"Yes, ma'am, he was."

But as he walked to the car, an uneasy feeling gnawed at him. Linda Logger had motive to kill her ex, but he didn't think the single mother had it in her to murder him, especially in the heinous way Logger had met his death.

Which left them with no viable suspects. All they had was that damn text to Brenda.

Would their unsub contact her again?

———————·———————

Brenda tried to shake off the incident at Amelia's house as she drove away. She wished Sadie, Amelia, and Jake could realize that she wasn't the enemy. Amelia had been wronged terribly, and any gossip that had dogged her over the years needed to be set straight.

Focus on the case—that was her first priority.

She mentally ticked over the facts she knew so far. The victim's name was Jim Logger. She pulled over at a gas station, grabbed her iPad and accessed the Internet, then entered the man's name on Google Earth. A few seconds later, she had his address.

She plugged it into her GPS, then pulled back onto the road and drove toward Logger's apartment, a complex outside town in an older development. She passed a small country church, the choir music drifting through the open windows reminding her that it was Sunday.

Her parents would be upset that she'd missed church today. They'd forced her to attend every Sunday when she was a child. And afterward, dinner, always banana pudding.

She hated banana pudding. Just like the hospital soap, it turned her stomach. A memory floated into her head, of eating rotten bananas.

Where had that come from? Agnes Banks had never fed her rotten food.

She turned off the main road into the apartment complex. Whereas her place was set on the ridge, taking advantage of the natural setting and the mountains in the background, this low-income complex had been thrown up off the main road into town, with an eye more to convenience than to the picturesque landscape.

Several cars were scattered across the parking lot, where the lines marking the parking spots were just as faded as the beige color on the building. The complex was two stories, with cookie-cutter one- and two-bedroom apartments.

Checking the number for Jim Logger's apartment—112B—she parked in front of the 100 building, not surprised to find Nick's black sedan already present. A crime unit van was also parked beside his car.

Of course Nick wouldn't want her here, but she steeled herself against his disapproval. Grabbing her shoulder bag with her notepad and recorder inside, she stepped from her car and walked up the cracked sidewalk to 112B.

The door stood ajar, but she rapped on it just to alert Nick she'd arrived before she pushed it open. Nick stood next to a crime tech who was dusting for fingerprints. Nick wore gloves as well.

His dark brown eyes reflected resignation. "I figured you'd show up here."

"I won't interfere, and I didn't bring cameras," she said. "I just want the story, Nick."

"Is that the reason you went to see Amelia?"

"Yes," Brenda said. "I know you and Jake and Sadie don't believe this, but I don't want to hurt her. I want people to know that she's strong, that she's not ill now, that her actions were all because of—"

"My father."

"I was going to say 'the experiment.'"

"You don't have to tiptoe around his name or what he did," Nick said. "I won't defend him."

Which indicated the depth of his pain. "That's sad in itself," Brenda said softly.

"Just don't hurt Sadie or Amelia," he warned. "They don't deserve it."

"Finally something we agree on."

A heartbeat passed between them, and Brenda thought he was going to say something else, that he might be softening toward her, but one of the crime techs walked in from the bedroom, and his hard look returned.

"We're about finished in there," the tech said.

"What did you find?" Nick asked.

"Several fingerprints, some bodily fluids on the sheets, a little blood in the bathroom. Maybe a shaving mishap."

"You took samples?" Nick asked.

"Yes, of everything."

"We're photographing the contents of the closet and bathroom now."

"I want to look around when you're finished," Nick said.

The tech nodded, stowed the evidence bags he'd collected in the collection kit, then disappeared back into the den.

Brenda inched inside the room, visually scanning it for details, careful not to touch anything. The furniture looked as if it had come with the apartment. A plain beige couch and chair, a scarred wooden coffee table, a dinette set that looked as if it was fifty years old.

Three cardboard boxes sat in the corner of the living room, suggesting that the man hadn't yet unpacked everything. No personal photos except for one lone eight-by-ten of a little baby girl wrapped in a pink blanket, hugging a stuffed bunny. Nothing stood out as suspicious.

Another crime tech was processing the kitchen. From where she stood, it looked as if Jim Logger rarely used it.

"What did you find out about Logger?"

Nick knelt to examine the CDs stacked by the television. "He was married, has a child, divorced now. His widow said they had problems when he returned stateside. He was moody, started drinking too much. Worked for a security firm for a while. But he was really hitting the booze by then, and left or was fired, she's not sure which. After that, he worked as a truck driver."

"Something to look into," Brenda said.

Nick gave a clipped nod, and Brenda walked over and glanced at the CDs. Some military flicks, a thriller, a sci-fi flick. Dozens of porn movies.

"Interesting," she said, noting the titles involved S & M, rape, and submission.

"Fits with the way we found him." He stuck the CDs back on the shelf, then strode toward the desk in the corner. An older-model laptop sat on the top, and Nick began to examine it. Brenda followed him and leaned over his shoulder, watching as he scrolled through Logger's browser history.

"More porn sites," she said in disgust. "Did his wife say he cheated on her?"

"She said he saw women and liked rough sex."

"You think he met someone online?"

Nick checked the man's e-mail. "I don't see any chat rooms or online dating sites."

"Maybe he hooked up the old-fashioned way, in a bar," Brenda suggested.

"Could be." He clicked a few more keys, then sighed. "No Facebook or Twitter accounts either."

"How about his financials?"

"I was going there next," Nick said. He found records of a bank account, but no savings account.

"Not much money," Brenda commented as she read over his shoulder. "And no big check deposits or withdrawals."

"Looks like he wasn't paying for sex," Nick said. "No paycheck from a security company, but there is one from Mountain Truckers. I want to talk to them."

"What was the name of the security company?" Brenda asked.

"The wife didn't know."

"There's no listing here. They must have paid him in cash."

"Which could mean either that he lied and wasn't working for a security company, or that the one he worked for wasn't exactly legitimate."

"What does his job have to do with his death?"

"I don't know. Maybe nothing, but the more we learn about him, the easier it'll be to piece together this mess."

"His death could be random," Brenda said. "He died simply because he hooked up with the wrong person."

"It's possible," Nick said, although he didn't look convinced. "But if the unsub chose this victim for a reason, we need to know what's special about him."

"Maybe his ex-wife discovered he liked it rough, agreed to play his game, then killed him."

She saw the wheels turning in Nick's head, but he didn't answer.

"You talked to her," Brenda said. "Do you think she killed him?"

"On paper, she's the perfect suspect," Nick said. "Wife scorned, husband a cheater. She finds out he likes rough sex, lures him to a motel. He'd certainly trust her, would pay for the motel. He'd let her tie him up."

"But something's not right about it," Brenda said, sensing he wasn't liking the wife for the crime.

"First of all, she's a stay-at-home mom with a baby she dotes on." Nick swung his gaze toward her. "Second. The unsub texted you, led you to the crime to find the body."

"Maybe she wanted me to write a story about cheating men."

Nick made a low sound in his throat. "That's possible, except we can't forget that the text indicated the present was for my father."

"You think Logger was connected to your father somehow?"

Nick scraped a hand over his jaw. "Maybe. Or perhaps the killer is connected to him, and she just chose Logger because he was a convenient target."

"Then the kill, her MO, has to be significant," Brenda said. "But why repeatedly strangle the victim, then leave his body in a compromising sexual position for the Commander?"

It had felt so good to watch the man die.

He had deserved every painful second. They all did. They were all just like the Commander.

Every man she saw on the street, every man in the coffee shop, every man who'd ever touched her.

She thumbed through all the photographs she'd taken. Which one should be next?

She pasted them on her wall, like a scrapbook of memories.

Then she crossed Jim Logger's name off the list with a smile. One down…

So many more to go.

Chapter 8

―――――― o ――――――

Nick checked Logger's desk but found nothing but unpaid bills and a letter from his ex-wife's lawyer, citing him for missed child support payments.

The crime team was still working, one of them lifting trace samples of bodily fluids from the sheets. If the unsub had had sex with Logger in his apartment, it might prove to be a lead.

Brenda started to open the closet door, but Nick stopped her. "You shouldn't be here, Brenda, and you certainly can't touch anything."

Jake strode in, pulling on gloves, then glowered at Brenda. "I should have known you'd show up."

"You going to throw me out like you did at Amelia's?"

"I just want you to leave her in peace."

"Brenda, you'd better go," Nick said.

"But I can help," Brenda argued. "Just give me some gloves, and I'll search the closet."

"No," said Nick. "Wait outside."

Brenda huffed, her pretty face crunching into a scowl. "You'll tell me what you find?"

"I'll tell you when we have the unsub. Now get out of here."

"Fine—I'll just conduct my own investigation."

Nick caught her arm before she left the room, but regretted it when heat sizzled between them. "This is serious, Brenda. Stay out of it."

"We've been through this, Nick. I'm not dropping it."

"It's not a game," Nick growled.

"I know that, but I might be the link you need to communicate with her."

Jake opened the closet door and started rooting around inside. "Just let us know if the killer contacts you again. Now, let us do our jobs."

Nick released her arm. If this murder was related to his father, he didn't want Brenda anywhere near it.

A hurt look simmered in her eyes, but she turned and walked into the living room. He followed, afraid she would bother the crime techs, but she checked her watch, then stepped outside.

"What do you have so far?" Jake asked.

"I need to check out the trucking company," Nick replied. "Maybe it'll lead to information about the security company. Logger's wife said his drinking escalated after he took that job. But I didn't find any pay stubs or deposits from a security company in his bank account."

"Sounds suspicious," Jake agreed.

"What happened earlier at Amelia's?"

Jake rubbed his forehead. "Brenda was questioning Amelia before Sadie and I arrived. Sadie's sister is vulnerable. She could say something to implicate herself without even realizing it."

"I don't think Brenda would use it against her," Nick said.

Jake's brows arched. "You're defending Brenda?"

"No." Was he? Nick chewed the inside of his cheek. "That's not the point. Where was Amelia the night of the murder?"

Jake hesitated, making Nick's nerves jump.

"She still didn't say. But she claims she's never been to the Slaughter Creek Motel."

"Do you believe her?"

"I don't know." Jake exhaled. "But I don't think she's our killer."

Nick narrowed his eyes. "One of her alters might be. Just think about it. Viola picks up Logger in a bar, lures him back to the motel. Then things get out of hand, and Skid takes over and finishes the man."

"It's possible, I guess," Jake said. "Although Amelia appears to be getting better, to be merging her alters. And this killer... she seems organized, as if she planned the murder. She's certainly covering her tracks well. Amelia is too emotional and erratic to do that."

He was right. The unsub had left no prints, no clothing behind, not even a condom. She'd stayed out of sight of the manager, and left without anyone knowing.

Plus she'd sent that cryptic text to Brenda.

"That's true," Nick said. "And we can't forget the number she carved behind the vic's ear. That suggests she's going to kill again."

Worry lined his brother's face. "We have to find her before she does."

———————— · ————————

Brenda checked her watch again as she left the apartment. Too bad Nick and his brother were throwing their weight around and wouldn't let her tag along with them.

Although she *did* know the name of that trucking company. She didn't need their permission to have a conversation with the owner.

Decision made, she jogged toward her car, but when she spotted a blond woman parking three doors down from Logger's unit, she veered toward her.

"Excuse me, ma'am," she said as she approached her. "Can I talk to you for a minute?"

The blonde tucked her briefcase under her arm, then shoved her sunglasses onto the top of her head. Her eye shadow, which was a little too heavy, matched her startling green eyes. "If you're selling something, I'm not interested."

Brenda bit back a retort. Funny, since judging from the Mary Kay bag over the blonde's shoulder, she was a salesgirl herself. The name tag on her pink jacket read "Susie."

"I'm not selling anything. My name is Brenda Banks—"

Recognition dawned, and the blonde's frown morphed into a smile. "Oh, right, I recognize you from the news. What's going on?"

"Did you know Jim Logger, the man who lived in unit 112B?"

Susie hoisted her sample bag from the seat, then locked the car and picked her way over the ruts in the sidewalk. "Not really. I saw him coming and going a few times."

"Did you talk to him?"

"He helped me carry some groceries in once when it was raining, but we didn't talk about anything personal. Why?"

"He was murdered."

Susie pressed a hand to her chest. "Oh, my God, what happened? Was he killed in his apartment?"

"No. At a motel." Brenda fidgeted. Nick would never speak to her again if she revealed details. "The police are investigating. They're searching his apartment now."

Susie started toward the building, her stilettos catching in the broken cement. "Well, I'm sorry to hear about his death. I hope they find the killer."

Brenda walked beside her. "Did he have a girlfriend?"

"Like I said, I didn't really know him."

"Did you see a woman with him?"

Susie paused, shaking her shoe loose from where it had caught in the cracks. "Maybe a redhead once. Oh, and another time a blonde. Then two brunettes in one night."

"Ahh, he was a ladies' man."

She resumed walking. "I guess you could say that, but something about him...He gave me the creeps."

"What do you mean?"

"He seemed disturbed, angry all the time. I decided to stay away from him." She adjusted her sample bag in her arms. "Now I'm glad I did."

Brenda thanked her and dropped her business card in the woman's purse. "Call me if you think of anything else."

Susie hurried toward her apartment, and Brenda considered knocking on the neighbors' doors. But Jake and Nick appeared outside and glared at her, and she decided she'd better drive to her parents' for dinner.

Nick and Jake would canvass the neighbors. Then she'd find out what they'd discovered.

Although she could stop by that trucking company on the way to her folks' house.

After all, her parents had made her wait for answers.

They could wait this time.

———————

Nick took the right side of the building and Jake the left. He caught the woman Brenda had been talking to as she reached her condo.

"Listen," she said, tucking her sales kit beneath her arm. "I already told the reporter I don't know anything. I'm sorry about that man's death, but we weren't friends. I was never in his apartment, and we never socialized."

Of course irritating, nosy Brenda had gotten to her first. "Did you see him with any women?"

"A few came and went, but there wasn't anyone special."

"What about night before last or yesterday midday?"

"I didn't see anything. I was at a convention in Knoxville."

Nick thanked her, then gave her his card and strode to the next condo. He rang the bell, but no one answered, and when he looked inside, the place was empty.

The next unit had a For Rent sign in the yard and was also vacant. He rang the last doorbell and identified himself when an elderly man answered.

The man leaned on his cane. "Eh, sorry, I'm a little hard of hearing."

Nick nodded. "Sir, did you know Mr. Logger who lived in 112B?"

The man adjusted his hearing aid as he peered around the corner. "No, don't believe I did. Why? What's going on?"

Nick debated whether to tell him. He didn't want to worry the old man. "Just asking some questions." He showed the man a photo of Logger. "This is Mr. Logger. Did you ever see him with a woman?"

"A what?"

"A woman!" Nick hated to shout, but it was necessary.

"I don't pay no mind to the neighbors," he said. "My wife's been sick, so I stay in taking care of her."

"I'm so sorry," Nick said. "Thanks for your time."

He texted Jake that his canvass had turned up nothing, and that he was on his way to the trucking company, then headed to his car.

Maybe Logger's boss could offer more information about the victim.

And hopefully forensics would turn up something that would lead to the strangler.

Although he had a bad feeling that the killer hadn't left any evidence behind.

Brenda parked in the Mountain Truckers lot, noting three eighteen-wheelers and a row of rental moving trucks in a separate fenced-in area.

Sunlight was fading, the treetops shimmering a silver gray. The March wind added a chill to the air, a reminder that winter hadn't yet left the ridges and peaks of Slaughter Creek.

A metal fence surrounded the property, and the scent of gasoline permeated the air. She crossed the graveled lot, wobbling on the uneven surface. A double-wide trailer served as the office. She climbed the wooden steps, then rapped on the door.

She didn't bother to wait for someone to answer. She opened the screen, then the wooden door, and stepped inside. A metal desk sat to her left, and the rest of the space was divided into two offices, one on each side. A young girl with bleached-blond hair looked annoyed as she dropped her phone. Judging from the gooey expression on her face, she was obviously texting, not working. The nameplate on her desk read "Tia."

"Can I help you?"

"I'd like to speak to the manager."

"You need a rental?"

"No," Brenda said. "I'm actually a reporter."

The girl's eyes widened in recognition. "Oh, right! You're Brenda from the news!" She jumped up, grinning at Brenda as if she were a celebrity. "Can I get you something? We have bottled water and soda."

"I'm fine," Brenda said, deciding this girl might know more than the manager. "I need some information on one of your employees. A man named Jim Logger."

"Oh, Jim." Tia blushed. "He was a looker, but...he could switch moods on a dime."

"Did you and he ever—"

"No, God, no," Tia said. "Not that I didn't think he was sexy. But I'm engaged." She stuck out her hand, waving her fingers to show off her diamond.

Brenda barely resisted squinting to see it. "That's beautiful," she said. "When is the wedding?"

The girl's plump shoulders shrugged. "We haven't set a date yet. Benny—that's my fiancé—he had to do a little time. But soon as he makes parole, we'll start planning."

"Oh, I see. Well, good luck with the wedding," Brenda said. "Now tell me more about Jim Logger. What kind of employee was he?"

Tia fluffed her curly hair. "He usually volunteered for the long hauls. Said he liked getting away, being on the highway. He had trouble sleeping, so he was perfect for road trips."

"Did he have a girlfriend?"

"Not that he talked about. I think he was still hung up on his wife, but"—the girl leaned forward as if sharing a dire secret—"he had a bit of a temper problem. One day the boss told him he might have to lay him off, and Logger blew up."

"What happened?"

"He punched the wall with his fist," Tia said. "Boss said he wasn't puttin' up with that shit and fired him on the spot."

"When was that?"

"About two weeks ago."

Brenda twisted her mouth in thought. "Did he mention where he worked before he joined this company?"

Tia shrugged. "No, but he probably listed it on his application. Waylin tries to make sure his employees don't have serious rap sheets. I mean, he'll let some petty stuff get by, but not serious crimes like embezzlement or robbery or murder."

"Would you mind pulling his file for me?"

Tia shifted and dug through her file drawer, then removed a folder and rifled through it. "Oh, here it is. Hmm, says he worked at a placed called Stark Security."

"Is there a phone number for it?"

Tia read the number, and Brenda jotted it down.

"Wait a minute," Tia said, her nose wrinkling. "Why are you asking all these questions about Jim?"

Brenda hesitated. "I'm afraid he was murdered."

Shock flashed across Tia's face. "Good heavens, that's awful."

Brenda laid her business card on the desk. "Yes, it was. If you think of anything that might be helpful, please let me know."

She opened the door and stepped out just as Nick's dark sedan pulled to a stop. When he climbed from the car, his scowl pierced her.

"I told you to stay out of this, Brenda."

"I was just leaving." Brenda waved to him as she descended the steps. The wind caught her hair and swirled it around her face. "The manager's not in, but I talked to Tia, the receptionist. If you want to know anything, you always talk to the female in the office."

Nick's eyes were glued to her sexy swagger. She decided to torture him.

"Is that so?"

"Yes." She met him at the foot of the stairs, her hip hitched out. "Anyway, she said Jim Logger had a temper, that two weeks ago he and the boss had heated words, and Logger put his fist through the wall. Manager fired him on the spot."

"Sounds like Logger. What was he upset about?"

"She didn't know." Brenda toyed with the strap of her bag. "But maybe he cruised the bars to drown his sorrows."

"Maybe." Nick reached up and tucked an errant strand of her hair behind her ear. The touch seemed so intimate that her heart fluttered. Sunlight was fading, painting shadows across his face. Shadows that only made him look sexier.

Dear God, she had to get away from him before she did something stupid—like throw herself at him.

That would be a huge mistake. Nick didn't even like her.

"What else?" Nick asked, oblivious to her racy thoughts.

"She gave me the number for the security company where he used to work."

Nick held out his hand, palm up.

Brenda studied it for a moment, her fingers itching to grab his hand and cling to it.

Instead she huffed, then scribbled the number on a sheet in her notepad, ripped it out, and shoved it toward him.

"Let me handle this," Nick said curtly.

Brenda knew how to play the game. She'd let him believe he was in charge. "Of course, Nick."

His gaze met hers as if he'd read her mind.

But just then her phone dinged, breaking the moment. She had a text. She glanced at it and frowned.

Good job at the motel, Brenda. I knew when I saw you at the sanitarium years ago that you and I would be friends.

Brenda stiffened and scanned the property, her senses alert.

The killer had contacted her again. And she had definitely been in the sanitarium. Was she one of Blackwood's subjects?

And if she was, would she tell everyone that Brenda had been there as well?

———————— , ————————

Seven felt the burning ache rising in her again.

The need to kill.

The image of Jim Logger's face as he'd gasped for his dying breath flashed in her head, and sweat broke out on her upper lip.

His lips had turned blue, his eyes bloodshot, his skin a sallow color.

Adrenaline surged through her, and she slipped on a slinky black dress.

It was time. Time to send the Commander another present.

Anticipation like nothing she'd ever felt seared her.

Laughter bubbled in her chest. She didn't want him to think she'd forgotten him.

She knew exactly where to go, too. The place the military men liked to gather. There they were horny, drowning their troubles in booze and beer. Looking for a soft body to assuage the pain and the nightmares that dogged them.

Hell, she was doing them a favor, offering them one last night of pleasure.

Then she'd end their suffering forever.

Chapter 9

———— o ————

"What's wrong, Brenda?" Nick asked.

Brenda stuffed her phone in her purse. "Oh…nothing."

Nick had learned to read people in his training, an asset while interrogating the enemy. Brenda's eyes had blinked rapidly at his question.

She was lying.

"Who was the text from?" he asked.

She shrugged. "My mother. They're expecting me for dinner."

At the reminder of her parents and their status, a social level he would never achieve even if he had the desire to, which he definitely didn't, he stiffened. "Then you'd better get to the mayor and his wife."

An odd look pinched her face. He caught the door before she could close it and fixed his gaze on her. "You will tell me if you hear from the killer again, won't you, Brenda?"

She blinked rapidly again.

"Yes, of course," she said with a saccharine smile.

He wanted to shake the truth out of her. She'd just told another lie.

Which meant the killer *had* contacted her again.

"Brenda," he said in a dark warning voice. "Don't do anything stupid like trying to track down this maniac yourself."

Her gaze skittered sideways. "Trust me, Nick, I'm not a fool."

She slammed the door, started the engine, and tore from the parking lot.

Nick's pulse jumped. Despite her bravado, he'd detected a note of fear in her voice before she'd pulled away. And she hadn't made any promises…

He stepped to the side of the trailer and punched in the number for the security company where Logger had worked prior to the trucking company. An automated operator answered: "We're sorry, but this number is no longer in service."

Nick cursed, then stared at the dust stirred up in Brenda's wake. She'd said the text was from her parents, to trust her.

He didn't trust anyone.

Brenda was ambitious, smart, and a go-getter. She had beaten him here, and if the killer contacted her, Brenda might even arrange a meeting, which would be dangerous.

Damn her.

Pretty or not, Brenda was in the middle of his investigation.

He leaned against his car and phoned the agency, then asked to speak to Charlie, the best technical analyst he'd ever met.

"What can I do for you, Nick?"

"Access that trace on Brenda Banks's phone. Forward her texts to me."

"Sure. Hang on."

Keys tapped, then a few seconds later, Charlie spoke up. "I just e-mailed them to you."

Nick scrolled down and noted a couple of texts from Brenda's boss, praising her for the motel coverage and wanting to know when she would have more information.

But the last one stopped him cold.

Good job at the motel, Brenda. I knew when I saw you at the sanitarium years ago that you and I would be friends.

Goddammit. He was right. Brenda *had* heard from their unsub, and she was keeping it from him.

He reread the text, searching for clues.

What had the message meant, she'd seen Brenda at the sanitarium? Had Brenda visited someone there? He couldn't imagine her hoity-toity family spending time in that place for any reason.

Then again…what if Brenda or one of her family members had been admitted to the hospital for treatment?

His hand grew itchy, and he jumped in his car and peeled away from the trucking company. He needed his computer.

Then he'd hack into the hospital records, and find out what Brenda was hiding.

Brenda straightened her jacket as she entered her family's house. Her mother's maid, Geraldine, met her at the door. "Thank goodness you finally got here, Miss Agnes has been having a conniption fit."

Brenda squeezed Geraldine's arm. "When isn't Mother having a conniption fit?"

They both laughed. "This one isn't so bad," Geraldine said with a twinkle in her eyes.

So this was a setup. "Fix me a martini fast."

The housekeeper laughed again. "A dirty blue is waiting on you at the bar."

"Thanks." Brenda hugged her and grabbed the martini on her way to join the dinner party.

Still, she felt her father's disapproval as she entered the sunroom. Her mother was laughing at something another woman said, while her father was talking to a man much younger than him, with short brown hair. The younger man was dressed in a designer suit that he definitely hadn't bought in Slaughter Creek. His back was to her, so she couldn't see his face, but she instantly sized him up as a preppy lawyer, stockbroker, or something equally boring.

Diamonds glittered from her mother's hands and neck, and she wore a dark blue silk dress that flattered her slender figure. Agnes Banks looked fantastic for her age. She should— she divided her time between the gym, the country club, and the spa.

"Brenda!" Her mother waved her over with a smile, although Brenda detected a slight flicker of disapproval at Brenda's crumpled suit. "Come and meet the senator's wife, Julianne Stowe."

Her father paused, and the man with him turned toward her. Instant recognition dawned. He stood almost six feet, with olive skin, close-cropped hair, and charming eyes. Not the senator, but this was his son. His picture had been plastered all over the Internet and television, where he worked tirelessly on his father's campaign.

He also ranked number ten on the top one hundred eligible bachelors in the States.

"Hi, Mother, Daddy," Brenda said as her mother drew her up to her side. Brenda tolerated her air kisses. "I didn't realize this was a formal party, or I would have dressed for it."

Agnes's smile warned her to behave. "You're fine, honey." She introduced her daughter to the senator's wife, and Brenda shook her hand.

"Nice to meet you, Mrs. Stowe," Brenda said.

"Oh, please, dear, call me Julianne."

Brenda nodded, but her mother continued the introductions.

"And this is the senator's son, Ron. He works for his father's campaign."

"Yes, I recognize him." He was the good son.

Unlike her—the naughty daughter who went off on her own.

Brenda smiled and shook his hand as if she *were* the good daughter, though. His white teeth beamed as he grinned at her. "Nice to finally meet you, Brenda. I saw your piece the other night about that murder at the motel."

Brenda arched a brow. Was he trying to flatter her to earn publicity for his father's campaign?

"Hush, now, we don't want to talk about that awful stuff," her mother said. "Why don't you show Ron the gardens, while Geraldine gets dinner on the table."

"Agnes," her father said, as if he knew she was being obvious.

Brenda wanted to choke both of them. But her Southern manners kicked in, and she motioned for Ron to follow her. "Come on, we'll take a walk."

The scent of freshly cut grass, roses, and the hint of rain floated around her as they walked along the cobblestone path through the gazebo to her mother's garden.

"I suppose you're really interested in flowers," Brenda said wryly.

Ron's deep chuckle rumbled through the air. "Yes, although they smell faintly like a setup."

Brenda laughed, appreciating his good nature. "I'm sorry. My parents obviously think I need help in the dating department."

"Do you?" Ron asked. A teasing gleam glittered in his eyes.

She couldn't help but laugh. "I'm the reporter, I'm supposed to ask the questions."

He lifted his shoulders in a shrug. "Ask away. I'm an open book."

"Right." Brenda sipped her drink as she settled onto the wrought iron bench tucked inside the garden by the wall. "You're good-looking, slick, the perfect politician's son. No ghosts in your closet?"

He folded his arms, sat down beside her, and stretched his long legs in front of him. "Now, Brenda, we all have our secrets."

Brenda lifted her chin in challenge. "Don't tell me one of the most eligible bachelors in the States is actually hurting for women?"

'Well, not exactly hurting." He threw his head back and laughed. "I like you already, Brenda." The ice clinked in his glass as he sipped his drink.

Brenda couldn't help but like him as well. But how much of his charm was an act?

"When I saw you on television, I knew we'd get along," Ron said.

Brenda traced a finger along the rim of her glass. "Why would you say that?"

"Because you have spunk," he said. "Most of the women I meet are boring, plastic. They're money hungry and only want to talk to me because of my father."

"Sounds like we're soul mates."

He grinned. "Maybe we are."

Or maybe she would be just another conquest for him. That, and he wanted to use her for publicity.

Besides, she couldn't help but compare him to Nick, and there Ron failed miserably.

"Tell me about this murder you're covering," Ron said. "Was it related to the big story about that sanitarium?"

"You read my piece?"

"Of course," he said. "I'm sure the town was in shock when they learned those experiments were conducted under their noses."

Brenda shifted. "Yes, they were."

"Have you learned who the other subjects were?"

"Not yet," Brenda said. "I'm trying to set up an interview with Arthur Blackwood, but so far I haven't managed to. And he's not talking to the police."

He lifted a rose petal that had fallen to the ground and sniffed it. "Was someone working with Blackwood?"

Brenda shrugged. "The FBI suspect a higher-ranking power in the CIA or military headed the project."

Ronald dropped the rose petal, and the wind caught it. "Any idea who?"

She watched the petal float to the ground. "Not that I know of."

"Was the motel murder related?"

She stiffened, suddenly feeling as if she was at an inquisition. There was no way she'd tell him about the text from Jim Logger's murderer.

Fortunately, the dinner bell tinkled, and she stood. "We'd better put our murder talk on hold. Mother frowns on talk of dead bodies at the dinner table."

He chuckled as they walked back to the house. Inside, he morphed back into the charismatic politician's son. Dinner conversation revolved around the upcoming election and speculation over who might be appointed chief of defense.

Luckily Brenda kept abreast of politics for her job, and the conversation flowed smoothly.

But still she felt like a fraud at the table, as if she didn't belong in this group, in this fancy house.

She'd felt that way most of her life, as if she were an outsider.

Now she knew the reason—she *didn't* belong. She had come from someone else, not from Agnes and William.

And as soon as this case ended, she'd find out the name of her birth parents. She had to know the truth about who she was.

Even if the truth wasn't pretty.

———————— ⁄ ————————

Nick pulled into the parking deck across from the building housing the security company, a high-rise sandwiched between another building and a strip mall on the outskirts of Nashville. His thoughts strayed to Brenda and her dinner as night set in.

Her parents enjoyed the society crowd. Were they entertaining tonight? Was Brenda sipping drinks with some polished rich guy? Some slick man who'd talk his way into her bed?

Irritated that the idea bothered him, he struck her from his mind. Let her sleep with whomever the hell she wanted.

He didn't care.

Not one fucking bit.

He crossed the street, dodging traffic, then noted the sign advertising the businesses out front. The security company's name had been removed.

The fact that the phone number was no longer working had suggested that the company might have moved, but he'd hoped they'd simply switched numbers.

The small office complex housed three other offices, one an insurance company, the other a real estate office. He strode to the last one, where the security company was supposed to be, but the door was locked. He peered in through the glass in the doorway, but it was so dark he couldn't see inside.

Yet he thought he detected the dim glow of a light, somewhere in the back.

Glancing around him to make certain no one was watching, he picked the lock, then slipped inside and shut the door. A dead quiet echoed through the room, as if it were vacant. His visual sweep confirmed it had been cleaned out.

Hearing a creaking sound from the back, he reached for his gun. But suddenly someone jumped him from behind. The son of a bitch slammed something hard against the back of his head, throwing him off balance, and he swung around. But another figure appeared from the back room, gray gunmetal glinting just before he fired.

Dodging the bullet, Nick ducked behind the desk, and the two figures darted out the door.

He jumped up to chase them, but they disappeared around the back of the building, and when he followed, one of them fired again. The bullet zinged by his head, almost nicking his brow.

The men jumped in a dark SUV, tires squealing as the driver spun the vehicle around. He shot at the tires, but the SUV barreled straight toward him, and he had to jump to the side to escape being plowed down.

———————— , ————————

The bastard had cried and cried before he'd died.

Pitiful, weak man.

Even she hadn't sobbed like a baby when the Commander had forced the lungs from her air and deprived her of life.

No, she was tougher than him.

She pulled her car to the side of the road, the deepest part of Blindman's Curve, where more than one resident of Slaughter Creek had lost his life, and smiled at the memorial someone had erected for a lost one.

The flowers had dried up long ago. The heart-shaped pillow had been chewed and picked apart by animals, its stuffing scattered on the dry leaves. The ribbon had faded.

She glanced around to make sure no one was nearby, then rushed around to the backseat and dragged the man from the back. The rug she'd rolled him in had made it easier to haul him into the car. Now she shoved him down the embankment, smiling as his naked body flew loose from the rug and careened to a stop beneath a tree.

His limbs flopped out beside him, the frayed ropes still half tied around his wrists and ankles. His penis was a limp purple mess.

She rubbed her gloved hands together with a satisfied smile.

At the sound of an engine rumbling in the distance, she hurried back to her vehicle. She punched the gas and tore away from the curve, winding her way back around the mountain.

Sweet pleasure stole through her as she remembered the man's terrified eyes as she stole his last breath. All the fuckers should die like that, their bodies left to rot in the woods where no one would find them.

Except she *wanted* this one to be found. Wanted the Commander to know she'd left him another present.

Red Rover, Red Rover,
Send Seven right over…

Time to send Brenda another text.

She tapped her fingers along the steering wheel as she began to compose a new limerick in her head.

There once was a girl who cried
Then she died and she died and she died
But no one came
Cause they called her insane
So she lied and she lied and she lied.

Chapter 10

———— o ————

Nick had to dive over the railing of a back stoop to avoid being pulverized as the SUV careened toward him. His knees hit the pavement first, and he rolled, then came up on his haunches, ready to fire.

The driver shifted into reverse, then spun to the right and flew around the corner of the building. Ignoring the pain in his knees, Nick jogged down the steps, then chased after the vehicle, trying to read its license plate.

But it was too dark, and the SUV roared onto the street and disappeared out of sight before he had a chance.

He limped around to the front of the building. Obviously the gunmen had been looking for something in the office space.

But what?

His curiosity piqued, Nick entered again, the floor creaking under his boots.

The first office was empty, not a stick of furniture inside. The second held a metal desk and filing cabinet, but he looked through the cabinet and it had been emptied as well.

Everything had been taken.

Not even a piece of paper or a chewing gum wrapper remained. When had the company disbanded, and why?

Most small businesses failed because of financial problems. Had the company simply relocated?

If so, why had two armed men been searching the office space? Something of importance must have been here.

Something worth killing over…

Curious, he walked next door to the real estate office. A bell rang as he entered, and a twentysomething redhead wearing a blazer and capris smiled up at him. He wondered why she hadn't heard the gunfire, then realized she had earbuds in. She removed them, then clicked off her music. "Can I help you, sir?"

"Do you know what happened to the security office next door?"

She came around the desk and tapped her chin with one long red nail. "I sure don't. But it was odd. One day they were there, and the next, they just picked up and left."

"When was that?"

"Hmm." She tapped her chin again. "Right around the time that big story broke over in Slaughter Creek."

The timing did seem suspicious. "Did you know anyone who worked there?"

She shook her head. "Not really. But that man who was killed at that motel, Mr. Logger, I saw him hightail it out of there one day, pissed off."

Just like he'd left the trucking company. Logger's ex said he had trouble with his temper.

"You don't know who owned the company?"

She fiddled with her hair. "No—I saw a man leaving one day, though. He was a big guy, bald. Looked like he was tough, like he was a bouncer or something."

"Anything else?"

"I'm afraid not." She gave him a flirtatious smile. "By the way, are you looking for a place to live around here?"

"No, just information."

"How about a drink?"

He considered it. She was attractive. In fact, she might be good for a night of sex. And he needed that bad.

But she wasn't Brenda. And he didn't want to take this woman to bed when he was seeing Brenda in his head instead.

So he thanked her, then left. But as soon as he was in the car, he phoned his partner at the bureau, Special Agent Rafe Hood, and explained about the security company and the attack. "So far I haven't found out much about them. See if you can dig up anything."

"I'm on it," Rafe said. "Any hints as to who worked with your father?"

"Nothing yet. How about you?"

"The CIA is still stonewalling us."

Nick rubbed at his aching knee. "Figures. And the Commander is sitting back, enjoying the game."

Nick thanked Rafe, then drove back to Slaughter Creek, picked up a burger, and hurried into his cabin. The agency had suggested he let Rafe handle his father's case, claiming he was too close, so Rafe had the files from the hospital. But he'd learned hacking skills in the service, and a few minutes later he was studying the records from Slaughter Creek Sanitarium.

He'd expected to find out that Brenda's mother had suffered a mini-breakdown or had a drinking problem that required treatment, or maybe that an aunt had been institutionalized.

But that wasn't the case. Brenda had been admitted. When she was sixteen.

He stared at the medical report, knowing full well he'd broken laws and invaded Brenda's privacy by doing so.

But the woman perplexed him, and he couldn't look away.

Brenda had been seeing a therapist because of depression. The therapist had recommended a week of inpatient treatment.

He shouldn't read the rest of the report, but he had to know why a young girl who appeared to have everything, parents who doted on her, all the money in the world, was depressed.

A minute later, he discovered the triggering factor: Brenda was adopted. The Bankses weren't her birth parents—although the records didn't list their names or any information about the adoption.

Hell, not that it mattered to him. But obviously she'd been deeply hurt when she learned that the people who'd raised her had lied to her.

That wasn't the key factor here, though. The key factor was that she'd been in Slaughter Creek Sanitarium at the same time as the killer.

Meaning they had crossed paths. Brenda either knew the killer—or the killer knew her.

———————— , ————————

Brenda silently admitted that Ron was good company. But he was a politician—he'd been honed to be charming. He was also smart and educated, and had his finger on the pulse of the state's issues.

Nick was dark, intense, gruff, and he didn't seem to care what anyone thought of him. He definitely wasn't out to charm or flatter her.

But that intensity drew her to him anyway.

"Darling," her mother said. "Ron asked you a question."

Brenda sipped her water and feigned a smile, but her phone buzzed that she had a text.

She slipped it from her pocket and read the message.

There once was a girl who cried
Then she died and she died and she died
But no one came
Cause they called her insane

So she lied and she lied and she lied.

Brenda's hand trembled. When she looked up, everyone was watching her.

"Are you all right?" Ron asked. "You look pale."

She tucked her phone back into her pocket. "Yes, I'm fine. But I have to go."

"You're not going to work at this hour?" Her mother's expression was a mask of disapproval.

"Brenda." Her father gave her a stern look. "I hope this isn't about that murder. It's not safe for a young woman to go out by herself to crime scenes." He inclined his head toward their guest. "Is it, Ron?"

Ron slanted Brenda a smile, then threw up a hand. "Hey, I'm not stepping into the middle."

Brenda gave him a grateful look, then pushed away from the table. "I really do have to go. And no, Dad, I'm not going to a crime scene. But I'm beat, and I have some messages to return."

Her parents and Ron stood, and his mother was rising from the table, but Brenda waved for them to sit back down. "Don't bother getting up. Enjoy your dessert and coffee." She squeezed Mrs. Stowe's shoulder. "So nice to meet you, I hope we'll see you again." She circled the table and gave her mother and father a hug—if she didn't, her mother would chase her to the door.

"I'll walk Brenda outside," Ron said.

"That's not necessary."

"I don't mind." Brimming with politeness, he placed his hand at the small of her back as he accompanied her. His solicitous manner was irritating, and Brenda wanted to shake off his touch, but she forced herself to be civil.

"I'd like to see you again," Ron said. "That is, if you're interested."

She should be.

So why wasn't she?

Logic warred with her instinct. She didn't trust Ron's motives, or believe that he could be faithful.

But he had connections, and with the election coming up in the fall, she couldn't afford to burn any bridges. She might be assigned to cover the race.

"Sure—just give me a call when you're back in town."

He nodded, and Brenda reached for the door. He caught her arm and dropped a kiss on her cheek. "I really enjoyed our conversation."

Brenda murmured agreement, then rushed outside. But all she could think about when she drove away was that she wished that kiss had been from Nick.

Fat chance of that.

She waited until she was in her condo to phone Nick. It was nearly midnight, and she hesitated, thinking he might be asleep. But she needed to talk to him about this limerick, and he would want her to call him, so she picked up the phone.

To her surprise, he answered on the first ring. "Brenda?"

"Yes," she said, hating the way her voice suddenly sounded breathless. Damn her libido for thinking about kissing him earlier.

"What is it?" he asked gruffly.

No polite chitchat or flattery from this man. "I received another text."

"From the killer?"

"She didn't identify herself, but yes, it's from her."

"What does it say?"

Brenda read him the limerick.

"Fuck."

"What?" Brenda asked. "Do you know who it is?"

"No, but it confirms that the sender is connected to my father."

"How can you be sure?"

"Because he received a similar rhyme the day Logger was murdered. He showed it to me when I visited him in prison."

Brenda walked to the window, eased the curtains back, and looked out. The street was normally quiet this time of night, another reason she'd chosen the development, but tonight it seemed desolate and eerie, offering a million places for a predator to hide.

Had that dark car been parked at the curb when she'd arrived home? Had she seen it before?

A tingle traveled up her spine. Was she being paranoid, or was someone watching her?

"Did the message say anything else?" Nick asked.

"No." Brenda did not want to share the previous text.

Tension stretched between them for several seconds before Nick replied, "It must be from one of the subjects in the experiment."

Brenda massaged her temple, where a headache pulsed. "The line that she'd died and died and died, do you think that's literal?"

"It's possible," Nick said. "It fits the MO. Logger was repeatedly strangled and brought back to life. Maybe the same thing happened to her."

A sick feeling swept over Brenda. "God, Nick, how could anyone be so cruel? And what was the purpose of repeatedly murdering him?"

"You mean other than giving the depraved killer pleasure?"

Brenda's stomach twisted. "What kind of person takes pleasure in watching someone else die?"

"A sociopath." Nick muttered something else low under his breath. Something that sounded like he understood, that he would enjoy watching his father die.

"Nick—"

"She commented that everyone thought she was insane," Nick said, cutting her off. "Does that sound like anyone you know?"

An image of Sadie's sister sprang to mind. "It sounds like Amelia."

Nick cleared his throat. "Did you ever visit her at the sanitarium?"

Brenda began to sweat. "What? No. Why would you ask that?"

"Because this killer connected with you. Maybe you met her somewhere before."

"She could have seen me on TV," Brenda said. "Nick, do you think your father knows who she is?"

Nick's tired sigh echoed back. "If he does, he sure as hell won't tell me."

"But he might talk to me," Brenda said.

"I doubt it."

"You have to let me try," Brenda said. "Maybe he wants people to know his side, so he won't look so bad. I could flatter his ego. Make him think I believe he was a genius, conducting cutting-edge experiments."

"Sounds like you've already planned your angle."

"You have to admit it might work," Brenda said. "We all want the truth."

Seconds passed. "I guess it's worth a shot," Nick said. "I'll set up a meeting asap. But the fact that the unsub contacted you tonight has me worried. What if she's killed again?"

Brenda studied the car down the street again. "The message doesn't say anything about a body."

"That doesn't mean there isn't one," Nick said. "She might just be toying with you, with us."

Brenda didn't like the sound of that.

She closed her eyes, willing images of the week she'd spent at the sanitarium to return. For so long she'd tried to forget those horrible few days.

The cries and screams from the patients in the other wards. Grace Granger's incoherent screeching from the bed where they'd chained her to the wall. The hushed whispers and evil glares from the orderlies who'd muscled the patients into their restraints.

The time she'd wandered too close to the ward where she'd seen them take Amelia…

There had been others down that hall. Maybe a boy…another girl…

What had they been doing to the patients in those rooms?

She strained her memory banks, searching for details of their faces, but they were clouded by the terror that seized her when the orderly dragged her back to her room.

He warned her that bad things would happen to her if she went too far.

She'd never gone down that hall again.

Now she wished she had.

Then she might know the killer. And she might be able to stop her, before she took another life.

——————— · ———————

The room was closing in, the dark terrors coming again as night swallowed the mountains.

Seven rubbed her hands up and down her arms, desperate to chase away the chill. But the sliver of moon that seeped through the storm clouds outside looked exactly like the curve of the Commander's chin.

And the glittering stars—they started the patterns in her head.

She saw the patterns in everything. In steps. In buildings. In the cracks in the sidewalks. In mountain ridges. In the lines on a person's face.

In her dreams.

In the sky.

She counted the clusters of stars. Three here. Five there.

No…seven was the number.

The number echoed over and over in her head. She began to pace out the steps, just as she'd been trained. Never three, never four or five or six.

Seven.
Always seven.

Seven paces to the right
Seven paces forward
Seven paces back
Seven to the right again
A perfect square of seven

"It's time," the Commander's deep voice said as she fell backward into the endless tunnel. Back into the sea of monsters.

The orderly shoved her into the cold, dark room. The chill of death and the screams of the others started again.

Then everything disappeared except the fear.

And she began to pace the steps in her hole.

Seven is my number
Seven is my name
Seven is the size of my box
When we play our game

Seven times I strangle them
Seven times they'll cry
Then it will be the Commander's turn
Seven times he'll die

Chapter 11

Nick paced his den, willing Brenda to come clean with him about her time at the sanitarium. He couldn't ask her, or she'd know he was snooping around in her past.

"I'll talk to Amelia tomorrow," he said. "Then work out a visit for you with my father. That is, if he agrees to see you."

"He'll agree," Brenda said. "His ego won't allow him to resist bragging to me."

"Sounds like you know my father."

"Just instinct, reading through the lines."

Her instincts sounded on target to him. His father was a narcissistic egomaniac.

"I'm sorry, Nick. I know it must hurt, what he did. And having everyone know about it makes it worse."

Nick stepped onto the back deck of the cabin for some fresh air. What was the saying—the sins of the father shall be visited upon the son a thousand times?

"Nick?"

"I'm here."

"If you ever want to talk, I'm a good listener."

Yeah, for a story. She wasn't exactly trusting him with her own secrets.

"I'll call you tomorrow and let you know about the interview."

"Wait. Let me go with you to talk to Amelia."

"That's not a good idea."

"But I've established a relationship with her." Brenda paused. "She's lonely, Nick. She wants a friend, and I can be that friend."

Maybe she was right. Amelia might tell a friend about her stay at Slaughter Creek Sanitarium. Especially if they'd met in the hospital.

"All right, but I'll take the lead. You can't say anything to upset her. Understand?"

"Perfectly."

"I'll pick you up at eight."

"I'll be ready." Then she gave him her address.

He didn't tell her that he already knew where she lived. That he'd done his homework.

Worry seeped into him. If he knew where she lived, the killer might know, too. Was she in danger?

"Brenda…lock your doors tonight."

A soft sigh. "Don't worry, Nick. I sleep with a pistol under my pillow."

Did she have to put that erotic image in his head?

"I'm glad you warned me," he said, then berated himself for the husky timbre of his voice as he imagined crawling in bed with her. Surely she couldn't read his errant thoughts.

Her soft laugh indicated she had. "Good night, Nick."

He steeled himself, forcing his mind back to his father. That reminder destroyed any sexual fantasies.

"Good night," he said gruffly.

He hung up, then punched Jake's number. His brother answered on the third ring, his voice thick with sleep. "Nick?"

"Sorry, I woke you," Nick said, knowing Jake and Sadie were probably cuddled up, all cozy, in mad love. "Brenda received another message from the unsub."

Nick heard sheets rustling and knew his brother was getting out of bed. "What did it say?" Jake asked.

Nick recited the rhyme.

"Nothing specific about a crime or another body?"

"No." Not yet. "I'd like to talk to Amelia again, Jake."

A hesitation. "I don't know what good that will do. Besides, Sadie is guarding her like a dog."

"I'm not going to accuse her of anything. But she might know the killer."

"You have a point," Jake said, his voice worried. "I'll meet you at her condo in the morning."

"Okay, but I'll warn you. Brenda's coming with me."

A litany of curse words rolled off Jake's tongue. "Why the hell are you letting her tag along?"

Nick watched a deer roaming through the woods behind his house. He remained perfectly still, aware that the slightest movement would startle the skittish animal, and it would disappear.

Amelia reminded him of that deer.

"Nick?" Jake said, his voice rising an octave. "What are you doing?"

"I have my reasons," Nick said, deciding not to expose Brenda's secret just yet. Why, he didn't know.

But it just seemed wrong.

Still, if he discovered it had any relation to the case, he would tell his brother.

And it would be very informative if Amelia recognized Brenda from the hospital. "Just trust me."

"All right, Nick," Jake said. "Meanwhile, I'll be on the lookout for murder reports coming through, just in case our strangler struck again."

Nick would do the same. There was no *if* in his mind.

This unsub would strike again. In fact, he had a bad feeling she already had.

———————— · ————————

I'm glad you warned me.

Nick's husky tone as he'd murmured those words kept Brenda awake half the night. She grabbed a cup of coffee to go the next morning, a headache burgeoning from lack of sleep.

Heaven help her, but she wanted that man in her bed.

Not going to happen, Brenda.

She obviously wasn't his type. So what was his type?

Muttering a few choice words for letting her mind even venture into that territory, she stepped outside on her front stoop to wait for Nick. Maybe the cool morning air would clear her head, and dispel the images of Nick naked in bed, doing wicked things to her.

Her phone buzzed, and she checked to see if it was her boss. She'd sent him an e-mail the night before, assuring him she'd have a fabulous story when she finished her research; maybe even several personal profiles on the subjects of the experiment, as well as a piece on Arthur Blackwood himself.

But Ron Stowe's number appeared on the screen. She let it roll to voice mail. He should have been the man in her lust-driven dreams. At least she had a chance of sleeping with him.

Nick showed absolutely zilch interest.

Except his voice had turned husky last night. And he had warned her to lock the door as if…as if he might be worried about her.

Truthfully, she had been spooked by that car down the street. Of course it was gone this morning.

She was probably just being paranoid.

Maybe not. *A killer is sending you private texts. She might be watching you.*

Nick's sedan rolled up; he pulled into a parking space, but Brenda threw her purse over her shoulder, gripped her coffee, and hurried to his car. The grim expression he shot her when she settled in the seat wiped all sexual thoughts aside.

Not that he wasn't sexy with that stern, tough scowl on his face.

But he definitely hadn't stayed awake lusting after her all night.

"Did you hear anything else from our unsub?" Nick asked, not bothering with pleasantries.

"No."

"You're sure?" Nick asked as he drove from the parking lot.

Brenda folded her arms around her to ward off the chill. "Yes, I'm sure."

"I checked, but no murders were reported in the area, none that fit the MO of our unsub."

"Maybe she won't kill again," Brenda said.

Nick grunted. "She will. If Logger's murder had been an isolated event, she wouldn't contact you. She wants us to know she's smart, and that it wasn't an accidental asphyxiation. She wants to make a point. And the number she carved on her victim is significant."

Brenda ignored Nick's disgusted look as she made a note of his comments in her notepad. She had a good memory, but sometimes details were forgotten. And she wanted this story to be accurate.

They lapsed into a strained silence as he drove to Amelia's. When they arrived, Sadie and Jake were already there. They obviously wanted to protect Amelia. If she were in their shoes, she'd feel protective, too.

Jake led them into the entryway. "She's agreed to talk to you both," Jake said. "But I'm warning you, Brenda, don't report anything unless I give you the go-ahead."

"I know the drill," Brenda said. "You should trust me by now."

Jake and Nick exchanged questioning looks, as if that was improbable, then Jake escorted them to the kitchen. Brenda noticed that the dark, ominous paintings she'd seen before were gone, and wondered if Sadie had hidden them from her.

"Hi, Sadie, Amelia," Brenda said. "Thank you for letting me come."

Sadie's gaze met hers. "You did a nice job with the last story, Brenda. I just hope you respect our family and how much Amelia has suffered. Her condition is still delicate."

Brenda's heart squeezed. "I understand. I honestly don't want to hurt any of you." She turned to Amelia, who was sipping a cup of tea, and sank into the chair beside her. "You're a very brave woman, Amelia."

Amelia smiled, squaring her shoulders. She'd always looked as if she were in a fog before, mainly due to the drugs her caretaker had given her. Her eyes looked clearer, more focused, now. Maybe she was healing.

Sadie offered tea or coffee, but Brenda and Nick declined. Nick claimed a chair, and Jake joined Sadie. He laid one hand on her shoulder in a display of support, and emotions tugged at Brenda.

What would it feel like to have a man love her the way Jake loved Sadie? So deeply and unconditionally?

"Amelia," Nick said. "I hate to bring up this painful subject, but I need to ask you some questions about the sanitarium."

Sadie squeezed her sister's hand. "You don't have to do this if you don't feel up to it."

Amelia pursed her lips. Outside, the wind chimes tinkled again. "No, Sadie—my therapist said that talking about it might help me heal."

"You could help us save a life, too," Jake said gently.

Amelia's hand trembled slightly as she set her mug on the table. "I don't remember a lot about that time."

"Tell us about the CHIMES," Nick said.

Amelia's eyes darted to Sadie's, then back. "I don't know what all they did to us in the experiments."

"How about the other children?" Brenda asked softly. "Did you meet them?"

Amelia's hand moved as if she were playing an instrument. "*Ting, ting, ting.* The chimes are ringing."

Brenda frowned, and Sadie spoke up. "They played music that sounded like wind chimes, the same repetitious sound over and over, to hypnotize the kids."

Nick clenched his jaw, but Brenda forced herself not to react.

"What else do you remember, Amelia?" she asked.

Amelia looked at Brenda, and suddenly reached out and took her hand. "The clock. Ticktock. Ticktock. Ticktock."

Again, more repetition. She'd read about brainwashing and how terrorists used repetitive sounds or sensory stimulations or deprivations to torture their captives.

"They lined us up, and then we went through the tunnel of darkness."

"They forced them down to the basement of the sanitarium," Sadie said, her voice cracking.

The room grew quiet, still, the tension palpable.

"They took the others with you," Brenda said gently. "Who were they, Amelia?"

Amelia's eyes looked haunted, as if she were far away in a disturbing, frightening place. "We didn't have names. Just numbers." One lone tear trickled down her cheek. "I was Three. Always Three."

A sick feeling swelled inside Brenda.

"So far we know there were five of you," Nick said. "Joe Swoony, Grace Granger, Bertrice Folsom, and Emanuel Giogardi."

"Grace died," Amelia said as she wiped the tear away. "He killed her."

"I know," Brenda said. Amelia was still clinging to her hand, her nails digging into Brenda's palms. But Brenda didn't release her. "Were there more?"

"More numbers," Amelia said with a slow nod, as if a memory had surfaced. "A boy," she whispered softly. "A big boy—he always stood behind me when they lined us up."

"What was his name?" Nick asked.

"I told you we didn't have names, just numbers," Amelia said, agitation lacing her voice. "Grace was One, Joe Two. Emanuel and Bertrice, Four and Five."

"Who was the big boy you mentioned?" Brenda asked.

"Six."

"Was he the last one in the line?"

Amelia shook her head. "No, there was another girl." She looked up, her eyes darkening. "She tried to run away, but they caught her."

"She was Seven?" Brenda said softly.

Amelia nodded. "Seven and Six were his favorites," Amelia whispered.

"Do you know where Six and Seven are now?" Nick asked.

Amelia took another sip of her tea, but when she spoke, her voice was calm. Controlled.

"They went to live with the Commander."

As soon as they left Amelia's, Brenda checked her phone. She wanted the killer to contact her again, wanted to establish a two-way communication with her. So she quickly sent another text.

Seven? Where are you? Talk to me.

"Anything?" Nick asked.

Brenda shook her head. "Let's give her some time."

"If you can form some kind of bond with her, we might be able to use that to reel her in."

Brenda nodded, and they lapsed into silence as they drove toward the prison, the hills the road wound through giving way to farmland, ancient trailer parks, and countryside that was turning lush and green with spring.

An hour later, they slowed and entered through the security gates, then parked and walked to the front together. Several inmates played basketball on the court in the yard, while others congregated in groups to talk and smoke.

"Are you sure you want to do this?" Nick asked as they checked his keys and their phones at the security desk. "My father can be...dangerous."

Brenda's gaze met his. "Lives are at stake, Nick. If I can reach your father, it'll be worth it."

A war raged in Nick's eyes, but he finally murmured agreement, and they walked into the prison together.

Their conversation with Amelia echoed in Nick's head.

Seven and Six were his favorites.

Nick knew what it meant to be the favorite. "I'm going in with you," Nick said as they were escorted to a visiting room.

Brenda turned to him. "Don't you think your father might open up more if he's alone with me?"

Nick gritted his teeth as images of the way his father had brutalized him raced through his mind. He'd seen his father's crazed, detached look in the basement at the sanitarium when he was about to kill Sadie. Ruthless. Cold. A bastard. "My father is dangerous, Brenda."

"I know that, but there are guards everywhere."

That didn't alleviate Nick's anxiety. "Typically the inmates on twenty-four-hour lockdown are restricted in their visitation, and you could only talk to him through a Plexiglas screen. But I arranged for you to have a room today."

"Good—he'll be more relaxed that way, and maybe let down his guard."

"The Commander never lets down his guard." Nick scraped a hand over his chin, rubbing at the stubble already spiking up.

The guard showed them to the room. "All visits are taped for security purposes. There's a room next door with a TV monitor where you can watch, Agent Blackwood."

Nick took Brenda's arm, forcing her to look at him. "Be careful. If he says anything, tries anything—"

Brenda's eyes locked with his. "I'll be fine, Nick. I'm not afraid of your father."

Nick swallowed hard. "You should be."

Brenda's lips curled into a smile. "Don't worry, I can handle myself. Besides, I trust that you won't let anything happen."

She squeezed his hand, then disappeared into the room.

Nick grimaced. She might think she was equipped for anything, but she didn't know the depth of devious behavior his father was capable of.

The scars on the back of his neck itched.

If his father touched her, he'd kill him.

Brenda took a deep breath as she entered, and Nick slipped into the next room to watch. His father was already seated, his feet shackled, his handcuffed hands splayed on the table. Just like always, the son of a bitch appeared calm, confident, in control.

The sick monster.

Brenda sank into the chair facing him, removed a mini-recorder, and placed it on the table. "I hope you don't mind if I record our conversation, Mr. Blackwood."

"Of course not, Brenda. I'm glad someone in this backwoods town finally wants to hear my side."

Brenda offered him a smile. "I'm sure everyone is eager to know the motivation behind the research you conducted in Slaughter Creek. Maybe if they understood the purpose of the experiment, all the negativity would settle down."

The Commander leaned back in the chair, his eyes intense as he studied Brenda. "Yes, that's what everyone is missing. The fact that the research was intended to help our government. Back during the Cold War, people were terrified about the measures foreign governments were taking. The US didn't want to be caught off guard in a biowarfare attack."

"So your research involved chemical testing on subjects?"

"Yes, along with behavior programming and mind control." He rubbed a finger along the corner of his mouth, obviously enjoying her undivided attention. "Basically, a soldier's biggest flaw is that he's human. Emotions cloud his judgment. We were striving to eliminate that emotional factor so we could hone soldiers to be more efficient, to enable them to follow strict military orders and commands."

"So the soldier experiences no guilt or remorse when he kills?" Brenda asked.

"Exactly," the Commander said. He leaned forward, a sinister smile curling his lips.

"To do that, you sacrificed innocent children without their parents' consent?"

"As in all wars, there are casualties of the cause."

Nick balled his hands into fists. He wanted to make him a casualty.

"Let's talk about those casualties," Brenda suggested.

"Of course."

Brenda laid a piece of paper listing the names of the victims they'd uncovered on the table. "We have identified these subjects, but we know there are more."

"Where did you get that information?" he asked with a smirk.

"Amelia is finally talking," Brenda said.

A brief look of surprise flitted across his father's face before he masked it. "How can you believe anything that poor disturbed woman says?"

"The thing is, Commander, I do believe her." Brenda squared her shoulders. "Nick also showed me the note you received." She removed her phone, then flipped it around for him to see. "I received this message. I think it's from the same person."

Another smile creased the Commander's face. "And you believe I know who this is?"

"Yes, I do," Brenda said calmly.

His father stood and faced Brenda. "You're working with my son Nick, aren't you?" A seething rage darkened his father's eyes. "That's why you came, not to understand me or report my version."

Brenda stood as well, her posture confident. "The person who contacted me killed a man and sent me a note telling me where to find him. She said she'd left a present for you."

"She?" the Commander said.

"Yes, *she*," Brenda said. "I believe you call her Seven. Tell me about her. Why was she your favorite?"

"Ahh, my favorites. You should ask Nick about that."

Brenda narrowed her eyes.

But his father's tone made Nick's skin crawl. He wanted to yank Brenda out of there before the situation spiraled out of control.

"Tell me where she is, Commander, before she kills again."

Anger hardened the Commander's eyes, and his chains clanked as he moved closer to Brenda. "You want to know about Seven?"

Brenda lifted her chin. "Yes, I do. I want to help her."

"Seven was a good girl. She did what I said." He raked his gaze over Brenda. "But you don't obey your father, do you, Brenda?"

"I have a mind of my own," Brenda said. "But you tried to destroy Amelia's mind and free will. Is that what you did to Seven, too?"

"Oh, Seven thinks for herself," he said. "She was one of my strongest. She fought every test."

Rage heated Nick's blood at the cruelty the woman must have suffered.

"In fact, she was a lot like Nick," the Commander said. He lifted his eyes toward the camera in the corner. "I know he's here. He wouldn't let you talk to me if he wasn't watching."

Nick's breath caught in his chest. His father was escalating, wanting to make a point.

He needed to extricate Brenda from the situation.

Brenda lifted a defiant chin. "He's not like you. He wants to save lives, not take them."

"He's more like me than you know, Brenda." His father suddenly lunged toward her, pressing her against the wall. "But you don't see that, because you're fucking him, aren't you? That's why you're here. You're fucking him, and he put you up to interviewing me, hoping I'd smell your cunt and spill my guts."

Nick stormed into the room. His father had Brenda pinned, his handcuffed hands around her neck.

"Let go of her," Nick barked.

The Commander laughed and tightened his hands around Brenda's throat. "See, I knew he'd run to your rescue."

Nick didn't care if he had played into the bastard's game.

He'd kill him before he let him hurt Brenda.

———————— , ————————

The new voice called herself Rachel.

"Just look at these paintings of naked people," she shouted. "You're a sinner, Amelia. A whore."

"No, I'm not," Amelia cried. "It's Viola."

"You're Viola." Rachel jerked the paintings from where she'd hidden them when Sadie and Jake and Nick visited, then raised the knife in her hand.

"They have to be destroyed," Rachel said as she punctured the face of a woman on one of the canvases. "Just like you do."

"I'm not going to let you take over," Amelia shouted.

Rachel raised the knife and slashed the painting again and again, ripping through canvas, tearing the couple depicted apart.

The knife went too far, and the point slashed her wrist. She stared at the blood trickling down her arm and watched it drip onto the tattered canvas.

Ahh, the pain was easing. Another slice, and more blood, thick, red, pulsing with life. Emptying her agony onto the floor.

Rachel began to pray over her. To beg for forgiveness for her transgressions.

Amelia pricked her wrist with the knife again, her eyes glued to the blood dripping down her arm.

Yes, she felt freer already.

Chapter 12

———— o ————

Nick grabbed his father, jerked him away from Brenda, then spun him around. His father used his weight to anchor himself, then swung up his hands in a fight position.

Behind them, Brenda gasped for air, fueling Nick's rage, and he launched into combat mode, kicked his father's hands down, flipping him around and throwing him into a chokehold.

Just enough pressure, and the bastard would pass out.

A little more, and he'd be dead.

Nick squeezed harder, his father's grating laugh booming through the room.

Harder and harder, a little more force, and he'd never have to hear that sinister voice again.

Brenda yanked at his arms. "Nick, stop—please, stop now."

"He tried to kill you!" Nick shouted as he increased the pressure on his father's neck.

"This is what he wants," Brenda cried. "Don't do it. Don't play into his hands."

It took a few seconds for her words to register. But she was right.

He released his father and shoved him to the floor. The Commander looked up at him with a smug grin. "I told you, Nick, you are like me."

Nick shook his head, but he couldn't deny the truth. He'd never wanted anything more than to make the son of a bitch suffer and put an end to his infernal manipulations.

Brenda touched his arm. "Come on, Nick. We're finished here for the day."

"Women make you weak, Nick. Don't forget that, and fall into the same trap your brother did," the Commander said as he pushed himself up to stand.

"My brother is twice the man you are," Nick said.

Brenda snatched her recorder. "If you find your humanity and decide to continue our interview and tell me who the remaining subjects were, give me a call."

Nick stepped to the door, yelled for the guard, took Brenda's elbow, and ushered her through security and outside.

Brenda tried to hide how shaken she was by Arthur Blackwood, especially since she'd pressured Nick for a personal interview.

Perspiration trickled down Nick's forehead as he strode toward the car. She'd never seen him lose control like this. She could hear his teeth grinding.

She rubbed at her neck, still straining to suck air in through her aching vocal cords. "Nick..."

"Get in the car."

Brenda dropped into the seat while Nick did the same. But instead of starting the engine, he turned to her, raked her hair back, and examined her neck.

"Nick..."

"He could have killed you." His dark eyes flared. "I'm taking you to the hospital."

"Nick…" Brenda caught his hand as he reached for the keys. "Stop. I'm okay. I don't need to go to the hospital."

When he slanted his eyes back to her, pain and other emotions she couldn't quite define glittered in his eyes. "For God's sake, he tried to strangle you."

"But he didn't." Still, a shudder rippled up her spine at the memory of the attack. "I'm fine. Really."

"I never should have allowed you to go in there with him alone." He traced a finger over the marks on her neck.

Brenda gripped his hand in hers. "You couldn't have stopped me—I wanted that interview, and you know it."

"Maybe. But you're not going to see him again," Nick said. "Not ever."

"Nick—"

"I mean it—I won't let him hurt you." He pulled her into his arms and held her. "You're trembling."

"I'm sorry. I'm just rattled, that's all." For a brief second, Brenda allowed herself to lean into him. To accept his comfort.

After the attack, Nick felt so strong. Safe.

"You have nothing to be sorry about," he murmured against her hair.

She rubbed slow circles across his chest, savoring the feel of his heart beating wildly below her ear.

"I thought I had him," she said, trying for bravado.

"He used you to get to me," Nick said in a tortured voice.

Brenda nodded, then lifted her face and looked up at him. His dark eyes latched on to hers. Their breathing echoed in the silence. She trembled again, then dug her fingers into his chest.

He groaned, then lowered his head and closed his mouth over hers.

Brenda parted her lips in invitation. The first touch of his mouth stirred desires that she'd managed to keep from him for years.

Because she'd craved this kiss since she was a teenager. She couldn't believe it was finally happening.

And she didn't want it to end.

———————— , ————————

Nick drove his tongue into Brenda's mouth, deepening the kiss and pulling her closer against him.

She was the bravest, most infuriating, *sexiest* woman he'd ever met.

And she was driving him crazy.

Lust sizzled through his veins. The need to have her, to hold her, to taste every inch of her, rose inside him like a beast.

He stroked her back, one hand sliding around to tug at the buttons of her blouse as he dipped his head and kissed her neck. She moaned softly, her hands threading into his hair, lifting her body as if to offer herself to him.

He couldn't resist. His tongue trailed in a sensuous line down her neck, then lower to nip at the delicate skin above her breasts, where he'd parted the fabric. She tugged at his shirt, making his blood run hotter, and he eased the lacy edge of her bra aside and closed his mouth over one ripe nipple.

Her breath rushed out, and she moaned, the two of them frantic as she raked her hands across his chest. A button popped, and her fingers danced across his skin in an erotic tease.

He leaned into her, half climbing over the seat. He had to have her. Had to be inside her.

Suddenly the sound of another car broke into the sexual haze clouding his brain. Fuck. He was acting like a randy teenager.

He eased his hold on Brenda, then slowly lifted his mouth from her breast. His sigh sounded just as desperate as he felt. The last thing he wanted to do was stop.

He wanted to take Brenda right here in the car, in the middle of the prison parking lot.

Very romantic, Nick. You're a classy guy.

Disgust filled him, and he began buttoning her blouse. Why not maul her in the prison hallway?

"Nick—"

"Don't say anything," Nick murmured. "Just cover up."

Thank God for tinted windows.

Brenda's hands trembled as she finished buttoning her blouse. He fastened his own shirt, not daring to look at her.

"Nick—"

"Please, Brenda, don't talk."

She gripped his arms and shook him. "Why not? Because you wish that hadn't happened?"

His gaze met hers. There was wildness about her eyes, a flare of passion. Desire. Raw hunger.

All the same emotions and need consuming him.

"Because I'm not sorry," Brenda said. "Not at all."

Car doors slammed nearby, and a prison bus returned from a work detail, a line of inmates descending the bus stairs.

"You sure as hell should be. Look where we are," Nick said. "Look who I am."

"I know who you are, and I want you," Brenda said. "I—"

Nick threw up a hand. "Stop."

"Why?" Brenda said. "Because you're afraid I might care about you? That you might care about me?"

Nick refused to answer that question. Because she'd hit the nail on the head.

Instead, he started the car and drove toward the gate and guards' station. Things had spiraled out of control because he'd been furious with his father. Because his father had baited him.

But, hell, the truth was that he *did* want Brenda.

He'd wanted her half his life. Since back in high school, when Jake had dated her.

After graduation, Jake had left for the military, and Nick had seen Brenda around town and fantasized about having her.

And then again, the first time he saw her when he returned to Slaughter Creek.

But he'd played right into his father's hands and tried to kill him for touching her.

He couldn't lose control again.

———————— ‚ ————————

Brenda wanted to scream in frustration. Nick had completely shut down. Any intimacy or trace of closeness had completely vanished.

Nick thought that she didn't know who he was. The Commander had taunted Nick, saying that he was just like him.

Did Nick believe that?

He couldn't. Nick was courageous and strong, a man who risked his life to save strangers. He would never have used those children in a diabolical experiment, as the Commander had.

But he obviously didn't want to discuss a personal relationship now, so she remained silent as they stopped for a late meal, then turned to study the mountains as they drove back to Slaughter Creek. Farms, chicken houses, and rotting shanties clung to the sides of the ridges. Some homesteads were well kept up, while others looked deserted and run-down. But the tranquility of the rural setting drew outsiders on vacation; it made families feel as if they were retreating to a simpler, more wholesome life.

She was surprised Agnes and William, who seemed to thrive on being in the limelight, had settled here instead of in a big city. All her life she'd felt as if she didn't belong with them. That she was different, a misfit, because she didn't care about climbing the social ladder.

When she'd learned she was adopted, she'd finally understood the reason for these unsettling feelings.

If she met her birth mother, would she see similarities between them? Is that where she'd gotten her eyes, or her hair, or her stubborn insistence on digging for the truth?

When she was a child, some of the kids at school had talked about camping and hiking in the woods. Sleeping outdoors beneath the stars and chasing away bears that sneaked into their campsites looking for food. She'd wanted those kinds of adventures.

But Agnes and William Banks had never been campers.

Vacations for them meant cruises and traveling to Europe, sometimes taking her, sometimes leaving her with the nanny. The popular girls in high school had envied her. But most of those trips had been filled with boring museums, formal dinners where she endured countless lessons on being a lady, and endless adult parties, where she ended up in a corner or a hotel with a nanny wishing she was home.

Wishing her parents loved her for the way she was, not for the perfect daughter that she could never be.

Her cell phone buzzed, and she checked the number. Ron Stowe again.

"Who keeps calling you?" Nick asked.

Brenda cleared her throat. "The senator's son. I met him the other night at my parents' dinner party." Good grief, why had she volunteered that information?

Nick's jaw hardened. "You aren't going to answer?"

"I'll call him back later."

Nick turned his focus back to his driving, and she silently chided herself. Why couldn't she be attracted to Ron instead of Nick?

Her phone dinged that she had a text, and she quickly checked it.

Seven is my number
Seven is my name
Now it's time for us
To play a little game
You'll find the next body
At Blindman's Curve
Don't feel too sorry for him
We all get what we deserve.

Brenda's palms began to sweat. "Nick, it's from her. There's another body at Blindman's Curve."

————————— , —————————

Nick scrubbed a hand down his chin, punched the gas, and flew along the curvy mountain road.

"She identified herself as Seven this time," Brenda said.

"Jesus." Nick grabbed his phone and pressed Jake's number.

"How'd it go with our father?" Jake asked immediately.

"He was the same evil bastard he always is," Nick said, omitting the fact that he'd nearly killed him. "But listen, Jake, there's been another murder. The body's at Blindman's Curve."

"I'll call a crime team and meet you there."

Nick hung up and floored the gas, his mind churning. The first body had been left in a motel room, the victim tied to the bed in a graphic sexual position.

If this was the same unsub, why dump the body in the woods?

What was Seven trying to tell them by her choice of disposal sites?

Chapter 13

———— o ————

Nick parked a few feet from Blindman's Curve on the shoulder of the road. "Wait in the car—"

"No," Brenda said. "I can help you search for the body."

Nick wanted to spare her, but Brenda had proven she was tough.

The sun had set, gray storm clouds obliterating the stars, giving the woods an eerie glow. This curve, one of the worst switchbacks on this side of the creek, had taken more lives than he could count. Sadie and Amelia's parents had died in this very spot.

Of course, for years everyone'd thought it was an accident.

But now they knew the Commander had been responsible for their deaths. All because Mrs. Nettleton had overheard a conversation between one of the doctors heading up the experiment, and had grown suspicious.

Nick climbed out, opened the trunk, and retrieved two flashlights. Brenda's hand brushed his when she took one from him. He tried to ignore the heat of her skin, but when their gazes met, her eyes darkened with awareness.

Good God. She was distracting.

They had a body to find. He couldn't think about how close he'd come to having sex with Brenda in the prison parking lot.

The March breeze stirred leaves and trees, the sound of a coyote somewhere in the distance echoing from the woods. A truck barreled by, going too fast, and Nick pushed Brenda back from the shoulder as the truck crossed the line. Sparks flew as the idiot skimmed the guardrail.

"They should have called this Deadman's Curve," Brenda said.

Nick muttered agreement as they hiked over the guardrail into the woods. He shone the light along the ground ahead of them, cautioning Brenda as he nearly stumbled over a clump of branches that had blown off in a recent storm.

He paused, and she ran into him. "Sorry."

He gestured toward the right with his flashlight. "Look, there are marks, as if someone dragged a body."

"You're right." Brenda followed the trail. "It goes in that direction."

Nick swung the flashlight around in an arc and noticed a pair of footprints pressed into the dead leaves and mud.

"Don't step in the tracks," he said, pointing them out. "I want a plaster cast of that boot print."

"The prints look small, like a female's," Brenda commented.

"Fits with our theory."

A few feet over, Nick spotted a lump that looked like a body in a pile of weeds and bramble. "Over there."

Traffic noises from the road rumbled like thunder behind them. As they drew nearer, the stench of death swirled around them.

Brenda pressed a hand to her nose. "Oh, my God."

Nick handed her his handkerchief. "Stay here. It's only going to get worse."

"No, I'm fine," Brenda said, although she coughed as she moved up behind him.

Nick inched nearer the body, his flashlight landing on the corpse. Flies buzzed around, and ants and other insects swarmed over the naked corpse.

A siren wailed, the sound of cars screeching to a stop echoing from the road. "Go back and meet Jake. Tell him where we are."

Brenda whirled around and ran back through the weeds, grateful to get away from the stench and the grisly scene.

Nick inched closer, careful not to step on the boot prints and drag marks, then peered through the weeds at the man's arms. Rope burns marred his wrists and ankles, just as with Logger.

The ligature marks around the dead man's neck were also similar to the ones on Logger.

But this scene was much more disturbing.

Why had the killer left this body exposed to the elements, instead of in a motel room?

———————— · ————————

Brenda had seen Logger's dead body, but nothing had prepared her for the sight of this victim covered in insects. It also looked as if some animal had gnawed at his foot and chewed part of it off.

She leaned against a pine tree and struggled for a breath. She needed the fresh mountain air to cleanse herself from the putrid smells, but the odor swirled around her in a sickening rush.

She closed her eyes, but suddenly a memory assaulted her.

It was the first day her father had forced her go to the hospital. The counselor suggested she needed therapy and drugs for depression.

All she could think about was that she'd found that document. That the two people she'd thought were her parents were not.

That they'd lied to her all her life.

If she wasn't Brenda Banks, who was she?

Who had given birth to her and thrown her away?

Why hadn't her mother wanted her? Had she been young and immature, maybe a teenager? Had her parents forced her to give her up?

Or was she a product of a sexual assault? Maybe a terrible rape, and the girl couldn't stand looking at a reminder of the heinous crime?

Where was Brenda's father? Did he even know she existed?

Tears blinded her as the pain rolled through her. Even now, years later, she wondered why her own mother hadn't loved her enough to keep her. If her mother couldn't love her, why would anyone else?

Images of the sanitarium taunted her. The big iron gates. The stone building with its turrets, like a haunted castle from medieval times.

The dark corridors and locked doors and screams in the night.

The counselor prescribed medication to help her sleep, but it had only made her crazy.

Either she'd had hallucinations—

Or the things she'd seen had been real.

A siren blared, coming closer, and blue lights twirled against the night sky, drawing her from the memory. Still, for a brief second, she'd been back there. Back in that basement, where she'd followed one of the doctors.

Then running away, when he'd spied her. Running and running down the halls, terrified what they might do to her if they caught her.

Tires screeched, doors opened, and voices pierced the night as Jake, the crime team, and the ME arrived.

Brenda mentally pushed aside the images. She could not fall apart now, or no one would ever respect her as an investigative reporter.

Retrieving her phone from her pocket, she called her cameraman and explained the situation. "Yes, meet me here. The police and crime techs are already at the scene."

Quickly pocketing her phone, she met Jake at the edge of the woods. "Nick's over there with the body. I'll show you."

Jake and the crew followed her down the trail. Nick was taking pictures with his camera, while flies and other insects swarmed.

This time, Brenda braced herself for the sight. Nick's dark gaze met hers in a silent question, as if he was concerned about her.

Irritated that she'd shown any weakness, she gave a quick nod. She was human, after all. Maybe Nick had seen dozens of dead bodies in the military and on the job and had grown accustomed to the gruesome images, but this was new territory for her.

Nick greeted his brother, Deputy Waterstone, and the CSI team. The crime techs started taking photographs and combing the scene for forensics, while Jake's deputy roped off the area.

Jake paused, his hands on his hips as he surveyed the scene. "If this is the same unsub, why toss the body out here?"

"Good question," Nick said. "The location might have some significance to her."

"She could be making a statement about throwing him away, saying he's garbage," Brenda suggested.

Nick shrugged. "It's possible, especially if she knew the victim. Maybe he hurt her in some way."

"Or she just hates all men," said Brenda.

"I thought all serial killers hated their mothers," Jake said.

Nick cleared his throat. "That's a common theory, that the killer suffered trauma or abuse as a child."

"That fits," Jake said.

"Although most serial killers are men," Nick said. "And technically it's not a serial murder until there are three victims."

"She's over halfway there," Jake said. "And with this MO and the way she left the body, it appears like she's escalating."

"The Nettletons died on this curve," Brenda commented.

Nick and Jake both looked her way, then turned back to the scene. "She's right," Nick said. "Maybe she wants us to know that they were murdered trying to expose what was happening at the sanitarium."

"I guess that's possible," Jake said. "We need to identify the victim."

"I know," Nick agreed. "Victimology might lead to a suspect."

"If she's working alone, she must be strong," Brenda commented. "She dragged him from the car into the woods a good hundred yards."

Trees and brush rustled as the crime techs combed the area. The ME rubbed his forehead. "It definitely looks like the same killer—ligature marks the same size and depth, petechial hemorrhaging, rope burns around the wrists and ankles, compression marks where CPR was probably performed."

Nick eased the man's head to the side and checked behind his ear. "Yep, she carved a two on his neck."

"Time of death?" Jake asked.

"I'd guess sometime last night. I'll know more when I do the autopsy."

"What about his foot?" Nick asked. "What kind of animal got to him?"

The ME nodded. "The teeth marks look like they were made by a mountain lion, although they're virtually extinct in the area. Still, some folks say they've seen a few around here."

Headlights beamed from the highway, and the news van screeched to a stop. Brenda started back to meet Louis, but Nick caught her arm.

"Dammit, Brenda, I thought we made a deal."

"We did," she said tightly. "But I still have to do my job."

Uncertainty shadowed his eyes. Could he trust her?

"I won't cross the line," she said. "But I have to report this, Nick. The public, the people in town, need to know that a dangerous killer is loose."

"Fine—then tell them there was another murder, you can even mention that the victim died of strangulation, but don't mention the MO or our theories about the killer being female. We have to withhold details from the public to keep crazy grandstanders from coming out of the woodwork. We don't have time to deal with false confessions or phony leads."

"I understand."

"And you especially can't mention the piano wire or the number carved behind the man's ear. That's her signature, and I don't want it leaked."

"Don't worry," Brenda said. "I will protect the investigation, Nick." If she didn't, no law officer would ever trust her again. "You should hold a press conference. The men in Slaughter Creek need to be warned not to trust any strange women."

"Like that's going to keep a man from picking up a woman," Nick muttered wryly.

"You're probably right," Brenda said. "The danger might turn some men on. But you could release a profile of the killer."

"Not until I have more information. But when the time comes, I'll handle it."

Brenda wove through the trees to meet the news van. Time to paste on a smile for the camera and report the story—at least, the part of it she could tell.

Louis looked freaked out. "Are we going in those woods?"

"No, they won't let us film the body. We'll have to wait and talk to Agent Blackwood and the ME when they finish." Brenda gestured toward the shoulder of the road behind the metal guardrail. Occasionally a car whizzed by, a couple of vehicles slowing as if to see what was going on. She prayed they didn't stop. It was too dangerous on the curve for them to park.

"You ready?" Louis asked.

She nodded and smoothed down her hair. "This is Brenda Banks, coming to you live from Blindman's Curve in Slaughter Creek, where the body of a man has been discovered. At this point, the victim has not been identified, but Sheriff Jake Blackwood and Special Agent Nick Blackwood are on the scene."

Louis panned the camera over to their vehicles, then back to her.

"The medical examiner is conducting a preliminary exam of the body although an autopsy will be performed to establish cause and time of death. A crime unit is also searching for evidence the killer may have left behind."

Louis captured footage of the woods as she spoke. "Police have neither confirmed nor denied that this man's murder is connected to Jim Logger's, but they are looking into that possibility. If anyone saw or heard anything suspicious around Blindman's Curve in the last twenty-four hours, please report it to the authorities. We will bring you more on the story as it unfolds."

She wrapped up the tape by listing the phone numbers to call.

"Are we done?" Louis asked.

Brenda shook her head. "No, let's wait until the medics carry the body to the ambulance." As morbid as it sounded, viewers wanted to feel like they were part of the scene.

Nothing hyped up publicity better than a body bag with a man's corpse inside.

Of course, to have her handiwork shown off on the news was exactly what the killer wanted.

Brenda scanned the woods and hills, searching for a pair of eyes.

Was the killer watching now?

———————— , ————————

The ME motioned for Nick and Jake to follow him over to the body. He brushed away several insects, then pointed to the man's neck. "See the ligature marks?"

"Yes, it looks like repeated strangulations."

The ME nodded. "Although there are numerous marks from the piano wire where the pressure from the killer was uneven, there are seven distinct indentations in the skin." His brow furrowed as he looked up at them. "Those seven lines are deeper. It appears that the killer lifted the wire, then placed it back, increasing the pressure but forming a pattern."

"Amelia said the Commander didn't assign the subjects names, only numbers. She was Three," Jake said.

"And the killer gave her name as Seven in the last message she sent to Brenda," Nick said. A knot of anxiety squeezed his belly. "If Seven is her name, and her pattern on the killers is also seven, is she planning to kill seven men to make her point?"

———————————— , ————————————

Seven paced the top of the mountain ridge. Seven paces to the right, seven paces forward, seven to the left, seven to the right again. A perfect square.

Then she started all over again.

Seven times until she could stop.

She didn't want to miss the show down on Blindman's Curve. She'd seen Nick Blackwood and Brenda arrive and watched them find her gift. This one was a little messier than the last, but he deserved it.

She lifted her wrists and studied her own scars, remembering the brutal way the man had bound her. Even as she'd bled and begged him to finish her, he'd saved her.

All because of the Commander's orders.

She smiled as she watched Brenda in front of the camera.

Why wasn't Brenda taking the camera into the woods? Why was she staying on the side of the road?

Brenda was supposed to show everyone what Seven had done to the man. She was supposed to let everyone see his shame and humiliation, his corpse being used as a meal for the insects in the woods.

She began to pace again, her body twitching with adrenaline and anger. She'd chosen Brenda because she expected her to showcase her handiwork.

Because she'd make sure all the people in Slaughter Creek, especially the Commander, realized they weren't safe.

Because of who Brenda was.

But if Brenda didn't do her justice, she'd pay. Just like the others.

Chapter 14

Nick grimaced as the medics hauled the corpse from the woods and loaded it into the back of the ambulance.

Brenda headed toward him as the medics pulled away, her cameraman in tow. "Special Agent Blackwood, what can you tell us about the body you discovered here tonight?"

Nick forced his voice to be even. "The body belonged to a man, probably midthirties. We have no ID yet, but we're working on that now."

"Are you ruling this a homicide?"

Nick swatted at a fly buzzing past his neck. "I can't give an official statement in that regard yet. The ME will have to determine cause and time of death first."

"Judging from the way the body was discarded, you believe it was murder?" Brenda pressed.

A warning simmered in Nick's eyes. They both knew damn well it was murder.

"It appears that way."

"Are there similarities between this man's death and the death of Jim Logger?"

He fought to keep his temper. "I can't comment on that yet. We will release more information once we've had ample time to analyze the evidence."

He pushed past her and strode over to meet Lieutenant Maddison. "Did you find anything?"

"Dr. Bullock said the killer carved the number one into our first victim's neck. Did she do that with this victim?"

Maddison nodded.

Nick made a sound in his throat. "It's part of the unsub's signature."

"Do you know what it means?" Brenda asked.

Nick glared at her for following him. But at least she'd left her cameraman behind. "We believe she was one of the subjects in the Slaughter Creek experiments. Subject number seven."

A vein throbbed in Maddison's neck. "Just when I think they can't come up with something new."

"What else did you find?" Nick asked.

"A partial boot print that we're casting. Looks small, probably a female." He paused. "We also found fibers in the man's mouth."

"Just like before. I think the team is still researching where they came from, but the tech thinks it was from a woman's pair of panties."

Maddison's brows arched. "She stuffs her underwear in his mouth so no one can hear him scream."

"Then she takes all his clothes with her." Nick sighed. "Anything else?"

"We also found a small swatch of fabric caught on a bush over there." He gestured a few feet away to the right, slightly off the trail.

Nick mentally contemplated the crime. The killer could have ducked behind the tree to hide if another car appeared.

"Looks like the fabric yoga pants are made of."

Nick's pulse picked up. "Maybe you can get some DNA off of it."

"We'll try. If we're lucky, she left something on the body the ME can identify."

Nick hoped to hell so. He had a bad feeling the body count was going to rise.

His phone buzzed, and Nick checked the number. His buddy from the bureau, Rafe Hood.

He stepped aside to answer the call, his eyes glued to Brenda as she walked her cameraman back to his van.

"Nick?"

"You'd better have something for me, Hood, because I have another dead man."

"I've been checking into that security company your vic worked for. I cross-checked with other soldiers' releases, and had a hit on one who worked for the company. A guy named Darren James. He lives over at Willow's Peak. Report shows he was given a medical discharge due to panic attacks. He worked odd jobs since his release, spent some time as a mechanic, then a short-order cook, before he signed on at the security company."

Very different jobs. "Anything else?"

"He's divorced. Wife met someone else while he was overseas."

Poor guy. "Thanks. I'll have a talk with him. Maybe he knew Logger. If this victim worked at the same security company as Logger, we may have found our common thread."

Then it might explain Seven's method for choosing her victims.

Brenda waved to her cameraman, then smiled at the text her boss Harry had sent, congratulating her on another good segment.

But Brenda wanted more. She was intrigued by Seven and wanted to get inside her head, to know what made her tick. The story behind the story; the one only the killer could tell.

Just as only Amelia could tell what had happened to her as a victim.

Would Amelia remember Seven? If so, maybe she could give Brenda a description of the woman.

Then she could break the case.

She hurried over to see if Nick had any new information. "What do we do now?"

Nick made a low sound in his throat. "*We* don't do anything. You're going home, and let me do my job."

"Have you identified the victim?"

Nick shook his head. "Blood and DNA will tell."

"Do you have any leads?"

Nick leaned closer, his dark eyes resting on her. "I said go home, Brenda. You've done enough today."

Brenda's temper flared. "What did I do, Nick? Make you feel something for a change?"

She was referring to the kiss, and he knew it.

"What happened in that car was simply an adrenaline-charged reaction to a bad situation," he said in a low voice. "Nothing more."

Brenda traced a finger down his arm. "You can tell yourself that all you want, Nick, but we both know it's not true."

"Don't," Nick warned as she lifted her finger to touch his cheek. He caught her hand and shoved it down, then released her. "Whatever it was, it won't happen again."

Jake emerged from the woods with the crime team, and Nick walked toward them, dismissing her. Brenda wanted to hear whether they'd found anything, but obviously Nick was shutting her out.

So she headed over to ask Louis for a ride home, to get her car so she could visit Amelia again. If Amelia remembered Seven, she might offer Brenda a clue as how to find her.

Nick explained to Jake about the possible lead with the security company. "If we find out that our second victim worked at the same place, it might help."

"Are you going to question Darren James?" Jake asked.

Nick nodded and told Maddison to call him with the crime scene findings. Deputy Waterstone left to do rounds in the town and answer a domestic dispute.

"With two murders so close together," Nick said as he and Jake stood by his car, looking out at the woods where the body had been dumped, "our killer has to be staying somewhere nearby. She also has to know the area."

"Good point," Jake said. "Where has she been all this time? We know Amelia has been in and out of the sanitarium, but lived in Slaughter Creek with her family."

"Grace Granger and Joe Swoony lived here, too."

Jake ticked the names off on his fingers. "Emanuel Giogardi became a hired killer, but he still kept a place in Byrne Hollow, where he killed himself. And Bertrice Folsom's family lived outside town."

"I'll start checking out rental properties, cabins off the grid," Jake said. "Places a killer might hide. There are a lot of those in these mountains."

"A needle in a haystack," Nick muttered. "But it's worth a shot. Meanwhile I'll have a chat with Darren James. See if he knew Jim Logger or anything about the Slaughter Creek experiments."

They shook hands, then went their separate ways, each determined to stop Seven before any more bodies were added to the count.

Nick jumped in his car and turned onto the mountain road, taking the turns slowly as he drove toward Willow's Peak.

The wind kicked up, sending the trees swaying with its force, the cloudy skies threatening another storm. The tips of the ridges still sparkled with snow and ice that hadn't melted, the mountain temperature not yet warm enough to thaw out the freeze at the top of the ridges. Tornado season loomed, threatening to wreak havoc and take lives.

His shoulders ached from fatigue—and from the tension of his self-enforced control. Damn Brenda for shaking that control.

He veered onto a narrow road called Goat Pen Lane, his mind still trying to make sense of the crime scene. Cows grazed in the pasture to the right, two horses roaming by the wooden fence.

His car bounced over the ruts in the graveled road, gears grinding as he shifted and climbed the incline. A sharp drop-off to the side forced him to hug the center of the road, tires spitting gravel as he chugged up to the top of the ridge.

A few lone stars glittered as Nick parked in front of the log cabin. A Ford Bronco sat near the house, which was lit up, as if someone was at home.

He climbed out and walked up the front steps to the porch. The moon hung low, fighting its way through the clouds, and a coyote howled from somewhere nearby. Nick's hand automatically went to his gun, but he kept it in his jacket, pausing to listen for sounds inside the house.

The TV was blaring, so he pounded on the door with his fist. But no one answered. He tried it again, then stepped to the side of the door and peered through the window.

The den in the front of the house held a faded sofa and two mismatched chairs, but little else. From there, he saw a kitchen with an oak table and some scarred chairs. To the right, a staircase led upstairs.

He checked his watch. It was late. Maybe the man was in bed. But why leave all the lights and the television on?

He jiggled the door, and it swung open easily. Nerves knotted his shoulders, but he stepped inside. "Mr. James?"

The house was quiet except for the sound of the wind, whistling through a window somewhere in the house.

"Mr. James, are you here? My name is Special Agent Nick Blackwood." He inched through the den, flipped the TV sound down with the remote, and checked the kitchen. The window above the sink was open, the view of the valley below highlighted by the moon's glow. The kitchen looked clean, no dishes in the sink or on the counter.

He crept back to the front of the house, then climbed the staircase. "Mr. James, are you up here, sir?" He identified himself again, then paused, listening again, but nothing moved or stirred.

A quick look in the first bedroom to the left showed that it was clear. The bed was neatly made with a quilt. No clothing in sight.

He inched to the next room, then cursed.

A man's body lay on the floor by the window. He glanced at the bathroom, but it appeared empty, so he walked over to the dead man. Blood pooled on the floor below his head.

He had been shot in the head at close range. A through-and-through.

A professional hit.

Not Seven's MO.

Suspicions mounted. His father had hired a hit man to eliminate anyone associated with the Slaughter Creek experiments.

Both Logger and James had worked at Stark Security, and now both were dead.

Was that the reason they were killed? If so, what did the security company have to do with Seven?

Brenda checked her watch, hoping it wasn't too late, but she stopped by Amelia's anyway. The lights were on, so she rang the doorbell. The wind chimes tinkled in the breeze, the smell of honeysuckle and flowers drifting to her.

Spring had always been her favorite time of year. A time of regrowth and rebirth, of warm weather and barefoot days at the park.

Only she couldn't erase the images of the dead body from her mind.

The door creaked open, and Amelia stared at her with wide eyes. "Brenda?"

"I'm sorry to bother you so late, but I wanted to talk to you again."

"Sure, come in," Amelia said. "It's nice to have a friend. Everyone in town steers clear of me. They all think I'm crazy."

Her gaze met Brenda's, and the two of them laughed. "I guess I was...am," Amelia said.

Brenda shook her head. "You're doing great, Amelia. If I didn't think so, I wouldn't have come."

"Really?" Amelia pressed a hand over her paint smock as if embarrassed to be caught a mess. Her hair was pulled back in a ponytail, her face void of makeup, paint splattered on her hands and clothes.

She looked young and vulnerable. But the insecurity in her voice made Brenda's heart squeeze. "Yes. As a matter of fact, I thought you might be able to help."

Amelia's expression turned wary. "Another man died?"

Brenda narrowed her eyes. "How did you know?"

"I didn't. But I figured if you were back, it was because something bad had happened."

Brenda wanted to assure Amelia that she'd simply come to visit. But that wasn't true, and she refused to lie. Too many people had lied to Amelia already. "I'm sorry—if you don't want to talk, that's fine. I can leave." She reached for the door, but Amelia clutched her arm.

"No, come on in. I couldn't sleep anyway. That's why I was painting." She sighed as they entered the den, and Brenda shivered at the sight of the black shadows on the canvas Amelia had been working on. A gold cross hung above a window in the sketch, as if to ward off the demons. A corner bookcase now held a Bible and a ceramic angel that hadn't been there before.

"The nightmares come at night," Amelia admitted.

Crimson reds dotted the black. Blood, maybe? The colors in her nightmare?

Then she noticed a painting of a girl who looked familiar. "Is that Grace?"

A soft smile curved Amelia's face. "Yes—I tried to imagine how she'd look if she'd been happy and had led a normal life. She never got the chance."

Sadly, Amelia was right. "I'm really sorry about what happened to both of you," Brenda said, meaning it.

Amelia tucked a strand of hair behind one ear and gestured for Brenda to sit down. She made herself comfortable, hoping Amelia could relax with her. "Thanks for inviting me in. What else do you remember about Grace?"

"We played games in the waiting room before the doctor gave us our immunizations. Grace had a doll named Chatty Cathy. I wanted one so badly, but Gran never would buy me one."

"You went to the free clinic for your immunizations?" Brenda asked softly.

Amelia nodded and picked at a thread on her shirt.

The free clinic in town had served as the base where Nick's father and the doctors in the research project had chosen their subjects.

"Did you see Grace at the sanitarium?" Brenda asked.

A haunted look flashed in Amelia's eyes. "Yes, sometimes."

Brenda cradled Amelia's hand in hers. "You did such a good job capturing Grace on canvas. Do you think you could draw a sketch of the others in the project?"

Amelia's eyes lit up. "You mean Joe and Bertrice?"

"Yes," Brenda said. "And Seven."

Amelia stood, walked to the window, and stared out into the dark night.

"I'm sorry—did I say something to upset you?" Brenda asked.

Amelia shook her head. "It's just that I know I'm supposed to remember. But…"

"Sometimes you don't want to," Brenda said.

"Exactly." Amelia looked back at her. "Does that make me a coward?"

Brenda shook her head, then went to Amelia and stroked her arms. "No, Amelia, it makes you human."

"Sadie says you're only being nice to me because you want a story for the news."

An image of the five-year-old Sadie being taunted by the bigger kids on the playground rose from the graveyard of Brenda's memories. "I do want to tell your story, but not to embarrass or humiliate you. I want everyone to see that you aren't mentally unstable, that you're brave. That you're going to survive no matter what they did to you."

Tears blurred Amelia's eyes. "But sometimes I still feel crazy. When I hear the voices. I tell them to go away, but when it's dark and I dream about that basement where he took us, I want to give in and disappear."

"But you haven't," Brenda said.

"I promised Sadie I wouldn't give up."

"Good for you. You're stronger than people think."

"Thanks. But I still get confused."

Brenda rubbed Amelia's hand. "Believe it or not, I know what it's like to be confused about who you are."

Amelia's eyes narrowed. "You can't know. Everyone always liked you in school. You were popular." Amelia took a deep breath. "You always wore these pretty store-bought dresses, while Sadie and I wore faded hand-me-downs from the Goodwill store.

One day you wore a white dress with sparkles and these bright red shoes. You looked so beautiful."

"I called them my Dorothy shoes," Brenda said with a laugh. She'd forgotten about them.

"I thought you looked like a princess."

Brenda licked her suddenly dry lips. She knew the dress Amelia was talking about. Her mother had insisted she wear it to the country club, had screamed at her for wanting to play outside, had made Brenda pose with her parents for a photo for the newspaper because her father was running for town council.

"It appeared like I was happy, like I had it all, Amelia, but on the inside, I was just as insecure as you and Sadie." Brenda paused. "It's obviously not the same as the ordeal you endured. I wasn't tortured or used like you were, but…" She decided to confide in her completely. "When I was sixteen, I found out my parents, the people who raised me, aren't really my parents. They adopted me. They'd lied to me for years."

Amelia's face softened. "But you're Brenda Banks—you're on TV."

Brenda laughed softly. "I do like my job, but in here"—she pressed a hand to her heart—"in here, I don't know who I am. And that eats at me, because I need to know the truth."

Amelia squeezed Brenda's hands. "Sometimes I wish I didn't know the truth, that people didn't know. They look at me like I'm a freak."

"You're not a freak," Brenda said earnestly. "You were a victim, but you're taking charge of your life. I believe telling your story will help you heal."

A sad smile curved Amelia's face, but her eyes flickered with determination. "Maybe you're right. I'll try to remember what Seven looks like and draw her."

Brenda gave Amelia a hug, emotions overwhelming her. "Thanks. Call when you do." She turned to leave, then paused at the door. "I'm sorry, I didn't mean it like that. You can call me anytime, Amelia. Just to talk."

That wary look returned to Amelia's eyes.

"I promise you that I won't print anything or report anything you don't want me to."

Amelia's eyes glittered with tears. "Thanks, Brenda. I promise I'll try to draw a picture of Seven, but it's been years since I've seen her." She tilted her head to the side. "She was pretty, you know. Not in a movie-star way, but striking. But her eyes were so tormented. Even though the Commander called her his favorite, she cried just like we did when he took her to the dark room."

Brenda clenched her hands together. No telling what he'd done to Seven when they were alone. "Thank you. But listen, Amelia, if it's too painful to remember, don't push it. Take care of yourself first. We'll find Seven, even if you can't help."

Amelia gave her a hug, then Brenda left, her heart aching.

They had to find Seven before she killed again.

Nick phoned Jake and another crime unit, and he and Jake decided to include his coworker, Special Agent Rafe Hood, in the investigation of the murder on the ridge. The Bureau had assigned him to investigate the Commander, saying he and Jake were too close. The fact that the gunshot wound resembled a professional hit meant they could be dealing with a different killer.

But Nick had a bad feeling it was all tied back to his father's fucking experiment.

He just didn't know how this man's murder fit in. Had he worked for the Commander? Was he another hired gun, like the man he'd sent after Sadie in San Francisco?

Or a subject they wanted to snuff out before he talked?

Brenda rubbed her bleary eyes as she drove around the mountain toward her condo. Shadows jumped at every corner, the wind hurling leaves and debris across the road. Thunder rumbled, and a branch snapped off a tree to her right and tumbled across the road.

Suddenly a car raced up behind her, its headlights blinding her. She glanced in her rearview mirror, blinking and willing it to back off. But the car sped up, its motor roaring until it closed in, riding her bumper.

Brenda tapped her brakes, hoping to warn the tailgater, but instead of slowing, the driver gunned the engine and slammed into her rear. Clenching the steering wheel in a white-knuckled grip, she struggled to maintain control. But the car rammed into her again, and her car skidded and spun out of control.

Fear mingled with anger as she fought to stay on the road, but the curve loomed ahead, the mountainside rushing toward her as she slammed into its rocky face.

Her head snapped forward as the air bag exploded, the sound of the car racing away echoing in her ears as a black sea of nothingness swallowed her.

Chapter 15

Nick searched James's house while the ME examined his body and the forensic team dusted for prints and combed the log cabin. He opened the closet and noted the dead man's clothing: seven white shirts, seven pairs of dark gray slacks—one for each day of the week—on hangers spaced at half-inch intervals.

The man's two pairs of dress shoes were stowed in a line on the floor beside a pair of military boots, the distances between them neatly measured. His bedroom was orderly, the bed made military style. James might have left military service, but his training had stayed with him, making him almost obsessive-compulsive in his home.

Nick glanced around for a computer or cell phone, but didn't find one. In the prior cases related to the Slaughter Creek experiments, the victims had been either subjects or medical personnel.

Was this man's death related to the Commander, or to Seven and the stranglings?

But how?

Both James and Logger had worked for the same security company. Logger had been murdered by Seven. So had victim number two.

James had been shot in the head.

Nick checked behind the victim's ear, but there was no number carved there.

He searched the desk drawer, but it held only paper clips, pens, and rubber bands in neat compartments. He found a shoebox in the closet and looked inside. A 9 mm Luger. Hollow bullets. An extra magazine.

For personal protection? Or had he been a hired gun like the man who'd been sent to kill Sadie?

Nick examined the weapon. It hadn't been fired recently. Still, he gave it to the crime tech to log into evidence.

Frustrated, he went back to the kitchen and rummaged through the kitchen drawers. Barring the usual silverware, most of the drawers were empty. A mail holder on the corner of the counter held recent bills that were organized by due dates.

In the last drawer, he found a business card listing the number of a rehab facility.

If James had been injured or suffered psychological effects from his stint in the service, maybe he'd received physical therapy and counseling. Nick turned the card over and read the name. Angel Mount Rehab.

His phone jangled, and he snatched it up. "Special Agent Blackwood."

"Nick, it's Jake."

"Did you find anything?"

"I'm on my way to check out a building in the northern part of the mountains," Jake said. "There was a fire this past week that sounds suspicious."

Nick frowned. He didn't see a connection, but sometimes seemingly unrelated events were related. "Okay. I found Darren James. He's dead, shot in the head at point-blank range."

Jake cursed. "Doesn't sound like our unsub."

"No, but the MO is similar to Emanuel Giogardi's death."

"True. Did you find anything proving a connection?"

"No, but I'm with the crime team and ME now."

"Good. Listen, Nick—" Jake hesitated. "There's something else. A nine-one-one call just came in. Someone reported an accident on the mountain not too far from Amelia's." Jake's breath rattled out. "The car belonged to Brenda. An ambulance is on its way."

Nick had to clear his throat to talk. "Is...she all right?"

"I don't know any details, my deputy took the call."

Fear knifed through Nick. What if Brenda was seriously hurt? "With Brenda's face plastered all over the news working this case and her confrontation with the Commander, he could have ordered a hit on her like he did with Sadie."

"You could be right," Jake agreed. "Which means we're on the right track."

"I'll go talk to her," Nick said. And if he found out the Commander had put a hit on her, he'd finish choking him himself.

Brenda couldn't breathe. Something was smothering her. She opened her eyes, dazed, confused, a hammer pounding her head. Where was she?

Bright blue and yellow lights danced across the dash of her car, blinding her and intensifying the pain splitting her temple. Her chest ached as if a fist had slammed into it, and her leg and shoulder throbbed.

Her mouth felt dry, but when she swallowed, she tasted blood.

Noises from outside the car echoed around her, and someone yanked open the car door.

"Miss, are you all right?" a voice shouted.

The voice boomeranged in her ears, once, twice, three times, but it sounded muffled and far away.

Suddenly she felt the air bag being ripped away, and gentle hands touching her face. "Stay still, ma'am. I'm a paramedic. A deputy sheriff is here, too."

Brenda frowned. A deputy? Paramedic?

"What happened?" she whispered.

"You had a car accident. We're going to take you to the hospital." He tilted her head back to examine her eyes. "Are you hurt anywhere?"

"I don't know," she said. "My head hurts, and my chest, but I think I'm just bruised."

She tried to wiggle her toes and feet, but she couldn't move them. Her limbs felt heavy, weighted. "Oh, God. I...can't move my legs."

"Just stay still and try to remain calm," the medic said as he yelled for a board. "The dash is crushed in, so your legs are trapped right now."

The world swayed, lights spinning in a sick, drunken rush. The sound of men shouting at one another echoed again, then the seat shifted slightly, and she felt the medic sliding something around her neck.

She must have passed out for a minute, because the next thing she knew, she was lying on a stretcher, and they were loading her in the back of an ambulance.

"You have a nasty bump on your forehead," one of the medics said. "And the air bag probably did a number on your ribs."

Fear seized her, but this time when she tried to move her toes, they tingled and she could move them.

"My car," Brenda whispered. "What about my car?"

"The deputy will see that it's towed," the medic said.

"I'm right here, Brenda," Deputy Waterstone said in a gruff voice. "What happened?"

Brenda forced her eyes open, although the throbbing in her head intensified as the bright lights assaulted her. "I..." What had happened? She'd just come from Amelia's, was on her way home, then...another car ran up on her. "Someone hit me from behind," she murmured.

"Hit you?" Deputy Waterstone said. "You're sure?"

Brenda tried to nod, but the movement only made her head swim faster. "Yes," she whispered as she swallowed back nausea.

"Did they stop?" he asked.

"I don't know...I must have lost consciousness."

"So you didn't see who it was or what kind of car they were driving?"

"No...wait..." She clutched the blanket the medics had put over her. "It was a sedan. But I couldn't see the color."

One of the medics attached an IV, then closed the back door, and the ambulance jerked, tires grinding over gravel as they sped onto the highway.

She closed her eyes as the world rocked back and forth, the memory of the car ramming into her growing more vivid.

Dear God. Someone had tried to kill her.

———————— , ————————

By the time Nick reached the site of the accident, the ambulance had left. Deputy Waterstone was waiting on a tow truck and directing traffic with his flashlight.

"How's Brenda?" Nick asked.

"She was awake, had a concussion—the medics rushed her to the hospital."

Nick's stomach churned at the sight of the car. It had slammed headfirst into the mountain ridge and was twisted like a pretzel. He walked around the side of the vehicle and noted the way the axle was bent. The passenger side had borne most of the brunt, although glass covered the seats and blood dotted the dash.

A truck roared past, slowing as the driver noticed the police car and accident, but Nick motioned for him to keep going.

The deputy shined his flashlight along the rear bumper. "What are you looking for?" Nick asked.

"Brenda said someone hit her from behind."

Nick's blood ran cold. "Where's the other driver?"

"He didn't stop."

Damn. "Who called it in?"

"A nine-one-one operator said a trucker—he didn't think anyone was in the car, but thought we should check it out."

Nick knelt to examine the rear as well. "Did Brenda see the vehicle or the driver?"

"She said it was a sedan, but she didn't get the color or the driver," Deputy Waterstone said.

Nick grimaced as he spotted black paint on the rear bumper of the BMW. "Take a sample of that paint and send it to the lab. If this wasn't an accident, we need to track down that driver."

Waterstone scraped the paint off into a small envelope. "Brenda covered that story on the Slaughter Creek sanitarium. Maybe someone doesn't want her snooping around."

"You could be right. The Commander or whoever else spear-headed the project may still be trying to cover his ass." Nick gritted his teeth. "I'm going to the hospital to check on Brenda."

Deputy Waterstone jammed his hands in his pockets. "I'll wait on the tow truck."

Nick jumped in his car and raced toward the hospital.

At that late hour, there was hardly any traffic, but the minutes dragged by, and it seemed to take him forever to reach the building. He parked in the lot as close as he could get, then jogged to the entrance to the emergency room. The waiting room was packed with welfare patients forced to use the emergency room as their doctor's office. One family with a herd of kids were chowing down on food from McDonald's while they waited. A man in tattered clothes who smelled like stale alcohol and sweat lay groaning, probably in search of pain meds.

Nick crossed the room to the admittance desk. "Excuse me—"

"Sign in and take a seat," a strawberry-blond girl said between smacks of her bubble gum.

"I'm not a patient." Nick flashed his badge. Just as he'd hoped, the young girl snapped to attention.

"Oh, sorry, sir. What can I do for you?"

"I'm looking for a patient brought in from an accident. Her name is Brenda Banks."

"Oh, you mean that reporter." The girl stood and leaned closer. "She usually looks so pretty, but she got banged up real bad. I asked her if she wanted me to call her parents, but she said no."

Nick barely heard the last part. He was too busy imagining Brenda's face black and blue. "Can I see her?"

"I don't think she's in a room yet. They took her for X-rays and a CAT scan."

Those were just routine procedures, he reminded himself. It didn't mean her injuries were life-threatening.

"I'll let you know when they move her to a room." She gestured to the left. "There's snack and coffee machines down the hall."

"Thanks. Can I leave you my number in case you need to reach me?"

Her eyes flared with curiosity. "Sure. Most times we just call out names."

"I'd feel better if you had my cell number," he said, then slipped her his business card. "It's urgent I talk to her as soon as she's taken to a room."

She tapped the card between her bloodred fingernails, and he strode down the hall.

It was possible that some drunk driver or teenagers joyriding had hit Brenda, and that they hadn't meant to.

But if the hit had been intentional, then someone had tried to kill her.

Which meant Brenda needed a damn bodyguard. Or leave the town and go someplace safe until the case was solved.

Brenda felt as if she'd been run over by a truck. She clenched her jaw as the doctors and nurses forced her through X-rays and then a CAT scan. She hated hospitals. Hated the smells. Especially the cleaning chemicals and soap...

"I just want to go to sleep," she said as a nurse pushed her in a wheelchair to a room.

"You can soon," the nurse said. "But you have a slight concussion, so we'll be checking on you through the night."

Brenda didn't bother to argue. She'd had her tonsils removed when she was younger. Every time she'd fallen asleep, someone had come in to poke and prod her.

It reminded her of her visit to the sanitarium.

She'd have to go home to get some real rest.

The nurse rolled her into the room, then helped her into bed. They'd already confiscated her clothes and given her an ugly hospital gown.

She pulled the sheet up over her and closed her eyes, grateful to finally be left alone.

Maybe soon the room would stop spinning.

Finally she drifted into a fitful sleep. In her dreams, she was driving on the mountain, on one of the curves. A car raced up and rammed into her, sending her into the ridge.

She startled awake. It hadn't been a dream. She was sore and achy and felt like a punching bag.

Suddenly she sensed someone else in the room. Looking up, she saw Nick standing at the window. She blinked to clear her vision, then called his name.

He walked over to the bed, his jaw set in stone, his eyes feral. Brooding.

"How do you feel?" he asked.

Her head and body throbbed. "I'll live."

Her attempt at humor failed miserably. "What happened?"

The memory haunted her. "I went to see Amelia again."

Disapproval flickered across his chiseled face.

"I thought she might be able to draw a picture of Seven."

The disapproval disappeared, and something akin to admiration flashed on his face. "Did she?"

"She's going to try," Brenda said. God, her mouth was dry. She tried to reach the water on the tray table, but winced in pain.

Nick picked up the cup and handed it to her. She took a blessed sip, her parched throat desperate for more. But her hand trembled, sloshing water on her chest.

Nick grabbed a napkin and gently blotted up the water, then held the cup for her. He smoothed down her hair as she laid her head back on the pillow.

"Then what happened?" Nick asked.

Brenda massaged her temple. "A car came up behind me, tires squealed, then the car slammed into me."

"The driver intentionally hit you?"

Unwanted tears blurred her eyes, and she tried to blink them away. What kind of reporter cries? "At first, I thought he was just going too fast. But then he sped up and rammed me again."

A savage look darkened his eyes. "Did you see what kind of car it was?"

Brenda shook her head. "No…It was dark, and it all happened too fast."

Nick rubbed at his chin. "Do you have any enemies?"

She licked her lips, her eyes closing. "No—at least, not that I know of."

Suddenly the door to the hospital room opened, and her parents stormed in. "My God, baby, what happened?" her father asked.

"Brenda, are you all right, sugar?" her mother cried.

Nick tensed and stepped away from Brenda.

"What's going on?" her father said.

Her mother pushed past him and rushed to her bed, her makeup smeared with tears. "Oh, no, look at the bruises on your face, darling."

"I asked, what happened?" her father barked.

"Dad, Mom, calm down," Brenda pleaded as her mother pulled her into a hug that only made her sore ribs feel more brittle.

"Brenda was in an accident," Nick said.

Her father gave Nick a pointed look. "If it was an accident, why are you here?"

The brooding darkness returned to Nick's eyes as he introduced himself. "I'm Special Agent Nick Blackwood." He extended his hand, but her father stared at it without offering his own. "I came to ask Brenda about the accident."

"It's your fault that Brenda's here, that she's hurt," her father said sharply. "You and your brother and father—you've shamed this town."

"My father did, yes," Nick said. "But my brother and I are trying to help."

"Daddy," Brenda said, "please calm down. Nick is investigating—"

"You're in here because you're digging into things you shouldn't be," her father roared. "I told you to stay out of it, Brenda!"

He turned to Nick. "My daughter doesn't belong in your ugly world." Then he took Brenda's hand. "Now when you recover, sweetheart, you're coming home so your mother and I can take care of you."

Panic clawed at Brenda. The last place she wanted to be was at her parents' house, being smothered and criticized by them at the same time.

Nick's phone rang, and he checked the number. "Excuse me, I need to take this."

He stepped outside to answer it, then ducked his head in a minute later. "I have to go."

"Nick, wait," Brenda said.

Nick's cool gaze slid over her parents. "I'm meeting Jake. Your parents are right. When you're released, go home with them so you'll be safe."

Brenda started to argue, but Nick disappeared again. Damn him. He was not going to cut her out of this case.

In fact, if whoever had hit her was trying to scare her off the story, they didn't know her at all.

The attack had only fueled her temper.

Nothing would stop her from finding the truth now.

———————— · ————————

Nick hated to leave Brenda, but at least she was safe in the hospital. And her parents would watch her.

Adopted or not, they loved her.

Good God. He was starting to care for her, too. Starting to care too damn much.

Fuck. The first rule of police work was not to get personally involved with a suspect or witness. Caring about someone meant putting them in danger, making them vulnerable to criminals.

Maybe the mayor could convince Brenda to lay low for a while. Maybe he'd lock her in his house, and Nick wouldn't have to worry about her anymore.

He rushed out of the hospital and jumped into his car.

"I'm at that property in the north," Jake said. "A fire destroyed a lot of the main house, but it looks suspicious."

"How?"

"There's a dead body inside. A woman." Jake paused. "And this was no accident. Someone tied her inside and left her to die."

Chapter 16

———— o ————

Nick parked by Jake's car and climbed out, the scent of smoke striking him. His brother was right. This place was in the middle of nowhere, completely off the grid.

A perfect place to hide, or to hold someone hostage.

Although most of the house had burned down, the frame of the long L-shaped building remained. Two smaller buildings sat to the side, while barbed wire fencing encircled the property, making it feel like a prison yard.

Jake met him at the edge of the ashes. "It looks like there was a main room, a kitchen, and four bedrooms in the back. I'll have the arson investigator verify that this was no accident, but I smelled gasoline."

Nick grimaced at the sight of the charred body. "Jesus, she was handcuffed to that pipe and left to die."

Nick narrowed his eyes, then knelt to study the body. "It appears she was struck on the back of her head with something sharp."

"Maybe she was dead before she burned up."

"So who was here and why kill her?" Nick asked.

Jake shone a flashlight along the footprint of the structure. Here and there a smattering of bricks remained. The metal edge of an old bed. A bookshelf. "Hopefully the fire investigators will be able to find something in the ashes."

"The area to the left looks like it might have been a dorm of some kind," Nick said, noting the way the rooms appeared to be lined up. The metal desks looked the same, each with a bookcase beside it, a single metal bed against the wall. He examined the ashes by the bookshelf. "These might have been textbooks."

"There's not a college or school anywhere near here," Jake said with a frown.

"It could have been some kind of home for troubled kids where they conducted their own classes."

Jake frowned as he pointed to metal restraints by one bed. "Not a school—a prison."

Nick's insides chilled. A deserted compound in the mountains, rooms with handcuffs and restraints, two outbuildings. "Do you know of any homes for troubled kids in the area?"

"There's a ranch, but it's farther north. I never heard of any school or home out here."

Nick gestured to one of the chains. "That looks like blood."

Jake arched a brow. "You think this place might be related to the Slaughter Creek project?"

"It's hard to say. Could be some other maniac who abused his wife and children. Or a kidnapping case involving a psycho." Nick pulled at his chin.

"I'll check police reports for missing women or children when I get back."

Nick found a business card that had partially burned in the fire, but he could make out enough of the letters to know it was for Stark Security. "Someone from that security company was here."

"Maybe Logger discovered that a predator was holding a woman or child hostage," Jake suggested.

"That's possible. It would explain why Logger was upset about the job." Noticing something shiny, Nick stooped down, raking ashes from the corner by the bed. A ring, a plain silver band covered in soot, lay in the pile. Sliding on gloves, he picked it up and examined it.

It looked as if there might be some kind of etching inside, but he couldn't tell what it was.

"You called a crime team?"

'They're on their way."

"Have them see if they can lift a print off this ring." Beside the charred beds, smoky ashes and debris littered the floor.

"It's worse in the other building." Jake gestured toward the outbuildings and led the way, the stench of smoke and blood swirling in the air as they entered.

Nick grimaced and aimed his flashlight toward the side. "There are restraints attached to the walls in those stalls."

"Jesus Christ," Jake muttered. "Someone was obviously held captive here."

They walked to the next building, a sense of dread congealing in Nick's stomach. A second later, his fears were confirmed when he saw two rooms that resembled labs. "This looks like some kind of torture chamber. There are medical instruments, a stainless steel table, and a medicine cabinet, although it's been cleaned out."

"No computer," Jake commented.

"This place was definitely hidden from the road." The mountains surrounded them, the compound set in a pocket that shielded it from view. It was so damn dark, he could barely see his feet.

Nick shone his flashlight across the door to another room, then stepped inside. Bile rose in his throat. Two wooden boxes that resembled coffins sat against opposite walls.

Jake threw up a hand. "I don't want to even look inside."

Neither did Nick, but he forced himself to open the lid, and shone his light on the inside of the box. Blood and hair and something he guessed might have been skin cells were evident in the box, and there were scratches on the sides and top. "Someone was locked in these boxes."

Jake knelt and pointed to a wooden slat on the floor, and Nick stooped down and pried at the boards.

"It's a fucking hole," he muttered.

"There are fingernail marks on the inside as well," Jake said, horrified.

Rage at the demented person who'd used this place boiled inside Nick. Was this torture chamber related to the Slaughter Creek project? To his father?

To Seven?

Was this the place where she'd been kept after she was moved from Slaughter Creek?

Or was there another psychopath on the loose?

Brenda swallowed her pain medication and silently willed her parents to leave, but they'd been hovering over her like mother hens. It was driving her crazy.

"Exactly what happened again?" her father said.

Brenda pulled the blanket up over her. "I told you, a deer ran in front of me, and I swerved to miss it. I lost control and ran off the road."

"That must have been so frightening," her mother said.

More frightening that someone had intentionally tried to kill her. But she didn't intend to share that with her parents. They'd chain her to a bodyguard for the rest of her life.

Her mother fiddled with her earring. "What can we do for you, sugar?"

"Go home, get some rest, and stop worrying," Brenda said. "I'm fine. The doctor just wanted to keep me here tonight for observation."

Her father rubbed his hand over his bald spot as he paced by her bed. "I thought when you first worked for the paper that you'd get all this nonsense about investigating out of your head. This line of work is no place for you, Brenda."

"Your dad is right," her mother said. "The pieces you wrote about the garden club and that nice story on Janie Tudor's debutante ball—those were perfect for you." She patted the sheet covering Brenda. "Why don't you go back to writing those interesting pieces, honey?"

Because she had a brain. "Investigative reporting is a step up for me," Brenda said, biting back a retort. "A chance to show the network what I'm worth."

"What you're worth," her father said sarcastically. "I'll tell you what you're worth. More than that federal agent whose father just about destroyed our community. His sons need to pack up and leave town, so everybody can heal."

The throbbing in Brenda's head grew more incessant. "Daddy, Nick and Jake Blackwood are honorable men. They're trying to correct their father's wrongs and locate the victims so they can help them."

"I don't give a rat's ass what they're doing," her father said. "I want you away from them so you'll be safe."

"He's right," her mother murmured. "When the doctor releases you in the morning, you'll come home where you belong. Then we can take care of you."

Good heavens, she wasn't a five-year-old with a cold.

Brenda gripped the rails of the bed, her cheeks aching from biting her tongue. "I know you mean well, both of you, but in the morning, I'm going to my condo. Please, you two, go home. I need some sleep."

She faked a yawn and closed her eyes in an effort to shut them out. Thankfully her mother got the hint and bent over to plant a kiss on her forehead. "All right, sugar. But we really want you to come home with us."

"Mom," Brenda said with an edge to her voice. "Please, let it go."

"Brenda—"

"Dad, I mean it." Brenda twisted the sheets between her fingers. "I can take care of myself."

He continued to rub his head in a nervous gesture, his eyes unusually concerned, his jaw strained. He had always looked so calm when she was young.

Now, he looked old and...worried, as if something deeper was troubling him. The town expressed its shock over the Slaughter Creek project, and he was probably exhausted from the gossip and anxiety in the community.

Then again, maybe there was something he wasn't telling her.

"Dad," she said as she looked into his eyes. "What's wrong? Do you know something about Arthur Blackwood or the research project that you haven't shared?"

"Of course not." A spark of anger dashed across his face, then he blew out a breath and took her mother's elbow. "Let's go, Agnes. Brenda needs her rest."

Brenda reached for his arm. "Dad?"

He leaned over and kissed her on the cheek. "Be careful, sweetheart. You're playing a dangerous game, working with Arthur Blackwood's son."

Before she could reply, he ushered her mother into the hallway.

Brenda studied the closed door. Had she misread her father, or had his warning sounded almost like a...threat?

No, that was crazy...

Her father wouldn't threaten her. He loved her. He was simply worried about her and wanted her off the investigation.

Because almost everyone who'd known about the research project had been murdered.

And now Seven, a serial killer, was making contact with her as if they were friends.

Nick wanted to go back to the hospital and see Brenda, but that might give her the wrong idea, that he cared more than he should.

Dammit, he did care more than he should, but he refused to let her know that.

"Call me if they turn up anything," Nick said. "I'm going to visit that rehab facility and see what I can find out."

Jake glanced at his watch. "Tonight?"

Nick swatted at a fly. "You're right. I'll go first thing in the morning. Surely by then, our ME will have an ID on Seven's second victim."

"And on this poor woman," Jake said as the CSI team photographed the charred body.

Nick wasn't quite as sympathetic. "I hate to say it, but if she had something to do with whoever was shackled and kept here, she probably got what she deserved."

The scent of smoke, ash, and burned flesh floated to him in the wind. "Look, Jake, I'll wait here. You have a wife and daughter. Go home to them."

Jake's gaze met his. "Times like these, I'm glad I have a family."

Nick was more the glass-half-empty type. "And I'm glad I don't. No one to answer to if I don't come home." And no one to worry about getting hurt or losing.

Brenda's face flashed in his mind, and relief that she was okay surged through him.

Fuck. He had to keep his distance from her. She was getting under his skin in a way that he'd never allowed anyone to.

"Thanks, I think I'll take you up on that." Jake shook his hand, then strode back to his squad car.

Nick walked past the debris from the fire to the wooden structure housing the stalls, frowning as one of the techs lifted prints from the chains. A female tech sprayed luminol on the chains, and traces of blood glittered in the darkness.

"Mercy," she muttered beneath her breath. "Whoever was chained obviously cut themselves trying to escape." She used a pair of tweezers to pluck at something caught in the metal. She scraped a sample and held it up to the light. "These look like epithelial cells."

"Let me know when you get DNA," Nick said.

She nodded, then wiped at her brow with the back of her hand. "There's more blood on the wall of the stall. A significant enough amount to indicate that someone was seriously hurt."

Nick examined the section she was referring to. She'd already sprayed the luminol, and she was right—blood spatter covered half the wall.

Nick moved to the next stall, disgusted at the sight of blood on that stall as well.

Who the hell had been kept here? And where were they now?

Various scenarios pelted him, all disturbing.

The perp could have set the fire, then moved the hostages to another facility. If so, why leave the woman to be burned? To keep them from identifying her?

Was she a victim or the psychopath who'd held others captive?

Another possibility—the victim or victims had escaped, chained the woman to the pipe, then set the fire and run because she was the monster who'd tortured them.

Or the psychopath had murdered the victims and buried them somewhere nearby, then killed the woman and left her in the fire to take the fall.

Grimacing, he gripped his flashlight and went to search the property for signs of a grave.

Seven scrubbed her arms and hands with the sterile soap to wash away the blood. She'd read somewhere that cutters felt relief when they watched the blood flow from their wrists.

But nothing gave her relief.

Except watching the men die.

She searched the news for Brenda's reporting on the story and finally found a short clip.

Damn her to hell. She spent only a few minutes at Blindman's Curve, and didn't even describe how they'd found the man.

A fiery rage grew inside her.

Why wasn't Brenda showing photographs of the bodies? She hadn't mentioned that Jim Logger had been tied up and repeatedly strangled, either.

Or that her latest conquest had been dumped in the woods like a piece of trash.

Fucking assholes. They deserved everything they'd endured and worse. Did the police think withholding details from the public would enable them to find her quicker?

A bitter laugh escaped her. She wasn't an idiot.

No, the Commander had trained her well.

Did they allow him to read the paper in prison? Had he watched the news report and recognized her skills?

She placed the skin she'd taken in her treasure trove and slipped it inside the wall of the cabin, where she'd carved a nook to hide it.

The cops were probably anxious for a suspect.

She'd give them one soon.

But first...first she had to hunt again. She licked her lips, tasting the sweet scent of the man's fear as he took his last breath.

Yes, it was time for another man to die.

Chapter 17

—— o ——

The next morning Nick grabbed a cup of coffee at the drive-in doughnut shop on his way to Angel Mount Rehab.

He hadn't slept for thinking about Brenda and her so-called accident.

Irritable from lack of sleep, he punched the hospital number to check on her as he wound around the hills. Angel Mount sat on the other side of the mountain. The town had been named after a folk legend about an angel who could be seen in the fog over the ridges on a cold winter's day. Legend claimed that years ago her car had flown over the edge of the overlook, and that you could still hear her screams from the ridge at midnight.

Others said that she rose in the midst at dawn, whispering a song about the life ever after—that any time someone died in the valley, you could see her angel wings as she helped guide deserving souls to heaven.

The phone buzzed a dozen times before someone finally answered. At least it wasn't one of those aggravating automated machines that sent you through a thousand disconnected choices.

"I need Brenda Banks's room, please."

"Certainly—one moment." The sound of the phone ringing echoed over the line. Once, twice, three times.

Finally Brenda picked up. "Hello."

"How do you feel this morning?"

"Like I need to go home so I can sleep. You know they wake you up every hour to check on you. It's ridiculous."

"Glad you're in a good mood," Nick said wryly.

"What are you doing?"

Nick maneuvered a turn, forced to slow when a truck pulled out in front of him. "I'm on my way to the Angel Mount rehab facility."

"Why are you going there?"

"A man named Darren James worked for the same security company as Logger. I found a card with the address on it in his things."

"What did he tell you about Logger?"

Nick debated whether to tell her, but so far she'd kept her word not to disclose information without his permission. "Nothing. Darren James is dead."

He could hear the sheets rustling in the background. "What?"

"I found his body at his place. Shot in the temple at close range."

"I don't understand," Brenda said. "If it was Seven, why would she shoot him, when she strangled her other victims?"

"She didn't kill him," Nick said. "It looks like a professional hit."

"You think this murder has to do with your father and the project?"

"We'll definitely investigate that possibility."

Nick slowed into the curve, relieved when the truck in front of him turned down a dirt road. "But there's something else Jake found."

"What?"

"He was looking for abandoned cabins and areas where Seven might be hiding out, and found this place that had recently burned down. There were three buildings. The first was a dorm. There were chains next to the metal beds, and a dead woman in the ashes, handcuffed to a metal pipe."

"Oh, my God. Someone murdered her?"

Nick heard movement and decided she must be out of bed, pacing the room.

"It looks that way," Nick said. "But it gets worse."

"Worse than leaving someone in a fire to die?"

"Yes. One of the buildings held metal tables and medical equipment, scalpels and shit. There were also stalls with chains covered in blood, and there was blood on the walls. Another room had an underground pit. One where someone had been forced to stay." He paused for a breath. "I also found a card from Stark Security."

"The one where Logger worked?"

"Exactly."

Seconds passed. "Do you think your father performed experiments at that place, too?"

"It's one theory. If things had heated up at the sanitarium, he could have relocated there to avoid detection."

A heartbeat of silence stretched between them. "Nick..."

"I stayed there half the night with a crime team," Nick said. "They collected a shitload of forensics to analyze, and we have the female victim to identify."

"I'm getting dressed. Pick me up and—"

"No, Brenda, you need to stay in bed."

"I'm fine," Brenda argued. "I want to help."

"No, you're not fine. Now cut yourself some slack and trust me to do my job."

"I do trust you," Brenda said softly.

That trust did something to him, stirred emotions he didn't want to have.

He disconnected the call just as he reached the ridge where Angel Mount was located.

A silver angel was perched on the front of the stone building, a fitting mascot, given the facility's name. Nick parked next to a blue pickup, noticing a few other cars in the lot, along with an ambulance and a row of what appeared to be handicapped vans.

To the left, walking trails wove through a garden area, park benches set along them for resting or relaxing. Three other buildings were connected to the main one through covered breezeways. Wind swirled dried leaves around Nick's feet as he made his way to the front door.

When he entered, a perky blonde sat at a receptionist desk facing him. He glanced past her to what was obviously a therapy area housed with workout machines, bars, and exercise balls. Smaller rooms for individual therapy flanked this space, equipped with tables and relaxation tapes. The whir of machines, voices, and the grunts of a young guy gripping bars as he struggled to walk mingled with chatter from two men in wheelchairs in the far corner.

"Hi, I'm Teresa. Can I help you?" the receptionist asked.

Nick offered her a smile, then introduced himself and flashed his credentials. "I understand that a man named Darren James came here for therapy."

"Hmm, I don't know. I've only been here a couple of weeks, but let me ask Jose. He runs the center."

She bounced up from the seat and dashed over to speak with the men in wheelchairs. Nick was surprised when the Hispanic man rolled over to him. "I'm Jose. You're asking about a patient?"

"Yes, sir," Nick said. "A man named Darren James. What can you tell me about him?"

Jose rubbed a hand over the back of his neck. "I'm afraid I can't discuss my patients with you. Why are you asking about him?"

"Because he's dead," Nick said bluntly.

Jose's eyes widened. "What happened?"

"He was murdered. So anything you can tell me about him might help us find his killer."

Jose massaged his thigh. "What do you need to know?"

"What brought him here to the rehab facility?"

"He had a head injury when he first returned from Afghanistan, and a shattered ankle. But he also had emotional issues."

Sounded like Logger.

"Did he come for treatment voluntarily?"

"The physical therapy, yes. The counseling he balked at." Jose's face grew pinched. "Finally I convinced him to join one of the support groups for vets. I thought he was doing better, having fewer panic attacks. Dealing with his anger issues. He seemed excited about returning to work."

"Where did he work?" Nick asked.

"Some kind of security company. He said he couldn't talk about it, that he had to sign a confidentiality clause."

Nick arched a brow. "Did he have any family?"

"No, that was the shame of it. His mother died of cancer while he was deployed. He didn't even get to attend the funeral."

That would do hell to a man.

Nick removed a photograph of Jim Logger from his pocket and showed it to Jose. "Do you recognize this man?"

"Yeah, that's Jim. I believe Darren told him about the job. Got Jim pumped up, thinking about his future."

So the two men were connected through both the rehab facility and the security company.

Jose's brows furrowed. "Don't tell me Jim's dead, too?"

"I'm afraid so," Nick said quietly.

Jose mumbled a shocked word. "Did the same person kill them?"

"That's what I'm trying to figure out." Nick removed his phone from the clip at his belt, retrieved the photo of the dead man in the woods, and showed it to Jose.

"How about this man? Was he a patient here as well?"

The picture was grainy and dark, the man's face a muddy gray, his features distorted. Jose took a few minutes to study it.

"I don't recognize him."

Hell, he'd hoped to find a common thread between the three men. Then again, there might be one.

The security company.

Both Logger and James had worked for it.

And the company might have serviced that compound where the woman had been burned.

———— , ————

Brenda wanted to be working. But the doctor insisted she rest, and her parents had practically forced her to go back to their house for the night.

No amount of arguing had convinced them that she would be safe, left alone with a concussion.

"You can stay in your old room. It'll be just like it was when you were little," her mother said as she plumped the pillows on the white iron bed where Brenda had spent her youth.

Brenda crawled in bed and played nice, but she felt like a prisoner. "Thanks, Mother. I am tired—I think I'll take a nap."

"Of course." Agnes's diamond earrings twinkled in the sunlight streaming through the sheers. "Call me if you need anything."

In a rare emotional moment, her mother paused and brushed back her hair, tears in her eyes. "I know you're independent, honey, and you don't want me hovering, but I couldn't stand to lose you." She sniffed. "I may not be the best mother, but I've tried."

Brenda's throat swelled as déjà vu struck her. It felt as if she and her mother had done this before, as if her mother had cried over her bed when she was younger.

But she couldn't place the memory.

And she'd never been seriously ill before. No car accidents.

In fact, she'd had a charmed life. Lonely sometimes, but safe.

She knew she shouldn't complain, that the Bankses had given her everything she could have ever asked for. Compared to Amelia's life, and Grace Granger's, hers had been a fairy tale.

But she still wanted the truth. And that was something Agnes and William refused to give her.

"I'm lucky to have had you," Brenda finally said.

Her mother hugged her, then wiped her eyes as she left the room.

Too antsy to lie in bed, Brenda walked over to study the photographs on her wall, high school pictures of cheerleading, prom, and graduation. The pictures told the story of a happy, well-adjusted girl.

But something had always been missing, a part of her that was lost.

She slipped into her old desk chair and rummaged through the drawers. Movie ticket stubs from when she'd dated Jake, a concert ticket a stoner named Lonnie had taken her to in her rebellious stage, her old high school ring.

She dug in the bottom drawer, smiling when she discovered the book she'd started writing when she was twelve.

She flipped it open, laughing at the crude drawings, but her laughter died as she skimmed the pages. Her story evolved around the kids at school.

Amelia. She'd described how crazy Amelia was, that Amelia had an imaginary friend named Bessie. Little had they known then that Bessie was an alter personality triggered by Arthur Blackwood's mind-control techniques.

Another page showed a crude sketch of Grace Granger, annotated with Brenda's observations of the troubled girl. Then there was one of Joe Swoony.

Regret filled her for the nasty way she'd depicted them, not knowing what she knew now—that they had all been victims of horrific abuse.

An idea began to percolate, and she grabbed a notepad and began to sketch out her thoughts. She would do individual pieces on the victims, as she'd planned.

And she would title the series *The Slaughter Creek Seven.*

Even if she couldn't investigate with Nick this afternoon, she could start on these profiles.

She picked up the phone to call Grace Granger's mother. She would start with Grace.

And she would finish with Seven.

Nick met Jake at the ME's office. Dr. Bullock introduced them to his assistant, a thirtysomething brunette named Dr. Carrie Culpepper.

"I like bugs, she likes bones," Bullock said with a cheeky grin.

Nick simply nodded in response while Jake chuckled.

"Since you two keep shoveling the bodies in here, I called in reinforcements," Bullock said. "Dr. Culpepper is going to perform the autopsy on the woman in your fire. I've been working on the man." He led them over to the table where their victim lay. Bullock had already washed off the dead bugs and made the Y incision.

"You've identified him?" Nick asked.

"Yes," Bullock said. "Since your first victim was in the military, I took a chance that this guy was too and searched those records. His name was Sergeant Luther Mason."

Bullock scowled. "Thirty-five years old. Also a man who worked out, although his liver indicates he was a heavy drinker."

"Tox screen?" Nick asked.

"Rohypnol in his system."

Jake cleared his throat. "Hmmm. That suggests our victim didn't go with the unsub willingly?"

"The drug definitely helped him along," Bullock said. "But there's no trace evidence of fluids from the female." He picked up the guy's wrist and pointed to the rope burns. "Just like Logger, he was bound, hands and feet."

He rolled the man sideways. "But unlike Logger, this guy sustained whip marks on his back."

"She's escalating," Nick said. "Becoming more violent."

"Either that, or this kill was more personal," Jake said. "Maybe this guy hurt her before."

Bullock nodded. "That fits with the degrading way she left his body in the woods."

"Sergeant Mason," Nick said, addressing the dead man, "did you work for the same security company as Logger and James?"

And if he had, what had those men done to Seven?

Seven arranged the dolls in the child-size chairs, around the table. They were beautiful dolls, each with her own hand-painted porcelain face. Each different, unique, just waiting for a little girl to love her.

Cora with the dark ringlet curls and baby-pink lips and dress made of blue satin. Amber with the golden-blond strands, sea-green eyes, and burgundy ball gown. Tamara with hair as red as leaves in the fall and an emerald necklace that showcased her white wedding gown.

Tears blurred Seven's eyes as she placed a china cup in front of each of them.

You're too old for dolls.

But now that she was free, she would have them.

Images of her childhood taunted her, and she squeezed the teacup so tightly that it shattered.

Seven watched the little girl on the street skipping rope and laughing. Her friend, a chubby girl with red hair and freckles, hugged her doll to her.

The happy little girls didn't belong in this neighborhood. Not where he lived.

Oh, he acted like he loved little children. But that was a trap.

Love wasn't supposed to hurt like that.

What if he hurt one of these little girls?

She shivered, her knees knocking together.

She was scared. Lonely. Still hurting from the latest beating by the Commander, this one because she'd failed another one of his tests.

They were standing at the edge of the schoolyard, where kids were playing tag, riding the teeter-totter, and swinging. She could see more kids inside, building with blocks and painting with their fingers and playing dress-up. One tiny blonde held a baby doll to her.

"I want a baby doll like that," Seven said.

The Commander gripped her hand. "Soldiers don't have dolls."

"But I don't wanna be a soldier." She stomped her foot. "I wants a doll."

He slapped her so hard she stumbled backward. Then he dragged her toward the hole.

"Sit in there, and then you'll forget about dolls."

"No!" Seven cried. "I don't like the dark!"

But he shoved her in that deep dark hole where all the bad kids went.

Then the metal lid clamped shut and the light went away, and she couldn't breathe or see or hear anything at all.

Chapter 18

———— ◦ ————

"Come on, baby girl, we have to get moving."

Brenda's chest hurt too bad to move. She didn't like the places Mama took her. The dark alleys where men smelled like smoke and that stinky brown stuff they had in their brown bags.

But Mama dragged her along behind her. "I'm sick," Mama said. "He's got stuff that'll make me feel better."

Mama smelled too. Like sweat and dirt and some kind of smoke that smelled funny and made her head hurt.

"Please, Mama," Brenda said. "I don't feel good." Her head hurted and she started coughing. Coughing so bad she spit up gunk in her throat. Her legs felt rubbery, too, and she was shaking. Cold one minute, burning up the next.

"We'll rest after I get my stuff," Mama said in a low voice, 'cause they were walking past one of the police that Mama said was a bad person.

The streetlights from the stores were shutting off now. The cars passing by as if they couldn't see them.

Mama made sure no one did. They hid behind the corners of the buildings else the po-po, that was what Mama called the police, else the po-po runned after them. They would take her away from Mama if they saw her, Mama said.

Mama tugged her hand, and Brenda stumbled. Only her feet didn't want to move, especially toward that street. Two big, mean-looking men were huddled around a garbage can they'd lit a fire in.

Her legs gave way, and she sank onto the dirty street by a Dumpster that stank like rotten food. The world looked fuzzy now, the lights spinning so fast the world looked blurry.

She started shaking harder, and the smell was so bad that her stomach started rolling. "Mama," she whispered.

"Get up, Brenda. The po-po gonna take you and put me in jail."

But Brenda was too tired to move, and her chest felt like it would explode.

"We'll find something to eat soon as I get my stuff."

The mention of food made Brenda's stomach hurt more. She started coughing again, coughing so bad that she throwed up.

"Good Lord," Mama said. "Just wait there. I'll be right back, then we'll find a place for you to lay down."

"Don't leave me, Mama," she whispered.

But the sound didn't come out and then her mama was gone, and she was heaving on the street, choking on her own spit and feeling like she was going to tumble right over into it.

She heard screaming from down in the dark alley, and some-thing that sounded like a balloon pop, then more running. She blinked back the tears running out of her eyes. Then she hunted for her mama in the dark, but she didn't see her anywhere.

More tears leaked down her face, then the world tilted again, and she fell backward against the Dumpster. She wanted to find her mommy, but her head hurted too much, and her eyes were stinging, and she was coughing again and shaking so hard that her head banged against the metal trash can.

She needed to find the sun. If she could find it, she'd be warm. She and Mama were always chasing it. Mama said it would lead them to something good.

But it was dark in the street, and there was no sun to be found, as if it had left her, just like her mama.

She crawled into the corner and curled up, wrapping her arms around her and rocking back and forth to stop the sickness, but it didn't work. Finally she closed her eyes and gave in to how tired she was.

And then there was nothing.

Brenda jerked awake, trembling and disoriented. She shivered as if she was still in the throes of that nightmare, a nightmare that felt as if it had really happened.

The painkillers the nurse had given her must have sparked the weird dreams.

Because it had to be a dream.

Although it felt so real…like she had been living that life with that other woman she called Mama.

A deep, gut-wrenching loneliness filled her, making her ache all over. As much as she told herself that she hadn't been that little girl, that she'd been raised in the lap of luxury by Agnes and William, she couldn't shake the feeling that maybe she had known that little girl and her mother.

A soft knock sounded on the door, and Agnes poked her head in. "You okay, honey? I thought I heard you crying."

Brenda shoved her hair from her face. "Just a strange dream."

"What happened?" Agnes asked.

Brenda sighed. "I dreamed I was with some homeless woman, a junkie. She was dragging me behind her while she went hunting dope."

Agnes' face grew pinched, a look she'd tried to eliminate from her facial expressions because she claimed it aged her. "Must be the medication they gave you in the hospital. It'll do strange things to your mind."

Brenda nodded and waited until her mother closed the door, then climbed from bed and headed into the bathroom to shower.

She couldn't afford to lie in bed all day while Nick investigated without her. A murderer was out there hunting her next victim, and she needed to stop her.

———————— . ————————

Nick called a meeting of the task force to review the details they had uncovered so far—Jake, Deputy Waterstone, Agent Hood, Dr. Bullock and his assistant Dr. Culpepper, along with Lieutenant Maddison, the lead officer in the crime lab.

Everyone filed into the back room at the sheriff's office, where Nick had requested a whiteboard.

"I thought it might be helpful if we review what we have so far and see if anyone has a theory or finds connections we've missed. Time is of the essence; our unsub is probably already looking for her next victim."

He wrote Seven's name on one side of the board, then used the other to tack up photos of the victims they'd discovered so far, along with a line to track the chronology.

"You think we're dealing with a serial killer?" Lieutenant Maddison asked.

Nick nodded. "Yes. We also believe she's escalating." He indicated Logger's photo. "First she killed Jim Logger. He was former military, divorced, had a temper, and worked for Stark Security before he lost that job. Then he moved on to work for Mountain Truckers."

"Is his place of employment important?" Dr. Bullock asked.

"We aren't certain, but two murder victims worked at the same security company, although they were killed using different MOs. We don't know yet if Sergeant Luther Mason worked there, but Darren James, the man we found shot on the ridge, and Jim Logger did."

"What about the female body the sheriff found in that fire?" Deputy Waterstone asked.

Nick glanced at Jake. "We think that her death may be connected to the Strangler case but are still trying to piece things together." Waterstone started to ask another question, but Nick gestured for him to let him finish. "The fire he's referring to," he explained to the others, "was at an abandoned compound in the mountains. Sheriff Blackwood was searching for deserted properties where our unsub might be hiding out when he discovered it. Evidence from that scene indicates that at least two people were held and tortured at the facility."

He pointed at the photographs of the compound. "This building that burned down had bedrooms and a common area. This woman"—he gestured toward the photograph of the dead woman who'd been chained to the pipe—"died in the fire." He tapped the next photos of the other two outbuildings. "These two buildings held medical equipment as well as a pit that had been dug in the ground, where we believe whoever held these victims punished the captives."

"What does this have to do with our serial killer?" Deputy Waterstone asked.

Nick rubbed his chin. "We'll hear from Lieutenant Maddison about the forensics, but our theory is that this place was an extension of Commander Blackwood's research project, possibly where he kept the two subjects we haven't located yet. One of those we believe to be Seven, the woman we suspect murdered Logger and Mason."

"Do you think she killed Darren James?" Lieutenant Maddison asked.

Nick shrugged. "No. The MO is different. We know that the Commander hired guns to kill all those who could expose him, and we believe this hit might be related."

"Which means that someone else is still trying to cover up the project and those involved," Jake said.

Concerned murmurs echoed through the room. "You still think that someone higher up than your father spearheaded the project," Deputy Waterstone commented.

Nick gestured toward Rafe, and Rafe nodded. "Yes. We're working on that angle now."

Nick pointed to photos of the corpses. "Please fill us in on the autopsies, Dr. Bullock."

The ME adjusted his glasses. "Sergeant Luther Mason died of asphyxiation due to repeated strangulations, just as the first victim, Jim Logger, did." He tacked photos of the bodies on the whiteboard. "If you look closely, you can see that the ligature marks are consistent with the same type of piano wire. The pressure and length of the wounds also indicate they were inflicted by the same person."

"We know that the unsub chose to leave the bodies in different locations, and that the second victim was left in the woods," Nick said. "He also sustained whip slashes on his back. The S & M might have been consensual, but the drugs in his system indicate he may have been coerced. The manner in which he was left suggests that the unsub is escalating, and that the crime was more personal. That she was angry, either at him or at the circumstances of her life and that she blames the victim."

"Which brings us to Darren James," Special Agent Hood said. "He was shot at point-blank range, execution style. Definitely not the same killer."

Lieutenant Maddison spoke up. "Actually, about the forensics we found at the compound. The blood spatters we collected in the stalls where victims were held belong to a male."

"No female samples?" Nick asked, surprised that Seven's blood hadn't been present. He wanted to know her real name.

Then again, Amelia claimed the Commander had assigned them numbers, not names. So how had Seven come to be involved in the project? Had her family sent her to the sanitarium for treatment, as Grace's, Joe's, and Amelia's families had?

Maddison shook his head. "We did collect strands of female hair from the pit, but so far we haven't matched the DNA to anyone in the system."

Nick tensed. Had Seven been forced down in that hole? And for how long?

"We've linked Logger and James to that security company," Jake said. "What if they were hired to guard the compound? Perhaps that's how our unsub met Logger? Maybe James and Luther Mason both worked at the security company."

Nick's heart picked up a beat. "That would definitely serve as Seven's motive. The men could have abused her while they guarded the compound." He drummed his fingers on the table. "Logger's ex mentioned that he grew more disgruntled when he worked at the security company, and that he signed a confidentiality clause. Maybe he was struggling with what they were doing."

Nick turned to Dr. Culpepper. "What about the woman who died in the fire?"

Dr. Culpepper gestured to the whiteboard. "We identified the burn victim as the fifty-three-year-old Mildred Hoppinger." She pointed to the woman's left temple. "She suffered a contusion that was the result of blunt force trauma premortem."

"So someone knocked her unconscious, then handcuffed her to the pipe and left her to die in the fire," Nick said.

"Or was she dead before the fire started?" Jake asked.

"The actual cause of death was smoke inhalation. But there's something else," Dr. Culpepper said. "All her fingers were broken."

Nick chewed the inside of his cheek. "All of them?"

She gave a quick nod. "That has to be significant."

"It doesn't fit Seven's MO," Jake commented.

"Perhaps she was another Ms. Lettie," Nick suggested. "The Commander hired her to guard the captives."

Dr. Culpepper nodded. "She did serve in the military twenty-five years ago."

"How do we know she's not one of the subjects of the experiment?" Special Agent Hood asked.

Jake listed the names of the subjects they had confirmed so far. "Her age. All of the subjects are now in their twenties."

"This is my working theory right now," Nick said. "I think our unsub, Seven, was held, along with at least one other subject, in this compound. According to the timing of the fire, it's possible that the Commander's arrest triggered Seven and the other subject to break out of the compound." He gestured toward the burn victim. "They left her to die because she kept them locked up. And because she was an accomplice to the abuse and torture inflicted on them."

Deputy Waterstone removed his hat and scraped a hand through his hair. "So you're saying that we have two psychos loose, not just one?"

Nick tasted grit in his mouth as he swallowed. "I believe so. At this point, we don't know if Six, the subject unaccounted for, is dangerous. Seven killed Logger and Mason."

"But a hired hit man killed Darren James," Special Agent Hood said. "That would account for the difference in the MO."

Jake stood. "Correct. If the Commander didn't order the hit, then whoever his accomplice was ordered it."

And the bastard still wasn't talking.

"Then who ran Brenda off the road?" Deputy Waterstone asked. "The psycho Strangler or the hit man?"

Nick stiffened, the image of Brenda in that hospital bed taunting him. "Good question. I don't think it was Seven. She's sending messages to Brenda to gain publicity. If another subject escaped with Seven, he has no reason to go after Brenda either."

"But somebody did," Jake said. "Maybe because they thought she was getting too close to Seven."

Nick contemplated that suggestion. That was possible. But Brenda had shared everything she'd learned with him, hadn't she?

Unless…she knew something about Seven from her stay at the sanitarium. Something she was hiding.

———————— , ————————

Seven had known he would come. She knew his weaknesses. His penchant for tawdry affairs, solicitous women, his secret desires.

Desire he kept well hidden from the press.

But she would rectify that. Or at least, Brenda Banks would.

Hatred burned deep in her soul as she waited for him to arrive at the bar. She checked her face in her compact, studying her dark hair and eyes, wondering if he would remember her.

She doubted it. When she'd seen him, they were children.

The memory made perspiration bead on her neck. She'd cried out for help that night, but no one had heard her.

Now he would be the one shouting for help.

Laughter bubbled inside her. But no one would come to his aid either.

Stowing the compact in her purse, she fingered the vial of pills. She'd done her research. She wouldn't need drugs to make Ron Stowe follow her or to tie him up.

He liked it rough. Liked to be dominated and abused. Liked to be forced to his knees and to beg.

A smile curved her lips. The bartender slanted her a suggestive grin, but she aimed a cool look his way. Then, quickly reminding herself that she needed to blend in, she wet her lips with her tongue and leaned over the bar so her breasts strained at the top edge of her satin tank top, well aware that half the men at the bar fidgeted and adjusted themselves like dogs in heat. Any minute she expected them to salivate and attack.

The urge to teach each of them a hard lesson teased at her nerve endings.

But she had an agenda to follow.

And she couldn't allow indulgences with irrelevant parties to distract her.

The senator's son slipped into the dark bar, his face shadowed by a fedora that she supposed was a disguise. No doubt he'd had to ditch his security team to meet her, just as he'd ditched his daddy's campaign fund-raiser tonight.

She'd promised him it would be worth it.

Lifting to her cheek the red rose she'd brought with her so he could easily spot her, she watched him maneuver through the throng at the door. Other patrons danced on the crowded dance floor, cigarette smoke blending with alcohol and cheap perfume.

Her mind began humming, as if she were locked in that room again. Seven steps to the right, seven to the left, seven back again, seven across.

Her finger traced the square on the bar, over and over and over again.

Goddammit, Seven. Stop it. Someone will notice.

She gripped the rose tighter with the other hand, her breath hitching as a thorn pierced her skin, the pain a reminder to focus.

Ron Stowe noticed her then. She felt his eyes on her. Felt the moment his breath hitched in his throat as he approached.

Her tits hardened at his heated gaze, her thighs growing moist.

A moment later, he dropped onto the bar stool beside her. "You're even sexier than you sounded on the phone."

Seven smiled, her heart fluttering with excitement as he ordered a drink. She wasn't good at conversation, but a man like him preferred to talk about himself. So she let him.

A half hour later she led him outside to her car. "Get in," she ordered.

"What will happen if I don't obey?" he murmured.

Seven lifted a bloodred nail, then pinched his cheek so hard he winced. "Then you'll have to be punished."

He climbed in quietly, then she drove them to the cabin she'd rented and ordered him into the bedroom she'd prepared for their night together.

"This rendezvous has to remain between you and me," he said. "I'm paying for your discretion."

Anger heated her blood. He was paying her? Like a common whore? "Did I say you could speak?" she asked in a lethal voice.

"No, but I need to know—"

"If you speak again without permission, your punishment will be much more severe."

A frisson of fear darkened his eyes at the sight of the whips and the chains attached to the poles in the wood floor, but he obviously believed she was still playing out a fantasy.

So he allowed her to attach the restraints.

Anticipation bubbled inside her as she picked up the whip and began his torture.

Chapter 19

---------- o ----------

Brenda showered and dressed quickly, her nerves on edge. She didn't belong here in this princess fairy room with the white provincial furniture and the pink polka-dotted curtains and the dozens of perfume bottles that her mother had collected on her travels as a gift to her darling, precious little girl.

Her dream had disturbed her almost as much as the fact that someone had run her off the road the night before.

Almost, but not quite.

Still, she couldn't stop thinking about it. It was almost as if the nightmare had been real, a memory, not just a figment of the concussion and the hydrocodone she'd been given at the hospital.

Maybe it was a memory.

No…that was impossible. Agnes said she'd adopted her at birth. She and William even had pictures of them holding her as an infant.

She chucked the pills in the trash, worry needling her. She did not want to get hooked on painkillers.

When the teenagers she'd befriended in high school had experimented with pot and dabbled in other recreational drugs, she'd pulled away from them. She'd been terrified of becoming like the drug addicts she'd seen on television. Or maybe it was because Agnes had pounded a strong fear of addiction into her.

Not that her mother didn't enjoy her cocktails. But she'd stressed moderation to the point that it had been ingrained in Brenda the same way her Southern manners had.

She glanced again at the childhood sketches of the kids in her school, then dialed Nick's number, eager to hear if they'd made progress on the case.

He didn't answer, so she left a message asking him to call her. "I'm going to talk to some of the mothers of the subjects and start compiling the personal profiles on the families."

But she should stop by and see Amelia first. Maybe she'd drawn that sketch of Seven for her.

Downstairs it was quiet, and she strained to remember what her mother had said the last time she'd peeked in on her. In the kitchen, she found a note saying she and her father were attending the fund-raiser for the senator's campaign.

Grateful she didn't have to deal with saying good-bye and a lecture about her leaving, she snatched the keys to her father's extra car, a Lexus sedan, let herself out the door, and phoned Amelia.

But Amelia didn't answer either, so she phoned Joe Swoony's mother. The older woman welcomed her call and agreed to the interview.

"As long as you don't paint my son as an idiot," she said. "No telling what kind of future he could have had if that awful Arthur Blackwood hadn't stolen it."

"I promise to honor and respect him," Brenda said, surprised the woman didn't hate Blackwood even more than she did.

If it had been her child he'd abused and subjected to his cruel experiments, he wouldn't have seen the inside of a jail cell.

She would have killed him.

"Someone tried to kill your father."

"What?" Nick gripped the phone as the meeting broke up. "When? Who? How?"

"In the chow hall," the prison warden said. "I don't exactly know how it happened, but a fight broke out, a guard's gun was ripped off him, and the inmate fired."

Hell, he half hoped his old man was dead. He deserved worse.

"Was he hit?"

"A flesh wound. A gang fight broke out then, and the guy who shot at your father was killed."

Something about the scenario nagged at Nick. Stabbings and gunfights were the norm in maximum-security prisons. But if this inmate had targeted Blackwood because of his Slaughter Creek crimes, someone might have put him up to it.

Not that most of the town didn't hate his father or have reason to want him dead.

"We isolated him for now and are looking into the matter," the warden said.

"Did the Commander have any interaction with this inmate? An altercation maybe?"

"Not that I know of, but of course we'll investigate the situation."

"Has he received any mail or visitors?"

"We're still examining the mail. Same as before. Hate mail, love letters. People are so fucked up."

"Get me all the information you can on this inmate," Nick said. "I want to know everyone and anyone he had contact with in the last three months. Check his snail mail, phone calls, and visitors. If someone paid him to kill my father, I want to know who the hell it was."

"All right," the warden said. "But you know your father isn't exactly popular in here. He's ranked with the worst."

The pedophiles, Nick thought. Because his father was a child predator.

Now that someone wanted to silence him, maybe his father would finally talk.

Nick hung up, then explained the situation to Jake and Agent Hood.

"You think whoever was behind the project is afraid Blackwood will talk?" Agent Hood asked.

Nick hissed. "Maybe. They certainly went to a lot of trouble to keep it quiet before."

"I'll follow through on his mail and the visitor log," Hood offered.

"I'll question the inmate's cell mate," Jake said. "Maybe someone inside the prison knows what's going on."

"We'll go together," Nick said as he jangled his keys. "Hopefully now that his own ass is on the line, the Commander'll talk."

But Nick remembered the cold lessons his father had taught him about surviving interrogation tactics when he was a child, and he doubted it.

Still, they had to try.

He had a bad feeling, though, that Arthur Blackwood would take his secrets with him to his grave.

Brenda parked at Amelia's, her conversation with Joe Swoony's mother reverberating in her head. Joe had appeared normal at birth and for the first two years, yet he'd started regressing around the age of two and a half—after he'd visited the free clinic, where he'd received a series of vaccinations. At the time, no one had suspected they were tainted, that the doctors had created them specifically for the research project to engineer and alter the young persons' minds.

Brenda's heart had literally hurt as Mrs. Swoony described the terror and helplessness she'd felt.

And the agony of watching her son deteriorate while other children thrived.

What had she done wrong? Mrs. Swoony had wondered. Had she somehow caused her son's problems?

And then the cruel taunts and ridicule from other children, from teenagers and insensitive adults.

Even worse were the pitying stares.

Brenda cut the engine in front of Amelia's, having gained a new respect for the young woman who'd fought her way back from the trauma she'd endured to reclaim her life.

She checked her phone, annoyed that Nick hadn't called. Obviously he wasn't concerned about her accident.

Then again, maybe he had new evidence on the case, a lead.

Lamplight glowed in the front, so hopefully Amelia was home.

Brenda grabbed her notepad and mini-recorder, then hurried up the sidewalk. Classical music from another condo drifted in the breeze and the smell of roses blooming from the flower garden scented the air, reminding her of her grandmother's house.

Odd, but she hadn't thought about her grandmother in ages. Agnes's mother had been harsh and rigid the few times she and her mother had visited, so much that finally Agnes had stopped going to see her. Brenda had never understood what she'd done wrong to make the woman dislike her so much, but it was almost as if she couldn't stand to look at her.

Then she'd discovered the adoption papers and understood. Agnes's mother couldn't love a child that wasn't her real granddaughter.

The sting of her dismissal had hurt so much, though, that for years Brenda had dwelled on trying to earn a place in the older woman's heart.

Amelia's wind chimes tinkled, dragging Brenda from her thoughts, and she rang the doorbell. Two doors down, a muscular-looking guy in army fatigues with a black hat tucked low over his head opened the door, then headed toward an old Corvette.

He glanced up at her and frowned, his expression wary as he ducked his head and jumped in a battered old Jeep. Seconds later, he gunned the engine, tires screeching as he roared from the parking lot.

Brenda gripped her shoulder bag tighter, then punched the bell again, but no one answered. The shades to her studio were open, so she peered through the window.

The canvas on Amelia's easel caught her eye.

A line was drawn in the middle of the canvas, a charcoal sketch of Amelia on one side. Or maybe it was Sadie. Who could tell?

But the other half depicted another woman—or rather, a girl. She had long straight hair and bangs and big, dark, wide-set eyes. Her nose was slightly flat, her lips thick, her angular features stark but attractive, striking even.

A memory tickled at her conscience, a past she'd thought she'd forgotten and would never visit again.

She had seen the girl before.

At the sanitarium.

She closed her eyes as images flooded her. The girl screaming, trying to escape, clawing at a guard and crying that the men there hurt her.

A chill engulfed Brenda, and she staggered sideways, then looked at the picture of the girl again.

She had met her in the sanitarium. She'd even tried to help the girl break out.

But the guards had caught her, and…the memory slipped away as if a vessel had carried it from her mind into a tunnel.

Emotions clogged her throat.

That girl, the one she'd tried to save, was Seven.

But Brenda had failed to help her back then.

Was that the reason she'd contacted her now?

———————— , ————————

She rolled to her side and lay for a moment, cradled in Ron Stowe's arms. His dying breath bathed her cheek as she yanked on the piano wire.

Tears rolled down his cheeks as his eyes widened in shock.

She had already killed him twice.

But this time was the last, and he seemed to know it, the fight draining from him, as if he realized that the more he fought, the more she would punish him.

And the more times he would have to die.

It really was a shame. He was so handsome that if she were a normal woman and he hadn't been…the man he was…she would have let him live.

Regrets and the misery of knowing that she'd never be that normal woman ate at her like a festering sore, and she closed her eyes and draped his arms around her, snuggling into him as if he'd just promised sweet nothings to her and the forever-after she would never have.

Tears blurred her eyes, blinding her.

His cheek still felt warm against hers, and she kissed his jaw, pretending that he loved her and that they were starting a life together.

But the blood from his cheek smeared against her own, and his hand felt cold and was growing stiff, reminding her that forever-after and love and family would never happen for her.

She had been born bad. Hadn't the Commander pounded that into her brain enough times for her to accept it?

Back to the hole…

His voice tore through the haze of her fantasies, and she felt like that little girl who'd wanted dolls and dresses, and to play with the other little girls when they jumped rope in the street, and to have Christmases with real trees and ornaments and presents and hugs from people who loved you.

But there was no love for girls like her. No forgiveness or holidays or light. Only shadows and punishments and darkness.

Great gulping sobs racked her, the body next to her growing stiffer and colder with every second, just as she imagined her mother's body had done before she'd left her with the Commander.

But as she purged the grief from her soul, her tears slowly subsided, and disgust at her weakness rose. She looked into Ron Stowe's handsome face, and hatred mounted.

He could have helped her. Just as Nick and Jake Blackwood and Brenda Banks and all the others who'd stood by and done nothing could have.

Swiping at the infernal tears, she climbed from bed and hurriedly dressed. The lessons she'd learned from the Commander kicked in, and she used the sterile soap to clean Stowe's body, then rolled him in heavy plastic.

His wide, listless stare met hers, but the fantasy she'd had earlier had vanished, and she saw only the vileness of another man who had betrayed her.

Red Rover, Red Rover
Send Seven right over...

The childhood game replayed in her head as she carved the number three behind his ear and placed the skin she'd drawn from her carving into a baggie.

Then she dragged Stowe out to her SUV and drove to the sanitarium.

She knew the guards' schedule when they made their rounds. Knew visiting hours had long come and gone. Knew that half the safety lights in the parking lot didn't work, and that the shift change for employees was still three hours away. That the security cameras in the south side of the parking lot were broken.

Angry at herself for her emotional outpouring, she made quick work of dumping the naked body. She checked to make sure no one was watching, then propped him against the sign for the hospital.

Let the residents of Slaughter Creek wake and see what their children had become because of them.

Chapter 20

———— o ————

Brenda tossed and turned all night, images of the sketch Amelia had drawn of Seven taunting her. She tried to piece together the disjointed memories of her short stay at the sanitarium, but they were clouded with fear.

She hadn't heard from Nick either.

What was he doing?

The fact that he hadn't called or checked on her hurt.

Antsy, she pulled up her computer and spent the next hour ironing out the piece on Joe Swoony. When she finished it, she'd talk to Grace Granger's mother.

She jotted down a few notes on Amelia, but she was going to be the hardest one to capture.

Because she was starting to feel close to her.

Getting close to a subject in an article was dangerous.

She needed to be objective, but how could she be when she connected with the young woman? When she'd seen her troubled mental state and the effects her illness had on the entire family?

When Amelia's parents and grandfather had been murdered to keep people from learning what had happened at Slaughter Creek Sanitarium.

Maybe Brenda couldn't be detached, but she would still write Amelia's story. Helping the town to understand Amelia would soften criticism and prevent more gossip.

She started the piece twice, but couldn't find the right opening line. Frustrated, she studied the childhood journal of the kids at school that she'd found at her parents' house.

An opening line teased at her mind—"Who am I?" No. She scratched that out and wrote, "Searching for Amelia."

The quest for the truth about her identity fit Amelia and the other victims, and it was a topic most individuals could understand.

She certainly could. Hadn't she been struggling to find her own identity all her life? To feel like she belonged?

Amelia's psyche had split into three personalities, a manifestation of the abuse the research experiment had inflicted on her. She spent the next half hour writing what she knew of Amelia's life, then realized she needed to talk to Sadie to verify the details. She also needed her approval, since Sadie guarded Amelia like a mother bear protecting her cub.

If Brenda had a sister, she would protect her, too.

Her cell phone buzzed, and she automatically tensed. It was barely morning. It couldn't be good.

She reached across the bed and snagged her phone from the nightstand, tensing as she read the text.

There once was a girl who was mad
Because nobody cared she was sad
So she took them to bed
And made them all dead
So everyone would know they were bad.

———————— , ————————

Nick's head had just hit the pillow when his phone trilled. He had set the ringtone to alert him who was calling, and the bluesy jazz tune indicated it was Brenda.

Blues and jazz because the music sounded sultry and sexy, just like her.

He glanced at the clock. Five a.m.

It couldn't be good news.

The ringtone started again.

Or…maybe she was just pissed that he hadn't returned her calls. But hell, he was doing his job. And he hadn't liked the desperate worry that had clawed at his gut when he'd heard about her accident.

Better to distance himself.

The phone trilled again, and he reached for it. "It's Nick."

"I just received another text from Seven."

"What does it say?"

The idea of sleep fled as Brenda read him the limerick.

"It sounds like she's killed again. But she didn't tell you where she left the body?"

"No." Brenda sighed. "Not a clue."

Nick's phone beeped that he had another call. "Hang on, Brenda. Jake's calling."

He didn't give her time to reply. He hit the connect button.

"Sorry to wake you," Jake said.

"You didn't—I was on the phone with Brenda."

"She heard from the unsub?"

"Yes, how did you know?"

"The director of the sanitarium just called. A body was dumped outside the building at the Welcome sign."

"Jesus."

"It's bad, Nick. We have an ID this time."

Cold dread curdled in Nick's belly. "Who is it?"

"The senator's son. Ron Stowe."

Nick released a string of expletives. "Brenda knows him."

"She does?"

"Yeah." Nick sighed. "Have the senator and his wife been notified?"

"I called them before I phoned you. I was afraid someone at the mental hospital would spread the word before he and his wife heard."

"All right. I'll meet you at the crime scene." They disconnected, and he clicked back to Brenda.

"Jake found the body?"

"Yes, Brenda…I hate to tell you this, but the victim was Ron Stowe."

Brenda gasped. "Oh, my God, Nick. Are you sure?"

"Yes. Jake's already informed the parents."

Nick yanked on a shirt, his jeans, socks, and boots.

"Ron was supposed to be at his father's campaign fund-raiser last night," Brenda said in a strained whisper.

"Looks like he didn't make it," Nick mumbled.

"Come and pick me up. I'm going with you."

"Brenda—"

"If you don't, I'll drive myself."

He pulled at his chin. She shouldn't be driving after her accident. "Fine. I'll be there in a few minutes."

Nick grabbed his weapon and jacket and rushed outside. The chill of the morning air hit him, but it invigorated his sleep-deprived brain. During the short drive to Brenda's, he debated on how to extract her from the investigation, but the moment he arrived and saw her dressed and ready to go, bruised face and all, he realized that any attempt would be futile.

Brenda deserved this story. Seven had *chosen* her to cover the murders.

The predawn lights streaked her face in shadows, her complexion pale, making the bruises look even more stark.

"Brenda, you should stay home and rest," he said as she opened the car door.

She shot him a look of disbelief. "Your unsub wants to see me covering this story, and I'm going to do it."

"Look," he said, the urge to stroke her cheek hitting him. Dammit, he didn't like the fact that someone had hurt her.

He liked even less that he cared that someone had hurt her.

"I admire you for standing up for yourself, for chasing the story and wanting to help, but it's dangerous. Someone's already tried to kill you."

"We don't know that," she said. "Seriously, the driver of that car could have been drunk. Or a bunch of out-of-control joyriding teenagers."

"You don't believe that, and neither do I."

Brenda rubbed at her forehead, reminding him that she'd had a slight concussion the day before. "Brenda, please go back inside and go to bed."

"I can't, Nick." Her voice cracked. "I have to see this story through."

Nick's gaze met hers. "How well did you know Stowe?"

A fine sheen of tears glittered in her eyes, making him wonder if they'd been closer than he realized.

He didn't like that idea either.

"We met at my parents' dinner party the other night." She wiped at her eyes. "I don't understand why Seven chose him. He never worked at that security company."

"Good point," Nick said. He dragged his gaze from her battered face before he could pull her into his arms and comfort her.

But as he drove, her question plagued him. He'd seen photographs of the senator and his son. Ron Stowe was a ladies' man, a politician's son. And she was right. He'd never worked for the security company where Logger and Darren James had been employed.

Which meant they might be wrong about the victimology.

Either that, or Seven was all over the place with her MO. And she was choosing victims at random.

Which would make it more difficult to find her.

Brenda battled her emotions as they drove toward the sanitarium.

If she'd attended the fund-raiser with Ron, would he still be alive?

Her phone buzzed, making her jump, but it was her boss, so she answered it. "I'm on my way to the crime scene now. I already called Louis. He's meeting me there."

"Be careful, Brenda. You need to talk to the senator, but be respectful."

What the hell? "Don't worry, I'm sensitive to the family's situation."

She ended the call, irritated that he'd felt the need to forewarn her.

"Do you know if Stowe served in the military?" Nick asked.

"I don't think so. I've researched the family, and there's no record that he did. Although his father served in the marines years ago."

Nick rolled his shoulders. "I wonder if he knew the Commander."

Had the senator worked with his father?

"Did you find anything shady on the senator?" Nick asked.

Brenda shook her head. "Nope, squeaky clean."

"Too clean?"

"Maybe."

Nick pulled down the drive and turned into the parking lot, both of them falling silent for a moment as they parked. Jake's squad car was in the lot, along with the MEs, and Louis rolled in with the newsman.

Brenda glanced around for the senator's town car, but he hadn't arrived yet. Her father's Cadillac caught her eye.

"My dad is here," Brenda said.

Nick reached for the door to get out. "I suppose he's playing politics."

Brenda frowned at his comment. Unfortunately a politician's son's murder would draw more media coverage and put more pressure on the police to solve the case than an average civilian's death would.

And William and the senator were friends.

Sucking in a breath to calm her nerves, she and Nick headed toward the cluster gathered around the body. Deputy Waterstone had roped off an area to keep onlookers from getting too close, and was ordering the staff at the hospital to stay behind the line.

The crime unit had arrived and erected a privacy screen to protect the body from being photographed by curious spectators while they conducted their preliminary investigation.

Nick radiated a take-charge demeanor as the two of them shouldered their way through the people gathered outside.

Two crime techs were snapping pictures while two others canvassed the crowd for witnesses. Jake stood in a conversation with Brenda's father.

Her father spotted her as she approached, the muscle in his neck jumping as his gaze fell on her face.

She didn't understand his anger. But she wouldn't give in to his demands for her to give up the case.

The tech closest to Ron finally moved, giving her a view of the body. Brenda staggered slightly. Nick caught her arm, steadying her, his voice low in her ear. "Are you all right?"

She nodded. But no, she wasn't all right.

The last victim had borne whip marks, but they were minor compared to the bruises on Ron's body. Scrapes and contusions covered his arms, legs, and chest. The crime tech eased his body forward, revealing deep, bloody slashes across his back. It also appeared that the killer had used a knife or sharp instrument— maybe a scalpel—to carve cuts on his upper body and thighs.

But the piano wire around his neck was identical to that on the other victims.

The only part of Ron Stowe's body that hadn't been beaten was his face. It was almost as if the killer had preserved his handsome image for some twisted reason.

"She made him suffer before she killed him," Brenda whispered.

"She's escalating even more," Nick commented.

Suddenly they heard a car screeching to a stop. Loud voices rose above the hubbub of spectators and crime techs as the car door opened. Bodyguards for the senator and his beautiful wife spilled out and shoved their way through the crowd, creating a path for the couple.

When Ron's mother saw her son's body, she collapsed against one of the bodyguards. A nurse from the hospital hurried to tend to her.

The senator's face blazed with pain and rage as he glanced at her father, then at Jake, then at Nick, and finally at her.

"This is your fault," he bellowed. "You've been covering this madness and making the Strangler famous."

"Mr. Stowe—" Nick said.

"It is her fault," he shouted. "If she hadn't glorified the killer, maybe you could have caught the sick bitch by now. In fact, she may have killed Ron because he knew you, Brenda."

Guilt suffused Brenda. What if he was right?

———— , ————

Amelia used the hospital soap to scrub her skin as the hot shower water pummeled her.

You're a whore.

You have blood on your hands.

You need to repent for your sins.

Tears fell as the images of her tawdry sexual acts replayed through her mind. She scrubbed harder and harder, desperate to obliterate the man's scent and the memory of his hands on her.

But even as she did, her body felt titillated, as if he was touching her again. Licking his way across her naked body. Thrusting inside her.

Taking her to oblivion.

Only she'd lost herself there for a while.

Sadie mustn't know. She would be worried. Afraid Amelia wasn't really improving.

And she was. Wasn't she?

Then who is that other voice in your head? Who likes the nasty stuff you do? Who gets off on pain and chains and suffering?

Chapter 21

———— o ————

Nick wanted to wring the senator's neck. He knew good and well that the man was in shock, but blaming Brenda was inexcusable.

"Senator Stowe, I realize you're distraught, but throwing accusations at the police or Miss Banks is not helpful. Why don't you take your wife home and call some family or friends to stay with her? She doesn't need to witness this, and neither do you."

"But I have to be here," Senator Stowe said.

Nick took him by the arm and spoke in a low, authoritative voice. "No, you don't. Think about your wife, for God's sake, not your political agenda."

Outrage flared in the man's steely gray eyes. "How dare you—"

"I am extremely sorry for your loss," Nick said, grateful to see that Brenda was recovering from the man's vicious onslaught. "Trust me, we will find out who did this to your son, but you can be more helpful by allowing us to do our jobs."

Mrs. Stowe made a strangled sound in her throat, then seemed to pull herself together.

"Just tell us how we can help," she said.

"Can you tell us where your son was last night?" Nick asked.

The Stowes exchanged a furtive glance. "I don't know," Mrs. Stowe said.

"He was supposed to attend my fund-raiser," the senator replied. "But he never showed."

"Did he call and tell you why he wasn't coming?"

"No," Mrs. Stowe said. "He just left a message saying that he couldn't make it."

"Was it unusual for him to miss a function like that?" Nick asked.

Another exchanged look between the couple. "No," the senator finally said. "He liked politics, but he liked his personal life more."

Mrs. Stowe wiped at her eyes. "And we didn't pry."

Brenda's father approached, his brows furrowed. "I'm so sorry, Stan."

The senator shook the mayor's hand and accepted his condolences. "Don't let your daughter plaster his picture all over the news like this. My son deserves more respect than that."

"I won't," Mayor Banks assured him. "And I promise we'll see that your son gets justice."

The senator turned to Nick. "Was my son killed by the same maniac who murdered those other two men?"

"We won't know that until we investigate, but it appears that way."

Senator Stowe glanced at his wife, misery on his face, the smooth politician gone. But rage flared in his eyes when he looked at Brenda.

Nick's heart stuttered at the pain on Brenda's face. This was not her fault, and he'd make damn well sure she knew it before it was over.

But for now, he had to do his job.

And that meant asking questions the Stowes might not want to answer.

Brenda struggled to don a professional expression as Louis walked toward her with the camera, but her father's disapproving scowl was almost more than she could bear.

At least Nick had made an attempt to defend her.

"Brenda, what do you know about Ron's death?" her father asked in a hushed voice.

Brenda clenched and unclenched her hands in an effort to calm herself. "Nothing."

"Don't lie to me. Your mother told me that you were supposed to go with Ron to the fund-raiser last night. But we were all there, and neither of you showed up."

Good Lord. Had Ron told them she was coming as his date? She had considered the invitation just so she could cover the event, but her boss had assigned someone else to do the job, wanting her to focus on the murders. Who knew they might cross at some point? "Dad, Ron did ask me, but I told him no. I have no idea where he was last night."

"You weren't with him?"

"For God's sake, you know that I was resting from the accident."

Uncertainty drew her father's mouth downward. "I know we left you in bed late in the afternoon, but you were gone when we arrived home last night."

Anger mushroomed inside Brenda. The last thing she'd expected was for her own father to interrogate her. "I went home to sleep in my own bed." Louis wove through the small crowd, his camera on his shoulder. "Now, I have work to do."

"Your work almost got you killed," her father said. "And look what it did to Ron Stowe."

Brenda was seething inside. "My job didn't get him killed, Dad," Brenda said. "But I am going to help find out who murdered him." She motioned to Louis. "Why don't we start with an interview with the town's mayor? That is, if you can be objective and not crucify me in front of the camera."

"What should I say, Brenda? The sheriff and that agent haven't given me any information."

"Just tell the people what they want to hear, Dad. You've always been good at glossing over the truth."

Another glint of anger registered before he tamped it back down and straightened his collar. "All right. Let's do it."

Brenda strategically led him over to a shade tree, positioning the interview to showcase the sanitarium in the background. "Mayor Banks," Brenda began. "We're here for another breaking story. Unfortunately, Slaughter Creek has seen another murder. This time, we sadly report that it's Senator Stowe's son, Ron, who has been killed. His body was left in front of Slaughter Creek Sanitarium."

"Yes," her father said, his voice grave. "It is tragic, and we're all saddened by his loss. Ron Stowe was an advocate for the senator as well as a gifted and talented spokesperson himself. The senator and I are personal friends, and he had aspirations that his son was going to follow in his footsteps."

Brenda swallowed against the lump in her throat. "Mayor, with the recent revelations about Arthur Blackwood's arrest, and now four murders in our town in the last two weeks, what would you like to say to the residents of Slaughter Creek?"

He rubbed a hand over his bald spot, a dead giveaway he was ticked off at her. "I would like to encourage residents to please be cautious, to report any suspicious activity or person to the police, and if you know anything about Ron Stowe's murder or any of the other victims, to come forward." He paused and cleared his throat. "That said, I am mayor of Slaughter Creek, and I promise each and every resident that I won't stop until the police arrest the Slaughter Creek Strangler, so we can restore peace in the town."

Brenda gripped the microphone and smiled at her father for the television. But inside she was furious. He had just glorified

Seven by pinning her with a nickname, one that would no doubt stick. "Thank you, Mayor Banks." She gestured to Louis. "Now let's see if Sheriff Blackwood has any details to share with us."

She strode toward Jake, still shaken by the fact that not only did the senator blame her for Ron's death, but her father did as well.

———————— , ————————

Nick corralled the Stowes into the hospital cafeteria, then sent one of the bodyguards for water and coffee. Mrs. Stowe dug some pills from her purse and knocked them back with the water.

Her face looked ashen, her makeup smeared, her hands trembling as she set down the cup. The senator had taken a seat beside her and spoke in a hushed voice, trying to calm her. But it was obvious they were both suffering from shock and grief. And a good dose of anger.

Who could blame them?

He should have caught this unsub before now.

He gave them a minute to console each other while he sipped his coffee.

Unfortunately every minute he waited constituted another minute that the unsub could use to hide, escape—or take another victim.

"Why would someone hurt our son?" Mrs. Stowe said in an anguished voice. "And why leave him naked and beaten like that?"

Senator Stowe squeezed her hand, but his penetrating gaze stabbed Nick. "Was that the way the other men were left?"

"Yes and no," Nick said. "But before we talk, you have to agree not to repeat anything we discuss in private."

"Trust me, Brenda Banks is not getting a word out of us," Senator Stowe said.

"I'm not referring to Brenda. I'm talking about your staff, friends, business acquaintances, and the media." Nick folded his hands on the table. "The police have withheld details of the other crimes to enable us to solidify a case when we catch this perpetrator. And trust me," he said in a tone that brooked no argument, "we will catch her."

"You think a woman did this?" Mrs. Stowe said, her eyes widening in shock. "How? Why?"

Nick inhaled. "The sexual nature suggests a female killer. The MO of the stranglings are the same. The unsub used piano wire to choke the men."

Mrs. Stowe shuddered.

"But there are some differences. Victim one was left in a hotel room. The second man in the woods at Blindman's Curve." He omitted the gruesome details. "Victim one worked for a company called Stark Security. We're not sure if the second victim was connected to it, though." He studied the senator's face. "Do you know anything about Stark Security?"

The senator shook his head. "No, should I?"

Nick shrugged. "We're just trying to piece everything together and looking for connections." He waited, but neither of the Stowes elaborated. "For instance, the other two men served in the military. Did your son?"

"No," Mrs. Stowe said. "Ron attended Yale, where he earned a business degree."

"What the hell would the military have to do with anything?" Senator Stowe asked.

"I'm not sure yet," Nick said. "Like I said, we're looking for connections that might indicate how and why this woman targets her victims."

Mrs. Stowe jerked her head up. "You think she knew our son?"

"I don't know that either. Why don't you tell me about Ron."

"He was a good boy," Mrs. Stowe said, wiping at her tears.

"He was smart and educated," Senator Stowe said, his tone defensive, as if he sensed Nick was digging for dirt.

"What about enemies? Did he have any?"

"Everyone loved our son," Mrs. Stowe said.

Nick aimed an inquisitive look toward the senator. "What about you? Any enemies?"

The senator's nostrils flared. "All politicians have enemies, but none that would kill my son to get back at me."

Nick wasn't convinced. "What about threats?" Nick asked. "Any specific e-mails or mail that stuck out?"

They both shook their heads.

"We'll need to look at all of your correspondence, as well as your son's, including phone calls, e-mails, texts," Nick said. "And I'll need access to your son's computer."

"What good will sifting through his life do?" Senator Stowe asked, his voice strained.

"If we see commonalities with the other victims, maybe we can narrow down our search."

The senator glared at Nick. "It sounds to me like you're going to make this about Ron's personal life."

"My intentions aren't to malign your son or your reputation," Nick said. "But it's imperative we study his actions to find his killer."

The senator started to protest again, but his wife laid her hand over his and cut him off. "All right," Mrs. Stowe said. "Whatever you need, do it."

"Was your son dating anyone?" Nick asked.

Mrs. Stowe shrugged, but the senator gave a noncommittal reply. "He's a single man. He dates."

"Has he mentioned anyone specifically?"

"No." Mrs. Stowe sipped her coffee. "In fact, he dates around, but I thought it would be nice if he settled down. I'm friends with Agnes Banks, so she set him up with her daughter."

Nick forced himself to breathe. Had Brenda been interested? "And?"

"They seemed to get along, but apparently he asked her to attend the fund-raiser last night, and she turned him down. He could have asked someone else later. I don't know."

Nick nodded. "Maybe we'll find something in his computer or phone to tell us where he was last night."

The senator folded his fists on the table. "Men have needs. If you print anything about what you find out, I'll sue you, the TBI, and the police department."

That pissed Nick off. "If you want me to find out who killed your son, I will have to dig into his life. And if it gets dirty, Senator, you'll just have to live with it."

"But—"

"Instead of blaming Brenda Banks, look at your own past. It's possible that the killer may have murdered your son to exact revenge against you."

Brenda felt helpless as she watched Jake and the crime techs work the crime scene. Two techs, having combed the trash cans outside, were heading inside to see if the killer had discarded Ron's clothing or phone on the premises.

She doubted it. Seven had probably killed Ron at another location, then brought his body here.

The shock should be wearing off, but seeing the man she'd met at her parents' house murdered in such a vile manner stirred rage at the killer, who'd sent her texts as if they were playing a game.

She reminded herself that Seven was a victim as well, that the abuse she'd endured as a subject of a diabolical experiment had altered her behavior and emotions and turned her into a sociopath.

But whatever the cause, she was still a dangerous psychopath, and she needed to be stopped. She was taking lives, cruelly and without remorse.

The bottom line—Ron Stowe didn't deserve the brutal beating and degradation she'd inflicted on him.

Nick and the Stowes exited the sanitarium, the senator's bodyguards hovering close by, scanning the parking lot for trouble. Brenda tracked the crowd; it made her feel marginally better to know that Nick would make sure every person present at the scene had been interviewed.

Louis nudged her and turned the camera toward the Stowes as they crossed the grass to the area where their son's body had been left. Thankfully, Nick blocked the couple from getting close, or seeing inside the protective screen the police had erected.

Louis trained his camera on the couple as they paused beside Jake. Brenda sucked in a breath. She had to do her job. But now wasn't the time to confront the Stowes, not when the senator had already accused her of causing his son's death.

They spoke to Jake for a moment, then her father gave Mrs. Stowe a hug and shook the senator's hand, no doubt assuring him that he'd make certain their son's killer was caught.

A couple of people still lurking by the crime scene tape darted toward the senator.

"What are you going to do to stop this crime spree?"

"Did your son know the other men who were killed?"

Jake rushed to block them while the bodyguards surrounded the Stowes.

Louis hurried toward them with his camera. The senator paused in front of it. Brenda realized he intended to address the public, so she gripped her microphone. "Senator, I know that I speak for everyone in Slaughter Creek when I express my sincerest condolences for your loss. Would you like to make a statement?"

His eyes seared her with contempt, but he nodded, his grief-stricken face solemn as he spoke. "My wife and I are devastated at our son's death and need time to grieve and make arrangements for his funeral." He paused, voice choking.

"No parent should have to bury his child," Brenda said sympathetically.

He swallowed hard. "No. Ron was a good man who didn't deserve to be murdered." He cast a scathing look toward Jake and Nick while his wife hung back, looking faint. Then he looked straight into the camera, his face determined. "I don't know who you are or why you killed my son, and I don't care. But I promise you that I won't stop until you're rotting in prison."

Then he took his wife's arm and led her back toward their town car, his bodyguards fending off questions from the crowd.

Nick strode toward her. "Come on, I'm heading to Stowe's apartment to search his things. I'll drop you at home."

"I'll go with you," Brenda said.

"No way." Nick motioned to Jake that he was leaving. "I have to do this by the book, Brenda, especially with the senator's attitude toward you."

"I promise I won't get in the way or touch anything, Nick. I just…need to do something to help."

Nick lowered his voice. "Brenda, for all we know, Stowe's home might be the crime scene."

Bile inched up her throat as she imagined what that might look like. A bloodbath, probably.

Nick helped her into the car, closed the door, then went to the driver's side and got in. "Go home, or to your office if you have one. Do all the research you can on Ron Stowe while I search his apartment. Maybe you'll find something in his background to indicate the reason Seven chose him as a victim."

Brenda nodded. Yes, she was good at research. And dividing the tasks would help them work more efficiently.

After all, Seven was growing more violent, taking more risks. And the clock was ticking.

——————— · ———————

Seven watched the scene unfolding from the window in the sanitarium.

When she'd left this place, she'd vowed never to return.

She smiled. Now it was fitting that she be an observer to the drama below.

How many times had she stood by a window here and hoped someone would come for her? That they would look up and see her crying in the window? That they'd rescue her?

But no one had.

Then the Commander had taken her to another horror.

Laughter bubbled in her throat. The only thing that would make the moment sweeter was if it were the Commander's body lying down there for all of Slaughter Creek to see.

It would be, in the end.

But first she had to finish with the others.

She gripped the paper she'd stolen from her father's files years ago and looked at it. Although there was no real need.

She'd memorized it long ago.

Brenda Banks's name was on it. Brenda, the little girl who was supposed to be part of the project.

Brenda, the little girl who'd grown up with parents who loved her and gave her all the dolls and Christmases she wanted. The little girl who'd had nice warm blankets and pillows to sleep on, for whom punishment had meant sitting in a room by herself for a few minutes, not being buried in a dark, deep hole. Brenda, who'd had hugs and kisses and spoiling and all the doting a little girl could handle.

Yes, she would take care of the others who'd hurt her.

Then she'd take care of Brenda.

Chapter 22

―――――― ○ ――――――

It took Nick a couple of hours to obtain a warrant for him to search Ron Stowe's apartment, as well as his phones and computer. Knowing the senator would try to prevent him if he suspected that his son had skeletons in the closet, he decided it was better to cover his bases. With the election coming up in a few months, Senator Stowe would definitely be protecting his campaign.

Even if it meant withholding pertinent information in his son's murder investigation?

Possibly.

Nick flashed his badge to the security detail at the gated community where Stowe lived, then parked in front of the multimillion-dollar high-rise condo and walked up to the entrance.

The automatic doors parted to reveal a two-story entryway with gleaming marble floors, ornate columns, and a security desk to the left.

He stepped up to it, flashed his ID again, and explained the reason for his visit.

"We were so shocked to hear about his death," Sonya, the woman behind the desk, said. "He was such a charmer. And always so polite."

"Was he seeing anyone?"

She tucked a strand of silver hair behind one ear. "This is an exclusive community," she said. "Our owners value their privacy."

"I understand that, and trust me, I'll use discretion. But the man was murdered," Nick said, emphasizing the word. "So anything you can tell me about his personal life might help us uncover his killer."

She glanced around as if to make sure no one was listening. "Honestly, I never saw him with any women. If he dated, he didn't bring them to his condo. It made me wonder..."

Nick narrowed his eyes. "If he was gay?"

She shrugged. "I can't confirm, one way or the other. Like I said, he was always polite and friendly. He kept busy running his father's campaign."

Nick nodded, then handed her the warrant. "Can you let me into his place?"

She checked the warrant, then reached behind the desk and retrieved a key card. "Here you go. It's the penthouse unit."

Of course the senator's son would own the best. He had probably thought his exclusive address would protect him from harm. "I'll also need to question the other people in the development."

"All right. I hope you find who murdered him."

"I intend to." Nick took the key, strode to the elevator, and rode it to the top.

The entire top floor belonged to the man. Had Brenda been attracted to his money and status?

It doesn't matter. You and Brenda Banks are strictly on a professional level.

And that was all it could ever be.

Resigned, he unlocked the door and slipped inside. Chrome and glass dominated the space as he entered, the modern furnishings of the living room—a massive entertainment center, white couches, and white carpet—stark in their clean lines. The effect was cold and impersonal; not a place where he'd feel at home, Nick thought, though the condo did have an enviable view of downtown Nashville's skyline.

The kitchen was stocked with Perrier, expensive wines, and gourmet coffee, but the cupboards and refrigerator held very little food; Stowe probably dined out most of the time. A take-out container from a local Chinese place was half empty, and the date on the eggs had expired.

Searching the kitchen desk, he found an organized tray of assorted bills. He rifled through them but detected nothing out of the ordinary. Next, he headed into the bedroom. The king bed was covered in a gray satin comforter, the neatly organized closet filled with designer suits, with separate bins for sweaters, and casual shirts still encased in plastic from the dry cleaner's.

Nick rummaged through his dresser but found only socks and underwear organized in built-in compartments. He then checked beneath the bed, but there was nothing hidden there either.

He searched for a cell phone, but obviously Stowe had had it with him. The killer must have either kept it or disposed of it. Hopefully their tech department was savvy enough to trace the number and any incoming or outgoing calls.

He returned to the living room and searched through Stowe's video collection, looking for S & M or porn but finding only political dramas, documentaries, and an occasional science fiction movie.

Finally he crossed to the man's office on the other side of the living room. Political posters, charts of campaign strategies, and a wall calendar detailing future plans scheduled for his father's campaign covered one wall.

If Stowe was in charge of the campaign, why had he skipped the fund-raiser?

Because he'd had a more enticing offer?

Nick booted up Stowe's computer and spent the next hour examining his e-mails. The large majority focused on work, social events for the campaign, meetings to discuss campaign strategies—everything he would expect.

Dammit, the man looked perfect on paper. *Too* perfect.

Nick scrolled through Stowe's browser history and again found dozens of politically related sites. He had to be missing something. Nobody was this squeaky clean.

He searched the man's desk drawer. No photos of naked women, porn magazines, or erotica-related material.

The bottom drawer stuck, though, and he had to yank it hard to open it. He found several files on financial matters on top, then dug deeper and realized a false bottom had been built into the drawer.

Curious, he set the file on the floor and lifted the insert. A smile creased his face.

Stowe had a separate computer hidden in the drawer.

His fingers itched as he opened it and booted it up. Seconds later, he discovered what he was looking for. Dozens of porn sites Stowe had visited, S & M and erotica chat rooms, and videos he'd made of himself with various women in compromising sexual activities. Several featured Stowe being dominated and even abused.

But in all of them he was alive. And he walked away with a satisfied look on his face.

Had he taped himself with the killer? Or had she taped the two of them and then kept a video of their sexual escapades—and his murder?

He studied the faces of the women, who enjoyed controlling and dominating their sex partner. Whips were involved, as was punishment and humiliation in ways that made Nick's skin crawl. Although none of these depicted autoerotic asphyxiation, in one video, a brunette was strangling Ron with a silk scarf.

What if Stowe had had sex with the killer prior to the night he'd died? Her face could be on one of these tapes.

And if Stowe realized she was the Slaughter Creek Strangler, could that have been her motivation to kill him?

---·---

Brenda stopped by the station to research the senator and his son, avoiding her coworkers so she didn't have to answer questions about the bruises on her face.

Jordan Jennings, the weather girl, poked her head into her office. "Good work this morning on the senator's son's murder. But why didn't you push the senator and his wife to talk?"

"Because they deserved a few moments to recover from shock," Brenda said.

"You get the best interviews when you catch people off guard." Jordan shrugged. "If Stowe has something to hide, now's the time to strike."

Now the weather girl was giving her advice?

Still, Jordan's comment triggered Brenda's curiosity, and she turned back to the computer and began to dig into the Stowe family's past.

The senator had been born in eastern Tennessee, had grown up under humble circumstances that won him favor with voters, and had worked his way through college as an office assistant for the town council. After graduation, the senator had served for eight years in the marines, where he worked on a tactical unit during the Cold War.

His wife had been raised in the lap of luxury by a blue-blooded family in Knoxville, had earned a business degree, and had been working at the mayor's office, where she met Stan Stowe, when she was thirty-one.

Brenda kept looking, but she couldn't find anything on the senator's military career except that he had received several commendations for valor and been honorably discharged.

When he'd left the service, he returned to politics, first by running for town council in his hometown, where he met his wife. She utilized her degree to help organize fund-raisers for his first campaign as mayor of his town, and he'd risen up the chain from there.

His record looked pristine. No arrest or skeletons in his closet.

Next Brenda accessed files on the senator's son, and found the same thing. Several photographs of him at graduation and at political events and parties, usually with an attractive woman on his arm.

But there was nothing incriminating or negative, nothing the senator wouldn't want the press to find.

Which made her more suspicious. Everyone made mistakes. But Ron Stowe didn't have so much as a parking fine or speeding ticket.

Something about the dates of the senator's military stint tickled her mind, though. Determined to verify her suspicions, she pulled up the file she'd organized on Arthur Blackwood.

They had served in the marines at the same time.

Nick stared at the photo of the senator and his father that he'd found in the archives of fund-raisers. He hadn't realized that his father knew the senator.

He needed to know more about that relationship. But after searching for more information for an hour, he came up empty.

Damn. He took Ron Stowe's computer, left the condo, and drove to the TBI office in Nashville.

"I want you to analyze Stowe's computer, especially his chat room conversations." He explained about the limericks and his suspicions that the unsub had been one of the subjects in the Slaughter Creek experiments.

"Check for common word usage, inflection, a code, anything to connect Stowe with a specific woman."

Nick knew it was a long shot, that Stowe could have easily picked up the woman in a bar. But they had to explore every possibility.

"Also analyze his phone and text records," Nick said. "Send me a list of anything suspicious."

The analyst agreed, and carried the computer back to the computer forensics lab.

Nick's nerves were on edge as he left the TBI and drove toward Slaughter Creek. This unsub had been one step ahead of them since the first murder. She was smart, knew how to stay off the grid, knew how to clean up her crimes, and so far, she hadn't left any evidence behind.

She had to make a mistake at some point.

Although, if Arthur Blackwood had trained her to be a soldier, she'd undoubtedly been taught everything she needed to survive and escape attention.

Still, there had to be some method to her madness. He thought he'd discovered it with the security company, but Stowe certainly hadn't been employed at the company. And he hadn't served in the military, as Logger and James had.

The one person who could explain her behavior was his father.

His phone buzzed as he swung his vehicle toward Riverbend State Pen, and he clicked to connect.

"Nick, it's Brenda."

The strained sound of her voice made his heart stutter. "Are you okay?"

A slight hesitation, then she said, "Yes. But I found something. I don't know if it's important, but I was researching the senator and saw that he served in the marines during the same period that your father did."

"You're sure?"

"Yes, I checked the military databases. They even served in the same assault unit at one time."

Nick took a moment to absorb the information. "That explains their connection. I found a photo of them together from years ago on Ron Stowe's computer."

"What if the senator knew about the project in Slaughter Creek? That might explain why Seven would target him. Maybe she wanted to punish the senator by killing his son."

"That's a possibility." Nick swiped at a bead of perspiration trickling down the side of his cheek. "But I discovered something, too, Brenda. Ron Stowe was heavy into S & M. I found dozens of explicit sex tapes of him and other women on a second computer hidden in his desk. So he could have crossed with our unsub on a personal level before he was killed."

Brenda's gasp echoed over the line. "He certainly hid that side well."

"Not so well that Seven didn't know about it." Nick hesitated. "Or if they had previously engaged in sex, he could have figured out she was the Strangler, and she killed him to keep him from talking."

"So she left him at the sanitarium as a message that she'd been a patient there against her will," Brenda finished.

Nick slowed, then flashed his ID to the prison security guard at the gate. "Listen, I'm going to question my father again. Someone tried to kill him yesterday, so maybe he'll be more cooperative now."

"Do you want me to go with you?" Brenda asked.

Hope laced her voice. But he didn't intend for her to ever go near his father again. Not after what had happened the last time.

"No, I'm pulling into the prison now. Just go home and rest." He hesitated as he parked. "And be careful, Brenda. We don't know what Seven will do next, or if the Commander ordered a hit on you. So watch your back."

Brenda agreed, and he ended the call.

Jake was beeping in. "I'm at the prison now to talk to Dad," Nick said after connecting.

"Good luck," Jake said. "I questioned the cell mates surrounding him but got nowhere. One of the antipedophile prison gangs has it in for him, though, so I doubt this is the last attempt on his life."

"Serves him right."

"I can't argue with you there. Oh, and I found Sergeant Mason's house. There was a business card with Stark Security printed on it in the fireplace."

"So that is the connection. What else did you find?"

"Not much. He wasn't killed at his house either. I don't know where Seven is killing her victims, but we need to find it."

They agreed to keep each other posted, and Nick hung up, then slid from the car. Ten minutes later, he sat in an interrogation room, waiting on his father.

When he finally shuffled in, shackled and chained, the Commander looked ten years older than the last time Nick had seen him.

Dark bruises marred his face and arms, a knife's slash mark ran from his temple to his chin across his right cheek, and he was limping. Prideful, though, the Commander lifted his chin with that evil, defiant tilt that made Nick want to jump across the table and cram his fist down his throat.

"I heard you were attacked," Nick said.

His father shrugged. "Don't tell me you're worried about me, son."

The word *son* sounded dirty coming from Nick's father's mouth, and resurrected memories Nick wanted to keep buried. "No. Sooner or later, you'll get what you deserve. I just hope one of your subjects gets the pleasure of pulling the trigger."

The Commander threw his head back and laughed.

Nick didn't. He laid the file folder he'd brought on the table, then began to spread the pictures of the murdered men across it, lining them up in order.

"What are we doing now?" the Commander asked. "Playing a game?"

"That's what our unsub calls it," he said. "She wanted you to see what she's done for you."

The crazed look of a sociopath fell over his father's face. "And?"

Nick tapped each man's photo. "Jim Logger served in the military, as well as Darren James, who we think ran the security company where Logger worked. This victim, Sergeant Luther Mason, also worked there." He pointed to the ashes of the compound and the dead woman's charred body. "She was left handcuffed to a pipe to die in the blaze. We think that our unsub, who calls herself Seven, and another subject, escaped from this compound, and then Seven began her killing streak."

The Commander showed no reaction.

"We also believe that you are responsible for the heinous acts that occurred at this compound, and we'll be adding them to your list of charges."

"You have no proof of any of this," the Commander said.

"No, but when we catch Seven, I'll convince her to testify against you and tell everyone what you did to her."

The Commander shook his head. "She will never do that."

"Why not? Because you think you still have control?" Nick slammed his finger on the photos one by one. "The sexual aspect of the crime, is that because you sexually abused her?" He jammed his face into his father's, disgust seeping from his pores. "What did you do to her, Father? Rape her? Force her to have sex with dozens of men? Beat her until she had no choice, sodomize her, then choke her over and over?"

His father's eyes met his. "These men obviously failed the test," he said. "But she didn't. That means you'll never find her."

"Oh, I will," Nick said. "And when I do, I swear to God if she wants to kill you, I'll give her my damn gun to do it."

Brenda drove to her house, hoping Nick would stop by after he'd seen his father. But he appeared to be doing everything he could to avoid her.

Her phone jangled, and her father's name popped up on the screen. A wave of nausea washed over her as she remembered the senator's accusations, and her father's condemning look.

She was tempted to let the call roll to voice mail, but if she did, he'd show up at her apartment, and that was the last thing she wanted tonight. Not another confrontation with the mayor.

She caught it on the third ring. "Hello, Dad."

"Brenda, where are you?"

"Almost home. What do you need?"

"Do the sheriff or that federal agent have any leads as to who murdered Ron Stowe?"

"They're working on it, but even if I did know something, Dad, I wouldn't be allowed to discuss an ongoing investigation."

"We're talking about the senator and his wife. Friends of mine and your mother's."

"I'm well aware of who they are, and you have no idea how sorry I am about Ron. Jake and Nick are both doing everything possible to find out who murdered him."

"The police should have already stopped this mad person," her father said. "I had to meet with the town council today to calm everyone down. We've asked the sheriff to impose a curfew in town."

"That's probably a good idea," Brenda said, although she doubted it would help. Seven wasn't targeting children or random people in Slaughter Creek. She obviously had a plan.

If only Brenda could figure out exactly what it was.

"I want you off this story," her father said. "It's too damn dangerous—"

"Dad, I'm not quitting my job. If anything, I intend to work harder to help Jake and Nick solve this case so Ron gets justice. Now, I'm home and I'm tired. I'll talk to you later."

She hung up before he could launch into another tirade. Exhausted from the day and worried that Seven might already be stalking her next victim, she parked and let herself in.

But as soon as she did, she sensed that something was wrong. A faint hint of something strong, like hospital soap, scented the air. And her curtain sheers had been pulled back.

She froze, then reached inside her purse for her derringer, pulling it out as she listened for sounds of an intruder. But she heard no voices or footsteps, only the whistle of the wind seeping through the open window in the kitchen. The window that overlooked the backyard and patio.

The window she'd left shut.

Gripping her gun at her side, she inched inside, checking the den, then her office space. Nothing amiss.

But when she crept into her bedroom, her heart accelerated.

Something was lying on the pillow on her bed. A roll of piano wire. The kind of wire the killer had used to strangle her victims.

And something else.

Something in a plastic bag.

Swallowing back a scream, she inched closer, peering down at the bag and its contents.

Dear God. It looked like slices of skin. The skin Seven had taken from her victims.

Brenda turned to run, but suddenly something hard slammed against her head and she went down, the world tilting until there was nothing left at all but the darkness.

Chapter 23

———— o ————

Nick needed to purge his anger over his father. Why he'd thought Arthur Blackwood would ever give up the killer, he didn't know. The man was a monster who had no compassion or feelings for anyone.

Including his two sons.

Ancient feelings of betrayal and anger festered inside him, threatening to explode.

His cell phone trilled, causing him to jump. Goddammit, he had to get a grip.

He saw it was Jake, so he jerked the phone up. "Hello."

"Nick, you won't believe this, but I just received an anonymous call saying that Brenda is our killer."

Nick scratched his head. "What in the hell are you talking about?"

"I know it sounds crazy."

"Was it a female who called?"

"Hard to tell. The voice had been altered by a computer."

Nick's stomach rolled. "What exactly did the caller say?"

"That Brenda had been in Slaughter Creek Sanitarium as a patient at one time."

Jesus. That was true.

"That she killed the senator's son."

"I don't believe that," Nick said, although his mind raced over the past few weeks' events. "The killer was one of the Commander's subjects. Brenda wasn't part of the experiment."

"But..." Jake hesitated. "I checked, and Brenda was in the hospital at one time, Nick. She's also the right age. What if she was part of the experiment, but she didn't exhibit the same overt side effects as the other subjects? She could have sent those texts to herself."

Nick turned his car around and headed the opposite direction toward Brenda's. There had to be another explanation. "I still don't believe it. The Bankses would never have allowed their daughter to be used like the others."

"Maybe they didn't know," Jake muttered.

Nick contemplated that possibility.

Jake cleared his throat. "You know some criminals insinuate themselves into investigations just for the thrill of watching the police chase their tails."

And to throw off the cops. "It's not possible, Jake. We've known Brenda half our lives."

"Find out what's going on," Jake said. "Why Brenda was at the sanitarium."

He knew the reason, but he didn't want to share that with Jake. Not yet.

But he would if he had to.

"I'll go talk to her," Nick said.

He hung up, agitated, as he sped around the mountain. Every phone call and conversation he'd had with Brenda repeated itself in his head. Brenda's shocked reaction to the murders—she'd nearly been sick when they'd found Mason's body in the woods. And she had known Ron Stowe.

She'd also insisted on coming with him to the crime scenes and to see his father. And the Commander had tried to choke her.

Why had he jumped her? Because she was one of his subjects?

Disbelief made him grit his teeth. He had been with Brenda, he *knew* her...

Except he'd thought earlier that the killer had been one step ahead of them since the first murder. Was it possible that he'd been blinded by his feelings for Brenda? That his lust for her had prevented him from seeing that she was using him to keep abreast of the investigation?

Had she known his father in the sanitarium?

Hell, she could have insisted on meeting with him to reconnect.

And what about the Bankses? Wouldn't they have known something was wrong?

She was adopted...

Good God. She could have been part of the experiment before Agnes and William Banks took her into their home and raised her as their own.

He punched the number for the forensics lab and asked to speak to the computer analyst. "This is Special Agent Nick Blackwood. Did you find anything on Stowe's computer?"

"Yes. Three of the women in the tapes are high-priced call girls. They work through a service called Maiden Delights."

So Stowe was paying for sex. "Send me and Sheriff Blackwood a list of their names, as well as the contact information for the site."

"It's on its way."

"How about Stowe's e-mails and social media sites?"

"He scoured several porn sites and chat rooms for sexual sadists. His user name was Honey Bear."

Nick frowned. "Can you cross-reference names of women on those sites and at Maiden Delights with anyone he may have had contact with in a work situation? Look for employees and volunteers, especially ones who've just come on board."

"That'll take a while. I'll get back to you."

"Thanks." Nick hung up just as he veered into the parking lot at Brenda's development and threw the car into a space. He texted Jake that the analyst was sending over some names for them to check out, then opened his door, jumped out, and jogged up to Brenda's condo.

His stomach clenched when he found the front door ajar. "Brenda?"

He reached for his gun as he crept inside. The sheers fluttering in the den drew his eyes to the open patio doors. He ran a quick visual check of the living area and kitchen.

But no one was inside.

Still, his senses told him something was wrong. Where the hell was Brenda?

He slowly inched his way toward the bedroom and found her lying on the floor, unconscious.

Dear God. He hoped she was alive.

Brenda stirred, the sound of a voice drifting through the fog in her brain. Nick?

"I'm here," he said softly. Then she realized that she was on the floor, and he was kneeling beside her. "Wake up, sweetheart."

She twisted her head, and felt him gently stroking her cheek. "Just lie still. I'll call a medic."

"No, I'm okay," Brenda said, blinking to bring him into focus. Her memory returned abruptly, and she jerked at his shirt. "Someone was here," she whispered. "She left something on the bed."

He glanced sideways, and she tried to sit up, but she was so dizzy she swayed. He scooped her into his arms and eased her onto the chaise in the corner. "Did you see who broke in?" Nick asked.

"No, I just saw the open window. Smelled...something... then she hit me." She rubbed at her head, angry now that she'd let the killer escape.

Nick's feet pounded as he crossed the room to the bed. "What the fuck?"

"It's piano wire and a baggie—"

"With skin she took from the victims—her trophies," Nick finished in a disgusted tone.

Tension vibrated in the air, electric with questions and Brenda's own fear.

Nick removed gloves from his pocket and pulled them on before picking up the baggie. "I need to send this to the lab. Maybe the killer's DNA is on it."

She hoped so. She wanted to stop this madness now.

Her head throbbed, but she massaged the knot, her mind beginning to process what had happened. "If Seven was here, Nick, why didn't she just kill me?"

Nick turned and faced her, his face cast in shadows, the angles and planes harsh in the dim light. "Good question."

Brenda frowned at his impersonal tone. "Why would she leave me her trophies? Do you think that means she's finished?"

"No." He walked over to her, then stood, his hands on his hips. "Are you sure you didn't see anyone when you arrived?"

Brenda nodded. "I don't understand. First she contacts me with these limericks, and now she brings me this creepy stuff and knocks me unconscious."

Nick dropped the baggie onto her dresser, flipped on a light, his gaze troubled.

"Did your attacker say anything?"

Brenda searched her brain. "No…at least not that I remember." She stood and walked over to Nick. He was still staring at the baggie of skin, his jaw rigid. "Maybe she's angry that I haven't printed anything about the numbers she's carving into the victims."

The heat kicked on, whirring softly in the silence. "That's possible."

"What other explanation could there be?" She gripped his arm. "If she wanted to kill me, she could have."

Nick's voice dropped a decibel. "Maybe she has other plans."

"Like what?" Brenda cried, frustrated. Her head was pounding like a jackhammer. Then the truth dawned.

"You think she's planning to frame me for the murders?"

Nick's eyes darkened, then he gave a slow nod. "Jake received a call earlier suggesting that you might be the unsub."

Brenda's heart began to pound. "Does Jake think I killed those men?"

The second it took Nick to answer made Brenda feel sick. Surely Nick didn't believe that she was capable of murdering a man in cold blood...

Nick looked into Brenda's tormented eyes, and knew she couldn't be the demented woman who'd committed these serial murders.

Not Brenda.

She was tough, smart, obstinate, and infuriating at times, but she didn't appear devious. And she certainly didn't behave like a sociopath.

Sociopaths can look like normal people. Just look at the famous ones who blended into the crowd.

He walked to the window and glanced across the back wooded area. Was he allowing his lust for Brenda to cloud his judgment?

Brenda's footsteps sounded behind him, then he heard her hiss of outrage. "Nick, you don't really believe I'm the Slaughter Creek Strangler, do you?"

He should have answered more quickly, but the rational side of him was still running scenarios through his brain, filtering out the details and compartmentalizing what his gut told him and the facts the evidence pointed to.

"Killers often insinuate themselves into an investigation," he said. "Jake received an anonymous call incriminating you. And now I find the killer's trophies in your bedroom."

"Nick?" This time her voice sounded agonized. "I realize this looks bad, but I sure as hell didn't fake a head injury."

His gaze met hers, and he didn't try to hide the war in his eyes. Because he knew she had been at the sanitarium. And she still hadn't opened up and shared that information.

But he was seasoned and trained to detect the truth. He wouldn't be so attracted to her if she were lying, would he?

Then again, he did have his own dark side. And she'd gotten under his skin in a way no woman had.

Enough to blind him to the truth about her?

"Nick?" Brenda's voice cracked. "I don't know why Seven would implicate me, but I would never hurt someone the way she did."

For the first time since they'd started the case, Brenda looked vulnerable. And not because someone had assaulted her— because she was worried about what he thought.

That touched him more than anything.

"I know." Unable to resist, he thumbed a strand of hair from her forehead. "Are you sure you're okay? You don't need a doctor?"

"My head will be fine." Her eyes glittered with unspoken emotions. "But I'm not okay if you think I'm capable of these crimes."

Nick's hard heart softened, and he traced a finger over her mouth. "I don't think that, Brenda. But I do think that Seven has an agenda, and that for some reason that we don't understand yet, you're at the center of it."

Relief echoed in her soft sigh. "I agree, but I don't understand the reason," she whispered. "If I did, I'd tell you, Nick. I respect you and your devotion to the job."

Nick's lungs constricted. He'd tried for years to win his father's respect, but becoming a monster was the only way to do that.

And he refused to turn into his father.

"You don't really know me," he said, his voice thick as images of his military missions bombarded him. The bodies lying dead, the secret attacks…"Don't know what I've done."

Brenda lifted her hand and pressed it against his cheek. "I know everything that's important."

Heat built inside Nick, the urge to kiss her blinding him to any rational thought. He had wanted Brenda as a teenager, and even more desperately since they'd been working together.

How could he not steal this one moment?

All he needed was a taste to satisfy the raging hunger inside him.

Then Brenda wet her lips with her tongue, and he was lost. He cradled her face in his hands, angled his head, and lowered his mouth to hers. Brenda parted her lips in invitation and slid her hands up to grasp his arms, holding on to him as if she never wanted to let him go.

That was all the encouragement he needed. He dragged her to him and deepened the kiss, savoring the way she felt in his arms, the soft purr she made in her throat as his tongue explored her mouth. Body hardening, he backed her against the wall, one hand trailing down to her hips to yank her up against him.

She fit perfectly into the V of his thighs. His cock strained against the fly of his jeans.

He wanted her like he'd never wanted another woman.

Brenda ran her hands over his back, urging him closer, and he dragged his mouth from hers and trailed kisses along her ear and down her neck, nibbling at the soft skin of her throat.

She tasted like sin and forbidden desires that he'd never allowed himself to indulge in.

Because she had been with Jake.

He'd vowed never to be second best to Jake, to make his own way, and now here he was about to take Jake's first girlfriend to bed.

Anger at himself for falling into the same trap he had as a teenager slammed into him, and he pulled away. Brenda's breathing rasped out, and she reached for him.

"Nick—"

"Don't," he said. "That was a mistake."

"Why?" she asked, need still flaring in her eyes.

At least the passion hadn't been just one-sided. She truly looked hungry for him.

The desire in her eyes made it more difficult to walk away.

But he had a case to solve. And the killer had left evidence here that he needed to get processed. Not that he thought it would lead them to anything that their unsub didn't want found.

She was too clever for that.

He walked over to the bedroom window and looked out, determined to regain control.

"Nick?" Brenda grabbed his arm and swung him around to look at her, but he remained rigid. "At least give me a reason. I want you, and it's obvious you want me. Why shouldn't we be together?"

"I told you, you don't know me."

"I know that I feel the heat between us. I've wanted you for years—"

"Even when you were sleeping with Jake?" The moment he uttered the words, Nick wished he could retract them.

"That's the reason you keep pushing me away?"

Nick strode past her, determined to get back to business. The sooner he left, the less chance he would have of revealing all his hand.

And his feelings for Brenda.

Because, whether he wanted to or not, he felt something for her. Call it lust and concern mixed together, but he felt *emotions* he hadn't felt in a long damn time.

Brenda's fingers dug into his arm. "I never slept with Jake, Nick."

His gaze met hers. "But—"

Her eyes pleaded with him to believe her. "It's true, Nick. Jake and I were...only friends."

He studied every nuance of her body language and inflection of her voice for the truth. And there it was. "But you dated for months—"

"I went through a difficult period at home," she said, her voice quavering. "And Jake was...nice. He talked to me, helped me fit in, make friends. But early on, we both realized there was nothing more between us. No chemistry."

Nick struggled to remember all those years ago, but he'd been messed up by his father and jealous of Jake, his easier manner with the girls and his popularity in school.

He'd assumed his brother and Brenda had slept together. Now that he thought about it, Jake never claimed to have bedded Brenda. At the time, he assumed Jake was being modest. Jake had never been the type to brag about how many girls he'd slept with, like some of the other jocks.

Brenda slipped a hand up to stroke his cheek. "I wanted you back then," she whispered. "But Jake was safe, and I was afraid to let you know that I had a crush on you."

He gripped her hands, stopping her when she reached for the buttons on his shirt. "You aren't afraid now?"

A sultry smile lit her eyes. "Yes," she whispered. "But I want you anyway."

Brenda's soft admission unraveled the last shred of his restraint, and he dragged her up against him and claimed her mouth again, this time allowing himself to finally express the heat and hunger exploding between them.

Brenda gave in to the desire she'd felt for Nick for years and teased his mouth with her tongue as she unbuttoned his shirt. He yanked her blouse over her head and tossed it to the floor, his mouth nipping at her neck as he trailed kisses and tongue lashes downward.

She curled into him, her breath catching at the hot passion in his kiss. His hands were everywhere, stroking and rubbing and feeling, bringing her to life with titillating sensations.

The buttons popped on his shirt in her haste to touch him, then he helped her by yanking off the shirt and throwing it to the floor with hers. Brenda had known Nick was strong, but seeing his well-honed muscles tensing as she raked her hand over his torso, then her lips over his chest, sent a wave of pleasure rocking through her.

"I've wanted this for so long," Brenda whispered as she trailed her fingers south to unsnap his jeans.

"So have I," Nick admitted gruffly.

The hushed sound of his voice against her breasts nearly drove her to her knees. She shucked her jeans and his followed, his perusal sending a thousand mind-numbing sensations across her body.

"You're even more beautiful than I dreamed."

"You dreamed about me?" Brenda said as she gripped his hips and pulled him to her.

His eyes darkened with a raw need that tore at her heart and made her kiss him again. God, she was falling in love with this man.

But telling him would send him running.

So she told him with her eyes, and her hands, and her mouth.

He pushed her to the chaise, then climbed above her and cupped her breasts with his big hands.

Her nipples stiffened to peaks, aching for more, and he unfastened the front clasp of her lacy bra so her breasts fell into his hands.

"You're even more spectacular than I imagined," Nick said as he lowered his head and tugged one turgid nipple into his mouth. Sensations surged through Brenda, and she traced her fingers over his back, silently begging for more.

He didn't disappoint. He laved one nipple, then the other, suckling the tips until she shoved at his boxers, needing to be closer.

Needing more. All of Nick. Inside her.

"Nick…"

His wicked chuckle tickled her belly as he trailed his tongue lower. He knew he was torturing her, and he loved it. His teeth tugged at her panties, then he peeled them off her. Brenda groaned and shoved at his boxers, and he complied, kicking them to the pile with the rest of their clothes.

She laughed as he leaned over to grab a condom from the pocket of his jeans, but her laughter died when she felt his thick length pulsing between her thighs.

He was huge, hard, more impressive than any man she'd ever been with. But there was more—it was his strong, tough, masculine body that made him even more exciting.

She wrapped her fingers around the head of his cock and stroked him, her body yearning for completion. But Nick shook his head with a lecherous grin, dipped lower, and placed his mouth on her aching damp center.

Brenda clawed at the sheets, mindlessly succumbing to his ministrations as he lifted her hips and dove deeper. One tongue swirl against her clit and she came apart, moaning as sensation after sensation splintered through her.

"I need you, Nick," she moaned.

He drew her sensitive nub into his mouth, sucking her until she cried out his name. "Please…"

She dug her hands into his hair, pleasure rocking through her as he rose above her, wrapped his hand around his thick length and teased her with it. She kissed him fiercely, tasting herself on his lips as he thrust inside her.

Brenda moaned again as his big cock filled her. She had never felt anyone so big, so powerful, so all-consuming.

With a soft groan, he pulled out, leaving her shaking and hungry for more. "Nick, please…"

His dark gaze latched on to hers, a sexy grin on his face. "Tell me you want me. That you want more."

"I want you," she whispered hoarsely. "I want more, please, Nick, I want more."

———————— · ————————

The sound of Brenda's whispered moans and pleas nearly made Nick come. But he wanted to last, wanted her to know he'd claimed her, wanted her to remember what it felt like to have him inside her.

He teased her sweet, slick folds again, then gripped her hips, angled her for his taking, then rammed his cock inside her.

Brenda's body spasmed around him, her shudders exciting him more, and he pulled out, then thrust into her again, building a frantic rhythm as his own hunger took over and drove him to drive deeper and faster. Deeper and faster, deeper and faster, until she cried out again with another orgasm.

He pulled out one last time, his heart racing as she grabbed his sex and guided it back inside her. He was so hard and aching that his control snapped, and he built the rhythm again, pounding inside her over and over, filling her, until his own release spilled from him.

Even then, he wanted her again.

The thought terrified him. He'd never needed a woman so intensely. Never felt such emotions pummeling him.

Never wanted to hold a woman forever.

But that was what Brenda did to him.

Inhaling to calm his raging emotions, he kissed her again, then rolled her to her side and pulled her into his embrace. Whatever happened, he intended to enjoy himself tonight.

Tomorrow morning, they would face Seven and the fact that for some reason she'd left damning evidence of the murders in Brenda's apartment.

Chapter 24

───── o ─────

B renda silently admitted to herself the truth—she was in love with Nick.

She had been all her life.

That was the reason she'd never been able to love another man these past few years.

The words teetered on the tip of her tongue, but she bit them back. Nick was not ready to hear a confession of love.

She wasn't sure she was ready to declare her feelings, either.

His labored breathing rattled in the air, making her smile, and she stroked circles on his chest. He had scars on his body that she hadn't expected.

Scars that could have come from his military service, or… knowing his father, they could have come from him.

She touched a jagged red line that rippled from his thigh all the way down his calf. He had burn scars on his calf as well. "What happened?"

Nick instantly tensed and rolled away to get up, but she tugged his arm. "Don't pull away, Nick. It's just you and me."

He shot her a dark look, his gaze meeting hers. "You don't really want to know about my ugly scars."

Brenda kissed him tenderly. "Yes, I do."

Nick heaved a weary sigh, his big body stretching out beside her again. She settled next to him, giving him time to decide how much he wanted to confide in her.

"I picked up a few scars from my stint in the service," he said. "I was shot in the abdomen, and in the chest." He indicated the puckered ridge of both old wounds.

"But you survived?" she said softly.

"I was trained to be tough, to kill, to survive no matter what."

"By the military?"

He shrugged, pulling her closer. She wrapped her arm around his waist and laid her head on his shoulder.

"Yes, but first by the Commander."

Brenda rubbed a slow circle on his chest. "He treated you like a soldier?"

"He trained me and Jake both, only he was softer on Jake for some reason. He seemed to hate me from the moment I was born."

"Nick—"

"It's true," he said. "I'm not saying this to solicit pity, Brenda. It's simply a fact."

She breathed deeply, not sure she wanted to hear what his father had done to him. But she had to, so she could understand him. "What did he do?"

Tension whispered between them, then Nick spoke in a low voice. "He put us, me, through rigorous survival exercises. Long trips into the woods and mountains, where he left me for days to see if I could find my way home. If I'd succumb to the elements."

"You obviously passed the tests."

Nick shrugged again. "I failed, according to him. That always brought severe punishments. Beatings. Isolation. Being thrown into a dark pit for days without a light, without a sound, without…hope."

Brenda swallowed tears. "Like the pit you found at that compound."

Nick's body shook slightly, as if the memory haunted him. "Yeah." He hissed between his teeth. "But at least he didn't resort to the more horrific things he did to the subjects of the experiment."

Brenda fought revulsion. Grace Granger had had a lobotomy. Others had endured shock treatment, sensory deprivation, psychotropic drugs, as well as behavior modification techniques.

Anger at his father fueled Brenda's tone as she said, "You and Jake were children. Your father was a monster who abused you."

Nick angled his head and looked at her, and Brenda's heart melted. He had endured so much pain as a child, while even though she was adopted, Agnes and William had protected her.

She stroked his wide jaw. "But even though he did, you're a strong man. A protector. You fight to put bad guys like him away."

"Don't make me into a hero," Nick said in a deep voice. "I'm not, Brenda. I have my own dark side."

"But you used that darkness for good." She pressed her lips to his. "I want you, Nick."

"Brenda—"

She shushed him with another kiss. "Make love to me again."

Nick moaned her name, then cupped her face in his hands and thrust his tongue in her mouth as he slid his cock back inside her.

———————— , ————————

Nick woke from a dead sleep to the sound of his phone buzzing. Sometime in the middle of the night, he and Brenda had made it to the bed. Maybe the fifth time they'd made love.

He hugged her warm, naked body next to him, dread balling in his belly as he remembered the case.

The evidence in Brenda's house he should have logged in last night.

The phone call from Jake, informing him about that anonymous tip.

The fact that Seven might have been trying to frame Brenda for her crimes.

But why? What did she have against Brenda?

The phone buzzed again, a grating sound that made him slip from bed to grab it. Still Brenda's voluptuous naked body sprawled on the sheets temped him to chuck the call and go back to her.

But Dr. Bullock's name flashed on the caller ID screen, and he punched connect. "Special Agent Blackwood."

"This is Dr. Bullock, I have you on a three-way with the sheriff."

Nick and Jake exchanged hellos.

"What's going on?" Nick asked.

Dr. Bullock spoke up, "I have some interesting results from Ron Stowe's autopsy."

"What did you find?" Jake asked.

A hesitation, and Nick heard Bullock moving around. "There were two blood samples that I extracted from his body."

Nick's pulse jumped. "Two?"

"Yes," Bullock said. "The first belonged to the victim. But the killer must have drawn her own blood because the second type belongs to a female."

Meaning they had DNA. Finally a break. "Have you identified her?"

"Yes and no," Bullock said. "I've run it through every database I have, and there's no match in the system."

"Then it'll only help us if we find her and then run the match," Jake said.

"That's not entirely true," Bullock said. "The blood does have genetic markers that link it to two people in our system."

Nick scraped a hand through his hair, his agitation mounting. "Spit it out, Doctor."

Bullock exhaled noisily. "The genetic markers indicate the woman is related to the two of you."

Silence fell for a strained second, and then he and Jake both spoke at once.

"What the hell?" Jake mumbled.

"That's impossible," Nick said.

"You two don't have a sister or other close female relative?" Bullock asked.

"No," Jake said quickly.

"We *had* a sister," Nick said, his mind searching for answers. "But she died at birth."

"I don't have the explanation, only the facts. Science doesn't lie," Bullock said. "This blood definitely belonged to a female, and it matches your blood, as well as the Commander's."

Nick's head rolled.

"The Commander could have had another child," Jake said, obviously thinking out loud. "Perhaps with another woman."

Nick had never considered that possibility. "That's true. He was missing for ten years. He could have another entire family we know nothing about."

Brenda had awakened and sat up, tugging the covers up over her. He missed the sight of that gorgeous naked body already.

But he had to focus, and she was a distraction, so he turned away from her. The very idea that he had a sibling he didn't know about was shocking, but to think she was the killer they were after stirred doubts and anger.

"He probably kept this family a secret for a reason," Jake suggested.

"Because he abused this girl," Nick said, his mind desperate for answers. "She probably realized what happened to her when the Commander was arrested. That was her trigger to start killing."

"There's another possibility," Jake said.

Nick's blood ran cold. "That our sister didn't die like he told us."

Jake cursed. "Yes. He faked his own death. He could have faked hers."

Nick sank onto the side of the chaise and dropped his head into his hands. "Then what did he do with her?"

The second that stretched between them filled with the answers both of them wanted to avoid.

"He put her in the experiment," Nick finally said.

"We don't know that." Jake shifted. "We don't even know for sure if she was the sister we thought died. The idea of another family is entirely possible."

Yes, it was. But still…"There's one way to find out," Nick said. "We have to exhume her body. If the grave is empty, we'll have our answer."

"I'll make the arrangements," Jake said.

"I'll meet you at the cemetery. And Jake—"

"Yeah?"

"There's something I have to tell you." He glanced at Brenda, who was still watching him, waiting for answers. "Last night someone broke into Brenda's apartment and left a roll of piano wire and a baggie of the skin samples the killer took from the victims on her bed. I'll bring those to send to forensics."

Jake grunted. "You didn't feel the need to do that last night?"

Nick hated the disapproval in his brother's tone. "Brenda walked in on Seven and took a blow to the head. She was unconscious when I arrived. The killer planted the evidence here to incriminate her."

Another muttered curse. "All right. But get that evidence logged in and analyzed asap."

"Did you find out anything on those names the computer analyst sent from Stowe's computer?"

"The head of the Maidens vouched for all her girls."

"I'm surprised she talked to you."

"It took some persuading, but once I assured her I didn't intend to prosecute her or bust up her escort service, she agreed. In fact, she looked into her clients, and all of them had alibis for the night Stowe was murdered."

Dammit, another dead end.

"I'll call about a warrant," Jake said. "I want that grave exhumed this morning."

Nick mumbled agreement, then ended the call and reached for his clothes. "What's going on?" Brenda asked. "What's this about blood work and a sister?"

Nick's emotions snowballed. He'd allowed himself to get way too close to Brenda. He'd spilled secrets about his father's abuse, knowing she was writing a story about the Commander and the subjects.

Knowing she could expose private thoughts he didn't want divulged.

"I have to go."

Brenda grabbed his arm. "Wait, Nick, talk to me. Tell me what's going on."

He gritted his teeth. "You want me to tell you what's going on, but you don't share, Brenda. You just dig around in everyone else's lives and expose their secrets for the world."

"That my job, Nick," Brenda said. "This town deserves to know what happened to their children."

"What about your secrets?" Nick said, his voice harsh. "Why don't you write your own story instead of everyone else's?"

Shock flared in Brenda's eyes. "What do you mean?"

"You know what I mean." Nick had protected himself for years from letting anyone know the truth about what his father had done to him. Yet Brenda had seduced the truth right out of him.

"No, I don't, Nick. Last night we shared an incredible night, and I thought we were close. I just want to help you."

"If you want to help me, tell me what you know about Seven."

Brenda's eyes widened with uncertainty. "I don't know anything about her except that she's contacted me for some reason."

"Stop lying!" Nick shouted.

Brenda took a step back. "I'm not."

"Yes, you are!" Nick clutched her arms and shook her. "You were at the sanitarium. For God's sake, you met her there, didn't you?"

———————— , ————————

Anguish robbed Brenda's breath at the condemnation in Nick's tone. She shook her head in denial, but the screams of the teenager needing help taunted her.

She hadn't shared that memory with Nick.

Nor had she told him about her stay in the hospital.

So how had he known?

Realization dawned, and hurt spiraled through her. "You investigated me, didn't you?"

Nick's mouth compressed into a straight line. "Brenda—"

"You did, didn't you?" She pushed her tangled hair from her face. Hair tangled from his hands and their night of frenzied lovemaking. He'd taken her on the chaise, the bed, the floor, in the shower...

She'd given him everything she had, including her heart.

But Nick had never trusted her. Instead, he'd dug up dirt in case he needed leverage against her.

"What were you going to do with what you found, Nick? Blackmail me with it if I decided to reveal something you didn't like?"

Nick started to respond but clamped his mouth closed. She had her answer.

"I think you'd better leave." She gestured to the disgusting baggie and piano wire. "And take that with you."

What was she going to tell her boss? She had to finish the story.

But she couldn't work yet, not when Nick's masculine scent still clung to her body and sheets and...when she wanted him again, even though he'd betrayed her.

So she shoved him toward the door, struggling to hold back the tears until she'd slammed it shut and locked it behind him.

———————— , ————————

Nick's stomach knotted into a fist as he drove to the cemetery. He had hurt Brenda.

Fuck. He hadn't meant to reveal that he knew anything about her past, but the shock of Bullock's phone call, the anonymous tip the night before, the evidence Seven had left at Brenda's, and the fact that he'd just slept with her and poured out his soul had triggered him to lash out at her.

She hadn't deserved it.

He wanted to go back in and apologize and pull her back into bed with him. For the two of them to forget this case and concentrate on making love again.

But that wasn't who he was.

He was a lawman.

He had to chase the leads wherever they took him.

Dr. Bullock and Jake were waiting for him at the graveyard when he arrived, Jake's face as grim as his. "It took some time to get the paperwork in order," Jake said, "but under the circumstances the judge readily agreed."

A team was in place to exhume the grave, had already placed a tent around it for privacy purposes. The extra coffin was waiting in the hearse in case they needed to transport the remains to the medical examiner's office for an autopsy.

"I requested the medical records on Mom and the baby," Nick said. "But apparently they couldn't be found."

"What a surprise," Jake muttered as he gestured for the team to begin digging.

Nick and Jake grew quiet, each of them turning inward as the gravity of the situation settled in.

All their lives, they believed they'd lost their mother in childbirth, and that the baby hadn't made it either. A little girl that they'd never met or known.

And now she might be alive.

"There is a coffin," one of the workers said a few minutes later, his shovel hitting stone.

"Let's pull it up," Nick said.

Jake crossed his arms, his anger as palpable. Had their father lied to them all these years? Was their baby sister really alive?

Chapter 25

———————— o ————————

B renda scrubbed herself in the shower, desperate to erase Nick's scent from her skin.

She was such a fool.

She'd fallen in love with him, and he'd dug into her private past. Tears blurred her vision, and she doubled over as a sob escaped her.

He knew that she'd been at the sanitarium.

Knew her deepest, darkest secret, that she'd had a breakdown, an identity crisis.

She soaped and rinsed her hair, closing her eyes as the tears fell.

Was that the reason he'd questioned her about that phone call tip? Had he thought that she was so emotionally unstable that she'd actually resort to murder?

No...

Memories of him kissing her flooded her. Surely he hadn't made love to her with those doubts in his mind.

No, he hadn't made love to her. Any emotions were all in *her* mind. To him, he'd simply had sex.

Maybe he used women all the time.

The shower water was turning cold, so she flipped it off, grabbed a towel, and dried off. She yanked on her robe, then combed her hair and stared at her face in the mirror.

Bruises from the accident still discolored her cheeks, her eyes were puffy and red from crying, and she looked...haunted.

As she calmed, the conversation she'd overheard between Nick and his brother echoed in her head. Nick had been talking to Jake about his sister. But his sister was dead.

Or at least they'd thought so. Did they now have reason to believe that wasn't true?

Why did Seven contact you?

Originally she'd thought it was to gain publicity for the crimes.

But had she planned to frame Brenda all along?

And if so, why?

Her head was swimming.

Her reasons must have to do with that sanitarium...

For years, Brenda had tried so hard to block out her stay there, but she needed to remember.

Maybe Seven thought Brenda had abandoned her, like everyone else in her life had.

Was she exacting revenge against her by setting her up for the murders?

———————·———————

Nick stared at the empty grave in shock.

Jake squatted down to examine the small coffin. "Fucking unbelievable."

"But why?" Nick asked. "And what the hell did he do to her?"

"Good question," Jake said as the ME shook his head in disbelief. "He could have given her up for adoption when Mom died."

"Because he didn't know how to raise a girl?" Nick said aloud.

"Hell, he didn't know how to raise us," Jake said.

A million scenarios ran through Nick's head, none of them pleasant. "I hope he did give her to a nice family."

"I don't believe that, and neither do you," Jake said. "The blood work tells the story."

Nick nodded, then raked a hand across the mounds of twigs and debris that had blown across their mother's grave. A bone-deep ache stole his breath. "If he lied about our sister, maybe he lied about Mom, too."

Jake shaded his eyes with his hand. "At this point, we can't believe anything he said. We'll have to exhume her grave to find out."

Nick agreed, grateful Jake had had the foresight to obtain a warrant for both graves in advance. Memories of his childhood years tortured him, though, as he watched the gravediggers start working on his mother's grave.

All those times his father had abused him, verbally and physically—if his mother was alive, had she known and allowed it to happen?

He'd assumed that his father had hidden the episodes from her when he was little. In fact, he had only been two when she died, and barely remembered anything about her. Except her sweet smell, like some kind of perfumed powder, and her tender, soft voice as she sang lullabies to him before bedtime.

He remembered talk about a new baby, and one night touching her big belly and feeling a movement as the baby kicked.

But the next night he woke to her screaming and remembered blood, and his father had rushed her to the hospital.

When his father returned, he was alone.

The wind had been howling that night, the screen door slapping against the frame as the Commander told them their mother and the baby were gone.

After that, the Commander became a monster.

Now, the ominous sound of the shovel scraping away dirt and rock reverberated in the tension-filled air as the men heaved dirt off the grave and threw it into a pile to the side.

Jake stepped aside to phone Sadie, while Nick watched. He couldn't wrap his head around the idea that his mother might be alive. If she was, where had she been?

With his sister?

Somehow, he couldn't imagine the woman with the sweet scent and soft voice standing by and allowing her husband to abuse her children as the Commander had.

He couldn't imagine *any* mother allowing that kind of abuse. Yet he knew that it happened. He'd seen it on the job. Heard stories that still shocked him, made him wonder if there was any good left in the world.

The wind swirled dead leaves around his feet, then voices shouted as the steel casket came into view. They all stood back as the machine lifted the slick gray coffin and maneuvered it to the ground beside the grave.

Jake returned, his gaze meeting Nick's, full of unspoken questions, as the men pried the lid of the coffin open.

───────────── , ─────────────

Brenda needed to talk to her source at the hospital. Maybe she could fill in the missing pieces in Brenda's memory.

Jake had pushed her to reveal her source's name during the investigation into Walt Nettleton's death. But Brenda had promised to keep the woman anonymous, to protect her.

She dialed the number from memory. If she'd programmed the name into her contact list, anyone, especially the police, could have gained access to it, and Brenda refused to endanger her.

The phone rang a half dozen times, then rolled to voice mail, and she left a message. "The Slaughter Creek Strangler killed the senator's son. I think she's trying to frame me. Please call me."

The clock struck ten, and she frowned. Ron Stowe's funeral was at two o'clock. She had hours before then.

Taking a chance that her source might be at work, she quickly dressed for the funeral in a black dress, then, deciding that Ron would have liked a little color, added a red scarf. She grabbed her phone and purse and drove to the sanitarium.

A storm was brewing outside, the wind hurling debris across the winding road as she climbed the mountain. Headlights from an oncoming car nearly blinded her, and she braked, hugging the side of the road, her earlier accident flashing through her mind. The car raced on, leaving the deserted stretch of road pitch-dark.

When her parents admitted Brenda to the hospital for treatment, she'd been angry and resentful. She'd also been plagued with awful dreams about who her real mother could have been.

Sometimes she imagined that a rich teenage actress had given birth to her, and was now famous and living in Hollywood. Other times she thought maybe her mother had been raped and couldn't stand the sight of her. And sometimes she imagined that her mother had wanted her desperately, but that she'd died and was watching her from heaven.

But then there was the recurring dream about the homeless crackhead.

Come on, baby girl, a voice inside her head whispered. *Just crawl in this alley and we'll hide for a while. We'll find something to eat when the restaurant closes down.*

That *had* been a dream, hadn't it?

Because the crackhead reminded her of the woman in her other nightmares. Especially the one in which she was four, living on the streets with this woman.

An image of a particular nasty day flashed back. It had been pouring down rain and freezing, and Brenda's head was stuffed up. One minute she was cold, the next burning up.

The woman was tall, rail thin, had scraggly brown hair and hollowed-out eyes. Her skin was an ugly yellow color, and sores covered her arms and face.

"I'm cold." Ice crunched below her feet. Her socks had holes in them, the toes of her sneakers worn so thin she felt the sludge from the alley bite at her toes. "Mama, I don't wanna go in there."

"Shut up." Mama's thin body trembled as she dragged Brenda inside a rotting building that smelled like vomit. The faint light of a cigarette glowed in the corner.

"Please, Mama," Brenda cried.

"I said shut up! This won't take but a minute."

Brenda bit her tongue. She hated it when her mama yelled like that. Hated the dark places they hid and slept. She wanted to go someplace nice and warm with real food her mama cooked on a stove, not the scraps other folks throwed in the trash.

Sometimes Mama found peanut butter sandwiches behind the school, but they had bugs in them that crunched between her teeth. And spaghetti from the Dumpster, but the cheese tasted funny and something green was growing on the bread.

Her stomach was growling now. She tried to remember when they'd last eaten. Yesterday. Or maybe the day before.

Men's voices rumbled from the corner as her mama's shoes shuffled across the concrete floor. There were three men, all big, nasty looking, and they smelled rotten like old bananas and sour milk and sweat and pee.

She ducked behind her mama, hanging on to the tail of her shirt.

Her mama reached out her hand to the man. "Here."

The big man with the lizard drawing all over his arm took the cash her mama handed him. "You know the price. This ain't it."

Mama's knees were shaking so bad they knocked together. "Just give it to me now, and I'll bring the rest later."

"You want it, Jo-Lynn, you gotta play nice."

"I'm good for it, Leroy—"

The man's big hand grabbed her mama by the neck. Brenda was so scared she thought she was going to wet herself.

Mama's neck looked like a chicken's, it was so skinny, and blue lines crisscrossed her thin hands. "Just give it to me, and I'll do whatever you want."

The man's nasty laugh bellowed through the building. "Damn right you will, bitch."

Mama swayed for a minute, her bones cracking. Sweat broke out on her mama's arms. She needed the medicine bad.

"All right." Mama turned to her. "Go over in the corner and wait, baby. I'll be back."

Brenda clutched her mama's hand. "No, don't leave me, Mama—"

Mama's eyes turned wild then, and she slapped Brenda across the face. "I said get over there and shut up."

Brenda's face stung as she hit the floor on her butt.

"Move it!" Mama yelled.

Tears flooded Brenda's eyes as she crawled to the corner by a bunch of cardboard boxes. If the men left them here, maybe they could sleep in one of the boxes tonight. It would be better than on the wet ground.

But she didn't want to stay if those bad men were here.

Noises sounded from the corner, the big man cussing.

Scared he'd come after her, she hugged her knees to her and buried her head in her arms. But she peeked up to see what they were doing to her mama.

The man with the cigarette stubbed out his cigarette. They pushed her mama against the wall and started tearing at her clothes, making animal noises.

Mama's cries and grunts blended with the men's. Brenda closed her eyes and tried to drown them out. But suddenly she heard footsteps. She smelled one of the men coming closer. His hand touched her hair.

"Come on, girl."

Brenda screamed as his fingers curled around her wrist. He dragged her up, pulling her toward the other corner. Mama shouted, tore loose, ran over, and started beating the man with her fists.

"Run, Brenda, run!" Mama shouted.

Brenda kicked and screamed, then finally sank her teeth into his big hairy fist. He tasted gross, but she bit him harder, and he bellowed, then let go of her...

The sanitarium slipped into view, tearing Brenda from the disturbing images.

But a bad feeling seeped through her. Maybe that hadn't been a dream...

She parked at the sanitarium, reminding herself that she'd come on a mission. The trees rustled with the wind as she walked up to the front. The stone turrets and gray mausoleum structure triggered other memories, ones that bordered on her memory banks but were still out of reach, as if obscured by a thick, dark fog.

Once in the building, she walked to the nurses' desk and checked to see if her source was on duty. She was, so Brenda rode the elevator to the second floor.

A bustling hubbub of carts and voices greeted her as the elevator doors opened, and the pungent odor of alcohol, medicine, and fear permeated the air, making her stomach cramp. She turned, tempted to leave. Desperate to escape this place.

But she couldn't. She needed answers. She needed to see the basement, where the experiments had been conducted. After Arthur Blackwood's arrest, the police had sealed off the basement as a crime scene, and a forensic team had spent hours investigating and searching for evidence.

Now, she spotted the person she'd come to see.

Mazie.

The nurse motioned for Brenda to follow her to the break room.

"I want to see the basement," Brenda said.

Worry deepened the grooves around Mazie's age-lined eyes, then she gestured for her to follow her. "I guess it's time you did."

———— , ————

The bones in the coffin looked stark against the satin lining.

Jake raked a hand through his hair. "Well, he didn't lie about Mom."

Nick released a sigh. "It appears that way. But I want an autopsy to verify that these are her remains." He struggled to wipe emotion from his voice. "And to verify cause of death."

Jake's face paled. "What are you suggesting? That she didn't die in childbirth?"

Nick shrugged. "After all of Dad's lies, he could have killed her."

———— , ————

Seven carefully cut out the photograph of the senator's son from the article on the front page of the newspaper, then added it to the collage on her wall. The other men who'd paid were there as well.

Brenda Banks's photograph was situated in the center.

Even though the men had hurt her, had kept her prisoner so the Commander could continue his torture, she hated Brenda more than the men.

Because the Commander had spared Brenda, had saved her, when he had used *her* in his experiments as if she were nothing more than a lab rat.

The anguished face of the senator and his wife mocked her from the paper, and she took the scissors and slashed at the image, slicing straight across the senator's face. Sweat dampened her palms as she mutilated his eyes and chin and nose until there was nothing left but tiny pieces of yellowed paper that she dusted off the table into the trash.

Pinpricks of joy mingled with rage, inciting her to mentally scroll down her list.

Brenda had to pay for leaving her there all those years. For being who she was.

Then she would deal with the Commander.

Chapter 26

———— o ————

Brenda's nerves tingled as Mazie led her down to the basement.

The dusty concrete walls echoed with the screams of children. Or maybe that was all in Brenda's head, put there by what she'd learned.

"You knew what they were doing, Mazie?" Brenda asked.

The older woman shook her head. "No, not exactly. I got suspicious later, but Mr. Blackwood always had answers to cover things up. And Dr. Sanderson and Dr. Coker were always so generous donating their time at the free clinic that I never dreamed they'd hurt a child."

"But they did." Brenda touched the old gurneys that were pushed against the wall, disturbed at the sight of the restraints attached to the beds. The scent of chemicals, blood, and body wastes still permeated the air, the floor discolored with stains that had come from God only knew what.

"I didn't know about the basement until the sheriff and his brother found out what was happening here," Mazie continued.

"Why did you decide to call me?" Brenda asked.

"Grace Granger," Mazie said. "I was in her room the night we thought she was coming out of her coma. She said some things that made me think back."

"What kinds of things?" Brenda asked.

Mazie scratched her head. "About being taken to the basement," Mazie said. "I don't know if it was the coma, but it was like she suddenly remembered being here as a little girl and was describing things in detail. I started remembering then, and wondering."

"Then Grace died?"

Mazie nodded, the dark circles under her eyes more pronounced in the dimly lit basement.

"Do you remember being down here?" Mazie asked.

Brenda glanced at Mazie, a snippet of a memory assaulting Brenda. She was four years old, hiding in the corner, her hands pressed over her ears. Noises...the carts clanging, the instruments scraping against metal, voices...

The cries...

"Yes, I was here," Brenda said, her heart hammering. "I don't understand why, though..."

She slowly turned in a wide circle, her body trembling as she was launched back to that day.

A loud scream, a woman's voice, then sobs louder than she'd ever heard before. "Take her, get rid of her, I don't want her anymore."

Brenda lay limp on a bed, like a rag doll. Her body ached all over. Her head and stomach hurt. What had happened?

Why was Mama screaming? Where were they?

Clang, clang. More rattling. A terrible smell like medicine. A man's deep voice ordering them to stick a needle in her.

She tried to fight it, kicked and yelled. She hated needles. But they stuck it in her anyway, and she started to cry.

Then it was dark. So dark she could barely see. Her eyes felt heavy. Her stomach twisted, like she was going to throw up. The room was cold, and she cried for her mama.

But no one was there.

Except in her mind there were men, men reaching for her. Pulling her down with their dirty hands. Tearing at her clothes.

No! She screamed and kicked. She didn't want them to take off her clothes…

Then she looked down and realized she had on some kind of gown. She was in a bed. A real bed. But this bed had metal bars on the side. And it smelled stinky.

Someone was crying. Screaming. Was it her?

She rolled sideways. She had to get away.

She grabbed the metal bar and slid down from the bed. It was a long drop to the floor, and she hit it and fell on her bottom. Her foot hurt, but she rubbed at it and stood. Then she sneaked to the door and peeked outside. A chubby lady in a white uniform rushed by. More noises down the hall.

A man in a white coat.

She must be in a hospital. Was Mama here? Had she come here to get her medicine?

Maybe that was Mama crying down the hall…

She pushed open the door and snuck into the hall, then followed the sound. Two steps, three. She was dizzy and stumbled. She reached for the wall, but it was cold and slimy.

Tears pushed at her eyes, but she swiped them away. Crying didn't do no good. Mama told her that.

She had to find her now. But it was dark all around her. Just a little thin light streamed from down the hall. If she could make it to the light, maybe she'd find Mama and get out.

She stumbled again, then dragged herself up and walked to the end of the hall. The door was cracked. That was where the light was coming from. There were steps, too.

She held on to the rail and inched down the first step. But her stomach quivered when she heard another cry.

This time it didn't sound like her mama. It was another little girl.

Were they hurting her?

Trembling with fear, she started to turn around and run back up the steps. Then she saw the girl. She had long dark hair and big dark eyes.

"Help me," the little girl cried. "Please, help me."

Brenda couldn't swallow. What were they doing down here in the dark?

Then she saw the tall man standing over the girl. His hair was black, his ears big. He had something shiny in his hand. And something else shiny on his finger.

A ring. Gold. It had a black middle with some letter on it.

The girl screamed again.

Brenda turned to run for help. But big arms snatched her up. Then everything disappeared as she was pitched into the dark.

"Brenda, are you okay?"

Brenda stumbled and found herself hugging the wall, her breath coming out in sharp, uneven pants. She was confused. She'd been admitted to the hospital as a teenager, not as a young child.

Or had she been here when she was little as well? "I was here," she said. "I have to find out the dates."

Mazie rubbed Brenda's back. "We could check records."

Brenda nodded. "Then let's check them. I have to find out what happened back then. I think the woman who's strangling men in Slaughter Creek was here at the same time I was."

Seven must have recognized her from the news story and reached out to her, hoping she wouldn't let her down this time as she had back then.

Nick finished his cup of coffee and tossed the Styrofoam cup into the trash as he paced outside the ME's office. It had taken forever to move his mother's body to the morgue, and now he was waiting on the ME to confirm that the bones belonged to his mother.

He and Jake had considered interrogating their father again, but they'd decided to go armed with all the information they could gather when they did.

He sucked in a sharp breath, wondering where Brenda was. She'd been so upset this morning, misunderstanding everything. He slid his phone from his pocket to call her, but Dr. Bullock poked his head out of the door.

"Come on in, Agent Blackwood."

Nick shoved his phone into his pocket and followed the medical examiner. Dr. Culpepper, the forensic anthropologist Dr. Bullock had called in, stood over the bones on the table.

For a moment, Nick couldn't breathe. The remains had once belonged to the woman who'd given birth to him. The woman who'd changed his diapers, cuddled him when he was a baby, and rocked him to sleep.

Dr. Culpepper peered through her goggles. "We haven't confirmed her identity yet," she said. "I've requested dental records to verify. They're being faxed over."

Nick nodded. "What can you tell me?"

"Judging from the skull and hip bones, I can confirm that this body belonged to a female, late twenties. The bones indicate that she sustained a fractured arm and that she was anemic when she died. Also, she gave birth more than once."

A fax machine made a noise, and Dr. Bullock went to check it.

"My father said my mother died in childbirth," Nick said. "Is that true?"

Dr. Bullock cleared his throat. "Come here, Agent Blackwood. The computer is running a comparison of your mother's dental records to the teeth we found with the bones."

Nick stepped over beside the medical examiner and watched as the computer presented various images, comparing angles and different teeth.

"This program makes identification fast and accurate," Dr. Bullock explained. "I had to fight the county to buy it. Good thing, with all the trouble we've had in Slaughter Creek lately."

And all due to his father.

A noise sounded, and a positive match showed on the screen.

The ache in Nick's chest held tight. He hated to admit it, but some part of him had latched on to the hope that his mother might still be alive.

God. He wished his father had died instead.

"So my mother was buried in that grave, but my sister survived," Nick said.

And now she was on a killing spree.

The forensic specialist made a low noise in her throat. "You probably want to look at this, Agent Blackwood."

The anxiety in his belly intensified as he walked over to stand beside her. Emotions he didn't want to feel rose, but he swallowed them back, forcing himself to remain in professional mode.

Instead of struggling to remember the face that had gone with these bones.

"Look at these markings on her skull. These were caused by a blow to her head." She stepped to the head of the table, carefully angling the skeleton to point out the indentations. "That blow cracked the bone here and caused a brain hemorrhage, which in my opinion was the cause of death."

Nick saw red. His mother hadn't died as a result of childbirth complications. Someone had murdered her.

And he knew who it was.

He reached for his phone to call Jake.

"I'm not supposed to show this room to anyone," Mazie said as she led Brenda into a neighboring storage room where old files were stacked. The room was dark and musty, the boxes damp with mold.

"We're looking for *my* file," Brenda said. "It's not like we're violating someone else's medical history."

"I suppose you're right." Mazie's shoes squeaked on the cement floor. "But I'd still get into trouble."

Brenda jumped at the sound of a mouse in the corner, then silently chided herself. "I thought the old files burned."

"The ones from the free clinic did, and some of the hospital files were lost in another fire," Mazie said. "But some were saved and moved in here."

Mazie gestured toward the third row, and they began examining the dates and years on the sides of the file boxes.

"Why haven't the police seen them?" Brenda asked.

"Because no one told them about these files." Mazie's face paled. "I suppose I should do that."

Brenda nodded. "The files need to be examined," she said. "We might discover the names of other victims in here." She visually scrolled down the dates on the boxes on the next shelf, wiping away dust to read the year.

She stood on tiptoe and dragged the first box off the shelf, then the other two, and set them on the floor. Mazie took one, and Brenda grabbed another, wiping dust from the top as she lifted the lid. File folders were crammed into the box in alphabetical order.

Dust motes swirled in the air as they plowed through each file.

"There's nothing under the name Banks," Mazie said.

Realization dawned. "That's because I was adopted," Brenda said. "Look for a little girl around four who was brought in for an injury."

"That's odd. This has always been a psychiatric hospital," Mazie said, yanking out a file and thumbing through it.

"I can't explain," Brenda said, desperate to sort out the truth. "I just know I was here. That I was hurt. And that my real mother might have been here, too. Maybe for rehab."

Mazie's eyebrow twitched as she examined another folder. They worked for another few minutes, and Brenda checked her watch. Another hour before she needed to be at the senator's son's funeral. Not that they would welcome her, but she wanted to pay her respects. And Seven might show.

"Here." Mazie waved a folder at her. "A four-year-old girl named Ann was brought in with her heroin-addicted mother. The mother was raped, and the child…beaten and traumatized. The doctor who saw her thought she had witnessed her mother's attack."

"Who was that doctor?"

"Dr. Sanderson," Mazie said, her voice cracking. "Good lord, he was part of the project."

Nausea rolled through Brenda, but the memory fit. "Ann is my middle name."

Mazie handed her the file. "I'm sorry, hon, but there's not much here. Just a notation that Child and Family Services was called."

Brenda frantically skimmed the file, hoping to find something Mazie missed, but the nurse was right.

At least now the nightmares she'd had over the years made sense.

Because they were real.

But why would people like Agnes and William Banks adopt a traumatized child through Child and Family Services, instead of paying to privately adopt a healthy newborn?

———————— . ————————

Seven pressed her foot on the man's chest and smiled as a whimper gurgled from his throat.

"Who are you?" he rasped. "Why are you doing this to me?"

She dropped down and straddled him, her bare crotch rubbing against his naked chest. The friction felt heavenly, giving her a rush. "You don't remember me, do you?"

His eyes narrowed as he searched his memory banks for some lost thread of a recollection. But his eyes registered blank.

That was one reason he had to die.

If some fuck was going to hold her hostage, make her do unspeakable things, the sick cocksucker should at least remember her.

She gripped the ends of the piano wire around his throat. His eyes bulged with shock and fear as it bit into his neck.

"Please...I'll do anything," he moaned.

"Too late for bargaining." She raked her tongue up the side of his face.

Elation filled her as she closed the wire, pressing it into his flesh so deeply that he coughed and his legs began to kick as he bucked, fighting to get free. An image of Arthur Blackwood filled her vision, and pain rocked through her, driving her to tighten the wire, squeezing and pressing as she held his body down with her legs.

Finally he choked and gasped and gave in to death.

A smile creased her lips.

Time to revive him and watch the horror on his face as he realized he had to die again.

Chapter 27

B renda had to rush from the sanitarium to Ron Stowe's
funeral.

The parking lot was packed with Mercedes, BMWs, Lincolns,
and other expensive cars. She spotted her mother's silver Jaguar
two rows from the side entrance of the chapel, but she had to
park across the street in the overflow lot.

Slaughter Creek had never had such a turnout for a funeral,
and probably never would again. Since the senator had lived in
Slaughter Creek years ago and had buried his parents here in the
local cemetery, he'd chosen to bury his son with them.

Security for the senator was obviously on high alert; guards
flanked the entryway and side exits to the chapel, and Deputy
Waterstone stood at the door as well. There were probably more
bodyguards inside.

Two other guards manned the entrance to keep the press
out. Both the senator and police had agreed to ban them out of
respect for the family's loss. One reason she'd left Louis behind.

Again Brenda wondered why Seven had murdered Ron. He
had nothing in common with the other victims, or with Arthur
Blackwood. Still, somehow he'd crossed paths with Seven.

Unless Seven simply wanted to up her game by murdering someone in the public eye.

Sliding on her suit jacket, Brenda climbed from her car, falling in behind an elderly couple and another couple in their thirties who looked familiar. Maybe from the senator's campaign?

A twentysomething brunette dabbed at her eyes as she entered, sparking Brenda's curiosity. Had she dated Ron?

No…she'd seen her picture in some of the photos documenting the senator's campaign.

Organ music flowed from the chapel, the bodyguards studying each individual in case the killer showed up and attacked the senator or his wife during the service.

Brenda's heart picked up a beat. Maybe she was here already. Hiding among the crowd so she could observe the mourners crying over the loss of the young man she'd brutally strangled.

Senses alert, she discreetly used her cell phone and snapped photographs of all the young women in the crowded chapel. Three—no, four—blondes, two more brunettes, a woman with striking red hair, another with a short spiky brown cut.

Someone nudged her from behind, and she shifted, but realized it was a white-haired woman with a cane who'd lost her balance. The woman's husband gripped her arm to steady her, and Brenda slid into a back pew to let them pass.

The service began, the sound of sobbing echoing through the room as prayers, scripture, and music honored the man's death. The coffin at the front was draped with a blanket of red roses, every space available filled with sprays of fresh flowers.

Ron's father stood to give the eulogy. "I don't know if I can get through this," he said, "but unfortunately Martin Laddermilk, my assistant, had a last-minute emergency and couldn't be here." The senator wiped at his eyes, and grief laced his voice as he began.

Brenda scanned the chapel for Nick but didn't see him or Jake. Odd.

The senator's speech was eloquent, emotional, touching. There wasn't a dry eye in the chapel.

The service finally ended, the pallbearers lifted the coffin, and the Stowes rose and followed behind, hands clasped, heads bowed in grief. Brenda's parents went next, obviously hovering close for support. Her father's eyebrows narrowed into a frown as he passed her.

A pang of regret sliced at her, but she swallowed back the guilt, determined to remain alert and study the crowd for Seven.

Would she recognize her if she saw her?

Fellow mourners rose, and the chapel emptied, hushed voices and sniffles trailing outside. Car doors slammed as people departed, a small crowd gathering in the cemetery for the graveside service.

Senator Stowe cradled his wife's arm and helped her into one of the lawn chairs set up beneath the funeral home tent, a few close friends taking seats while another small cluster of the senator's constituents stood respectfully by.

Brenda remained on the periphery, once again scrutinizing the women. Driven by the wind, a cluster of faded plastic flowers from another grave skittered across the grass, and tree limbs bowed as if a ghost had just passed.

Brenda turned to search the trees in case Seven was hiding there, but shadows flickered, the skies casting a dismal gray across the woods and making it difficult to see through the dense copse.

Brenda's phone buzzed, and people turned to glare at her. Instantly hitting the button to mute it, she walked a few feet away to check the message.

If you want my story, meet me at the old 4-H camp. Seven.

She scanned the crowd to see if anyone was using a cell phone, but all heads were bowed in prayer. Gathering her coat around her, she headed to her car, walking slowly, as her heels kept sinking into the soft, wet ground.

As she climbed into the driver's seat, Brenda punched Nick's number to tell him about the message, but his phone rang a half dozen times with no answer. She left him a voice mail asking him to call her, then sped from the parking lot.

If she could convince Seven to turn herself in, maybe the Stowes and her parents could forgive her for Ron's death.

———————— , ————————

Nick studied the layout of Martin Laddermilk's house as he got out of his sedan and climbed the steps to the Georgian home. Panicking when he couldn't reach Laddermilk before his son's funeral, Stowe had called Jake.

But Amelia was also missing, and Sadie was frantic, so Jake was searching for her, leaving him to check out this call.

He rang the doorbell a dozen times, scanning the immaculately kept grounds in case a gardener or worker was around. The security gate and location of the estate provided privacy and spoke of old money, just as the statuesque Georgian home did.

But Nick was unimpressed. He'd watched Laddermilk's interviews during the senator's campaign, and he thought something about the man was seedy. Maybe it was that pencil-thin mustache, or the glint of deception in his eyes.

Satisfied no one was going to answer, he turned the doorknob, but it was locked. He took out his tiny lock-picking device and pried open the door, surprised that the house's alarm system didn't launch into a pealing tirade.

Because someone had already disarmed it?

The scent of an expensive cigar filled the air, mixed with the odor of some kind of cleaner, and he drew his gun and inched inside.

"TBI—Mr. Laddermilk?" Nick called. "If you're here, please show yourself."

Silence met his voice, his words echoing through the two-story foyer. The place was decorated like a showcase, with glistening marble floors, expensive artwork, vases, and antique gilded mirrors.

Nick swept from room to room, identifying himself and calling the man's name. Photographs of a family adorned one wall in a study overflowing with books, several photographs of Laddermilk with the senator at various functions arranged on a bookcase.

One in particular drew his eye, three men smiling at the camera—Laddermilk, the senator, and Mayor Banks.

They had all chosen the political route, and obviously ran in the same circles.

Of the three, Stowe looked the most distinguished, with his charismatic Kennedyesque face. Laddermilk was short and stocky with small round wire-rimmed glasses. Definitely the sidekick, not the star of the show.

And Brenda's father—he was slimmer in the photo, his round face and pudgy body less astute looking, signs of early baldness already evident in his thinning hair.

"Laddermilk?" he shouted as he cleared the kitchen and living area, then started up the winding staircase to the second floor. Storm clouds darkened the sky outside, but a faint stream of sunlight bled through the ten-foot window, illuminating Nick's path as he checked the first bedroom suite. It appeared unlived-in. No clothes in the bedroom, no toiletries in the bath. Judging from the photos downstairs, Laddermilk's children were grown and must be living on their own. He'd read that the man's wife died of a heart attack two years ago.

Nick's boots melted into the thick, plush carpet as he inched down the hall to the master suite.

He halted in the doorway, his gut clenching at the sight before him.

Laddermilk's naked body was tied to the bed, just as they'd found Jim Logger's, a piece of piano wire wound around his neck, his eyes gaping wide in death.

Seven had struck again.

And now it seemed she was targeting people close to the senator. Would he be next?

———————— , ————————

Brenda Googled directions for the old 4-H camp, then programmed it into her GPS. A faint memory of attending one of the summer sessions when she'd won first place for her potato-head doll surfaced, making her smile as she wound through the dark mountain roads.

She was eight and had cut and hand-sewn a dress for the doll, which she'd fashioned by attaching the head to a paper cup. She'd been in that wonderful stage of childhood where she still had an imagination and an openness to friends of all types. And for once, Geraldine had convinced William and Agnes to allow her to attend the camp.

Had Seven been there?

She racked her brain for specifics. A little girl with red pigtails who'd made a Christmas tree skirt out of fabric scraps from her granny's closet. A skinny, quiet girl who'd baked cookies, then decorated them like faces of famous African American women.

A troll of a teenage girl who'd made fun of them, then got her due when fellow campers had fixed a paint can above a doorway and lured her beneath it. It had taken the girl days to wash the orange paint from her blond strands.

The road leading to the camp was long and winding, surrounded by thick rows of pines, oaks, and cypresses. The buildings that housed the 4-H'ers were nestled into the side of the mountain to offer seclusion as well as camping, hiking, swimming, and other nature-related activities.

Brenda retrieved a copy of the sketch Amelia had given her, her rendition of Seven, and mentally tried to match the face of the lonely-looking child in the drawing to girls she'd met at the 4-H camp, but nothing fit.

The forest folded her into its depths as she climbed the hills to the peak where the main part of the camp had been built. Her nerves vibrated with hope that she was finally going to meet the girl she'd left behind at the hospital.

Somehow she had to convince her to stop taking lives.

Slivers of light fought their way through the leaves, dappling the inky darkness as she rolled into the center of the camp. She searched for a car and finally spotted a dark blue Jeep perched at the overhang of the ridge, teetering there as if one wheel had already slid over the edge.

She checked her purse for her weapon, praying she wouldn't need it, but knowing she'd use it if necessary to protect herself. The car door screeched open as she swung her feet around to get out. Gravel crunched beneath her shoes. The last remnants of snowdrifts were beginning to melt, creating a muddy sludge, the scent of spring blending with the smell of damp earth.

She scanned the perimeter, praying Seven didn't jump from the shadows and attack her. There were at least twenty bunkhouses for campers and acres of land donated to the camp for activities, acres where Seven could hide.

Somewhere in the woods animals skittered, and the sound of a gunshot blasted. A hunter?

Was it hunting season?

Jittery with anticipation, Brenda checked her phone again, suddenly wishing she'd waited until Nick had returned her call. But he'd obviously written her off, now that she'd served her purpose.

Still, her text should have made him realize that she was still his best link to Seven.

Inhaling to fortify her courage, she had just decided to try Nick again when she heard piano music wafting from the main lodge at the top of the ridge. She froze.

Seven had killed her victims using piano wire.

She must have brought Brenda here to explain the reason.

Brenda's shoes slipped in the icy sludge as she strode toward the lodge, and she wished she'd changed into boots. The bunkhouses looked run-down and in need of repairs, making her wonder when 4-H had stopped using the camp. Had they chosen another location for their summer retreats?

She stumbled over an uneven patch and slid, windmilling her arms to keep her balance and barely righting herself before she hit the ground. The music grew louder as she approached, the tune a macabre number that she recognized from *The Phantom of the Opera*.

She almost turned and ran back to the car, but she was too close now. She wanted answers.

So she opened the door, the music pounding louder as she stepped inside, the walls vibrating with the bleak intensity of the tune.

The lodge looked dismal and deserted inside, the only light seeping in from the fog-coated windows. The wood floors were dusty and squeaked as she pivoted to search for Seven. Assuming she was playing the piano, Brenda walked toward it, but a board behind her creaked, and suddenly she felt the barrel of a gun stab her back.

"Hello, Brenda," a low, throaty female voice murmured.

Brenda stiffened, forcing herself not to react. She really didn't want a bullet in her back. She took a deep breath, bolstering her courage. "Surely you didn't ask me to come so you could kill me."

A bitter laugh rent the air. "Maybe."

A knot of fear clogged Brenda's throat. She thought about Nick and how they'd left things. How she still wanted him, even though he'd been prying in her past.

"No, I don't think you did. I think you wanted to see me again." Brenda slowly turned to face her. "That you want me to hear your side of the story."

The woman's face was steeped in the shadows, her clothing all black, a dark hoodie over her head.

But a thin stream of light filtered through a hole in the ceiling, and Brenda nearly gasped at the wild look of insanity in her eyes.

"That is what you want," Brenda said quietly. "You want to tell me your story, so everyone will know what happened to you."

Seven's slow smile sent a frisson of alarm up Brenda's spine. "All in good time." She shoved a phone at Brenda. "First, call the Blackwood brothers. I might as well explain it to everyone at the same time."

Brenda's hand felt clammy as she lifted the phone. "Are you going to turn yourself in?"

Another laugh, this one harsh and sinister. "No—I'm going to finish what I've begun."

Brenda's mind raced. Seven wanted her to lure Nick and Jake into a trap. Then she would kill them all.

Chapter 28

———— o ————

"I'm fucking sick of this," Nick muttered as he phoned Jake to relay the news that Laddermilk was dead.

The crime scene unit was already on the way.

"Whoever killed him got past his security system," Nick said.

"Your theory about the killer knowing her victims could be right."

Nick contemplated the killer's signature and checked behind the man's ear. The number four.

Jake cleared his throat. "Hell, she might have posed as someone working with the campaign."

"So he trusted her and let her in."

The crime team's van zoomed into the parking lot. "Pull up photos of a list of all of the senator's staff and volunteers. And let's focus on the ones who recently joined his campaign."

"Good idea, I'll get on it asap," Jake said. "I paid Ms. Lettie a visit today."

"What did she have to say?" Nick asked.

Jake heaved a weary sigh. "She's still not talking. The Commander must have done a number on her head."

"She's probably too afraid to talk. Afraid she'll end up dead." Nick huffed as he hurried down the steps to let the crime techs in. "Did you find Amelia?"

"Yes—she told Sadie she has a boyfriend."

Nick opened the door for the team. "Is she mentally ready for that?"

"Good question," Jake said, his voice worried. "She won't tell Sadie who the guy is either. Sadie encouraged her to talk to her therapist about the man. And she's going to persuade Amelia to let them meet."

Maddison met Nick on the steps. "Which way?"

"Upstairs." Nick's phone was buzzing again, and he checked the number. Brenda.

He led the team inside, hoping they'd find evidence this time. But other than that blood droplet, Seven had left only bread crumbs, teasing them with the fact that, so far, she had escaped detection.

His phone went silent, and he pointed out the master bedroom as they reached the top of the stairs. "In the master suite."

His phone started up again. Brenda.

He punched connect and stepped into the hall as the techs went to work.

"Brenda, I'm in the middle of something. What's going on?" Hell, maybe she knew Laddermilk was dead and was on the way with the news van.

"Nick, please don't hang up," Brenda said in a strained voice. "I'm with Seven."

Nick froze. Seven had Brenda?

———— ⁄ ————

Brenda clutched the phone, desperately searching for a way to warn Nick that he was walking into a trap.

But the odds were that he already knew that.

A deep breath echoed back. "Are you okay?"

The thick ropes Seven had used to tie her to the chair cut into her wrists and ankles. "Yes. But she wants to see you and Jake." So she could kill them all and move on with her killing spree.

"Hang on." He rushed in and told the tech he had to leave, then strode down the front steps of Laddermilk's mansion, already on the way to his car. "Where are you?"

"The lodge at the old 4-H camp. But, Nick—"

"I'm on my way," Nick said. "Just try to keep her calm."

Brenda started to speak again, but Seven grabbed the phone from her hand and disconnected the call.

"Why are you doing this?" Brenda asked. "I thought you wanted me to be your voice, to speak for you and the other subjects, but I can't do that if I'm dead."

Seven's eyes darkened to black, accusing, in the dim light. "You were at the hospital. You know what they did to us."

Brenda shook her head. "I didn't remember what I saw," she said. "Just that I was taken there when I was small, and then again when I was a teenager. But everything in between is a blur."

"You wrote a news story about the experiments," Seven snarled as she circled Brenda. "You painted Jake and Nick Blackwood as heroes. But they aren't. No one is. No one saved us back then."

"Because the families were in the dark," Brenda said, desperate to help Seven understand that the people of Slaughter Creek hadn't intentionally abandoned her. "They were all snowed by the doctors because they were giving free services."

"Then there you were, and you were special," Seven whispered in a voice laced with pain and accusation, as if Brenda had betrayed her.

Brenda dug one finger beneath the rope around her wrist, struggling to untie it. "What do you mean, I was special?"

Dark pools of anguish lined Seven's face. Brenda saw her enormous brown eyes, the eyes that had pleaded for help so many years ago, and felt a pang in her chest.

"He let you go." Seven counted the steps as she circled Brenda. Seven to the right, seven back, seven more...

Brenda's fingers paused in her work. "I don't understand," she finally said. "What do you mean, he let me go?"

Seven waved the knife blade in front of Brenda's eyes, then pressed it to her own arm and punctured the skin, watching as blood pooled on the surface. Brenda noted old scars, fresh ones... Had Seven tried to kill herself or was she a cutter?

Images from her nightmares flashed in Brenda's head.

"That little girl in the basement was you, wasn't it?" she asked.

Seven watched the blood drip from her wrist with a sadistic smile. "Yes. See, you do remember."

"Not everything," Brenda said. "I was brought into the sanitarium because...well...I don't exactly remember everything. I have nightmares about being with a crackhead."

Confusion marred Seven's expression. "No, you were *his*," she said in a high-pitched voice. "So the Commander let you go."

A wave of terror washed over Brenda. "You mean I was part of the experiment?" Brenda asked.

Seven shook her head, a strand of her unruly hair sliding across one cheek. She pushed it back with the hand holding the knife, and a faint stream of light from the window illuminated the scars on her throat.

They were similar to the markings on her victims. The abused had become the abuser.

"Was I part of it?" Brenda asked.

"No!" Seven shouted as if Brenda was an idiot. "I told you he saved you because you were special."

Memories twisted in Brenda's mind. Was Seven delusional, or did she know more about Brenda than Brenda did?

A frisson of panic clawed at her. Faced with the daunting reality that something horrible had happened to her at the hands of her own mother, she wasn't sure she wanted to know the truth. "I wasn't special," Brenda said. "I think my real mother was a drug addict, that she…" What? That she allowed those men to have Brenda, in exchange for drugs?

No…in her dream, the woman had fought for her, told her to run.

So how had they wound up at the hospital?

"Yes, you were special. You belonged to him. He gave you a name, not a number," Seven said, her voice filled with hatred and envy and other emotions Brenda couldn't define.

"Who gave me a name?" Brenda asked, her heart hammering.

Seven held the tip of the knife to Brenda's cheek. "The Commander. You were his."

Panic surged through Brenda. "What do you mean—*his*?"

"His daughter," Seven shouted, her voice brittle. "You were his little girl, so he gave you to a family to keep you safe from the experiment he conducted on us."

Brenda gasped. She was Arthur Blackwood's daughter?

No…that was impossible. She had slept with his son Nick.

———————— · ————————

Nick met Jake on the outskirts of town so they could drive to the 4-H camp together.

"What exactly did Brenda say?" Jake asked as Nick veered onto the mountain road.

"Just that Seven wants to meet us."

"You know it's a setup," Jake said.

"Of course it is." Nick tightened his fingers around the steering wheel. "But we have to go."

Jake nodded. "Maybe this means she's done with her killing spree. That we're her end game."

A frown pulled at Nick's brows. "Then she must know who we are."

Nick checked his weapon. "But why involve Brenda?"

"Good question." Nick didn't like any of the answers that came to him.

If Seven had killed the senator's son to punish the senator, then he might go after Brenda to get revenge.

Nick's phone jangled, and he snatched it up, hoping it was Brenda, but it was the crime lab instead. "Agent Blackwood, we found a paint match to the sample Deputy Waterstone scraped off of Brenda Banks's car."

"And?"

"It was a black 2009 car. Brenda said it was a sedan, so I did some research. There are two matching that description that belong to residents in Slaughter Creek. One to a Wade Willingham, age sixteen. But he's been out of the country on a study program, and the car has been at his parents' home."

"And the other?"

"The other belongs to Jordan Jennings, a weather girl who works with Brenda."

Nick's pulse jumped. Maybe the woman was jealous that Brenda had gotten the lead investigative reporter spot. "Thanks. I'll have her picked up for questioning."

He hung up and explained the lead to Jake. Jake phoned his deputy. "I'm with Nick right now. We have a lead on the Strangler, but we think we know who ran Brenda Banks off the road. Her name is Jordan Jennings. She drives a black 2009 Toyota Corolla. Bring her in for questioning and impound her car."

"Sure," Deputy Waterstone said. "About those photos you asked me to dig up from the senator's employee and volunteer files?"

"Do you have them?"

"Yes."

"Send them to Nick's tablet." Jake hung up and thanked him, then retrieved Nick's tablet from the backseat while Nick maneuvered the curves.

Rain began to drizzle down, making visibility on the narrow road difficult. Nick flipped on his defroster and rubbed at the condensation on his window. Headlights from an oncoming car nearly blinded him, and he flashed his lights, warning the driver to slow down before he killed someone.

Behind him, another car approached, and he decided to keep an eye on it as he veered onto a dirt road leading to the camp.

"I wonder why she came out here," Jake said, obviously thinking out loud. "Just because it's deserted?"

Nick shrugged. "Could be. Or maybe the location has some significance to her."

Jake made a disgusted sound in his throat. "I can't imagine the Commander sending his subjects to 4-H camps."

"Me neither. And I can't see a sadistic man-hating killer playing with 4-H'ers as a little girl." The headlights on the car behind him fell back some, and the tension in Nick's shoulders eased slightly.

"Some of the famous serial killers led normal lives as a child," Jake said as he tapped the screen to accept the incoming photos Deputy Waterstone had sent. "Or at least they seemed normal."

"You're right," Nick said. "Maybe she's here because she plans to kill us and dump our bodies in the river. It's so isolated, no one would be the wiser."

"We're not going to let that happen."

Nick glanced sideways as Jake scrolled through the photographs. Several were shots from personnel files, which included background checks on the employees. But the volunteers' backgrounds hadn't been examined as carefully. Another set of photos showcased various social functions with guests and workers mingling.

"Here." Jake tapped the screen. "Look at this woman."

Nick gripped the wheel and took a quick look. Jesus. It had to be her.

She had the same intense dark brown eyes, wide cheekbones, black hair as they did.

But her eyes looked vacant, empty, and although she wore a scarf around her neck, he saw the faint telltale markings of a scar.

"That's her, Seven," Jake said.

Nick wiped his hand over his mouth to stem the sudden bile in his throat. "If she knows we're her brothers, she must hate us for not rescuing her."

Silence fell, thick with horror, regret, and grief.

Jake pointed ahead to a crooked wooden sign carved into a post. "There's the turnoff."

The rain continued to drive down, the tires of Nick's sedan clawing at the wet ground like quicksand.

"Did we camp out here when we were small?" Nick asked.

Jake shot him an odd look. "Once. He left us for three days, and we nearly froze to death."

Nick swallowed hard. Jake had taken care of him, had shown him how to start a fire with two sticks.

The sedan bounced over the ruts, and the car skidded in the mud. He cut the wheel into the skid, barely missing a tree by inches. Shrubs and foliage flew past. Finally the camp's huts slid into view.

"Brenda's car's by the main lodge," Jake said, gesturing to the left.

"That Jeep must belong to Seven," Nick noted.

Nick flipped off the lights and slowed, then parked a few huts down, hoping to go in on foot and surprise the woman holding Brenda hostage. He couldn't let himself think too much about the fact that she was the sister he thought he'd lost.

You did lose her. To the Commander and his sick, twisted games.

Leaves scattered down in the rain, sticking to the windshield and clogging his wipers as he cut the engine. Nick eased open the car door and stuck one foot out, his hand reaching for his weapon as he scanned the property.

Seven could be holding Brenda in any of the cabins.

"We should divide up," Jake said. "I'll check out the huts, and you head toward the lodge."

Nick nodded brusquely, although he wondered for a brief second if they should stick together. But no telling what Seven was doing to Brenda.

He just prayed they weren't too late and that she was still alive.

———————— , ————————

Brenda's fingers ached from trying to untie the ropes cutting into her wrists. "Why do you think that Arthur Blackwood is my father?"

Seven toyed with the piano wire she'd wrapped around Brenda's neck. "I heard them talking about you," she said. "The Commander and the bald chubby man he gave you to."

The bald chubby man—her adopted father, William Banks.

"They were arguing. The bald man said he would adopt you and keep you safe," Seven said in a shrill voice. "That he'd raise you as his own."

A dozen different memories teased Brenda's mind as Seven pinched the wire into Brenda's neck, but none of them involved her adopted father knowing Arthur Blackwood.

"But if I was his daughter, why don't I remember being with him? And who was that woman I was looking for in the hospital?"

"I don't know," Seven said again, as if Brenda was an idiot. "But I heard them arguing, and the mayor told him he didn't need to keep you, that he and his wife would take care of you."

Brenda shook her head in denial.

"It's true. He and the senator and the Commander were all friends," Seven said.

If Seven was telling the truth, then her father—William Banks—had known about the experiments. Had he stood by, watched and allowed those horrible things to happen to the innocent children of Slaughter Creek?

God…she felt queasy.

"Maybe you misunderstood." *She had to have misunderstood.*

Seven ground the wire tighter into Brenda's neck.

"That's the reason you killed the senator's son?" Brenda asked, mentally piecing together the fragments of the past few days.

Seven released a bitter laugh, her eyes wild, demented. "The senator should die, but killing his precious son hurt him more than losing his own life."

"Cruel, but true." Brenda had to keep Seven talking. Surely Nick and Jake would be here soon.

"So what now?" Brenda asked. "You kill me, then Nick and Jake, and then you're finished?"

An odd expression darkened Seven's eyes as if she didn't know how to answer that question. Maybe she didn't plan on ending her killing spree at all.

Seven didn't have time to answer, though.

A board creaked, and they both swung around as Nick walked into the room.

———————— , ————————

Nick's inventory of the situation did nothing to alleviate the anxiety that had clawed at him when he'd stood outside the lodge and listened to Seven's rant.

That damn piano wire was wound a little too tightly around Brenda's neck for comfort.

Seven's gaze shot to the door behind Nick, then around the room. "Where's your brother?"

Nick studied his sister, yet she was a stranger.

A killer who had ruthlessly taken several men's lives.

Her hair was just as dark as his, her eyes as deep a muddy brown. A harshness slashed her features that indicated she'd suffered at their father's hands. "It's just me," he said, keeping one eye on Brenda, whose face looked pale in the murky light.

"I don't believe you." Seven lifted the knife in her hand and placed it against Brenda's neck. A drop of blood trickled down Brenda's throat.

"Nick," Brenda said in a choked whisper. "I'm sorry—"

"You're wrong, Seven," he said, knotting his fists at the sight of that blood. "You have it all wrong."

Challenge glinted Seven's eyes. "What are you talking about?"

"Brenda is not the Commander's daughter."

Brenda gasped. "Nick—"

He saw the anguish in her eyes. "You aren't," he said to her. "You may be adopted, but Arthur Blackwood is not your father."

Seven took a step toward him, waving the knife, the tip red with Brenda's blood, a reminder that this woman could snap at any time. "You're lying. I heard them talking, arguing about using her in the experiment—"

"You misunderstood," he said sharply. "The mayor and senator knew my father, but Brenda isn't his child."

"Yes, she is!" Seven cried.

"No. Brenda isn't the Commander's little girl, Seven. You are."

Behind Seven, Brenda's eyes widened in shock.

"What?" Seven's voice rasped a denial, but he saw the wheels turning in her head.

"We found your blood on Ron Stowe's body," Nick said. "We tested it, and you're related to me and Jake." He moved toward her, hoping to slip the knife from her hand. "We thought our sister had died at birth, but we just exhumed the grave, and the coffin was empty."

Seven's hand trembled. "He kept me so he could torture me."

"I know what a monster he is. Everyone in town knows," Nick said softly. "It's over, Seven. Just give me the knife, and I'll see that you get the psychiatric counseling you need."

Nick reached for the knife, but suddenly a shot rang out. He ducked against the wall, his gun at the ready. Where in the hell had that come from?

Brenda's chair rattled as she struggled to free herself. Seven ran for the door. Nick started after her, but another shot blasted, the bullet zinging past his face. Brenda leaned sideways to dodge the bullet, and the chair fell to the floor.

Then he saw the blood pooling beneath her.

Dammit. She'd been shot.

Chapter 29

———— o ————

Panic flared in Nick's chest at the sight of the blood seeping from Brenda's abdomen. Her face looked gray, but her eyes blazed with courage as he yanked out his pocketknife and cut the ropes tying her to the chair. "Brenda?"

She clutched his arm. "I'm fine. Go after her."

Except she wasn't fine, and they both knew it.

He punched 911 and got an operator. "This is Special Agent Nick Blackwood. I need an ambulance at the old 4-H camp. A woman has been shot." He gave her the address, and she told him to stay on the line, but footsteps clattered, a back door slammed, and Nick realized the shooter had gone out the back.

He had to catch the bastard, so he left the phone beside Brenda. "Hang in there, Brenda. An ambulance is on its way."

Where the hell was Jake?

He gave Brenda a quick kiss, then jumped up and ran toward the back. Jake bumped into him on his way out, and was rubbing the back of his head.

"Some bastard coldcocked me by one of the huts."

"He shot Brenda and went out the back. Go after him."

"How about Brenda?"

"I'll stay with her. An ambulance is on its way."

A car engine rumbled somewhere to the right. Nick tossed Jake his keys. Seven's Jeep was already gone.

"I'll issue an APB for Seven's Jeep," Jake yelled as he darted to the car. A second later, he jumped in and sped off, gravel spewing behind him.

Nick cursed and ran back inside. His heart hammered with fear as he crossed the room to Brenda. She lay on her side, the pool of blood growing larger.

He yanked off his jacket and shirt, then his T-shirt, balled it up, and pressed it to her abdomen.

"Did you catch her?" Brenda whispered.

"No, she's gone. Jake's chasing the shooter." He pulled his shirt and jacket back on, then smoothed a strand of hair from Brenda's face and gently unwound the piano wire from her neck. Grooves where the wire had cut into her throat looked raw, and she gasped for air as he peeled it away.

Brenda moaned and he gathered her in his arms. "Just rest, sweetheart, the medics will be here soon." He pressed his shirt more firmly into her abdomen, but blood was soaking through fast.

Way too fast.

If the ambulance didn't get there soon, she might not survive.

———————— , ————————

Brenda fought to remain conscious. She couldn't believe they'd gotten so close to Seven and that she'd escaped. "Nick, you don't have to stay with me," she whispered. "Go find Seven."

Nick pressed a finger to her lips to shush her. "I'm not leaving you, Brenda."

The pain in her stomach had turned to a dull throb. Or maybe it was because she was so weak.

Nick stroked her hair, and she couldn't help but close her eyes. She was so tired. Her limbs felt heavy, her head so dizzy that the last few minutes blurred in her mind. "Who was shooting?"

"I don't know." Anger hardened his voice. "Jake said a man coldcocked him outside by one of the bunkhouses."

Brenda's legs were starting to feel numb. "Was he shooting at us or Seven?"

A heartbeat passed. "Us. Probably one of the Commander's hired guns. He must have followed you out here."

"I didn't see anyone," Brenda said, her throat raw. "Nick?"

He continued to stroke her face, gently brushing her hair away from her cheek. "What?"

"If I don't make it—"

"Shh," Nick said, cutting off her sentence. "Don't talk like that. We both know you're too stubborn to let a gunshot wound get you."

A smile tried to fight its way onto her face, but failed. Brenda's eyes felt glued together. She tightened her grip on Nick's arm. She wanted to hold on to him.

She wanted to live and finish the story and ask her parents what really happened at the sanitarium, ask them about the drug-addicted homeless woman.

Ask her father if he'd known about the experiments.

The thought made her ill, and she moaned as the world began to slip away.

"Brenda," Nick said softly. "Hold on—the ambulance will be here soon." He dropped a kiss into her hair, and Brenda relaxed in his arms and fell into the beckoning darkness.

——————— ˌ ———————

Nick cradled Brenda to him, rocking her back and forth, emotions pummeling him. She couldn't die.

Not now. Not here like this. Not when they hadn't settled anything between them.

Not when he thought…that he loved her.

He kissed her hair, holding her tight, determined to assure her he was there. The seconds ticked into minutes that felt like days as he waited on the ambulance. Finally a siren's wail blasted the air, and Nick released a breath he'd been holding.

They would get her to the hospital, and she'd be fine.

She had to be.

He eased her down on the floor, wadded his jacket up to serve as a pillow, then raced outside to meet the medics. The ambulance lights twirled against the night sky, then the vehicle roared to a stop.

"In here," he shouted as the medics jumped from the ambulance. "She's been shot in the abdomen, and she's lost a lot of blood."

"Adam and Joe here," the blond medic said. "Is she conscious?"

"In and out," Nick answered.

The men rushed around back to retrieve the stretcher and carried it into the building, along with their medical kit.

"Where's the bullet?" Adam asked.

"Abdomen, right side. I haven't looked for an exit wound yet."

Brenda looked pale, her face beading with perspiration, and she was shivering.

"Brenda," Nick said, then knelt beside her. "Help is here now. We're going to get you to the hospital."

She mumbled something he couldn't understand, then the medics began to work on her. They took her vitals and exchanged worried looks.

"Oxygen level is not good. Heart rate one-sixty."

Adam examined her wound, then rolled her to the side. "No exit wound. Bullet is lodged in the abdomen."

"Respiratory rate is elevated," Joe said as he started an IV drip in one arm.

Adam removed blood stoppers from the medical kit and pressed them onto the wound, then secured them with tape while Joe made quick work of attaching wires to her chest to monitor her heart. "Blood pressure low. Eighty-eight over forty."

"Let's start another IV with lactated Ringer's," Adam said. "We need to maintain volume."

Seconds later, they strapped Brenda to the stretcher and carried her to the ambulance. Nick followed, then grabbed Brenda's hand and kissed it. "Stay tough, Brenda. I'll meet you at the hospital."

"We're transporting her to the level-one trauma hospital," Adam said as he climbed in the back with her, and Joe headed to the driver's side.

"I'll follow in her car," Nick said.

The medics nodded, and he jogged over to Brenda's car. Thankfully the keys were still in the ignition and her purse on the seat.

The ambulance peeled away from the camp, siren wailing, lights flashing.

Nick fired up the engine and followed them. By the time they reached the main road leading to the hospital, he decided to call her parents.

The mayor answered on the third ring. "Brenda?"

"No, it's Special Agent Blackwood. Brenda's been shot, Mayor," Nick said. "She's on her way to the hospital now."

"Dear Jesus," the mayor mumbled. "Is she...all right?"

Nick's stomach clenched as he remembered all the blood. "I don't know. You'd better meet us."

"We'll be there as soon as possible."

They hung up, and Nick tried to focus on staying positive as he sped over the bumpy dirt road, then turned onto the main highway. The ambulance driver kept the siren going and flew around cars as they pulled to the shoulder to let the ambulance pass.

Twenty minutes later, he veered to the right into the hospital. The ambulance raced to a stop at the emergency entrance, and he threw Brenda's car into a parking space and jumped out.

By the time he'd reached the entrance, the medics were wheeling Brenda inside. He took her hand in his and hurried along beside the gurney as they pushed her to an ER room.

Nick rushed to the door, but a nurse blocked his way. "I'm sorry, sir, you'll have to wait outside."

He gritted his teeth. He wanted to be with Brenda, make sure she made it.

She *had* to make it.

He started to argue, and a heavyset guard motioned for him to step away.

Hating being helpless, he paced the waiting room and studied the clock, his panic increasing as each minute rolled by. An elderly couple glared at him as if he was getting on their nerves, but he didn't care.

Ten minutes later, the Bankses rushed in, both ashen-faced.

"Where is she?" Brenda's mother asked.

"They're prepping her for surgery."

The mayor's cheeks bulged with fury. "What happened?"

Nick grimaced. "She received a call from the Slaughter Creek Strangler and went to meet her."

Mrs. Banks's legs buckled, and her husband helped her into a chair. "We warned her not to pursue that case."

The mayor shook his finger at him. "She got into this because of you."

Guilt suffused Nick. They were right. If Brenda hadn't been so upset with him, maybe she wouldn't have gone to meet Seven on her own.

A vein bulged in the mayor's forehead. "Tell me you at least caught the person who shot her."

Nick heaved a frustrated breath. "Jake went after him. I stayed with Brenda to wait on the ambulance."

A doctor in surgical scrubs approached. "Are you the Banks family?"

Mrs. Banks jumped up, and the mayor rushed toward the man. "Yes. How is our daughter?"

"She's in serious condition," he said. "We're going to perform surgery to remove the bullet, which appears to be lodged in her kidney. I'll need you to sign some permission forms."

Nick's phone buzzed, and he stepped aside to answer it while the Bankses handled the paperwork.

"I caught the shooter," Jake said.

"Thank God." Nick pulled a hand down his chin. "Did he tell you who hired him?"

"Not yet—I'm on my way to the jail with him now."

Nick could meet Jake at the jail.

But he wanted to stay with Brenda. Even though her family didn't want him here. He didn't even know if Brenda wanted him here.

Seven's diatribe with Brenda echoed in his head. She'd said something about his father and the mayor...

He relayed the conversation to Jake. "I'm going to see what the mayor has to say."

"You think he knew about the Slaughter Creek experiments?"

"I don't know, but he sure as hell tried to dissuade Brenda from investigating the story. Maybe because he was afraid of what she'd learn."

"Keep me posted."

They hung up, and Nick hurried to talk to the mayor.

Mrs. Banks sat wringing her hands together, teary-eyed. The mayor was pacing, his hand sliding over his bald spot in a rapid, nervous motion.

"Mayor Banks, I need to talk to you," Nick said. "Let's take a walk and get some coffee."

That vein in the mayor's forehead throbbed again, stark beneath the hospital's fluorescent lights. "All right." He leaned over and whispered something to his wife, who nodded, but didn't bother to look up.

He and the mayor walked down the hall to the vending machines, then Nick stuffed quarters in the coin slot and hit the coffee button. The machine whirred and spurted out a cup of dark liquid.

The mayor accepted a cup as well, and they walked to another seating area near the hospital entrance. "All right. What really happened?" the mayor asked.

"I told you the truth," Nick said. "Brenda met the Slaughter Creek Strangler. The woman has been texting her about each murder."

The mayor stumbled backward. "She didn't tell me that."

Nick wasn't surprised. "A shooter must have followed her there and opened fire. Jake arrested him. Hopefully he'll tell us who hired him."

"I don't understand," the mayor said.

Nick studied his demeanor. The man was worried. But was he worried simply about his daughter, or about what Nick might uncover about his relationship to the Commander?

"We believe whoever was behind the project hired the shooter."

"Meaning your father?"

Nick studied the man's craggy face. "Possibly. But we also think someone with more authority oversaw it. Maybe a higher-ranking officer in the military or CIA."

The mayor's face blanched. "I thought the shooter was working with the Strangler."

"No. Hopefully when Jake interrogates him, we'll learn who that is."

"Did you at least catch this crazy woman?"

"I'm afraid not." Nick shook his head. "But before she escaped, she revealed some interesting things pertaining to her motive."

Mayor Banks swirled his coffee, then took a sip, his mouth working side to side. "Get to the point, Blackwood."

"The Strangler calls herself Seven. She was part of the Commander's experiment. In fact, she's his daughter."

The mayor's shocked gaze flew to his. "Arthur Blackwood had a daughter?"

Nick nodded. "My brother and I were told our sister died at birth, but we know differently now." He explained about the empty coffin. "But Seven was confused. For some reason, she thought Brenda was the Commander's daughter. That he gave her to you to raise to save her from the experiments."

The man's eyebrows drew together. "Where in the hell did she get that idea?"

"Apparently she heard you and the Commander talking at the sanitarium when Brenda was little." Nick paused, weighing his words. "Did you know what the Commander was doing back then, Mayor Banks?"

Chapter 30

———— o ————

"You listen to me," Mayor Banks said. "I did know your father back then through the town council, but whatever that maniac woman thinks she heard is a lie. I was not involved in those experiments."

Nick cocked his head to the side. He didn't believe that. "Really?"

"Yes," the mayor said. "And yes, we adopted Brenda, but that's a family matter."

"You and Senator Stowe and the Commander served in the military together on the same assault unit," Nick said. "I saw a photograph of you together at a fund-raiser for the sanitarium twenty years ago."

The mayor's face blanched. A breath later, he said, "Yes, we served together. And the senator may have been in on the experiment. But I wasn't." His chubby cheeks deflated, as if he were wrestling with defeat. "I admit that I suspected he might be up to something, but he never confided in me. When you arrested Arthur and revealed that he was conducting an experiment, it all made sense. That's the reason I tried to persuade Brenda to drop the story. I wanted her to stay the hell away from your father."

Suddenly Mrs. Banks rushed toward them, her eyes filled with tears. "William, it's Brenda! She's not doing well in surgery."

The mayor caught his wife by the arms. "What happened?"

"The surgeon said both kidneys were damaged." Her voice cracked. "She needs a transplant immediately."

Mayor Banks's face looked strained. "Dear God, we'll have to find her mother."

Mrs. Banks shook her head. "There's no time." She clutched her husband's arms. "They're going to test me to see if I'm a match."

The mayor nodded. "Yes, maybe that will work."

"I don't understand," Nick said.

Mrs. Banks took a deep breath as if she needed courage. "Brenda is my sister's daughter. My sister was a drug addict and lived on the streets. We took Brenda away from her when Brenda was four."

"So Brenda is your niece?" Nick said. "Does she know the truth about her mother?"

The couple exchanged a pained look, then shook their heads.

"You need to tell her the truth," Nick said.

"We will after the surgery," Mrs. Banks said. "But right now, I have to talk to the doctors. If I'm a match, they'll do the transplant immediately."

Nick's throat felt tight as the couple clasped hands and headed down to the lab.

———————— , ————————

Brenda felt herself rise from her body, as if she were weightless. The room was out of focus, and she felt weak, a bright light blinding her.

She blinked to clear the haze, then realized she was floating in a room of white.

And that she was dying.

Her body was lying in a hospital bed below, tubes, IVs, and machines whirring around her to keep her alive.

Gauze pads had soaked up blood, an oxygen machine pumped air into her, and another tube had been inserted down her throat.

She was so still, her complexion so pale, and there was so much blood. She strained to recall why she was here, then a brief flash of a gunshot sounding and a bullet stinging as it pierced her stomach came back.

"We're losing her," the doctor said.

"Hang on, Brenda," a nurse murmured. "We're going to find you a kidney." A terrible sense of loss overwhelmed her as her life flashed before her eyes. Nick…holding her as she bled on the floor.

Nick and the beautiful night they'd spent together.

The betrayal she'd felt when she realized he'd investigated her past.

Then other snippets of her life, back to when she was little and scared and hungry and cold. She felt that coldness now, all the way through her bones.

More memories bombarded her, like a movie she couldn't turn off. The homeless woman dragging her into an alley. Being sick and hungry.

Agnes soothing her after a nightmare.

The Christmases with the Bankses, candy canes and presents, warm and cozy by the fire, her mother cuddling on the sofa, reading stories to her.

Her sixth birthday party, when Agnes arranged pony rides for her and her first-grade class.

The lonely holiday when she'd been ten and her parents had dragged her on a holiday and left her in the hotel room with a nanny while they partied with their friends.

And her teenage years, when she'd learned about the adoption and rebelled against the Bankses.

Suddenly there was a commotion, as the operating-room door swung open. Doctors and nurses started bustling around. Machines beeped, there was a hubbub of harried voices, and a big man in a hospital uniform pushed another gurney into the room.

Brenda gaped in shock.

Her mother—Agnes—was on the other bed, an IV hooked up to her arm.

The nurse patted Brenda's hand, but she was still floating above her body, too numb to feel it. "I told you we'd find you a donor."

Her mother looked over at her. "I love you, Brenda. Everything's going to be okay. I promise."

The same nurse that had patted her arm squeezed her mother's shoulder. "You're very brave to do this, Mrs. Banks. Now start counting backward from ten."

"Ten, nine, eight…" Her mother's voice faded as the doctors draped a sheet over her, then intubated her.

"Scalpel, please." The surgeon held out his hand, and one of the assistants laid the instrument in his palm. Seconds later, they lifted Agnes's kidney from her body, and Brenda watched them insert it into her own abdomen.

Slowly she felt herself floating back down, slipping back into her body…clinging to life as her mother's kidney began to work.

———————— · ————————

It was the longest night of Nick's life.

Finally, around four a.m., the doctor came out of surgery to talk to them. Nick hung close enough to the mayor to hear.

"So far the surgery is a success, but Brenda will need to stay on antirejection meds. She's in the ICU tonight, but we hope to move her to a room tomorrow."

"And my wife?" the mayor asked.

"She's doing fine, Mr. Banks," the doctor said. "We'll let you see her when we settle her into a room."

Relief echoed in the mayor's sigh. "Thank you, Doctor," he said as he shook the man's hand. "I don't know what I'd do if I lost either one of my girls."

Nick backed away, feeling like an outsider. He wanted to see Brenda, but only family was allowed. And he was nowhere near family.

He left the hospital and drove back to his cabin, but he was too wired to sleep. Tonight Brenda had almost died, and Seven had escaped.

Where would she go? Where was she hiding out?

He spread all the information he'd learned on the case on his kitchen table, then laid out the crimes in order. Seven had killed Logger and Sergeant Mason because they'd been hired guards where she was kept hostage.

Her accomplice, who he suspected was Six, had helped her burn down the compound, leaving the woman in the building to die.

Seven had tried to kill Brenda because she'd mistakenly believed Brenda was the Commander's daughter, and that she'd been spared the experiment because of her relationship to him. Because the Commander loved Brenda.

But the Commander had never loved anybody.

Which meant that now Seven knew she was his daughter—and that he hadn't loved her, because he sure as hell hadn't spared her.

She murdered Ron Stowe to punish the senator. She'd also known Stowe and Laddermilk from the senator's campaign.

He studied the senator's photograph. Had he known about the project? Had he spearheaded it? The mayor suspected that he had.

Nick would question him in the morning. But he wanted to be armed with more ammunition, so he booted up his computer and pulled up everything he could find on the senator, his life, and his career.

He found two more photographs with Seven in them. She'd always remained in the shadows.

Now he knew the reason.

Would she go after the senator next?

He checked the man's calendar to see where he would be the next few days, and discovered that he planned to attend a charity auction the next day. Nick was shocked the man hadn't canceled because of his son's death, but the event was still scheduled; in an interview, the senator had claimed he would attend in his son's honor.

Nick stood, paced to the window, and looked out at the mountains. In a couple of hours, he'd meet Jake at the jail to interrogate the shooter.

Then he'd go to the auction, in case Seven showed up to ambush the senator.

———————— . ————————

Brenda struggled to open her eyes, but her eyelids weighed a ton. Her body felt weak, drained, her mouth so dry it felt as if cotton candy were stuck inside it.

She tried to move, but pain ricocheted through her abdomen, and she realized that her arm was tethered to an IV.

She blinked, willing away the panic streaking through her. Then a warm hand closed over hers.

"Nick?"

"No, it's me—your mother."

A snippet of another memory invaded her consciousness. The surgery, floating above her own body, the realization that she was dying.

Then her mother being wheeled in beside her...

"What happened?" she whispered.

"You were shot." This from her father, his voice gruff.

Anguish lined his face. He was standing by her bed, but her mother was in a wheelchair. She looked weak and worried, her face milky white.

"You're going to be all right," her mother said softly.

Brenda's gaze met hers. Tears glittered on her mother's eyelashes, and an IV was attached to a pole beside her chair.

Her father cleared his throat. "You needed a kidney transplant, so your mother volunteered."

Brenda licked her dry lips. "But how…were you a match?"

A moment of silence lapsed, then her mother smiled sadly. "I guess it's time you knew the truth, Brenda."

"What do you remember?" her father asked.

Brenda forced her eyes to stay open. "I had nightmares…this dream about a homeless woman, drugs…a warehouse."

Sorrow bled from her mother's voice as she said, "I'm so sorry, honey. We hoped you'd forget, that you'd never remember that awful night."

"So it was real," she said. "I was hurt?"

Her mother wiped at her eyes. "The woman you were with, your mother—"

"Was a drug addict," Brenda said.

Agnes nodded. "She was my sister, Jo-Lynn."

Of all the scenarios Brenda had envisioned, none had prepared her for this. "But you…her…you're so different."

Her mother gently brushed a strand of hair from Brenda's forehead, reminding her of the way she used to brush it at night when she was a little girl.

"I tried to save her, to save you," she said. "I guess that's why I went overboard in spoiling you, making sure you had the best clothes. I wanted you to fit into society, to have everything, to forget the horrible places your mother took you, the rags you wore. The…Dumpster diving for food."

A cold knot of fear enveloped Brenda. "What happened to her?"

"I...we lost track of her," her father said. "You have to understand, Brenda. Your mother and I did everything we could to save Jo-Lynn. She was in and out of rehab, then she'd run off and get hooked again. We thought when she had you that she'd change, but her addiction was too strong."

"She turned to stealing to pay for her drugs," Agnes continued. "Stealing and selling herself on the streets."

Brenda clenched the sheets. "That night I was brought into the hospital, the warehouse?"

"Your mother was trading sex for drugs. But the dealers decided they wanted you, too," her father said, his tone harsh with disgust.

"But Jo-Lynn fought for you that night," Agnes continued. "They raped her and beat her, but she finally managed to get you both out. You were bruised, battered, dehydrated."

"You had a fever and were so dirty," her father interjected. "No telling when you'd had a decent meal."

"You were skin and bones," her mother said. "Sheriff Bayler called us, and we came to the hospital. When I saw you—" Agnes paused to swallow back more tears. "It broke my heart. You were so tiny and frail and...terrified. You had nightmares for weeks."

"When you were released from the hospital, we started paperwork to legally take you away from her," her father said.

"Jo-Lynn was furious at us, at me," her mother said. "But I was angry at her for making you live that life. I decided then that if I couldn't save her, I would save you." She squeezed Brenda's hand. "So we let my sister go and took you in as ours."

Her father stroked her cheek. "Try to understand how hard it was for Agnes," he said. "She had to give up her sister to save you. But if you want us to help you look for her when you're feeling better, we will."

Tears blurred Brenda's eyes. All those memories of life with the homeless woman—eating garbage, freezing to death, sleeping in alleys, and eating from Dumpsters—had been real. Memories. Not just bad dreams.

Her mother had chosen drugs over her.

Yet Agnes had loved her and given her a good life. And now she'd saved her again, giving up her own kidney to keep her alive.

"No, I don't need her." She clutched Agnes's hand and pressed a kiss to her palm. "I have my mother right here."

Tears flowed down Agnes's face. "Oh, Brenda…"

"I love you, Mom." Brenda swallowed against the dryness in her throat. "Thank you for loving me back."

Agnes pressed her cheek against Brenda's hand. "I love you, too, Brenda. Please forgive me."

"Forgive you?" Brenda said softly. "I owe everything to you, Mom. Thank you for being my mother. For showing me what being a mother really means."

Her mother hugged her, then laid her head against Brenda's hand until Brenda drifted back to sleep.

But this time, a peace fell over her. She knew who her real mother was. The woman who'd been there for her all along.

She would never forget it again.

———— , ————

"His name is Germaine Webber," Jake told Nick as he led him to the interrogation room. "He showed up in the system—prior for assault and battery. After he left the military."

"Why am I not surprised?" Nick mumbled.

"How's Brenda?"

"I called the hospital on my way, and they said she's stable. I'm sure her family is with her now." A family he wasn't part of—and never would be.

Jake opened the door, and they entered, Jake taking a seat across from Webber.

The man was a big brawny guy who looked as if he'd just stepped from a wrestling match. Chunky hands and short, stocky body. Scar on his left cheek. Some kind of tribal tat on his arm, and a cobra winding around his beefy neck.

"We have your gun, Webber," Jake began. "The bullets from it match the slugs the doctor removed from Brenda Banks."

Nick crossed his arms and remained standing, looking down at the man with a scowl. "Who hired you to shoot her?"

"Who says I was shooting at her?" Webber growled.

Nick and Jake exchanged irritated looks.

"Then who were you shooting at?" Jake asked.

Webber shrugged.

Nick rapped his knuckles on his chest. "At the two of us—a sheriff and a federal agent?" He wouldn't have put it past the Commander to put a hit on his sons.

A seed of panic flared in Webber's eyes. "That's not what I meant."

Nick slammed his fist on the table. "Then what the fuck do you mean?"

Webber's breathing sounded choppy in the ensuing silence. He unfolded his fists, then folded them back again, studying the hair on his knuckles. "All right, yes, I was supposed to shoot the Banks broad."

"Who hired you?" Nick asked, barely controlling the urge to beat the sense out of the man.

Webber chewed his lip. "What are you going to do for me if I tell you?"

Nick grabbed him by the neck of his tattered T-shirt. "I'm going to let you live instead of murdering you before you get transported to prison."

Webber's eyes widened, and he coughed and looked at Jake with panic in his eyes.

Jake simply shrugged. "I can step out if I need to, Agent Blackwood."

"Hell, no, don't leave me with this nutcase," Webber wailed.

"Then tell us who hired you," Nick bellowed.

"I don't know." Webber threw up his hands in warning when Nick reached for him again. "I swear to God. I received a text offering me ten thousand dollars to kill that reporter."

Nick's chest tightened. "You bastard. Who sent the text?"

"I told you, I don't know," Webber said, his voice breaking. "I picked up the first half in a gym locker that night. I was supposed to get the rest when the job was done."

"And the payment?" Jake asked.

"Hundred-dollar bills."

"Did the message say why this person wanted Brenda dead?" Nick asked.

Webber shook his head. "I didn't ask. I figured she was nosing around in something someone didn't want her to know about."

Jake silently cursed. "Do you have the phone?"

Webber rolled his fists again. "Cops took it when they brought me in."

"Where are you supposed to pick up the money?" Nick asked.

"He was supposed to text me the drop-off place when the job was done."

Nick snapped his fingers. "Jake, get that phone and have him set up the meeting. I'll call the mayor and have him talk to Brenda. We'll issue a statement that she didn't make it last night. Then we'll set a trap to catch the person who ordered the hit."

There were two suspects at the top of his list. One—his father.

The second—the senator.

Although Jordan Jennings, the reporter who'd tried to run Brenda off the road, also could have hired a hit man.

"And let's question the Jennings woman," Nick said. "She could have sent the text to get rid of Brenda."

Seven adjusted the straps on her silky black dress, fluffed her hair, then carefully applied her lipstick.

Ruby red. The color of blood.

The need for vengeance swelled inside her, and she slid on her black stilettos, grabbed her clutch, and headed into the country club where the senator was hosting the benefit auction for his favorite charity—the children's hospital in Knoxville.

A bitter laugh bubbled in her throat. How ironic and fitting at the same time. He was raising money to help sick children, when years ago he'd spearheaded the project that had destroyed so many children's lives.

Piano music filled the ballroom, drinks and appetizers floated around on silver trays, and diamonds glittered on the women. Chatter and laughter echoed through the room.

She slipped inside and mingled with the crowd, not surprised that Mrs. Stowe looked haggard. Less than twenty-four hours ago they'd buried their son.

But if the woman had stood by and allowed her husband to torture children, she deserved to suffer.

The senator stood out in his expensive black suit, the silver hair at his temples highlighted by his power-red tie. Well groomed, she was sure, just like his cover-up.

But the truth was about to come out.

She watched him chat and smile as he greeted the guests, although his face showed the strain of grief. Perfect.

She grabbed a flute of champagne and sipped it, then removed her phone and sent him a text.

There once was a man who stood by
And watched the little kids cry
So his son had to pay
For his father's cruel way
And now it's his own turn to die...

A waiter walked by and she took a canapé from his tray, watching the senator over her drink. The moment he read the text, his jaw snapped tight, and he scanned the room.

She smiled to herself, then wove through the horde of people entering the ballroom and made her way to the west wing to wait. A man exited the men's room, and she ducked inside to make sure no one else was there.

Then she made her way back into the hall, stepped into a corner, and hid until the senator passed, frantically texting as if to ask who'd sent him the limerick.

Padding quietly on the plush carpet, she walked up behind him and pressed her knife into his back.

"Step inside the men's room," she murmured in a low voice.

He twisted his head around to see her, but she dug the tip of the knife deeper. "Don't try anything, Senator, or I'll leave you to bleed out on this floor."

"You won't get away with this."

A sarcastic laugh escaped her. "I don't care. It'll be worth it."

His shoulders reared out, his posture went ramrod straight, and she pushed him inside the restroom, then flipped the lock.

"Who are you?" he asked as he spun around.

"You don't remember me, Senator?" Her voice was brittle.

He pivoted, his eyes narrowing when he saw her face, but he showed no sign of recognition. "Should I?"

"Yes. You and the Commander made my life a living hell."

Then she shoved him into a stall and slammed the back of his neck with the blunt end of the knife.

He staggered forward and collapsed onto his knees.

She wrestled him onto the toilet, then tied his hands and feet and began to strip off his clothes.

When she was finished, she'd leave him here dead, naked for all of his loyal followers to see.

Then she'd pay a little visit to Daddy Dearest.

Chapter 31

———— ○ ————

N ick studied the buxom blonde across the table from him in the interrogation room. "Listen to me, Miss Jennings. Tell us the truth, and we'll try to cut a deal for you." Not going to happen, but he'd lie to get what he wanted.

The bravado she'd had walking in faded from her face. "I told the deputy that I didn't do anything wrong."

Nick shoved the forensic report detailing the paint samples in front of her. "We impounded your car, and the paint matches. There are also scratches on your front bumper that indicate you had an accident, and paint on it matches Brenda's BMW."

The young woman fidgeted with the cheap rings on her fingers, her eyes averted. He'd seen her on the news, and she was a B-rate weather girl at best. Her skirts were always too tight, her makeup too heavy, her blue eye shadow more suited to a call girl than a serious anchorwoman.

She'd probably slept her way into the job she did have. "You were angry at Brenda for landing the job you wanted, weren't you?"

Her eyes cut down to her manicured nails. She was going to lose that privilege in jail.

"So you followed her and ran her off the road—"

"I didn't intend to kill her," she cried, then caught herself and slapped her forehead.

"What did you intend?" Nick asked bluntly.

"I just wanted her to be injured enough to have to take a leave of absence."

"So you could slide into her spot?"

She crossed her legs, tapping her foot up and down. "Yes. I figured once the director saw me outside the station doing some serious reporting, he'd realize he made a mistake and replace her with me."

He waited a second, making her squirm. "So you ran her off the road. Then when that didn't work, you hired someone to shoot her."

The woman's red lips parted. "You think I killed her?"

So she'd heard the false report they'd issued. "You found a source from an old news story or from a friend you have in prison—"

"I don't know anyone in prison."

Nick slammed his fist on the table. "Stop lying. I have records proving that your brother is in jail."

That shut her up fast. Then she began to sob. "I…was desperate. It wasn't fair that she got the job. She came from a rich family, her daddy bought her way up, she probably slept with the director—"

Nick wanted to strangle her. "Brenda is too classy and smart to do that. She has had her own share of trouble, but then again, if you were really an investigative reporter, you'd know that."

Her foot tapped faster. "What's going to happen to me?"

"You're going to jail." He produced a picture of Darren James. "Now tell me. Why did you kill this man?"

She shook her head violently. "I didn't. I don't even know him."

A rap sounded at the door, and Jake poked his head in, then pointed to the clock. "We'd better go. That silent auction has already started."

Nick gathered the photos and file and crammed them together.

"I may have done wrong by Brenda," Jordan said, "but I swear I didn't kill that other man."

Nick gave her a cutting look. "You'd better be telling the truth." Then he stalked from the room to meet Jake.

Jordan would be going away for attempted murder. But he believed her about James. She had no motive there.

Which meant that his father or possibly the senator had ordered the hit.

Brenda tapped her finger impatiently. The picture of her father and the senator was nagging at her. She had seen the ring the senator was wearing before.

Certain she was right, she phoned Nick.

"I was just about to call you," he said. "We just arrested Jordan Jennings. She ran you off the road and hired that guy to shoot at you."

"Oh, my God. She tried to kill me because she wanted my job?"

"Yes," Nick said through clenched teeth. "But we're still not sure who murdered Darren James. That was a professional hit. Probably the Commander or—"

"The senator."

"What makes you say that?" Nick asked.

"Because I remembered something. When I was little, at that sanitarium. A ring—it was shiny and had an emblem on it."

"A signet ring?"

"Yes. I was looking at an old picture of my dad and the senator. It's his ring, Nick. He was there, and he knew what was going on with the project."

"Jake and I are on our way to the charity auction where he is now. Have you heard anything else from Seven?"

"Not a word." Brenda ran a finger over her bandage. She hated being left out. She hated not being with him now.

"We think Seven is going after the senator."

"Let me go with you," Brenda said.

"No." Nick cut her off. "Rest, Brenda. When we catch her, you'll get your story."

He ended the call, and she clenched the phone in frustration. She wanted the story.

But there was one thing she wanted more than that.

She wanted Nick.

———— , ————

Nick's heart raced as he and Jake rushed into the country club. He'd skimmed the parking lot for Seven's vehicle, but there were hundreds of cars filling the spaces, the event having drawn a huge crowd.

No doubt the senator's son's death had spiked attendance; people would probably open their pockets a little wider out of sympathy for the man's loss and his efforts for the children's hospital.

Of course those same people had no idea that he might have been behind the research project in Slaughter Creek. They wouldn't feel quite so generous if they did.

Jake shoved open the door, and Nick flashed his badge at the security guard standing watch. Obviously after the senator's son's death, they were poised for trouble. "Where's the senator?"

The guard hooked his thumb toward the ballroom to the right. "They're about to start the speeches."

Nick flashed a photo of Seven from one of the other events. "Have you seen this woman?"

The guard shook his head, and Nick gestured for Jake to cover the right side of the ballroom while he took the left. Now that they knew what Seven looked like, it would be easier to spot her.

Voices, laughter, and piano music flowed from the open doorways, guests mingling throughout the ballroom, which was set up with cash bars and food stations to warm the guests into emptying their checking accounts for the senator's so-called cause.

In an adjoining ballroom, the items to be bid on were on display.

Jake rushed toward the doors at the far end, and Nick entered the left side, his gaze sweeping the crowded room. Dozens of young women in evening gowns, middle-aged couples dressed to the hilt, and yuppie men in designer suits crowded the floor and cash bar.

Dammit, it was going to be hard to find Seven in this mess.

An elegantly dressed woman near Mrs. Stowe's age climbed the steps to the stage, then tapped the microphone. "Ladies and gentlemen, we're delighted you all have come."

She prattled on about the generosity that had already brought in hundreds of thousands of dollars, then gestured toward a chart to the side, projecting estimated donations and goals.

Nick wove through the crowd, sweat trickling down his neck as he made his way to the front. He still didn't see either the senator or Seven anywhere.

Mrs. Stowe moved from behind a column, and he darted toward her. The strains of a grief-stricken night showed in the circles beneath her eyes, and her hand trembled as she sipped her champagne.

"Mrs. Stowe," he said. "I need to speak with your husband. Do you know where he is?"

She patted down an errant strand of hair. "No…he received a text and went to the lobby with his phone. But he should be back by now."

A text. Seven.

She would lure him away for privacy. Yet killing him here at the charity event for the children's hospital seemed fitting as her revenge. She intended to show the world what a bastard he was.

"Thanks." He wove back through the crowd, shouldering his way past a group of women chatting about their garden club, then out into the hall. He glanced left and right, looking for exits and escape routes, for hidden alcoves where Seven could corner the senator.

Jake had insisted they wear mikes, so he spoke into the one on his jacket. "Seven lured the senator out of the ballroom. I'll check the south and west exits. You take the north and east."

"Copy that," Jake murmured.

Nick passed a couple of women in expensive gowns, then noticed a guard at the exit at the end of the hall. The men's room was located in between.

He strode to the door, but it was locked. Heart thumping, he stepped back and slammed his shoulder into it, using all his weight. The door didn't budge.

He stepped farther back, then ran and hit it again, but no luck.

Knowing Seven might be strangling the senator, he couldn't wait. "I think they might be in the bathroom," he said into his mike. "I'm going to have to shoot the door open."

"I'm on my way," Jake said.

Nick aimed his weapon and fired at the lock. Two shots, and the knob twisted. He shoved the door open.

Hearing a grunt from the back, he bypassed the sinks and toiletry area, charging into the lavatory section. A muffled shout came from the far stall, where he spotted a man's shoes. Another strangled sound as the man's feet scrambled for footing, and then a woman's singsong voice.

There once was a girl with no name
But her daddy's friends liked her the same.
They could play with her mind
And treat her unkind
And if she cried they just thought her insane.

Nick braced his gun at the ready, walked slowly to the stall, and yanked it open. Seven was standing over the senator, twisting the piano wire around his neck as he gagged and choked for air.

"It's over, Seven," he said.

She pivoted toward him, her brown eyes staring back at him with crazed bloodlust.

"He has to pay," she said in a childlike voice.

"He will." Nick slowly moved toward her, his gun trained on her chest. "I promise you, everyone will know what he did."

She squared her shoulders, the wire still coiled around her fingers, the senator's eyes bulging in near death. Then he faded into unconsciousness.

Nick had to stop her before the man died.

Nick tightened his finger on the trigger, but his hand shook as he inched closer. Another step or two and maybe he could wrestle the knife from her. "I don't want to use this, sis, but I will."

An odd look flickered in her eyes as she realized what he'd said. Then she swung the knife toward him and lunged at him. "You should die, too. You and Jake left me with him, left me to be tortured."

Nick grabbed her arm and fought with her. She was amazingly strong, but then again, the Commander had trained her. "Let go of the knife, Seven."

She fought, kicking at him as she aimed the blade at his throat. But he caught her arm and knocked her backward, sending the knife skittering across the floor. Her fists flew at him next, rage fueling her strength as she pummeled his chest and face.

Nick gripped her in a chokehold to calm her, her back against him. "I'm sorry for what he did to you," he murmured as she struggled.

"If you're my brother, you should have saved me," she screamed.

"Jake and I didn't know about you. If we had, we would have, Seven. I swear." He loosened his grip enough for her to breathe. "But the Commander told us you were dead. He tortured me and Jake, too. He's a monster, and you can help us make him pay."

Blood from the cut on her wrist trickled down, dark droplets splattering against the white marble floor, and the fight slowly drained from her.

"I never knew I had brothers," she said. Her voice sounded weak and he realized she was losing blood, too much blood.

The senator stirred with a low moan.

Nick caught Seven before she collapsed just as Jake rushed into the room. "Get an ambulance, Jake."

For the second time in two days, he prayed that the bleeding woman in his arms would survive.

Only there was no justice in it.

Seven would spend the rest of her days in jail or a sanitarium, just as she'd spent most of her life.

———————— , ————————

Thirty-six hours later, Nick led Seven into the interrogation room to face his father. Her wrist wound had been treated, and she'd been placed under psychiatric care and a suicide watch.

Brenda's parents had taken her home to recuperate.

Nick wanted one last visit with their father; then he would be done with him forever. The bastard could rot in jail.

Seven was quiet as she sank into the chair across from the Commander. Jake pulled out a chair beside her, the big protective brother, while Nick remained standing, protective of Seven as well.

"We exhumed Mom's body," Jake said. "You killed her, didn't you?"

The Commander's stern face assessed them all with a calculating look that made the hair on Nick's neck rise. "She was supposed to give me another son. A soldier. She failed."

"You killed her because she had a girl?" Nick asked in an incredulous voice.

The Commander shrugged, an indifferent gesture that made it clear that he had no conscience.

"So you used our sister in your twisted work, as if she was just a plaything?" Jake asked.

"And you repeatedly strangled her?" Nick tried to control his rage, but his voice boomed all the same. "Why?"

"To make her strong," the Commander said.

"Strong?" Seven said. "You turned me into a killer." She shifted, then glanced down at her wrists. "That's what you wanted, wasn't it?"

"You did your job well."

Nick watched the interplay between his sister and father, anger mounting as he realized that his father had played him from the moment he showed him that first limerick.

The Commander had known the writer's identity, but he had sat back and watched her commit murder.

To toy with him? Or had he wanted Nick and Jake to discover that their sister was alive?

Maybe to rub in what he'd stolen from them.

Seven smiled, the crazed smile of a killer, and Nick's instincts spiked.

Was she still under his father's control?

———————— · ————————

Amelia tugged the sheet around her as her lover climbed from bed and dressed. The first time they'd met at the coffee shop by the complex, she'd felt connected to him. Had thought she'd recognized him.

Looking at the scars on his back confirmed her suspicions.

She reached up to kiss him, to look behind his ear for the number she was afraid was there, but he grabbed her hand and squeezed it so hard her knees buckled.

"You remember me, don't you?" he murmured.

She shook her head, but she was a terrible liar. She needed Skid for that, and she'd killed him months ago.

An evil grin contorted his features. "I remember you," he said. "We all have to stick together—you know that, don't you?"

She nodded, too afraid to argue.

Then he leaned over, raked her hair back from her neck, and pressed a kiss behind her ear. "Good-bye, Three."

She held her breath until he left. Then the trembling started deep within her, and she rushed to the door and locked it behind him, throwing the deadbolt.

But even as he disappeared down the road, she saw those piercing eyes watching her, just as they had years ago. Felt his hands on her.

And she knew she'd never be safe.

Chapter 32

———— o ————

Three days later

B renda still felt weak from the surgery, but her father had called a press conference to discuss Seven's arrest, and she intended to be present, even if he had to wheel her in.

"Honey, are you sure?" her mother said as her father helped them both from the car.

Brenda nodded. "I have to finish this story, Mom."

The past week she and Agnes had talked a lot about her birth mother. Brenda had asked about her father, but unfortunately they didn't have a clue as to who he was, and neither did Jo-Lynn.

She and Agnes had cried and laughed together, letting go of old hurts and teenage rebellion and insecurities, and were closer than they'd ever been. She would always be grateful that Agnes had rescued her from the hell she'd been living in and given her a good life.

The three of them walked together to the front of the court-house, then went into the press conference. As soon as they entered, Brenda spotted Nick in the background. If he thought he was blending in, he was wrong.

His strong, commanding body and intense expression would always make him stand out like a wounded warrior.

Even though he'd betrayed her, he'd also saved her.

"Ladies and gentlemen, thank you for coming," her father said. Then he shocked Brenda by turning to her. "I'm proud to say that my daughter Brenda Banks will be reporting on this story. She was instrumental in helping apprehend the Slaughter Creek Strangler, and we all owe her a huge debt of gratitude."

Applause rang out as Brenda stepped up to the podium. "Thank you, but the real thanks goes to our sheriff Jake Blackwood and Special Agent Nick Blackwood, who worked tirelessly around the clock to close this case."

Her eyes met Nick's, trained on her in a silent question. Was he waiting to see if she would reveal his past? The secrets he didn't want anyone to know?

She gripped the podium with clammy hands, hating that her body was still weak. But she was determined to finish this story and give the victims justice.

Hands began to wave, so to fend off an onslaught of questions, she continued. "Sadly, the woman who murdered three men in Slaughter Creek, including Senator Stowe's son, was the daughter of Commander Arthur Blackwood. She called herself Seven because that was the number given to her years ago when, as a young child, she was forced into the Slaughter Creek experiments.

"Seven is now in a psychiatric unit at the state prison. Investigators have discovered that her victims were all either directly related to the experiment or hired as guards to prevent her from escaping from the facility where Arthur Blackwood held her captive and tortured her."

"What about Senator Stowe?" a male reporter in the front row asked. "Didn't she try to murder him at the fund-raiser for the children's hospital?"

Brenda inhaled a deep breath. "Yes. We now know that the senator served in the military with Blackwood, and that he spearheaded the Slaughter Creek project. He is being held for trial now on numerous accounts of child cruelty, and for the murder of a man named Darren James."

"Is he being released on bail?"

She shook her head no. "Under the circumstances, the judge refused bail."

"Did the senator's wife know about the experiments?" someone asked.

"No," Brenda said. In fact, the poor woman had been so shocked that she'd had a mild heart attack and was still hospitalized.

Brenda caught sight of Nick weaving through the throng in the back near the exit to the lobby, and disappointment ballooned in her chest. He wasn't even going to wait around and talk to her.

———————— , ————————

Nick soaked up Brenda's strong but delicate features. He'd thought, *hoped*, that staying away from her would dim his feelings, but distance hadn't helped a damn bit.

Instead, it had only made him want her more.

He'd watched her with bated breath, half expecting her to divulge the abuse he'd told her about after they'd made love, but she'd relayed the story like a professional without stepping on his toes. She'd even painted his sister as a victim, even though Seven had sadistically murdered several men.

"Thank you for coming," the mayor said as Brenda stepped aside.

Nick waited until the pack of reporters and townspeople had disbanded, then stepped into the hallway.

The mayor and his wife hovered close to Brenda as they exited the room, and he almost changed his mind and left.

He didn't deserve Brenda. Didn't want to muddy her with the evil in his life. Or endanger her with his job.

But he couldn't drag himself away. He had to see her one more time, just for a few minutes, to make sure she was safe and healing as she should.

Brenda was shaking hands with someone as he approached. "Mayor," he said. "Mrs. Banks."

The mayor extended his hand, a newfound respect in his eyes. "Hello, Agent Blackwood."

Mrs. Banks gave him a hug. "Thank you so much for saving our daughter. We'll forever be indebted to you."

"You saved her life, Mrs. Banks," he said sincerely. "I was just doing my job." Although Brenda felt much more like a woman he couldn't get out of his head, now, than like a job.

Brenda said good-bye to the woman she'd been speaking to, then met his eyes. Nick felt as if he'd been hit with an iron fist. "Can I talk to you?" he asked, his breath hitching.

"Of course." She led him into a nook in the corner of the lobby, where it was more private.

"Brenda," he murmured, swallowing the lump in his throat. "You did a great job with the story."

A blush stained her cheek. "Thank you, Nick. I'm working on those personal profiles, and I think they're going to turn out well. Everyone wants their children's and family's stories to be heard."

"You know we're still missing one subject."

"Six," Brenda said. "Do you think he's responsible for the death of the woman in the fire?"

Nick shrugged. "If not, we have another psycho on the loose."

"I've been trying to get an interview with Seven, but so far she's declined," Brenda said. "In time I hope she'll open up to me."

He didn't think time would make a difference. His sister's mind was too warped by now to ever be repaired. But at least she'd had her vengeance.

"How are you feeling?" Nick asked.

Brenda pressed a hand over her side. "I'm better each day. But—"

"But what? You miss work?"

"I miss you, Nick."

Nick's throat closed. Dammit, she made saying good-bye impossible. "Brenda, I'm no good for you. Just look at my family, the bad blood…"

"For goodness' sake, Nick, you and Jake have both proven that there's no such thing as bad blood."

Nick fisted his hands by his side to keep from reaching for her. "I told you about my childhood, my dark side. I'll protect you if you need it, but I can't give more than that."

"We both had a rough time when we were little, Nick," Brenda said in a soft voice. "But it only made us stronger. It made you stronger."

He didn't know how to respond to that. He'd thought he was broken beyond repair, like Seven, but Brenda made him want to be whole.

The mayor walked past, his eyebrows quirked. Brenda seemed to stall for a moment, as if she wanted Nick to say more.

When he didn't, she reached up and kissed him on the cheek. "I love you, Nick. One thing I realized when I was on my death-bed is that if you love someone you should say it."

"Brenda—"

She pressed her finger to her lips. "It's okay if you can't say it back, but I do love you. I just wanted you to know that."

Then she walked toward the door.

Nick watched her go, his heart hammering. As tenacious and infuriating as Brenda could be, she wasn't pressuring him or demanding anything. She was simply being Brenda. Brave, com-passionate…daring.

He was the coward.

He wanted her back in his arms. Back in his life.

Back in his bed.

She had almost made it to the mayor when he vaulted into action and jogged after her. When he caught up with her, he took her arm. "Brenda, I love you, too," he blurted. "But we can't be together. Being with me would only put you in danger."

Brenda laughed softly. "I'm an investigative reporter, Nick. That means taking risks. Besides, my job might put you in danger."

His dark eyes twinkled with mischief. "You're right." He pulled her up against him. "But you're worth it."

"So are you, Nick." Brenda smiled and fell into his arms. He wrapped himself around her, then lowered his mouth and kissed her, putting all the need and desire in his soul into the kiss.

Thirty minutes later, he carried her into her condo, then took her to bed. She was still sore from her surgery, so lovemaking would have to wait.

But he kissed her again, loving her with his mouth and hands, then cradled her against him until they both fell into a contented sleep.

With Brenda by his side, he would never go to bed alone again.

———————— , ————————

A buzzing sound drew Nick from sleep. He rolled over, disoriented, then felt a warm body snuggled next to him and realized he was in bed with Brenda. A smile curved his mouth. He never wanted to be without her again.

But the buzzing continued, and his phone vibrated on the nightstand. Deciding to silence the thing and go back to sleep, he grabbed it. But Jake's number flashed on the screen.

It could be about their father or...sister. What if Seven had tried to kill herself? Or maybe she'd escaped and killed their father?

A man could hope.

Exhaling in frustration, he punched connect. "Jake?"

"Sorry to bother you, Nick, but I just received a call."

"About Dad? Seven?"

"No, they're locked up tight. But a couple of teenagers just called in a crime."

Couldn't Jake handle it? "Why call me? Was the MO the same as Seven's kills?"

"No. In fact they didn't find a body."

"I don't understand."

"They found a severed hand floating in Slaughter Creek."

———————— , ————————

Look for book three in the Slaughter Creek series, when Special Agent Rafe Hood is called in to track down Six—a serial killer with a shocking MO, who is severing body parts to keep as his trophy—in **WORTH DYING FOR.**

About the Author

Award-winning novelist Rita Herron's lifelong love of books began at the tender age of eight, when she read her first Trixie Belden mystery. A former kindergarten teacher, professional storyteller, and children's magazine contributor, she wrote nine books for Francine Pascal's Sweet Valley Kids series before shifting her focus to the adult market. Since then she has written over sixty romance novels and loves penning dark romantic suspense tales, sexy romantic comedies, and family-friendly romances, especially those set in small Southern towns. A native of Milledgeville, Georgia, and a proud mother and grandmother, she lives just outside of Atlanta.